SWISS SONATA

D1252853

SWISS SONATA

GWETHALYN GRAHAM

Cormorant Books

The publisher gratefully acknowledges the support of the
Canada Council for the Arts and the Ontario Arts Council
for its publishing program. We acknowledge the financial support
of the Government of Canada through the Book Publishing
Industry Development Program (BPIDP) for our publishing activities.

Printed and bound in Canada

NATIONAL LIBRARY OF CANADA CATALOGUING IN PUBLICATION

Graham, Gwethalyn, 1913–1965.
Swiss sonata / Gwethalyn Graham.

Originally published: Toronto: J. Cape, 1938.
ISBN 1-896951-62-7

I. Title.

PS8503.R775S8 2005   C813'.54   C2004-906527-0

Cover Design: Tannice Goddard/Angel Guerra
Text Design: Tannice Goddard
Cover image: Catherine Steele Archives, Havergal College, Toronto
Cormorant Books acknowledges and gratefully thanks Havergal College
for the use of the cover image.
Printer: Friesens

CORMORANT BOOKS INC.
215 SPADINA AVENUE, STUDIO 230, TORONTO, ON CANADA M5T 2C7
www.cormorantbooks.com

INTRODUCTION
⌒

by Elspeth Cameron

Swiss Sonata[1] is a remarkable and prophetic novel. Remarkable because it uses the unlikely setting of a girls' boarding school as a microcosm in which to address the volatile and ominous political situation of the western world in the late 1930s. Prophetic because it anticipates in 1938 the aggressive national policies of Hitler that later led to the Second World War. Its political verve — based on the author's close observation of events in Europe during her 20s — was so incisive that the novel was blacklisted by the Nazi regime. That the novel was written by a Canadian at a time when Canadian literature hardly existed is astonishing. That it was written by a woman at a time when women writers generally produced romantic novels like Margaret Mitchell's 1936 best-seller *Gone with the Wind* was stunning. Her main plot is not centred on a love story, but on the movement of several female characters towards

v

self-realisation. It richly deserved the Governor General's Award for Fiction, which it received the following year, the third year the awards were given.

But then, Gwethalyn Graham was a highly unusual woman. Born in 1913 just months before the outbreak of the First World War, Graham was politicized from an early age by her grandfather, James Frederick McCurdy[2], a scholar of Oriental language who was dismissed from Princeton for his overly-liberal religious views before heading the University of Toronto's Department of Oriental Language for twenty-three years. Both her parents further developed the tradition of this man who deplored racial slurs. Her mother belonged to, and usually headed, almost every liberal or cultural organization in the Toronto of her day: in 1923, the League of Women Voters; from 1926–29, the Women's Musical Club; in 1932–33, the Women's Canadian Club; in 1933, a large literary competition; the University Women's Club; the Lyceum Club; and Women's Art Association. She served on several patriotic committees during the First World War (receiving a medal from Serbia for her work with the Serbian Relief Committee in 1916) and was active in the movement to have milk pasteurized. As for Graham's father, barrister and King's Counsel Frank Erichsen-Brown, her older sister, Isabel Lebourdais, recalls "he was one of the best feminists I ever knew. He always said women could do everything men could; just give them a good education. Once he jumped onstage during a suffragette speech to a group of jeering men, silenced them and invited the woman speaker to continue."[3]

The Erichsen-Browns lived their politics: hosting British suffragettes and taking in refugees, the homeless and the lonely families of servicemen overseas to their Toronto Rosedale home. All four of the Erichsen-Brown children were encouraged to read widely, look closely and critically at the world around them, and speak their minds. According to Isabel, it was the intellectual foment of this remarkable family background that explained Gwethalyn's interest in sociology and human problems. "We argued all the time," she recalls. "It was possible to find several different political views in the house at any given time. Gwennie was a marvellous conversationalist. No matter who came to the house for mother's Sunday Open House — and that could be anyone from British suffragette Sylvia Pankhurst to Canadian artist A.Y. Jackson — she could talk to them. I didn't have the courage she had, and I envied her."[4]

From the age of six, Graham declared herself a writer. At eight she devised *The Goldfish News* about the goings-on in the family's aquarium, naming each fish after someone her parents knew. This concept of literature as a microcosm of life would be repeated in *Swiss Sonata*. Before this first published novel, Graham had written three novels and an experimental play. That play probably found its way into *Swiss Sonata* through Vicky Morrison, the novel's protagonist, who despairs of producing her experimental play because she has no idea where she will find a composer to write the original music for it. Graham destroyed all but one of these early works —"West Wind," an autobiographical novel about her brief, disastrous marriage.

Before marrying John (Jack) McNaught, a divorced father of three who was thirteen years her senior, in late September 1933, Graham had been given a privileged education: the girls' private school Havergal College in Toronto, which she hated; a year at the Swiss Pensionnat Les Allières, which she also hated; and Smith College in Massachussetts. She had left Smith right after beginning her second year, abandoning successful studies in music, history, art and literature to marry McNaught, whom she had known only a couple of months. She was either pregnant or feared that she was. Only a year later, after realizing that the penniless McNaught was an abusive, alcoholic womanizer, she left. McNaught's mother and her own supported her after her 1934 divorce for years. In *Swiss Sonata*, the faithless character Barry Gilchrist, who has been married to one of the teachers, as well as previously involved with one of the girls, is based on McNaught. As for McNaught himself, he soon remarried and later (after serving time in prison) re-invented himself as James Bannerman, a CBC radio talk show host, whose erudite and witty British-style programmes were popular in the 1950s and 1960s.

It was the end of that marriage in November 1933 that prompted Graham to begin writing *Swiss Sonata*. After a stint with the Bruce Housing Commission in Toronto helping the needy find homes, she moved to Montreal with her infant son, Anthony, and a Finnish nanny from London, Ontario, and began publishing articles in such journals as *The London Times* and *The News Chronicle* on Canadian and international social and political issues.

As the title indicates, Graham set up her novel in three sections that suggest the movements characteristic of the sonata. The three consecutive days — events in the novel take place on a Thursday, Friday and Saturday in January 1935 — roughly correspond to the sonata's exposition, development and recapitulation. On Thursday (the exposition) the theme and characters are introduced at a brilliant *allegro* pace; on Friday (the development) the situation is deepened through interaction and dialectic at a slower *largo* rate; and on Saturday (the recapitulation) loose ends are briskly tied together through various transformations in a quick, bright *finale*. This is an entirely fitting structure for a novel in which the main character frequently plays the piano, refers to musical works and entertains the thought that she might study at the Paris Conservatoire and make music her future career. The musical structure and content are echoed in several lyrical prose passages throughout the work.

These three days, covered with such Aristotelian economy of time, place and action, which immediately preceded the January 1935 plebiscite in the Saar, which was to determine whether this small territory, then owned by France, would remain under the aegis of the League of Nations or revert to Germany. The Treaty of Versailles — signed in 1919, which brought the formal end of the First World War — had formulated the terms by which vanquished Germany was to make reparations for the loss and damage inflicted during the war. This treaty, among other things, cut Germany's territory by about one-eighth and its population by some six and a half million. In some areas, where the population was a mixture of German and other ethnic groups, adjacent countries, plebiscites were used for the purpose of self-determination and to establish Germany's new borders. One of these was the Saar, which had been governed temporarily by the League. Under the terms of the Treaty of Versailles, France had been given special rights to mine the Saar's rich coal fields as compensation for German destruction of the coal mines in northern France.

The League of Nations, which began its official existence in January 1920, had been formed after the end of the First World War as an international peace-keeping body dedicated to making the world safe for democracy. Of the major world powers and several minor countries, only the United States declined to join. The League supervised the recovery period following what was commonly thought to be the war to end all wars.

As Graham recognized, the Saar plebiscite was a crucial choice. The fact that on Sunday January 13, 1935 this small province, rich in coal deposits, on the border of France and Germany chose to return to Germany was key, enabling the Nazis to manufacture military weapons, since coal was essential in making steel. Had the Saar chosen to join France, it might have been more difficult for Hitler to achieve his goal (as stated in *Mein Kampf*, 1933) of isolating France from the rest of Europe. Later — well after the publication of Graham's novel — Hitler was able to use the example of the Saar as evidence that Germany had a moral right to those countries or areas which "chose" to become German. This argument was used to support his invasion of Czechoslovakia (with its Sudeten German territory) in 1939.

The Pensionnat Les Ormes (Elms) in *Swiss Sonata* is a microcosm of these world events. Set in Switzerland, the three-nation country, with students from thirteen different countries and teachers from Switzerland, France and England, the novel's action involves conflicts and tensions among cliques and individuals that mirror its time. Most obvious is the conflict between the German nationalist Truda Meyer from Essen and the German Jew Ilse Bruning from Saarbrucken. Truda is the school bully who reads the *Nationalzeitung*, a periodical owned and controlled by Goring, and holds pro-Nazi views. She persecutes Ilse, among others, for reasons that echo the anti-Semitic policies gathering force in Germany at the time. Just as the Jews were scape-goated for economic reasons, Ilse is being scape-goated (wrongly, as it turns out) for money that has been stolen. Truda is also cruel to Anna von Landenburg from Nurnberg. Truda relishes the fact that Anna's father, a Bavarian Catholic who cares about the welfare of German Jews and has been in a labour camp, is arrested, endures a military trial, and is executed. It is no doubt Graham's lengthy and precise description of how the German labour camps and concentration camps were organized that caused this novel to be black-listed by the Nazis.

Many of the novel's dialogues stand for the political positions of the countries from which the twenty-seven characters come. These countries include England and the United States, Italy, France, Belgium, Poland, Denmark and Norway, Brazil and South Africa. When Truda defends her views of women's roles, for example, to the two Scandinavian girls, Else and Christina, Graham intends for the reader to contrast Germany's oppressive policies towards women to Scandinavia's more liberal views. Mme Tourain, the school's Swiss headmistress, recognizes the seriousness of such tensions as these at the Pensionnat Les Ormes and gives talks to the girls about the League of Nations in the hope of instilling peace.

The one student who does not belong to any clique is Vicky, the Canadian protagonist. Non-judgmental and equally available to hear out the distresses of all her classmates, Vicky seems to represent the firm individualism which Graham endorses, as well as the Canadian acceptance of many peoples. Vicky comforts the anguished French-Canadian Rosalie; spars with the rich, eccentric American Jew, Theodora Cohen; and even hears out the personal tribulations of the young Canadian athletic instructor, Mary Ellerton. Her uncanny ability (she is termed a "twentieth-century version of a mystic"[5] and Mme Tourain calls her "this species of Canadian saint"[6]) to connect in non-judgmental ways with others proves to be a threat to Mme Tourain, whose personal evolution from rational scholar to emotionally engaged administrator during the novel's three days occurs too late to bring her to an understanding of Vicky's non-conformist personality. As a result, Vicky is, somewhat improbably, dismissed from the school. She leaves, not to marry, but to seek adventure in the larger world with her friend Ted Cohen.

These events, alongside which the Saar elections are mentioned directly, position the novel as a document about the end of an era. Naziism is ascendant, with results Graham logically infers before they happened. As for a general approach to life, conducting it rationally by the book instead of by the heart and intuition (as Vicky does) no longer serves. And the nature and purpose of finishing schools (to create lady-like wives and "stamp out" individuality) no longer holds meaning. As Mme Tourain comes to see — largely through her attempts to understand Vicky — "the only thing that could be done would be to abandon the idea of finishing schools altogether, and attempt to get foreign students at twelve or thirteen, and equip them for any university in their respective countries which they might wish to attend, taking five years to do it."[7]

Meanwhile, just as Graham herself did at Les Allières, the students of Pensionnat Les Ormes receive their training in increasingly irrelevant subjects such as "social" French, the fine arts, skiing and deportment. Trivial rules, such as the mandatory wearing of woollen underwear in winter, offer Graham opportunities for ironic humour. More important, as Consuelo Deane from Brazil observes: all-female boarding schools represent an illogical "half-life" that does nothing to prepare girls in their late teens and early twenties for contemporary social and domestic life. "When there is such an inter-dependence between men and women, why in the name of common sense are we segregated from one another in this way?"[8]

Graham believed in democratic individuality for all people, regardless of race, nationality or gender. But because she sets *Swiss Sonata* in a girls' school with exclusively female characters (and no doubt because she herself had experienced an education she thought was inadequate, a terrible marriage, an unwanted pregnancy, single parenthood and a divorce) she emphasizes issues which would today be called feminist. Three decades before Kate Millett declared that the personal is the political in *Sexual Politics* (1970), Graham uses discussions about marriage, career and the role of women between and among the various students at Pensionnat Les Ormes to probe what she considered extremely important aspects of society and politics. The candid nature and wide range of these discussions is remarkable for the time. Graham touches on social and national attitudes to sexuality, menstruation, anorexia, lesbian crushes in boarding school, infidelity, arranged marriages and spinsterhood, among others. In doing so, she develops further some of the ideas she explored two years before the novel's publication in a December 1936 article for *Canadian Forum* called "Women, Are they Human?"[9]

In particular, Graham looks at the issue of marriage versus career. In her 1936 article, she protested against the "merely secondary existence" experienced by many women whose career ambitions were stifled. She noted the worldwide tendency to keep women at home, especially during the then-current economic depression. She also noted that the two fascist countries, Germany and Italy, extolled the virtues of domesticity for women. In *Swiss Sonata*, she dramatizes these ideas through her characters.

The German Truda and the Italian Maria-Teresa echo the Fascist position that women belong in the home. (A law passed in Germany in 1933 made the distribution of contraceptives and abortion criminal acts, both subject to severe punishment.) Maria-Teresa also represents the traditional Italian view of romantic love. She is so in love with love that she mistakenly worships the wrong man in a group photo her fiancé has given her. Natalia Babaian, an Armenian whose family have moved to Brussels and chosen a husband for her, states simply: "all

Armenian girls get married. They don't have careers."[10] It is a nice comic touch that Natalia, who is one of the top students at Pensionnat Les Ormes, spends her time compulsively re-arranging the furniture in her room. Graham implies that this may be the only area where she has the power to decide things for herself. It is Natalia's Polish roommate, Yasha Livovna, who finally convinces her to call off the arranged marriage and pursue the career in medicine she really longs for. In another comic twist, it is Yasha herself who sincerely choses to marry. The two Scandinavians, Elsa Michielsen from Denmark and the Norwegian, Christina Erichsen, are free of any notion that women should be denied careers. In fact, Elsa's mother is a writer (and "a vague woman ... when it comes to domestic matters"[11]) whose books — as *Swiss Sonata* was to be — were banned in Germany. Elsa's mother's response to this is far from submissive: "Now I *know* I'm worth reading."[12]

More serious treatments of the subject are found in dialogues between Vicky and Theodora, and between Vicky and Mary Ellerton. Theodora (Ted) compares the stereotypes of men and women, wondering why women, unlike men, are seen as incapable of friendship. Women, she argues, are thought to be emotional, catty and gossipy, whereas men are considered logical and loyal. Men are permitted to be individuals, while women — especially those groomed in finishing schools — are supposed to be uniformly docile. The two also compare sexual behaviours in North America and Europe. Ted (who admits to having lost her virginity in a parked car at age sixteen, for which she has been sent to school in Switzerland) concludes that the "necking" that maintains chastity in North America is inferior to the European acceptance of the full expression of sexuality before marriage: "At least they call a spade a spade."

Vicky claims that the whole subject of sex is overemphasized by the puritanical and the exponents of free love alike. That such discussions were radically frank for their time scarcely needs stating.

These discussions between Vicky and Ted seem forced. It is obvious that Graham is using her characters here, and sometimes elsewhere, as vehicles for her strongly held views. More successful are the personal discussions about love between Vicky and the young British sports instructor, Mary Ellerton. Both characters have autobiographical elements. Mary has recently come to the school for reasons that recall Graham's failed marriage. Like Graham, Mary married a man who has proved unfaithful. She has essentially put Barry Gilchrist on probation: if he can be faithful during their year apart, she will reconsider marrying him. He proves unable to meet this challenge (and Graham is remarkably non-judgmental about this). Mary's decision to make a commitment to the school instead of to Barry is seen in a positive light rather than as a loss. Their conversation gives Vicky the chance to acknowledge her own capacity for total involvement with some future husband and voice her belief that the closeness of marriage can be a positive thing.

The greatest flaw in *Swiss Sonata* is the portrayal of Vicky Morrison, the main character. Graham clearly intended her novel to focus on her protagonist, since she originally titled the novel "Vicky." But reviewers found this twenty-year-old with a "genius for self-obliteration"[13] too good to be true: beautiful, intelligent, talented, witty, and popular with everyone in the school. There are passages that suggest Graham meant her to be a "new woman" ahead of her time — one who thought for herself and trusted her intuitions. But Vicky's background as an illegitimate child foisted by an alcoholic mother onto an eccentric father at age seven is not only melodramatic, but is also improbable. Vicky's unusually mature and stable personality seems a highly unlikely result of such a background.

Another flaw in the novel is its stylistic unevenness. Confusion results from the sameness of voice shared by certain characters, although others are clearly delineated. For most of the novel, Graham is clear, witty, entertaining and thought-provoking. But occasionally, she is turgid and didactic. Sentences frequently cram in too many details, and the characters often seem to be lecturing each other on social and political mores.

Graham struggled long and hard to produce *Swiss Sonata*. It was drafted in Montreal while she was a single parent between November 1933 and July 1934. The London publisher Jonathan Cape rejected the manuscript in August 1935. After turning for a while to her "West Wind" and other earlier novels and plays, most of which she destroyed, Graham returned to "Vicky" and revised the manuscript between January and April 1937. It was finally accepted by Jonathan Cape in August 1937.

The novel was widely and favourably reviewed in England and the United States when it was published. In Canada, however, where literary criticism was almost non-existent and what little there was of the publishing industry had been levelled by the Depression, it was scarcely noticed. In fact, even the availability of the novel was severely limited in Canada. The Toronto publisher Thomas Nelson was the Canadian distributor for Jonathan Cape. They ordered the book in small lots of 50 copies, which were sent from London by ship. Only after each batch of books was sold did Nelson order another lot, which was inevitably delayed. Graham's tireless mother undertook a campaign to pressure Thomas Nelson and the Toronto bookstores to obtain more copies. But, according to Graham's sister, "they never had enough copies, and so the book just faded out."[14]

Gwethalyn Graham's political activism did not abate with the publication of *Swiss Sonata*. In the fall of 1938, after visiting Europe and England for six months, she returned to Canada. In response to what she had seen in France, Switzerland and England of the effect of Hitler's *Anschluss* (March 1938) and the Czechoslovakian crisis over the Sudetenland (May 1938), she circulated petitions and made speeches pleading for the admission of refugees — especially Jews — to Canada.

At the same time she worked as a freelance journalist, publishing articles on the political and social issues she was so passionate about. Two of these articles appeared in *Saturday Night* before the end of 1938. "Refugees: the Human Aspect"[15] was printed, coincidentally, two days after the infamous *Kristallnacht*, the worst Nazi pogrom against the Jews of Austria and Germany to that date. "Economics of Refugees"[16] was prompted by the July 5–16 international conference on the refugee problem at Evian, Switzerland. In this article, Graham argued that Canada had plenty of land and resources to accommodate new citizens. Refugees, she argued, gave back as much or more than they took from their adopted countries. She took Canada to task for its indifference to the plight of displaced persons, pleading for Canada to seize this "first real opportunity for world leadership."

Graham's political concerns about Canada's attitude to homeless European Jews would not take centre stage, however, until scholars Irving Abella and Harold Troper published their in-depth study *None Is Too Many: Canada and the Jews of Europe, 1933–1948* in 1982, forty-four years after *Swiss Sonata*. Her even broader humanitarian concern for all refugees, the homeless and the poor — as well as her egalitarian approach to both genders as well as all echelons and ethnicities in Canada — anticipated the multicultural society introduced by Prime

Minister Pierre Elliott Trudeau in 1971. By looking closely at the world around her, free of conventional attitudes, Gwethalyn Graham was a barometer of her time. And with her early death of brain cancer in 1965 at age fifty-two, Canada lost a writer whose voice might have taken a mainstream role in articulating and dramatizing an ideology of the toleration of difference she had just begun to explore in the 1930s.

NOTES

[1] Gwethalyn Graham, *Swiss Sonata* (London: Jonathan Cape, 1938).

[2] Sometimes spelled MacCurdy.

[3] Elspeth Cameron, interview with Isabel Lebourdais, Toronto, 25 Jan. 1995.

[4] Elspeth Cameron, interview with Isabel Lebourdais, Toronto, 22 Dec. 1994.

[5] *Swiss Sonata*, p. 227.

[6] *Ibid.*, p. 51.

[7] *Ibid.*, p. 30.

[8] *Ibid.*, p. 290.

[9] "Women, Are They Human?" *The Canadian Forum*, 16 (Dec. 1936), pp. 21–23.

[10] *Swiss Sonata*, p. 281.

[11] *Ibid.*, p. 115.

[12] *Ibid.*

[13] *Ibid.*, p. 175.

[14] Barbara Opala, interview with Isabel Lebourdais, Toronto, 2 Oct. 1979 as cited in "Gwethalyn Graham: A Critical Biography," Ph.D. thesis, Université de Montreal (Aug. 1980).

[15] "Refugees: the Human Aspect," *Saturday Night*, 12 Nov. 1938, pp. 8–9.

[16] "Economics of Refugees," *Saturday Night*, 19 Nov. 1938, pp. 8–9.

To F.E-B. and I.R.E-B.

CONTENTS

PART ONE

Thursday

I

PART TWO

Friday

147

PART THREE

Saturday

267

PRINCIPAL CHARACTERS

THE STAFF

Amélie Tourain	Lausanne, Switzerland
Rose Dupraix	Geneva, Switzerand
Sylvia Lange	Zürich, Switzerland
Henriette Devaux	Neuchâtel, Switzerland
Isabelle Lemaitre	Clermont, France
Mary Ellerton	London, England
Elizabeth Williams	Kent, England

THE GIRLS

Vicky Morrison	Toronto, Canada
Theodora Cohen	St. Louis, Missouri, U.S.A.
Ilse Brüning	Saarbrücken
Anna von Landenburg	Nürnberg, Germany
Rosalie Garcenot	Montreal, Canada
Truda Meyer	Essen, Germany
Consuelo Deane	São Paolo, Brazil
Yasha Livovna	Warsaw, Poland
Maria-Teresa Tucci	Genoa, Italy
Marian Comstock	Port Elizabeth, South Africa
Natalia Babaian	Brussels, Belgium

Aimée Babaian	Paris, France
Ina Barron	Brighton, England
Cissie Anderson	Manchester, England
Ruth Anderson	Manchester, England
Stephania Carré	Milan, Italy
Henriette Martin	Mulhouse, France
Rose Budet	Brussels, Belgium
Ida Samuels	New York, New York, U.S.A
Elsa Michielsen	Copenhagen, Denmark
Christina Erichsen	Oslo, Norway
Elizabeth Cummings-Gordon	Philadelphia, Pennsylvania U.S.A.
Helen Cummings-Gordon	Philadelphia Pennsylvania U.S.A.
Gretel Arnsbach	Berlin, Germany
Lotta Grosz	Berlin, Germany
Catherine Shaunessy	Seattle, Washington, U.S.A.

PART ONE

Thursday

I

୧

*P*ensionnat Les Ormes stands on the hill which rises above Lausanne so that it seems to overlook the world. Beyond the town is the Lake of Geneva; beyond the lake, the mountains of France. Somewhere across that stretch of water which separates Switzerland from France, somewhere behind those high hills are the Atlantic, America and England; up to the right lie Holland and Belgium, Norway, Sweden, Denmark and Germany; down to the left where the Rhône runs out is Italy, and at your back, across the Alps, are Austria, Poland, Hungary, and Czechoslovakia. Each year the girls who come from all over the world to Pensionnat Les Ormes, perched on its hillside, stand at their windows and look out over the lake, watching the autumn mists creep down from the Dent du Midi and obscuring the little villages of France. Then for months snow lies heavy on the world spread out beneath them, until at last the clouds come down from the peaks to float low along the shores and patches of green appear here and there; above the vague sounds of motor cars and lorries changing gear as they climb upwards come the cow-bells, clear and sweet. The boatmen of Ouchy, Montreux, Vevey and the little villages across the lake in France get out their barges, and once more the girls in Pensionnat Les Ormes linger at their windows watching them sail down the long broad lake from Geneva to the Rhône, or making their interminable lazy trips from Thonon to Evian.

They are in the heart of the world, yet curiously out of it, for no sound from Lausanne reaches them very clearly. Rather it is as though the town noises get lost in coming up across the playing fields and tennis courts, and by the time they reach the sloping terraces which flank the building there is nothing left of them but a suggestion that there is life and activity down in Lausanne, below this suspended little world on the hillside.

The main door of the school is on the side away from the town. The drive leading to it is long, cutting straight across between the tennis courts after it leaves the big wooden gates, then curving round the extreme edge of the gardens until, after a long, straight stretch up the slope, it ends in the courtyard by the front door. It takes about five minutes' fast walking to get from the gates to the grateful seclusion of the court during which you become thoroughly self-conscious as you notice the eyes watching you from the windows. Once you reach the corner of the house you are safe. You ring the bell, which is answered after a while by a young Swiss girl who shows you into a drawing room filled with brocade furniture and lithographs of genteel young ladies. On the mantelpiece is an ormolu clock which says seven minutes past three; you hastily consult your watch which says a quarter to four, wonder rather vaguely if it has gained, and settle down to wait. Every little while you look at that clock which continues to say seven minutes past three, but when Miss Ellerton comes in to inquire your business you forget about it altogether, in your surprise at finding anyone who looks like that in a Swiss pensionnat.

If you *were* to say anything about the clock, Miss Ellerton would tell you that it had been bequeathed along with six teaspoons, a Pekinese dog and many volumes on tropical fish to Mlle d'Ormonde, cousin of Amélie Tourain the present head-mistress, who had the school for twenty years before her, by an aunt who founded Pensionnat Les Ormes, and that it had stopped on its entrance to the school in the spring of 1884. Some day they are going to get it mended but at present they are too busy, for Mlle Tourain is correcting proofs for the second volume of her work on the history of Swiss independence, which will appear next autumn, and she, Mary Ellerton, has no time for anything, since she dismissed the housekeeper and has her job as well as that of assistant principal. Would you like to see the school?

2

All the rooms on the ground floor open off the T-shaped front hall. When you come in from the courtyard the doors of Mlle Tourain's study are directly opposite you; on your right are the kitchens and laundry rooms and between them and the study, occupying the whole corner, is the dining room. On your left, behind the big dark staircase which curves up to the first floor, is the girls' living room, and in front of it on the south-east corner, the main classroom. The dining room, study, drawing room and classroom all face south, through wide French windows which extend from the ceiling to within a foot of the floor and which overlook the terraces, gardens, tennis courts, Lausanne, and the Lake of Geneva.

The bedrooms on the three floors above are all more or less alike, with white woodwork, flowered wallpaper with a white background, light oak furniture and two white basins set in an alcove at the back of each room with a cupboard on either side, so that the only dark place in the school is the main entrance hall, which is poorly lit by small, stained glass windows on the north side of the house. There is nothing to be seen from those windows in any case but the courtyard, the steep slope of the hill, a few scattered houses and institutions ... an orphanage, an insane asylum, a jail, and more schools.

There are several hundred schools in and about Lausanne, Geneva, Vevey, Montreux and Neuchâtel to which boys and girls of all nationalities have come during the past fifty or sixty years to receive instruction in French, deportment, winter sports and internationalism. Pensionnat Les Ormes was founded in 1884 by Jeanne d'Ormonde's aunt, she who later bequeathed to her niece the ormolu clock, but the present building was erected by Jeanne herself in 1920. She was a quiet-mannered gentlewoman who was never able to reconcile herself to the sight of fifty young ladies skiing in trousers.

In 1930 she fell ill and appointed Amélie Tourain, her cousin, whose life had until that time been devoted to historical research, to take her place. For four years her successor remained in her study with her back to the china shepherdesses, cactus plants and potpourri jars with which Mlle d'Ormonde had seen fit to ornament her glassed-in bookcases, which ran along the west wall of the study and continued down the north wall as far as the door leading into the hall. Mlle d'Ormonde could not be said to have benefited greatly by the wills of her relatives; the husband of her aunt had found the atmosphere of a girls' school intolerable and retired to a small cottage in Gruyère where he devoted the remainder of his life to the study of tropical fish. It was from him that Jeanne d'Ormonde, upon the death of her aunt, had acquired the books; the rest of his belongings he had sold at public auction and given the proceeds to charity.

During her five years as assistant to her aunt, Jeanne d'Ormonde had frequently visualized herself sitting in the study, behind a large and imposing desk, aiding and inspiring the girls with a background of books, but her entire collection burned with the old building in 1920. There was nothing for it then but to install the fifteen hundred volumes on tropical fish. This she did, but had a cabinet-maker put on glass doors with very small leaded panes, to make it more difficult to read the titles, and to distract attention from them she covered the tops of the book-cases with cactus plants and china ornaments.

When Amélie Tourain came to take her cousin's place in 1930, she was mildly astonished at Jeanne's choice of literature. She had not known the uncle in Gruyère; her life in the little house at the end of the lane which ran down from Avenue Ruchonnet had been remote and tranquil, undisturbed by family antago-nisms. After a glance sufficient to tell her that all the books dealt with this curious subject, and two dismayed glances at the china shepherdesses and cactus plants, she called one of the maids and with her help turned the big desk which had always stood with its back to the French windows facing the door, so that it now stood with its back to the bookcases and faced the folding doors which separated the study from the drawing room. Then she sat down to think.

For four years she sat there, waiting for Jeanne to get better. Her honour and her sense of duty forbade her to find a substi-tute and retreat to her house off Avenue Ruchonnet, for she had promised Jeanne that she would stay until she was well again and able to come back. At the same time, the thought of abandoning her own work was intolerable, so for those four years she tried unsuccessfully to do both.

On Thursday, January 10th, 1935, she suddenly became dissatisfied with the school, herself ... in fact her whole life as she was living it at that time ... and called a special staff-meeting for three-thirty, although the regular weekly meeting was scheduled for eight o'clock that evening.

The next three days were to determine the course of her future, although, at the time, she was only partially aware of their difference from the thousand other days she had spent in the study, and it was not until Saturday, January 12th, the day before the Saar elections, that she was able to see the relationship which so strangely existed between the personal life of Mary Ellerton, the games mistress; the tragedy of Rosalie Garcenot; Anna von Landenburg, Ilse Brüning, Vicky Morrison ... and herself.

3

At twenty-nine minutes to four the teaching staff of Pensionnat Les Ormes met at the door of the study, came in together, and stood about awkwardly for a while, waiting for the headmistress, who was apparently lost in thought, to take some notice of them. She and Jeanne d'Ormonde were approximately the same age, but whereas Mlle d'Ormonde was small and delicately beautiful, with a black velvet ribbon always at her throat, her cousin Amélie Tourain was fairly tall, with greying brown hair piled on the top of her head, and no pretence to beauty of any sort. Her nose was broad and slightly aquiline, her skin naturally rather sallow, and sallowed still further by the rusty browns and blacks of her clothes. She took no interest in her appearance, and combined shapeless brown wool dresses with black or grey jerseys and shawls indiscriminately, without noticing the effect she created, exactly as she sat now, at her desk, unaware of her surroundings and either unaware of or indifferent to the presence of her staff. These, after more hesitations, settled down in the straight-backed chairs which Mlle Tourain had brought in from the dining room and arranged in a semi-circle before her desk.

Her black eyes swept over them in one comprehensive glance: she saw that Mlle Devaux's face had that mottled look which always betrayed her nervousness; realized that Rose Dupraix, who was sitting with her hands folded and her mouth set in a way designed to be pleasant, would oppose her politely yet vindictively no matter what she said, deploring any irregularity, disapproving of any action on the part of Amélie Tourain as she always did; wondered fleetingly what was the matter with Fräulein Lange to make her look so childishly and pathetically upset; observed with moderate satisfaction that Miss Williams at least looked as usual; and experienced her usual slight irritation at the sight of Mlle Lemaitre's thin, feverish face. The woman was as good a scholar as herself, so why was she so lacking in ordinary common sense that she could not take care of her health? That was the trouble with the whole French nation; they were, beyond a shadow of a doubt, the most highly educated and intelligent race on earth but with faces like pastry-cooks! They never ate the right food, never got enough exercise nor went out of doors if they could help it, kept their shutters closed at night, neglected their bodies for the sake of their minds from kindergarten onwards, and what was the result? A nation running on nervous energy, without stamina, without vitality ... without ordinary common sense!

Her eyes reached Miss Ellerton, the games mistress, who, after a few impatient glances in Mlle Tourain's direction, had got up from her chair and wandered over to the French windows where she was standing now, holding the curtain back with one hand and looking over the lovely grey town where dusk already lurked here and there. Some of the light which yet remained in the outer world was caught in her hair and outlined her small features so that the others, sitting patiently in their chairs, were aged by their contrasting dullness. Amélie Tourain leaned forward a little and switched on her desk light, then remained motionless looking at the girl by the window. An unaccountable conviction that Miss Ellerton was in some way connected with the turmoil in her mind had complete possession of her.

Mlle Devaux found it hard not to fidget. Whatever position she took was uncomfortable; she was troubled periodically by twinges of rheumatism in her legs, and for the whole day she had been moving restlessly whenever she sat down, the pain relieved only during those few minutes which she had been able to snatch after lunch, in order to lie down in her room. She became increasingly nervous and anxious as the silence contin-ued, her mind going over the events of the past few days in a rather haphazard way as she tried to remember whether or not she had committed any error, or been guilty of some neglect which might account for Mlle Tourain calling this entirely unprecedented meeting.

With a series of slow and almost imperceptible movements she managed to arrange her right leg so that the twinges were less frequent and transferred her eyes from the china shepherdess in pink ... who appeared to be poised on the edge of a precipice with her three sheep ... to Mlle Tourain's face. All her life she had been self-conscious in the presence of authority but during the past two months her uneasiness with Mlle Tourain had increased, due to the impertinence of Vicky Morrison, who had become the focal point of all her nervousness and dissatisfactions ever since Vicky had first noticed that Henriette Devaux was invariably panic-stricken during Mlle Tourain's weekly fifteen-minute inspections. Vicky had apparently then decided that it was up to her to relieve the general tension a little and thereby help out Mlle Devaux by drawing attention to herself. The third occasion on which she said something funny the headmistress had glanced at her over Ruth Anderson's notebook, then at Mlle Devaux, and after that things went much easier with the grammar teacher. She however became convinced that Mlle Tourain despised her because she could not keep order, for she was a rather unintelligent woman and failed to realize that the headmistress regarded her inspections of Mlle Devaux's class as the least dull of the lot, owing to Vicky's presence and ingenuity.

Fräulein Lange was thinking of her sister in Zürich who was expecting a baby in two months. She had written to her that morning saying that she was crippled with sciatica; Fräulein Lange did not think that was natural, and immediately, in her first free period, she had gone down to the Place St. François and bought a book on obstetrics. She had arrived back with the book just in time for her next class, which was a small one, consisting of Vicky, Theodora Cohen, the two Cummings-Gordon girls from Philadelphia, and Yasha Livovna. She had set them to translating a long poem of Heinrich Heine and then sat down on the opposite side of the table from them, with the book of obstetrics in her lap and the volume of Heine propped in front of her, so that they would think she was following them, and skimmed through the entire section on symptoms.

She was staring now at the bookcases behind Mlle Tourain, wondering whether her neglect of that class would be discovered or not, for she also feared authority and knew that German teachers were easy to come by. A moment later her mind returned to Maria, her sister. The book had said something about kidney trouble, and it might be that, rather than sciatica. There was no way of knowing. The book said that women ought to be examined very regularly; when she, Fräulein Lange had ventured to suggest to her brother-in-law Adolf that Maria should at least see a doctor once a month because she had always been rather delicate with a poor constitution, Adolf had paid no attention to her, beyond remarking that having babies was natural to women and that Maria should not be babied. The book said that kidney trouble was the most ... or one of the most ... dangerous of all complications; supposing then that Maria had kidney trouble and something happened to her?

She drew in her breath suddenly and sharply, so that Mlle Dupraix and Mlle Lemaitre on either side of her turned and stared. The Frenchwoman averted her feverish eyes quickly, but Mlle Dupraix continued to look at her disapprovingly. For once in her life Fräulein Lange was unmoved by her disapproval. Her hands, lying clenched in her lap, were cold and very red as she looked down at them. Her worry was turning to panic; she began to feel sick and looked about the room in a desperate effort to get her mind on something else. She must control herself; she was the German mistress at Pensionnat Les Ormes in Lausanne, and she had no right to let herself get into such a state; she had no right to be thinking of anything or anyone but the school and its forty-eight girls. Yet her heart cried that she cared nothing for the school and its forty-eight girls, she cared only for Maria.

Mlle Dupraix had been trying to make up her mind whether or not she should clear her throat, lean forward and ask deliberately, 'Mlle Tourain, is it possible that you are feeling ill?' In the end she decided to allow the headmistress her small triumph, her public exercise of authority in keeping them all waiting like this in that contemptuous and ill-mannered way, and resuming her former position ... she had been forced to shift a little in order to look disapprovingly at the German teacher beside her ... which spoke plainly of her well-bred self-containment, she turned her thoughts once more to Vicky. It required almost no effort of will on her part; she saved up Vicky for her unoccupied moments and might almost be said to have thought of her most of the time when she was not actively engaged in something else, ever since the girl's arrival four months before. Settling herself a little more comfortably in her chair, she gave herself up to the fulsome enjoyment to be derived from hating, cruelly and maliciously, someone twenty-five years younger than herself.

Her hatred was based on two things: that the girl knew more about Mlle Dupraix's subject, Beaux Arts, than Mlle Dupraix herself, and that no matter what she said or did, she could never feel that she had done more than very lightly scratch Vicky's surface, for the girl appeared to be imperturbable. Mlle Dupraix had, however, both said and done so much, that she suffered a certain amount of anxiety at times for fear Mlle Tourain should find out and dismiss her out of hand. But the headmistress could not do that, when it came right down to it, for during that woman's first day at school, when she had come in and discovered Mlle Tourain moving Jeanne d'Ormonde's desk from the place in which it had stood for ten years, she, Rose Dupraix, had made her position clear. She had said, looking down at the stout elderly woman sitting behind the desk and puffing a little from her exertions, who returned her look with that detached and unsmiling expression which was her outstanding characteristic, 'You realize, of course, that I have kept house for Mlle d'Ormonde ever since she took over the school, and have, besides that, been teaching Beaux Arts for the past eight years. You will be able to understand that although I am, of course, anxious to do everything I can to assist you, I find it impossible to look upon you as anything but my ... nominal ... head. I have worked for Mlle d'Ormonde for so long that she has come to be my ... my spiritual principal. I know you will understand what I am trying to say ...'

That shabby, fat, ill-dressed woman had remained looking up at her for a long time, nodding slowly, and then remarked at last, 'Tell me, Mlle Dupraix, what is this Beaux Arts which you teach? Or should I say what are these Beaux Arts ...'

She often asked herself how Mlle Tourain ... that brown lump of a woman ... could possibly be related to Jeanne, who was so refined in every way. At any rate, the headmistress could not dismiss her, because she was employed by Mlle d'Ormonde, who assured her of that fact every time she made her monthly journey across the lake to Evian to take her flowers. Mlle Dupraix saw to it that Mlle d'Ormonde was regularly posted on the happenings in her beloved school, and it had been *her* opinion that Vicky should be got rid of ... although she had added that since her cousin Amélie had charge of the school during her temporary confinement in the hospital at Evian, it was her affair, to be dealt with as she thought fit.

Mlle Dupraix was almost startled when the headmistress's voice at last broke into her thoughts. Mlle Tourain was sitting back in her chair now, and had begun to tap the rubber end of her pencil against the brass inkpot. The intermittent and irregular sound was an invariable accompaniment to her speech when she was in doubt or more than usually perplexed. The four teachers, seated in front of her, came to attention. Mary Ellerton hesitated a moment, then returned to her chair nearest the window and sat down with one leg crossed over the other, her arm along the back.

She was wearing a dark brown tweed skirt and a bright green sweater which increased her natural vividness. Her hair was the shade of reddish gold which Amélie Tourain had always imagined existed only in the minds of second-rate novelists; when Miss Ellerton had come to see her about the job that first day, she had actually hesitated to engage her. She was altogether too striking. She would never fit into the background of Pensionnat Les Ormes. Yet something about the girl ... a kind of quiet strength which suggested to the headmistress that at some time she had undergone a good deal of suffering ... had attracted her so strongly that she had taken her on, dismissing as being none of her business, the question which had been occupying the minds of the rest of her staff ever since: why such a creature should choose to go out in all weathers to give instruction in hockey, basketball, skating, skiing and tennis in exchange for twenty-five Swiss francs a month, board, lodging and the privilege of speaking French ... which she could speak fairly well already. The others continued to watch Miss Ellerton running up and down stairs, going at all her work with interest, almost as though she found the school entertaining, and supposed that she had an independent income since nothing else could conceivably account for that look of inner happiness, that look of separateness, as though she had an existence of her own quite apart from the school ... even while attending a staff meeting.

Mlle Tourain said, 'I called this meeting with the intention of asking your advice. I wanted to take these few minutes to tell you some of the things which are troubling me, so that you could think about them between now and this evening's meeting and possibly offer some suggestions then.'

Her mind was racing ahead of her speech; she was aware of her audience and at the same time aware of herself, looking at Amélie Tourain quite impersonally.

Her whole point of view had been, until very recently, that of a person looking through a window at something which is taking place in the room beyond. She had remained mentally ... which was the only way which really counted ... in her study, issuing from it to meals, to general assembly each morning after breakfast, for her rounds of inspection and the two hours which she was forced to spend each evening with the girls in their living room, but she had neither given one word of advice nor performed one action with the idea that she would be there to see that the thing was carried out. Since the doctors in Evian had said until very recently that it would be merely a matter of months before Jeanne could resume her position, she had simply sat and waited for four years.

The change had come imperceptibly; she could not have said when it was that she first faced the possibility of being saddled with the school for the rest of her life. Lately she had been drawn more and more from her mental retreat; there had been sporadic outbursts which had shown her the emotional pitch of the school so clearly that, try as she might, she could no longer avoid facing a few issues. She had heard, involuntarily ... for she would have given a great deal for her old serene and comfortable ignorance ... snatches of conversation hastily switched from German, English, Italian, Spanish into French as she went along the halls: someone was stealing, and Truda Meyer for quite obvious reasons ... her father owned steel mills in Essen and was ardently Fascist ... had started the rumour that Ilse Brüning from Saarbrücken was the thief. Ilse's mother was Jewish, Ilse was engaged to a Jew, and Ilse was too easily terrified. One does not expect forty-eight girls of every conceivable nationality and from every conceivable sort of background to be able to adapt themselves to living together in perfect harmony, under the best circumstances. When those circumstances appeared to be the worst imaginable, short of actual war between their countries, schoolgirl quarrels took on significance, pretexts were readily available, and adolescent imaginations started to work.

She tried to get some of these ideas across to her staff, seated in front of her. She was remembering, as she spoke, that the results of the little talk she had given the school the preceding Saturday night on the League of Nations, had not been all that she had hoped for. They had listened to her politely, all those children, agreeing with her in principle no doubt, but all having the idea ... this also she had gathered from chance conversations as they went about the school ... that the function of the League was to bring every other country into line with their own.

She had spoken with an undercurrent of passion running through her words, as she was speaking now. She believed intensely in the integrity and value of her country, although during her fifty-eight years of life she had come to the bitter knowledge that the rest of the world thought merely of a Switzerland which was divided into three parts, possessed no national language and no national identity of its own, and was distinguished for nothing but the manufacture of watches, cheese, lace, chocolate, and its winter sports. People seemed to know of the Swiss schools, but to think of them chiefly as a convenient way in which to familiarize their children with skiing and skating. She realized that culturally and economically the Swiss were relatively unimportant; educationally ... which was the only way in which they could hope to contribute toward human advancement in general ... they were attempting too much, for it was beyond the range of possibility that conventional, non-thinking adolescents could be made over in one year or even three. So far as she could see, the only thing which could be done would be to abandon the idea of finishing schools altogether, and attempt to get foreign students at twelve or thirteen, and equip them for any university in their respective countries which they might wish to attend, taking five years to do it. In that way the schools might complement the League idea.

The existing Swiss schools were in a curious position since, so far as the parents of their pupils were concerned, their chief function was to provide instruction in French and winter sports; the international idea was purely incidental. Yet, she supposed, they must have some vague idea of giving their children a chance to see through the eyes of other countries, or they would send them elsewhere. If you have a 'my country right or wrong' point of view, surely you don't send your children to a school where they will be forced to speak French, share rooms with a Norwegian or a Pole, and eat their meals with Armenians, Hungarians, Greeks, Danes, Germans?

'We are in a peculiar position,' she concluded. 'No one else in the world has our opportunity to ... to ... inculcate the international idea in minds which are not yet too set, too limited by prejudice, too mired in conventional patriotism, if you care to look at it in that light. However, although that ought to be our working basis, our actual raison d'être, we cannot attempt to remedy a situation as bad as the present one, through such a circuitous route.'

'What situation?' asked Rose Dupraix.

Mlle Tourain leaned forward with one elbow on her desk, looking at her with a faintly amused expression. 'I should have thought that after your twenty years in this school, you would have been the first to detect psychological changes, Mlle Dupraix.' She looked down at her pencil, still tapping impatiently on the brass inkpot, and went on a moment later, 'I put it to you like this ... if the atmosphere of this school continues to be as strained, as unpleasant, as it is at the moment, we shall lose our pupils ... and our means of livelihood. It's hard enough combining an American Jewess of Theodora Cohen's temperament with a hysterical fourteenth-century Fascist like Truda Meyer, without throwing in a peace-loving and devout Bavarian Catholic like Anna von Landenburg, a half-Jewish girl from the Saar who doesn't yet know what nationality she is, and adding a Swiss and English staff who are too detached to consider these girls as anything but so many troublesome children learning lessons in a schoolroom of a mountain village.'

She thought, looking from one to another, that none of these women would have been here had it not been necessary for them to earn their living ... no one, that is, but Mary Ellerton. Miss Williams took her remark in the spirit in which it was offered, and instantly looked apologetic; Fräulein Lange did not appear even to have heard her ... what *was* the matter with the woman? ... Mlle Lemaitre's black eyes said 'Fair enough' but the head-mistress was afraid that that was as far as she would go. Mlle Devaux was all ears and eyes as usual, but the headmistress had a shrewd suspicion that the grammar teacher had misunderstood her completely. Mlle Dupraix's chinless face ... she was the only one of the Swiss women who was free of obligations and could afford to buy good clothes ... was merely bored; Mary Ellerton smiled appreciatively.

'Somehow or other, we've got to smooth things over ...' She stopped, asking herself impatiently what good that would do. Somehow the school had to be brought back to its normal atmosphere; as it was now, the girls were all divided into their five or six cliques and when they went outside them there was immediate trouble. If this sort of thing was to continue, they might just as well stay home, thought Amélie Tourain. She had no desire to waste her time as headmistress of a school giving instruction in French, winter sports and deportment; someone else could certainly do that job equally well, if not better, and leave her free to return to her own work. The international aspect was the only one which appealed to her, and for the past few days she had had an uncomfortable suspicion that Jeanne had chosen her, uprooted her from her study in the house off Avenue Ruchonnet, for precisely that reason.

The task before her was taking hold of one corner of her mind, pulling on it gently, so that her history had begun to slide away from her. She was alarmed for a fleeting moment, not in the least attracted by the prospect of spending the rest of her life in Pensionnat Les Ormes, then once more her mind reverted to the immediate problem. What was a normal atmosphere? Even supposing there was such a thing, would it be good enough in these times? And how could it possibly be restored without censoring all the girls' mail and stopping all newspapers? She had borrowed a copy of Truda Meyer's *Nationalzeitung* and read it from cover to cover. It had once been owned or controlled by Göring; whether it was still or not, the propaganda which filled the issue, the urging of people to do this and that and feel this and that was so palpably obvious that she could not imagine a ten-year-old child reading it without feeling that it was an insult to his intelligence. So far as the other newspapers were concerned, they only served to increase her profound discouragement that after so many centuries of supposed civilization the truth should still be subject to so much distortion.

'You know that our common aim in this school is to weld together the various nationalities. I want you to try and break down the barrier which exists between the staff and pupils in almost all schools. You know as well as I do that as soon as these girls stray beyond their own particular little group, there's trouble. I have been forced to put the two Jewish girls on different floors from some of the Germans; I have been forced more than once to interfere in conversations which appeared to be going to develop along ... along undesirable lines. We are failing and failing badly, yet for some reason which I am at present completely unable to fathom, my staff refuses to recognize the gravity of the situation.' She stopped her incessant tapping at last and glanced from one to the other of the faces before her, poorly illuminated by the desk light, for it was almost dusk now.

When her eyes arrived at Miss Williams's face, the English-woman cleared her throat, peering uncertainly through her thick spectacles at the headmistress, and said doubtfully, 'I am sure we will all do anything we can, Mademoiselle, but the only thing which appears to me to be at all feasible at the moment is to carry on our dining room arrangements away from meals ... group the girls with as many different people as possible, and then have one of us with them. And surveillance of that sort would be rather trying for them.'

'Yes,' said Mary Ellerton from down the line. 'You can't stand guard over girls of nineteen and twenty.' She remembered Vicky's remark that the only place she could secure any privacy was in the toilet, and even there one was liable to be disturbed by Mlle Dupraix, who had lately taken to coming and rapping on the door if one were not to be found in one's room. She went on deliberately, leaning forward with her elbow on one knee so that she could see her audience on the right. 'Some of the girls haven't sufficient privacy as it is.' Her eyes reached Mlle Dupraix's face and remained fixed there. 'It would be better to pay more attention to the trouble-makers, and less to girls like Anna, and Ilse, Marian, Consuelo, Vicky and Rosalie ...'

'Really, Miss Ellerton, considering the fact that Rosalie has not been out of her bed these past two months, I hardly think

she need be included.' It was Mlle Dupraix and she was about
to express herself further when Mlle Lemaitre interrupted with
an impatient and irritable glance at the Beaux Arts teacher,
across Fräulein Lange's unhappy face.

The Frenchwoman could not forgive Mlle Dupraix her lack
of knowledge of her own subject, and her persecution of Vicky.
'Let us leave, for a moment, the question of keeping an eye on
the unfortunate Vicky ... I feel sure you were coming to that,
Mlle Dupraix ... for I should like to know what is to become of
that poor little Rosalie?'

The headmistress sighed, and relaxing against the back of her
chair for a moment said patiently, 'No one appears to know
where Madame Garcenot is. She simply set the child on our
doorstep as it were, telling us that she was rather delicate. To do
the woman justice, I do not think that she had any idea that
Rosalie has a heart condition. She has been in a convent since
she was five or six, and from what little I know of such places, I
think it unlikely that she ever had a thorough cardiac examination before she came to us. Dr. Laurent is not worried about her,
although he considers it vitally important that the child should
not be upset nor in any way troubled.' She met Miss Ellerton's
green eyes and, shaking her head slightly, looked beyond her at
the blank expanse of folding doors. The green eyes were warning her ... or that was the feeling she had ... that the less said
about Rosalie the better. She went on rapidly a moment later, 'I
would suggest, as a first step, that the teachers discontinue their
present practice of seeing the girls only at specified times.'

She stopped again, as though anticipating some objection,
then went on in silence. 'You are all, to a certain extent, in their
position. You, Miss Williams ... your heart is in England.' The
Englishwoman flushed, but continued to look straight at her.
'You, Mlle Dupraix, are not just in your dealings with the girls.'

'I beg your pardon, Mlle Tourain!' she said angrily, half-rising from her chair.

The headmistress ignored her, and said to her staff in general, 'I am taking the risk of offending you because the situation is so serious. You, Fräulein Lange ... you are ... preoccupied ...' Her voice trailed away as she looked at the German teacher's thin, troubled face, and she continued gently after a moment, 'I realize, of course, that at times it is impossible to be otherwise.' She made an apologetic and old-fashioned little bow which was returned by the German teacher. 'You, Mlle Devaux, are too concerned with grammar. I wish you would try to be a little more understanding, a little less rigid. Discipline is not everything.' Mlle Devaux looked as though she might cry, and the headmistress hastily shifted her gaze to Mlle Lemaitre's thin face with its flushed cheeks and hawk-like nose. 'It is a characteristic of the French to concentrate upon brains, to the detriment of bodies ...' she began, with the complete change in manner with which she always addressed Mlle Lemaitre, for whose brilliant, though too-early exhausted mind she had a wholesome respect.

'I find it difficult to reconcile myself to anything less than the most thorough work possible,' said Mlle Lemaitre, cutting short the headmistress's tactful preamble. She pushed back a loose strand of black hair and shoved her glasses a little farther up her nose. It was a characteristic gesture which had delighted hundreds of girls. She was a small, thin dark woman with an extremely nervous manner as though she were constantly over-stimulated, and small black eyes which darted here and there like a bird's, and were unnaturally bright.

'So do I,' said Mlle Tourain, looking down at her pencil again, 'but you and I ... in fact all of us ... must remind ourselves that this is only a finishing school, although our curriculum is a great deal heavier than in most such places.' She raised her eyes again and looked straight at each member of her staff in turn. 'So far as I myself am concerned, I have neglected my duty more seriously than any of you. That also must be remedied. When Mlle d'Ormonde comes back I should like her to find the school in the state in which she left it, if that is possible, considering the changes which have taken place in the world since then.'

'And I, Mlle Tourain?' asked Mary Ellerton.

'You have not been here long enough.' She looked at the English girl in silence for a moment, then went on quickly, with a change of expression and a slight movement of her chair, which suggested that she was throwing off some idea which had intruded itself. 'I do not feel that you ... really believe ... you are here. Sometimes I think that I should not be at all surprised to wake up one morning and find that you had gone ... exactly as you came ...' She leaned forward, without offering any expla- nation for her extraordinary remark and as usual not looking to see the effect of it, and began to address her audience again. 'Some people think that a school is a deadly and unnatural place for women. I have erred in the opposite direction; I have uncon- sciously tried to preserve my own life in the face of constant interruptions and distractions, resenting this place because it drew me into the world ... rather than away from it, as most people seem to think any school does.'

She seemed to be speaking to herself; with one last anxious look at the faces before her, she turned her eyes once more to the folding doors behind them and continued as though she were unaware of them, her low voice flowing in the stillness of the room, 'This is a microcosm; what we face here, the world faces; what we suffer, thousands of others suffer in the same way. Yet only we ... the schoolteachers and the parents of the world ... we, and we alone are granted the opportunity to work changes in the lives of other people, before change of any fundamental sort becomes impossible. I am not, of course, including that part of human experience which lies within the province of the Church. You think of this school as an isolated place in which there is no real *living*, as we understand the word.... The incidents of the day, when they vary from the incidents of every other day, are an intrusion, and often strike a false, hysterical note. We feel that monotony must be restored at any cost.' She glanced at them once more, and with her eyes on the brass inkpot again, she said, 'I am trying to make you see that what we are up against here is not exceptional, is not merely an undesirable ... manifestation of adolescent instability ... but life itself.' And after another brief silence, 'That is all, Mesdemoiselles....'

She looked up and watched them prepare to leave, bothered by a feeling of guilt which had crept into her halfway through her speech. She had put into words something which she herself only half apprehended; she had spoken the words as the ideas occurred to her, and had given the impression that she had been thinking about them for some time past. That was not honest. In actual fact, she as yet only partly conceived the truth in her remarks, and she needed time in which to think them out. These women before her were bored, bored. She was in a totally different position, since all along she had disliked and resented the very liveliness and activity of the school, had been irritated by the incessant interruptions and petty detail which constantly broke into her mind and scattered her thoughts. Whereas her staff seemed to regard the general tension, the flare-ups, the emotional currents, as melodramatic and exaggerated, she herself had an uncomfortable suspicion that they were a part of life, and as such significant. Unfortunately, however, she did not want life; she only wanted peace of mind.

Mlle Dupraix and Mary Ellerton had remained behind. The English girl closed the door behind the others and returned to her place beside the French windows, evidently wishing to see the headmistress alone. Mlle Dupraix stood in front of the desk, one hand straightening her very smart leather belt. She said deliberately, 'Vicky's been smoking.'

Miss Ellerton swung around and looked at her angrily. Before Mlle Tourain had a chance to speak, she said, 'I'm afraid you're mistaken. Vicky does not smoke. She ... she doesn't know how. I happen to know that.' Her head was thrown back a little and she stood rather stiffly, almost defiantly, as though she half-expected a fight and rather hoped that there would be one.

'Then possibly you can explain how it was she brought in a new package of cigarettes yesterday, after she'd been out shopping with you?' The Beaux Arts teacher was facing Mary now, leaving the still, heavy figure of the headmistress in the background behind the big desk.

'How did you come to know that Vicky had them?' asked Mlle Tourain curiously. She liked her position, just out of the light. She was able to watch what went on in front of her without being drawn into it, as it were, leaning forward on her arms and looking from the vivid girl by the window to Mlle Dupraix in front of her. Her indifference to the Beaux Arts teacher had not yet reached the stage of active dislike; she considered her such mediocre human material that she simply could not be bothered with her at the moment, that was all. Jeanne, who was surprisingly wise in most of her dealings with people, had certainly shown poor judgement where Mlle Dupraix was concerned. Amélie Tourain thought she knew how that had happened, for her cousin believed, with Ruskin, that those who think human nature high will usually find it even higher than they thought it. It was that essential part of her which had made her such an outstanding principal, but it had also made her incapable of seeing the few worthless people who came into her life in their true light. Either Jeanne had led Mlle Dupraix to believe, or the Beaux Arts teacher had come to believe on her own, that she would be the next head of Pensionnat Les Ormes. Amélie Tourain was able to appreciate her feelings when she herself had arrived instead.

'I was here when Vicky came for Rosalie's mail. She opened her handbag to take out a handkerchief and I saw them.' She switched her gaze back to the headmistress again, anxious to eliminate the undependable Miss Ellerton.

'Your eyesight is too good when it comes to Vicky,' said Mary, and pulling back the curtain, looked out over the town again. A few lights sparkled here and there on the hillside across the lake, and the atmosphere was heavy and grey. There would be snow during the night or the next day, she thought.

Mlle Tourain started to speak, and thought better of it. She was interested to discover that almost everyone suffered by comparison with Miss Ellerton, appearing lifeless, or rather only partly animated, and rather unfinished, as though they were still in the early stages of evolution. It was not only that her face and body were so finely moulded that she seemed civilized, while they appeared almost cloddish, but she had a spark of vitality, a lightness, which diminished those about her so that no one but that strange Canadian girl, Vicky Morrison, could retain their dignity beside her. The headmistress shook her head slightly, trying to rid her mind of Vicky's pale, disciplined face, knowing only too well that the rest of her staff were allowing themselves to become preoccupied with her to such an extent that the school was beginning to consist of forty-seven girls and Vicky Morrison. They met her on a level, and endowed her with a quite disproportionate importance by always showing their awareness of her, and by constant reference to her. The rest of the school formed a hazy background against which that girl seemed to move with extraordinary clearness. Mlle Tourain herself had felt that same impulse to look at Vicky when she was addressing the whole school, and if she could not prevent the others from making fools of themselves, at least she still retained some remnants of control over herself. The problem of Vicky, thought the headmistress uncomfortably, was further complicated by the fact that she was Mary Ellerton's best friend.

She wished, suddenly, that she were nearer Mary Ellerton's age herself, that there was not the gulf of thirty-three years' experience between them. She would have liked to see more of Miss Ellerton, for she had retained the idea which had flashed into her mind before she began to speak, that they were two people with, each of them, sufficient fire, vitality, enthusiasm ... however you want to put it ... to work well together. With the others, all the work, all the enthusiasm would have to come from her, for they were too limited by years of routine, of doing no more than they had to do, of keeping as much back as they could and still do their work efficiently. If someone would only act with her she might be able to follow up some of the various ideas which had been pouring into her mind during the past half-hour. She had the sensation, as she sat behind her desk just out of the light, of being in the hands of a sculptor intent on remodelling her; she was conscious of change, of being pushed and pulled by some force within her which was at war with all her preconceived, all her lifelong desires. It was a painful process.

Mlle Dupraix was talking in a stream of words to Mary Ellerton. The headmistress shook her head slightly, trying to clear it a little, and looked from one to the other in an effort to bring her mind back to the present.

'... and since no one seems to be aware of that girl's subtle Bolshevism, no one but me, *I* have to do the disciplining which should normally fall to half a dozen people. I assure you it is only for that reason.... I, apparently, am the only one who sees through her. You must remember that I have been dealing with girls for twenty years, and it is naturally easier for me to detect her ... her ...'

'... subtle Bolshevism,' said Mary, looking bored. She came back to the desk and picked up a pencil, fingering it absently. With her eyes on it she said, 'I'm afraid that I can't find anything wrong with Vicky. The only trouble with her is that she's too mature.'

'Mlle Ellerton!' said the Beaux Arts teacher in genuine astonishment.

The headmistress was both startled and annoyed. She sat up and stared across the desk at Miss Ellerton's pencil for a moment, then looked up at her. 'How do you explain the cigarettes then?' she demanded.

'I left her at the chemist's while I went to pick up some things I'd ordered at a shop in Rue du Bourg.' She looked up, from one to the other, then down again. 'I must confess that I don't quite see what Mlle Dupraix is getting at. Vicky may bring cigarettes by the dozen into the school, provided she doesn't smoke them here. I presume that you have not seen Vicky smoking them here, Mlle Dupraix? And that since you have scarcely left Vicky undisturbed for so much as an hour until midnight or later during the past month, that if she had smoked them you would have found it out for yourself.'

Mlle Dupraix decided to ignore her. Looking across the desk at the headmistress, she said, 'You will, of course, go into this ...'

Miss Ellerton cut in quickly, 'It's not my business, Mlle Tourain, but I imagine Vicky brought those in for someone else.

Everyone knows she doesn't smoke. If she's questioned about this, she'll certainly take the blame on herself and the whole school will realize it. That's bad for discipline. We don't want to make foo ... to put ourselves into an awkward position ...'

'An awkward position, Miss Ellerton ...' said Mlle Dupraix meditatively, and looked once more at the headmistress. 'We can hardly allow Vicky ...'

'Yes, Mlle Dupraix,' said the headmistress wearily. The whole petty incident had got on her nerves; she would have preferred to let the matter drop, but Mlle Dupraix was evidently not going to allow it. It was essential to keep the Beaux Arts teacher in her place, or she would go rushing over to Evian and detail everything mercilessly to poor Jeanne, who was in no state to be informed that her school was going to wrack and ruin through the negligence of Amélie Tourain. She sighed, then went on rather irritably, 'I am surprised that you did not immediately deal with Vicky yourself, Mlle Dupraix, knowing how ... er ... conscientious you are....'

'It was scarcely my concern ...'

'That has not restrained you in the past,' said Mary coldly. She looked straight at the headmistress and went on deliberately, 'Mlle Tourain, you know that I have only been here a little more than two months. There are some things which I am still not quite clear about. Is the staff permitted to enter the girls' rooms, at any hour of the day or night, without knocking? Are they supposed to limit the amount of time which a girl may spend in the lavatory, and after a period of a minute or so, rap on the door and order them to come out?'

'They are not,' said Mlle Tourain grimly.

'Thank you,' said Mary, and returned to her place by the window.

The headmistress was regarding Mlle Dupraix unfavourably.

The Beaux Arts teacher returned the look for a moment, then went on with a rising inflection, 'Smoking is not all she does. She reads by candlelight every night. Last night she was not reading French either ...'

'What *was* she reading?' asked Mlle Tourain, half-hoping that Vicky had been reading one of her volumes of Euripides in the original Greek. The idea of forcing Mlle Dupraix to admit that Vicky's nocturnal tastes ran to Greek drama appealed to her.

'Fogazzaro,' said Mlle Dupraix. 'A most unsuitable novel, *Daniele Cortis....*'

'I'm afraid I must disagree with you. I don't think we need feel concerned with Vicky's choice of novels. It's a long time since I read *Daniele Cortis*, but I should think that no one ... not even you, Mlle Dupraix ... could find anything in the least undesirable in that book. Both the heroine and hero always struck me as being considerably more virtuous than was consistent with my experience of people. As for her reading by candlelight, I never can bring myself to feel that that is very reprehensible. Perhaps it is because I myself read by candlelight for many years ... I remember,' she went on reminiscently, 'that I kept a copy of *Anna Karenina* under my cabinet de toilette for some months ...' A half-suppressed chuckle from Mary Ellerton who was still looking out of the window brought her back to normal. She said, with a return to her old unsmiling dignity, 'I presume you took the book away from her?'

'No.' And in answer to the headmistress's look of surprise she went on in exasperation, 'How could I? You know that she and Theodora are studying Italian with Signora Bellini ... and she gave her the book ... or told her to buy it ... it's the same thing. What I want to know is, however, how long you intend to allow that girl to be excused to play her piano, owing to bad eyesight, when she ought to be downstairs sewing with the other girls every night after dinner, if her eyesight is good enough to permit her to read by candlelight?' Her voice had risen in anger, and she continued with exaggerated emphasis, 'That girl is being treated as a special being. One would think she were a ... a ... well, what made her come here in the first place? How long is she going to stay? Who *is* she, when it comes right down to it? Do anyone of us know anything about her?'

'You'd better answer that, Miss Ellerton,' said Mlle Tourain wearily.

'I don't know,' she said, turning so that she was facing them. 'Vicky never talks about herself or her background. I know nothing whatever about her family. I know she was brought up in Toronto, but whether her parents were or are Canadian, whether they're living or dead ... I don't know. If you will forgive my saying so, Mlle Dupraix, I do not regard it as my business, and since she's twenty-two, I do not feel that it is *anyone's* concern but her own. I have too much respect for her to try and pry information out of her. Anyhow, it's not important to us ... what *is* important to us is her uncanny knack with people ... or her understanding, if you like. She's a very good influence.'

'A good influence!' said Mlle Dupraix. 'Well!' She started toward the door. 'I'm afraid you're due for disillusionment, Miss Ellerton,' she said, and went out.

Mary sank into one of the big leather chairs by the desk, rubbing her forehead with one hand, as she waited for the head-mistress to speak.

'You have a headache, Miss Ellerton,' said Mlle Tourain with concern.

'A little ... not very much,' she answered, looking up.

'I'm glad you stayed behind. I wanted to talk to you about Rosalie ... to ask if you know anything at all about her which might possibly help me to understand her a little better.'

Mary shook her head, looking over the corner of the big desk at the elderly woman seated behind it. 'I don't know any more for a fact than you do ... I *feel* a great many things, but that's not a great deal of help.'

She looked at Miss Ellerton swiftly, then down at her hands folded on the green blotting-paper in front of her. 'One can't help feeling a great many things. But it's not enough, as you say. Does anyone know anything about her? Has she any intimate friends?'

'There's only Vicky,' she said rather unwillingly.

'Vicky! Is Vicky running this school? She obsesses my staff, she ... really, Miss Ellerton, this is too much altogether. The girl apparently concerns herself with everyone and everything.' She shrugged impatiently and, rubbing her hands together, decided to question the girl about those cigarettes at dinner. The publicity might have a good effect on her.

Mary sat up, with one hand on either arm of her chair, and said decisively, 'No, she's the least interfering person here. Everyone talks to her, that's the trouble. Don't blame her for it, it's not her fault. I don't know what it is,' she went on meditatively, looking down at the floor as though she were thinking out loud and were anxious to find the answer for her own sake. 'There's something in her ... a certain quality which people are drawn to. With a different upbringing and a different environment, she might have been a religieuse. There's something more besides.' She paused, as though choosing her words very carefully. 'She has the gift of self-dismissal ... so that people are not afraid to talk to her, knowing that she won't ... I can't explain. They're simply not self-conscious with her, that's all.'

The headmistress was looking at her rather awkwardly. 'Well,' she said at last, 'I won't argue with you about that. I suppose I'll have to see if she can help me with Rosalie. Something's got to be done about her ... we can't leave her lying there alone in her room without having any real contact with her much longer. But I've got to have something to go on.' And as Mary said nothing she went on with growing annoyance, 'It's really too much to have to ask that girl about one of my own pupils....'

Mary said awkwardly, 'I'm afraid Vicky can't help you....'

'You mean she won't,' said the headmistress sharply.

'Won't then.'

'Why? Why?' she demanded impatiently. 'Yes, yes, I know all about the Anglo-Saxon objection to telling tales ... others have it besides the saintly English. It isn't a question of that. I simply want to *understand* ... I want to know why that little girl lies there all day and all night with a face like death, telling her beads, never smiling. Although I had never thought a child of that age could suffer mental agony, the last time I was up there in her room, I believed that she *was*. I came away with the conviction that whatever it was that was going on in that girl's mind, it's beyond my comprehension. I am perfectly powerless to help her, because I don't understand. There is something there, in that girl's mind, which is slowly taking her away from life ... I don't mean at all that I think she is mentally unbalanced ... it's not mysticism, because it's too personal ... it's rather a kind of spiritual resignation, a letting go of her vital forces which is extremely alarming, and yet, as you say, it is something that one feels rather than knows, and I will admit frankly that I would not say this to anyone but you for fear of being charged with ... hysterical ... exaggeration.'

She pulled herself up a moment later, as Mary said nothing, and went on, 'This doesn't seem to me to be the time for Vicky to take things into her own hands.'

Miss Ellerton stood up. 'I'd help if I possibly could, but I'm afraid ...'

'You mean that you yourself don't feel like trying to influence Vicky,' she said shrewdly.

Mary started to say something, then checked herself. She found that clear, dispassionate gaze rather trying. She moved a little, then said rather uneasily, 'I realize that it sounds absurd. But I do believe Vicky knows what she's doing. I couldn't bring myself to go beyond a certain point in trying to influence her, because, quite honestly, she knows people instinctively much better than I do.'

'She seems to have you all hypnotized. One half of the staff blame everything that ever happens upon her; the other half regard her as a species of saint. All this Vicky, Vicky, Vicky, is becoming farcical. Whether she intrudes herself, or whether, as you seem to believe, there is something about her which engrosses other people to such an extent that they force her to a place of undue prominence, I cannot have such an ... an incubus ... in a school which is run for the majority, not for the individual.' She spoke jerkily, because halfway through her speech she had suddenly recollected that the only opportunity she herself had had to talk to Vicky had been during the early autumn when the Canadian girl sat at the head table. During those weeks the headmistress had liked her because she had *not* intruded herself.

'This is too absurd. How am I going to run this school if I don't know what half my girls are thinking about? None of my staff know anything about them either. Do you know?' she asked abruptly.

'No,' said Mary almost inaudibly.

'I shall find out what's the matter with that child if I have to cross-examine Vicky for three hours. I will *not* be put in a position of inferiority and ignorance by this ... this ... species of saint from Canada....' She stopped, looking suddenly embarrassed, and sank back a little in her chair. She was making a most undignified exhibition of herself, but if you are wandering about in a room full of furniture, blindfolded, how on earth can you be dignified?

She shrugged again, then went on, utterly unaware that Mary was baffled and rather charmed by this sudden revelation of Amélie Tourain as a human being of fine, rich texture, 'We all run away from the idea that there is anything in the mind of an ordinary adolescent which is not straightforward and infantile. We only go so far as to allow them emotions such as love for their parents and friends, sports, a certain very limited amount of intellectual acumen and a conventional outlook ... when they suddenly show us something which doesn't fit into our conceptions of the normal, wholesome schoolgirl, we say, "Let us stamp it out, at whatever cost." It's a question of inconvenience to ourselves, of having to deal with individuals rather than with types, which is altogether too much trouble, and requires too much time and effort to understand ... for anyone to whom teaching is a simple method of earning a somewhat inadequate income, rather than a genuine vocation. I wonder why it is that this most important of all professions should be riddled with people who do it because other hopes have failed? Not through a knowledge of others, or a knowledge of themselves, nor from a desire to lead, to inspire, to teach something of the way in which life should be lived.'

And a moment later, 'There is, of course, something back of Truda Meyer's determination to dominate above all else; there is something behind this series of headaches which have kept Marian Comstock in bed for more than a week. And what about Anna von Landenburg? She is enduring something ... she *is* something besides a gentle, devout, sweet-faced young Bavarian girl ... and Rosalie. She is the greatest problem of all. I agree with you, as you know, that there is something besides her bad heart ... a great deal besides her bad heart, but what can a girl of that age know of life, or of suffering? She's been brought up in a convent! You would think that life would be as uncomplicated by doubts and fears for that girl as for anyone on earth. How can a sixteen-year-old endure ... whatever it is which she is undeniably enduring? I don't know. I'm living to see the total collapse of all my theories ... it seems that one's theories remain intact only so long as one generalizes from ignorance, and avoids particularizing from knowledge.'

Mary was astonished. She sat down on the arm of her chair and watched the face opposite her which had come alive during the past few minutes, half-perceiving at last that this woman was quite remarkable, that she possessed a mind which was not only objectively analytical, but subjectively analytical as well, and which was tempered by sufficient emotion to make her understanding almost unlimited once she was willing to rely on her intuition as well as on her intellect. Until this moment she had considered her brilliant, but humanly speaking, unimaginative. She had thought that Amélie Tourain might be of some use if she would only exert herself, but that even then her sphere of usefulness would be limited by her too-theoretical and academic experience of life.

With a swift, nervous glance at her, Amélie Tourain continued anxiously, 'I have everyone's tendency to judge others by myself. When *I* was sixteen, I was a bookish, heavy creature ... if I had my dreams, I never knew it.' She paused for one moment, looking upwards, her face tense, then apparently shook off some idea which had no connection with the present and went on, 'There may have been something more than that. Nowadays one is harassed by doctors and psychologists haranguing us about the unconscious mind. One doesn't know where one's at. There's no reasonable, logical answer to the argument that such and such is true of you, even though you have not been aware of it. You see ... until now, I have always believed that everything, including human beings, was susceptible to pure reason.' One of her rare smiles flashed across her face. 'I can't help feeling that these girls are all unnatural. I was never like that ... I'm not making the conventional, adult excuse either. I was *not* like that! A psychologist might say that I was, and have never realized it ... but it's the same thing, because my basis for understanding at the moment is what I can remember of my own actual experience ... not some psychical fact of which I am unaware. So I have the normal tendency to try to force them into being like myself ... to translate them, in other words, into terms I can understand ... since one cannot apprehend truth only with the intellect ... there is a spiritual and emotional apprehension as well. One's no good without the other. I have to be able to feel, vicariously, what they are feeling, and to do that I need a little knowledge of them ... I can't go on pure guesswork, any more than I can go on pure reason. And of course the problem is made all the harder by the fact that I know so well that if environment and suggestion count for anything at all, these girls cannot possibly be the kind of girls who were produced in Switzerland in 1890.'

She seemed to fall into thought then, allowing her mind to run backwards in one of her rare moments of mental relaxation. Mary made no effort to bring her back, but continued to sit opposite her in the dim, quiet study until the tea-bell rang with a sharp, discordant clanging. From then on their conversation was carried on against the noise of whispering, talking, shuffling, and clattering as forty girls rushed past the door to the dining room.

'These girls ... these extraordinary girls ...' said Amélie Tourain, bringing herself back to the troubled atmosphere of January 1935. 'I mean Vicky, Rosalie, poor little Ilse looking forward to Jewish persecution if Hitler gets the Saar on Sunday ... Yasha ... Anna ...' She dropped her hands wearily into her lap; she was wondering at the outgrowth of that bookish, heavy girl, and the woman whom she saw sitting in the book-filled study of the little house off Avenue Ruchonnet, a scholarly serene woman who was most strangely herself. Was it possible that the way to true living lay not through the rejection of human desires, trouble, pain and joy? Was it possible that she had lived for fifty-eight years in a world rendered sterile because there, in her little house down the hillside, there had been no ebb and flow of life ... only the slow passage of time, only so many days, weeks, months and years which now, as she looked back, melted into one another, an unbroken continuity.

She could go on in compromise no longer; that much she knew now, and no more. She had yet to be convinced that this way, through Pensionnat Les Ormes, lay her road, not the other life of contemplation and study.

She was wrenched back once more by Mary's voice asking: 'Is it necessary to hold the faculty meeting tonight?'

'I'm afraid it is. We've got to get to the bottom of this stealing ... we can't allow it to go on any longer.'

'It was because of that,' said Mary with difficulty, 'that I asked about it. I don't think Ilse and Truda should be left alone any more than is absolutely necessary. I don't know whether you know or not, but Truda thought she discovered Ilse copying during a test on Monday, and that gave her the idea that Ilse was the thief. Besides that ... you know how naturally uncongenial they are. Ilse's too mild and gentle ... Jewish cowardice and weakness, Truda calls it, inherited from Ilse's Jewish mother ... and Truda, as you said, likes to bully.' She stood up, glancing at her watch. 'I could ask Vicky to stay in the living room this evening to keep an eye on things,' she added tentatively.

'Certainly not,' replied Mlle Tourain, with a return to her old manner. 'Vicky's always gone upstairs after dinner to work at her piano ... I couldn't have her suddenly appear in the living room without everyone knowing that she'd been instructed to "keep an eye on things." And I couldn't have that. She's only one of forty-eight girls to me, whatever she is to the rest of you.'

II

Mary had intended to have her tea as quickly as possible and then hunt up Vicky, but on leaving Mlle Tourain's study she remembered that her skis were still lying in the snow down by the rink at the end of the garden, which necessitated a trip upstairs to get her coat and then a rapid walk down to the gates.

There she met the Bonne Femme, an ancient Swiss peasant woman who established herself each afternoon in the cellar-room beneath the floor of the east loggia with peanuts, chocolates, grapes, apples, dates, figs and other delicacies which she sold to the girls at exorbitant prices. She was trudging down the drive with her bag strapped to her shoulders. She stopped and peered uncertainly, then said, 'Ah, it's you, Mlle Ellerton.' She came close to the young English girl and stared at her, reaching up very slowly to her shoulder where the pack was pressing on it, trying to loosen the strap with one hand. 'It gets heavy,' she remarked, half to herself.

'Can I help you?' Mary asked. She was anxious to get back to the house, for the dreary cold wind which blows down from the Alps before a blizzard penetrated her clothes and made her ears ache. How did the old woman manage to stay warm?

'No ... no ... I know how it goes ...' She struggled for another minute, then relaxed with a sigh and continued to stand staring at her ... or through her, Mary thought, for the old woman's mind was wandering again, as it did occasionally.

'You're late today, Madame,' she said, looking upwards to the school where the lights beckoned her across the wide, snow-covered sloping terraces. The lights seemed to say 'Here is life, if you would only come here to live,' so distinctly that she was troubled, and had an impulse to run through the heavy gates into the outer world. Only half her being existed in the school; the other part seemed to vibrate just out of her reach beyond its windows. It was that other part which must be kept alive; she felt that so intensely that she never crossed the threshold of the school without consciously leaving something of herself behind as if to preserve the link between Miss Ellerton as she was now, and the Miss Ellerton ... or Mrs. Gilchrist ... she had been.

The Bonne Femme was giving her confused and disjointed explanations of her tardiness that afternoon. Normally she packed up and left shortly after two. Forcing herself to follow what the old woman was saying, Mary gathered that she had had to wait until Marthe, Mlle Tourin's elderly personal maid, had come off duty. Marthe, it seemed, was a distant cousin of the Bonne Femme who had once been attached to her son Henri, now a boatman with two barges of his own at Ouchy. Henri had recently fallen in love with a young girl, less than half his age, and proposed to set up an establishment of his own and send his mother back to the mountains. She suspected that the girl's father had some idea of personal advancement by sanctioning the match. In any case, it was all highly improper and she had waited this afternoon to consult Marthe about it, for she had always thought that Marthe regretted the quarrel between herself and Henri ... but now Marthe, who was approaching fifty, would not do anything about it. Could Mlle Ellerton suggest some way out of it? It was not that she minded going back to the mountains, for she had half a mind to die where she had been born, but the girl herself was pitiable ... Antoinette, her name was, and she was in love with a waiter at the German café ... it was wrong, all wrong, an offence against the Holy Virgin, although her son, surrounded as he was by godless Protestants, had become indifferent to his religion and neither she nor Father Antoine could do anything with him.

Mary shook her head. She was caught in one of those inexplicable moods which come suddenly and go as quickly, when one seems to be a harmonious part of the universe. She was aware of herself, talking to an old Swiss peasant woman about her son, standing by the gate of a school above Lausanne with the world and all its thrilling possibilities stretching out beneath her feet.

The old woman gave her a final, baffling look, turned and marched abruptly away toward the gates muttering to herself something about Vicky which Mary could not catch. She ran after her, caught her arm and said brusquely, 'What was that you said about Mlle Vicky?'

'I have forgotten.'

She looked at her quite helplessly, knowing that it was more than possible that the Bonne Femme really had forgotten, and there was no use in pressing her. She let go her arm, half-turned, then said on an impulse, 'Tell me, Madame ... you are clairvoyante, yes?'

'A little, sometimes.'

'What will happen to Mlle Vicky?'

'Oh ...' with a shrug, 'she will go. Why not? She should never have come ... with her will go Mlle Théodore....'

'And I, Madame?'

'Oh ... you. You will stay.'

For some reason she believed the maundering old woman, and watched her until she had turned the corner by the gates and disappeared into the street, almost bent double under her sack of delicacies, then started back towards the school, carrying her skis over her shoulder. The next day, she knew, the old Bonne Femme would be back in her dark cellar behind the improvised table laden with fruit and nuts, having forgotten all about it. She would be, once more, a white-haired, plump old woman with a neat lace cap on her head and a clean pinafore tied round her waist, sitting on an upturned box with her hands folded in her lap, bearing no resemblance to the sinister figure bent under the knapsack who had just disappeared down Avenue Closse. Her prophesying meant nothing. Mary was sufficiently clearheaded to realize that you cannot make a person believe anything unless that person has already had a conscious or unconscious vision of the same thing; you have no conviction of truth unless you have already apprehended it intuitively. The old woman might have said, 'You will go to live in Bangkok,' and she would merely have smiled.

Mary went doggedly on up the drive, unable to recover that single instant of mental poise. She looked about her at the trees on either side, then up into the dark sky. The school was ahead to the right now, for she had taken the turn where the drive left the south fence and started the long straight climb on the west side of the grounds. Between her and the lighted French windows whose shutters had not yet been closed for the night, a few elm trees cast their vague soft shadows across the snow, silhouetted against the lighted building. She wanted to take a long walk up the hillside beyond the school and sit down by herself where she could look out over the town and reorientate herself with the world, but there was not time, with all the things she had to do before dinner, and besides that one could not sit and think with the temperature down to zero.

Would this interminable winter never end? Each cold day since her arrival seemed to stretch downwards and backwards into the past, never merging with the day which preceded it, or the day which followed it but remaining separate, like a flight of steps up which she had dragged herself in almost unbearable loneliness.

The early months following her discovery that her husband was unfaithful to her and that the woman was one of her best friends, had melted into one another now, and seemed a long period of greyness and misery. She could not have said when it was that the days began to stand out individually, to become units of so many hours which must be got through somehow or other until night fell and reality slipped away, leaving her free to lie in bed and plan her future with Barry, her husband, as she wanted it to be.

That morning she had learned from Jack Emerson, who had shared Barry's apartment with him until he left Lausanne, that he ... her husband ... would not be back from Sicily until spring. Standing by the telephone in the linen-room ... there was another in Mlle Tourain's study, but one could not be sure that Mlle Dupraix would not drop in there, whereas the linen-room could be locked from the inside ... surrounded by sheets, pillow-cases, napkins and tablecloths fresh from the laundry stacked in piles all around her, she had felt sick with nervousness when she dialled the number. She had tried a hundred times during the past two months to summon sufficient courage to call him; the knowledge that she might meet him in the street had made every trip to town a mad adventure and she had walked about Lausanne weak in the knees, as a woman does who goes to meet her lover. It takes courage, she thought, to gamble all you've been able to salvage of yourself after months of suffering, to risk the death of this new, enriched person, who has somehow in spite of immense loss, emerged from the ashes of the old. That explained why she had tried a hundred times, and why she had often found herself thinking that if she did come across him looking in a shop window or posting a letter, she would turn into the first doorway and let him pass without speaking to him.

When she had telephoned that morning and asked for Barry, Jack Emerson had not recognized her voice. He had merely said that Mr. Gilchrist had gone to Taormina to paint, and would not be back until spring. It seemed odd to her that he had not remembered her, until she realized that the only reason *his* voice and his whole personality were so impressed on her was that when one suffers an intense shock one's perceptions become over-acute, and her memory was playing her the unhappy trick of retaining every sight and sound of that evening when she had first come to know that Barry was unfaithful to her. He had said the night before that he intended to go down to Devon to spend the weekend with his family, and she had believed him. Why not? She herself never lied, and when you don't lie yourself, you do not expect lies from others. Anyhow, she remembered ... how well she remembered ... that she had been standing at the bar with her young cousin, who had come down from Oxford demanding that she go out dancing with him ... and she had looked up to see Barry and Ethel, one of her best friends, reflected in the mirror in front of her. Something in the way they were looking at each other instantly recalled to her mind something in the way they had looked at each other when Ethel had been down in the country visiting herself and Barry the preceding summer, and the truth broke in her mind, sending long, sharp splinters into every corner of it.

Well, put up a partition between yourself and your memories if you cannot by any effort of will rid yourself of them. Who had invented telephones? Half the shocks of her life had come to her by telephone; she could look back to the person she had been and see her standing by a whole series of telephones listening, while an impersonal mechanized voice at the other end of the wire knocked away the foundations of her world. There was that girl who was herself at seventeen, standing in a wide hallway listening to a voice from Croydon reporting that her father's plane had been found floating in the Channel, and four years later that same girl trying frantically to get the office of the track at Brooklands where Stephen Ellerton, her brother, was trying to break some record or other. She was twenty-one then, and was phoning from the Gilchrist family place on the cliffs above the Bristol Channel, spending the weekend with them to mark her twenty-first birthday and her engagement to Barry.

In another sense, the most sickening conversation she had ever had with anyone had come at the end of that long, hellish afternoon during which she and Barry had talked and talked, during which he had explained, describing his emotions about Ethel beautifully and assuring her, Mary his wife, that this was not just an affair, but that he wanted to marry her best friend. Just as the door closed behind him, Ethel herself called on the phone. She said she hoped that they could still be friends; that she knew it would all work out in the best way for the three of them, and that Mary would realize after a while that her marriage to Barry had been a mistake from her, Mary's point of view. After all, they were modern, civilized people and there was no need for all this outmoded bad feeling which previous generations had seen fit to indulge in under similar circumstances.

Well, they had not married each other after all. A decree *nisi* takes too long to become absolute for such easy lovers to stave off boredom. In the end he had wanted to come back to her. Mary had said that they would wait a year. If at the end of that time he still wanted her, if he wanted her enough to be faithful to her in the meantime, she would see him then. This also by telephone, and in some ways it was the most difficult moment of her life, for the very sound of his voice pulled her to pieces, so that with the few fragments of herself which she could summon to her aid in such a moment, she had had to make that overwhelming decision. The rest of her clamoured 'Come back! Come back!' so that the aching desire for him might be appeased if only for a while, leaving the future ... who cares about the future if only I can see you and touch you again? ... to take care of itself.

The year would be up in April. Soon after that last time when he had telephoned to ask if he might come back, he had gone to Lausanne. It was his sister Betty, a sympathetic soul, who had suggested to Mary that if she simply couldn't stand London without Barry, she might try for this job at Pensionnat Les Ormes, which another friend of Betty's had recently vacated, leaving Mlle Tourain without a games mistress, so that she could at least be near him.

Which all sounded very level-headed and self-controlled, she thought, coming round the corner of the school into the courtyard, but the trouble was that she had to force herself to live up to this conception of herself. If she had been able to talk to Barry this morning ... if he had not departed for Sicily ... the year would have been up then, so far as she was concerned. It was as though her intelligence superimposed on her outward existence a course of action which had nothing to do with the actual life she led within herself. By day she was able to think clearly and sanely, but at night when she was alone she lay in bed terrified for fear something should happen ... for fear she should discover that Ethel had had a successor and he had not kept his word for the second time ... and she be left without the hope which had, once more, in spite of herself, become the core of her being. She had taken no particular pains to build up the first Mary Ellerton, but the second, the person she was now, had been put together slowly and with labour, and the whole welded by suffering.

She put her skis on the rack by the door, and stripping off her coat crossed the hall and entered the dining room. It was Thursday, she remembered, the day on which Pensionnat Les Ormes got fresh bread, which accounted for the mob in the dining room. By Saturday it would have started to thin out, by Wednesday ninety per cent of the school, not being particularly fond of bread six days old, would take tea in their rooms, the meal consisting of fruit, nuts and candy bought from the Bonne Femme. She shook off her mood as she closed the dining room door behind her and choosing the most congenial group of girls, went over to Fräulein Lange's table. The German teacher was not there; she was sitting in the art room on the third floor listening to Vicky playing the *Italian Concerto*.

The dining room had windows along the south and west sides. The north wall, which separated it from the kitchens and which was on your right as you walked in, was bare, but for a long table covered with clean, thick white dishes and a sideboard in which the bread and silver were kept in drawers. The west wall directly opposite the door had three casement windows and three tables placed at right angles to it, Mlle Tourain's, the head table, Mlle Devaux's, and Mlle Lemaitre's in the corner. Between the two French windows on the south side was Miss Williams' table, in the left-hand corner Fräulein Lange's table, and next to it, on the east wall, Mary Ellerton's own table, which, she saw on entering, was occupied by eight German girls, none of whom she particularly liked.

At Fräulein Lange's table where she sat down, with her back to the wall so that she could see the whole room, were Yasha Livovna from Warsaw; the two Armenians Aimée and Natalia Babaian; Stephania Carré from Milan and Maria-Teresa Tucci from Genoa; and at the end, the only two German girls who were *not* at her own table, Mary noticed ... Anna von Landenburg from Nürnberg, and Ilse Brüning, the little half-Jewish girl from Saarbrücken, both of them very obviously choosing neutral ground. Ilse would naturally want to get as far away from Truda Meyer ... who was sitting at the head of the next table with her seven sycophants ... as possible, but why Anna, Mary wondered.

There were no other members of the staff present; either they had already had their tea or they were not coming at all, for it was already close to four-thirty. Tea was the only meal which was an entirely voluntary affair; one might take it or not as one saw fit, and sit where one liked. Mary was always amused to notice how different the grouping ... for which Mlle Dupraix in her capacity of housekeeper was at other times responsible ... was in the afternoon. Then nationalities, and congenial nationalities, sat together. The rest of the time they were all mixed up.

The table in front of her was littered with tea cups and plates, as well as the inevitable heavy china pitcher containing milky tea, a dish of jam, a plate of butter, and three large stacks of fresh French bread. She was served by Yasha beside her as soon as she sat down. Yasha, she noticed, was in a silent mood ... a mood which might have been described as morose if she had a less enigmatic countenance. She sat and sipped her tea with the cup held in both hands, and her elbows on the table. She was a small, dark-skinned Polish girl with fair hair and brown eyes which were naturally shadowed. She was slender and voluptuous at the same time, passionate, generous, and about as pliable, Mary knew, as a piece of granite. She was extremely reserved, preferred not to draw attention to herself in any way, and was beginning her third year at Pensionnat Les Ormes, having been sent back unexpectedly during the early part of December.

Mary said, rather awkwardly, 'You don't look as though you're very pleased to be back, Yasha.'

She gave a barely perceptible shrug, turned her head and looked speculatively at Mary for a moment, then returned to her tea, saying rather coldly, 'My mother decided suddenly to go to Stamboul for Christmas. It's a waste of time for me to be here, since I already speak French and German better than I speak Polish, but she *would* go to Stamboul, and there was no place else to put me.'

'And your father?' asked Mary.

'My father? He spends most of his time in Vilna anyhow,' she answered with an obvious shrug, this time.

'You might learn English,' suggested Mary rather lamely.

'I already speak English,' said Yasha, in English, without a trace of accent. Then in French again, 'I had an English governess.' It was unlike her, Mary knew, to give an explanation for anything, so she might take that as a compliment.

The eight Germans at the next table were talking rather loudly in their own language. Mary ignored it for a while, then turned at last and said peremptorily, 'Speak French, please.'

She wished that she had Yasha's command of languages; it was obvious that what Truda and her friends were saying in German was bothering Ilse and Anna at the end of the table on Yasha's left, but she could not understand it.

Ilse, a thin dark girl with unusually fine brown eyes and an unhealthy pallor, said at last, as though in answer to Mary's unspoken question, 'They're talking about the Saar, Mlle Ellerton.'

'Everybody is, Ilse,' said Mary quickly.

Anna glanced across at the games mistress, past Ilse, buttering a slice of bread, and Yasha, sitting back in her chair and looking straight in front of her. She was white, except for a spot of colour burning over each high cheekbone, and her hair was dark, a cloudy frame for her face which already showed unusual character and the traces of unusual suffering for a girl of only nineteen. She was slender and rather tall, unlike little Ilse beside her, with greyish green eyes which appeared flat, dried as they were by fever and fatigue. She had a bad touch of flu but she was doing her best to keep those in authority from finding out about it for fear they would send her to bed. Her mind revolved around her father (who was head of the Bavarian group of counter-revolutionaries), escaping only now and then into work. If she were sent to bed and forced to stay there for perhaps a week, she would have nothing to prevent her constant fear for his safety and his life from closing in on her. She had been fighting to prevent that, ever since her arrival four months before, as the number of arrests, persecutions and death sentences increased each day.

She said, in her quiet low voice, 'Germany will get the Saar,' as though there were no more grounds for doubt than if she had said that there was snow on the ground outside the dining room windows.

'You can't be sure of that, Anna,' said Mary. 'No one can, until after the elections.' It was hard to talk to some of these girls now, she found; most of the time when she tried to be cheerful she felt that what she said was irrelevant and that she was taking them for children, which they were not.

The Bavarian girl shook her head. 'Germany will get the Saar, Miss Ellerton,' she repeated almost mechanically.

Ilse looked so upset that Mary, remembering her Jewish mother and Jewish fiancé, was alarmed, watching the little Saarlander bite her lip, struggling to control herself. Anna glanced at her with an unhappy expression, and the two of them fell into silence again, sitting side by side and somehow withdrawn from the group.

Maria-Teresa remarked from the other end of the table, 'This bread is meraviglioso! Every night I dream of bread from Saturday on ... the stale bread gives me indigestion, Mlle Ellerton ... but it's never so good as this.' Beside her, Stephania smiled at the table in general, as though asking for leniency in the case of Maria-Teresa Tucci.

Natalia and Mary began to discuss skiing at Gstaad where the school was to spend its annual fortnight in the middle of January. Mary had never been there, and listened to the heavy-featured Armenian girl's description of it with some interest. She liked Natalia, having recovered from her first instinctive antipathy to the girl's broad dark face and thick coarse hair; to her full, soft contralto voice and too-affectionate manner, when she discovered that Natalia was one of those rare people who see only good in others, who are kind, considerate and self-forgetful. She took the younger girls under her wing, was always knitting, sewing or darning for someone else, and could be depended upon to recognize incipient quarrels before it was too late. She also possessed, astonishingly enough, a remarkably clear, logical and well-balanced mind.

Her cousin Aimée, very similar to her in appearance but mentally and physically smaller, had never been heard by anyone to utter more than 'Oui' or 'Non' although Natalia became distressed periodically and assured Mlle Tourain that she really spoke beautiful French en famille. Because she was always silent, no one knew anything about her. Both girls had been born in Smyrna, but after the persecutions the two brothers had fled with their families, Natalia's father to Brussels where he grew rich from the tobacco trade, Aimée's father to Paris where he proceeded to grow equally rich in the Oriental rug business.

'Where's Vicky?' asked Mary of Natalia at the close of her anecdotes of the year before at Gstaad.

It was Yasha who answered her. 'She's in the art room with Fräulein Lange, or was when I came down.' A moment later she added, with unusual irritation. 'Something's up with Fräulein, so she goes running to Vicky like everyone else. C'est trop fort!'

Which might, thought Mary, mean anything. She was worried about Vicky, but unable to get at the cause of her worry. Perhaps it was the Bonne Femme working on her nerves, which were, like everyone else's at the moment, in a rather uncertain condition. There were a hundred small things which, totalled up, meant trouble for Vicky, but you cannot send for a girl and say that there is this thing and that thing which have been reported to me and which, taken together, lead me to believe that we would get along better without your presence at this school. You have to have some specific, grave charge to lay against a girl before you can expel her.

She began to be aware of fitful giggling and spasms of half-smothered laughter at the next table, but a quick glance at the eight German girls told her nothing. Something was in the air, though; she could tell that by looking at Ilse and Anna who were watching Truda and the others and looked ill at ease. Mary's anxiety for them in that heaven-sent period after dinner when Truda could pick a fight undisturbed if she chose, was gradually increasing to such a point that she almost decided to go against Mlle Tourain's orders and tell Vicky to stay down and keep an eye on things.

If the headmistress believed that Vicky was deliberately taking it upon herself to influence the other girls, or that she was preening herself on her inside knowledge, the headmistress was quite mistaken. Mary knew that from her own experience, for it was only when she tried to get something out of her about Rosalie, or what was worrying Anna, that Vicky closed up like a clam and refused to talk. Once she had said almost violently, 'I came here in order to live quietly by myself. I've had too much melodrama, too much excitement, and I wanted for once to be able to fade into a background; I wanted to live my own inner life as it seems to me only possible to live it when your external life is governed and simplified by a general routine. I wanted to be freed from all responsibility for my own or anyone else's existence. Now look at the mess I've made of it!'

Mary had asked Vicky about Ilse, because of all the girls in the school she seemed to be in the least happy circumstances. Her father, a lawyer in Saarbrücken, had been ill for a year, during which Ilse's fiancé, a young Parisien Jew, had taken care of his business and supported his family. Three months from now, two months from now, two weeks, one week, six days, five days, three days ... and Ilse's country would decide whether or not they should throw in their lot with Hitler and his cohorts. That was what Ilse had been living with, and Mary did not know how she had stood it. Supposing Germany got the Saar, Paul would not have much of a chance, for in the intervals when he was not conducting Brüning's law business or playing with Ilse whom he apparently adored, he was acting as some kind of officer in the remain-under-the-mandate-of-the-League-of-Nations party. So Ilse had his actual safety to worry about as well as Truda's unpleasantness. And there was Ida Samuels from New York and the other sensation-minded adolescents talking pogroms, Jewish persecutions in Essen, Munich, Heidelberg ... Jews or part-Jews were not allowed on the Wilhelmstrasse, they rode in the corner of the Berlin trams with their faces hidden, skulked along the gutters living on garbage and what charity the poverty-stricken German public could give them ... How on earth did little Ilse endure it, with Truda openly sneering at her approaching marriage to a Jew, and half the school discussing stories of the latest atrocities in her hearing? And now, into the bargain, she was supposed to be a thief, according to Truda and half a dozen others.

Yet Vicky had said, 'I think she'll be all right. Bad as it is, at least they're all in it together ... her father and mother, and Paul. Incidentally, he must be a very decent sort. He used to be in his father's firm in Paris ... it's quite an important one, evidently ... until he elected to salvage the Brüning's business. Anyhow, you can stick almost anything if you're not alone ... as Anna is.'

'Hasn't she got a father?' Mary had asked. 'It seems to me that I've heard Graf von Landenburg mentioned ... he's her father, isn't he?'

'Yes,' Vicky had said shortly. 'That's the trouble.'

Mary had been completely nonplussed. 'But what's the mystery then, Vick?'

'You'll probably find out, sooner or later. I promised her to keep it under my hat. The trouble is, she's as near to being mad with worry as anyone I've ever seen.'

Remembering that, Mary turned once more and scrutinized the immobile, feverish face of the Bavarian girl, still sitting beside

Ilse and now, like the little Saarlander, studiously ignoring the eight giggling girls at the next table. What on earth was it all about, Mary wondered. Truda and her friends obviously had something up their sleeves, but what could they possibly do in the dining room? Some of the girls had already drifted away and it was emptying fast; still, it was no place for a quarrel. She shrugged, and decided to wait until the last of them were out of the room. If nothing had happened by that time, then it was merely her own ... and Ilse's and Anna's ... imagination at work again.

Maria-Teresa Tucci at the other end with her back to the German girls at the next table, shivered and said, 'Dio mio! I ask myself each morning, "Maria-Teresa Tucci, shall you ever be warm again?" It's no wonder the Swiss have no music, no love and no art; all their energies must be spent in maintaining life. They are so busy trying to keep on existing that they have no time to live.'

'Who told you the Swiss have no love?' demanded Yasha.

'Theodora. She said that the government offers prizes to induce people to marry, and once married it is the custom for the women to grow enormously fat, and the men to grow beards, smoke large pipes, and put their feet on the mantelpiece. È vero?' she asked, looking acutely distressed.

Yasha threw back her head and laughed, while both Mary and Natalia smiled appreciatively. Maria-Teresa was very interested in all questions concerning love; she was engaged to an officer in the Bersaglieri, but she had asked every teacher and every girl individually not to mention it please, for her parents thought her too young (she was fifteen).

This fact, according to Vicky, who suffered more from Maria-Teresa's attachment to the officer in the Bersaglieri than anyone, should be suppressed, for she was forced to live next door to

Maria-Teresa who passed all her spare time playing the piano in her room with one finger and shouting:

'Sul cappello, sul cappello, che portia-ah-ah-Ah-AH-mo ...'

She had tried closing the door and stopping her ears, but while the 'sul cappello' part was then lost, she still heard the merciless pounding of Maria-Teresa's finger and then the 'ah-Ah-AH-mo' suddenly cleave the air, which was more upsetting than having to listen to the whole sentence and working up to it gradually. In desperation she bought Maria-Teresa the song and implored her to learn the rest of it, 'per l'amor di Dio, Maria-Teresa!' but so far she had not done it. She continued to sing, in a voice like a high-pitched trombone, 'Sul cappello, sul cappello, che portia-ah-ah-Ah-AH-mo,' accompanying herself inaccurately with the first finger of her right hand.

Vicky had given up, for a few days. Then, being occupied with the almost impossible task for a person with an unmathematical brain, of trying to teach herself counterpoint, with Maria-Teresa's lusty regimental song shattering the silence at unexpected intervals, she marched into her room one afternoon and demanded:

'For the love of heaven, Maria-Teresa, *what* do the Bersaglieri wear on their hats?' trusting that the little Italian would refer to the music she had bought her, and trying to inveigle her into learning the rest of it that way. But Maria-Teresa darted across the room to her dressing table and scrutinized the photograph of her beloved which had been taken with his own and several other regiments, and was so small and indistinct that 'Only the eye of a great love could possibly distinguish between him and the three thousand other gentlemen present,' said Vicky admiringly.

After looking at it closely for some time, Maria-Teresa raised her head at last and said dreamily, 'I don't know. I think it is a cock-feather.'

Vicky gave up, remarking bitterly to Mary, 'I was always led to believe that when Italians fell in love they suddenly acquired enough musical ability to make up for what they lost in the way of humour!'

'What's the matter?' asked Vicky in alarm, for Maria-Teresa's usual expression was one of joy mixed with happy anticipation; the entire staff went in constant suspicion of her motives and intentions owing to that look.

'Cosa c'è?' she repeated tragically. 'Enough to upset anyone, no matter how *stolide*!' She scrambled to her feet and shoved the letter into Vicky's hand pointing to the lines which read, 'I am not the thirty-second from the left in the tenth row as you seem to think ... those, my dear Maria-Teresa, are *privates*. That man, which you seem to have believed is me, is a private in the 7th. I am the sixteenth from the right in the third row, with the *officers*. I, as I thought you knew ... io sono tenente nel Secondo!'

Theodora struggled through it, then took refuge in the hall, leaving Vicky to deal with the situation. Vicky swallowed twice and then managed to say solemnly, 'I do not think that anyone could be blamed for that ...'

'He thinks I wished to insult him,' she said tearfully.

'Listen, Maria-Teresa. No man could fail to appreciate the ... the ... er ... devotion of a girl who would count thirty-two from the right ...'

'Left,' she corrected dismally.

'Left, then, and ten from the bottom, a hundred times a day ...'

Maria-Teresa was an almost ludicrous contrast to Stephania Carré, the only other Italian girl in the school and her inseparable companion. Stephania was the daughter of an official in the government in Rome, but lived with her mother and brother in Milan and hardly ever saw her father. She had had a very strict upbringing, and was extremely quiet and unobtrusive. Her mother, a worldly and rather bored woman, had impressed Vicky as both selfish and egotistical in her relationship to her daughter. Beyond seeing that Stephania was constantly chaperoned and that she wore childish clothes which did not become her thick, dark skin and mediocre face, she ignored her completely. The boy, who was nineteen and a year older than Stephania, was constantly out, and during the ten days which Vicky had spent in the Carrés' home at Christmas, they hardly ever saw him. The two girls were left with six servants to amuse themselves as best they could in the huge marble, velvet-hung rooms of the Carrés' apartment, to look through the grilled windows at the people passing in the street below, most of the day. The place was like a mausoleum where Stephania lived her life of quiet hopelessness, saying nothing about herself except once, during a long afternoon when she had remarked that she was in love with a second cousin who lived in Ferrara and whom she never saw except during the few weeks he spent with the Carrés in their villa near Tresa each summer.

They were sitting on one of the window-seats in the drawing room, their voices pitched low. The only sounds which reached the quiet room came from the streets which seemed very far away: motor horns, the clanging of tram bells, the intermittent cries of street vendors selling fruit and flowers, and the deep bells of the cathedral, tolling vespers. Vicky sat with her head against the window-frame, avoiding Stephania's eyes, while the girl talked, hesitatingly at first and then with increased feeling, to the only human being who had ever been interested in what she had to say about herself. There had been only that one sign of confidence and trust; the remainder of their days together were spent in mental isolation, and only her infallible instinct told her that Stephania was glad she had come, and that she was sorry to see her go.

Maria-Teresa was devoted to her, although she frequently expressed to Vicky her exasperation at Stephania's lack of spirit, remarking one afternoon, 'She simply sits and waits for things to happen to her. She waits for her family to marry her off to a man she does not love. She looks ahead and all there is in sight is a marriage with no love but with many children, and after a long time, death.' She was sitting cross-legged on Vicky's bed peeling an orange, while Vicky lay stretched out on the floor writing a two-part invention, or what she hoped might turn out to resemble a two-part invention, with luck. 'What sort of life is that?' demanded Maria-Teresa.

'I said, what sort of life is that?' she repeated, throwing a piece of peel at Vicky's head to attract her attention.

Vicky looked up and said politely, 'I never know whether you're more of a nuisance here with your incessant chatter, or more of one in your room with your incessant "sul cappello." Which do you think, dormouse?'

'It's up to you,' she said deferentially. 'I was asking what sort of life that is?'

'Whose?'

'Stephania's,' she answered, with remarkable patience.

'Oh! One no doubt behaves according to one's nature,' said Vicky sententiously. 'Probably Stephania will be as happy that way as any other. You see, Tessa, she was brought up to accept things ... so she accepts them. It's not in her nature to go against a social system. If it were, she'd probably be happy just revolting, even if she didn't get anywhere. I think most people act in their own best interests in the long run, whether they appear to be doing it for themselves, or for the sake of humanity. Some gifted individuals manage to do both. They're the actively good people of the world. The passively good ones, like Stephania, merely do nothing in their own interests, which works out for the good of the race in the end. Some do neither, like me.'

'What *do* you do?' asked Maria-Teresa with interest, spitting seeds into the waste-basket below her on the floor.

'I haven't the slightest idea.'

Maria-Teresa was puzzled. She fidgeted for a while, watching Vicky lying lazily on the floor with her dark head on one arm, her eyes half-closed as she looked sideways at the notebook beside her. 'Gesu Maria, but you're beautiful,' she said at last. 'It's not fair. There's Mlle Lemaitre with much brains and no beauty, and me with much beauty but no brains, and you with both so that each seems more, if you see what I mean.'

She would say periodically of Stephania, 'She is so *good*,' as if in explanation of her devotion to her. They were always together, but when one of the staff became suspicious and set out to investigate the night life of the school, it was always Maria-Teresa who was caught in Stephania's room or just leaving it, armed with cigarettes, foie-gras, and a bottle of Chianti under her dressing gown. No one ever knew where the Chianti came from; the bottles were too big to smuggle into the school, but she always had one or two on hand. It was one of the most baffling mysteries of Mlle Dupraix's life.

The girls had fallen into a desultory discussion of skating. Mary continued to worry about Vicky, drinking cup after cup of weak tea, half-conscious of the crowd at the next table and the invisible line which seemed to have been drawn between them and Ilse and Anna during the past few minutes. There was trouble of some sort brewing.

Yasha was saying, 'It's really time they found out. It's unpleasant not to know, for you can't help doing half a dozen people the injustice of half-suspecting them. Until we *do* know who's been stealing, we're all possible thieves.'

'The worst of it is that someone's getting away with it,' said Natalia, her normally pleasant, dark face rather bad-tempered.

Yasha's uncommunicative brown eyes opened wide. 'I don't agree with you,' she said calmly. 'At present we're all going about distrusting one girl after another. That makes forty-eight dishonourable people. Only *one* girl is *really* guilty ... unless she's formed a syndicate,' she added, with a look of faint amusement. 'It's not good for us, not good for our minds, to be eternally speculating on such a disagreeable subject.'

Natalia looked unconvinced, too preoccupied to think in any but a limited way while Yasha continued to develop her point. It occurred to Mary after a while that Ilse was becoming more and more upset at this philosophical discussion; she began to cry a little, while Anna held one of her hands and whispered to her in German. Mary, realized that neither Yasha nor Natalia liked Truda and her group of followers, it was likely to occur to them that Ilse might think they were referring to her. It was even possible that Truda's gossip about Ilse and the stealing hadn't even reached their ears. She said quickly, 'Change the subject, Yasha, you're bothering Ilse.'

The little Polish girl looked startled, glanced at Ilse, smiled at her warmly, then got up and went out, followed by Natalia and Aimée. The dining room began to empty slowly, as groups of two and three girls drifted toward the doors and out into the hall. Mary continued to sip her last cup of chilly tea, waiting for Ilse and Anna to leave. Their delay became more noticeable after a while, for they had finished eating and drinking long ago, and appeared to be merely sitting. It became plain to her suddenly that they were waiting for the Germans to leave in order to avoid meeting Truda and her friends in the hall, while, judging from their expressions of poorly concealed amusement, the girls at the next table were equally determined to sit them out. She did not know whether Ilse and Anna were actually afraid of them or not; Ilse quite possibly was but Anna was too isolated in her own troubled mind to be greatly affected by anyone.

The room was gradually falling into silence as one girl after another became aware of the game which was being played in the corner. It was still in the half-joking stage but it would soon develop into something different if she did not get the two factions separated. If she told Ilse and Anna to go, the German group would immediately get up and leave with them; if she ordered Truda and her friends to leave, it would be putting a label on it which she was anxious not to do ... perhaps lending it a seriousness which it did not yet possess. At any rate she would be letting everyone in the room know that she herself recognized the trouble between Ilse and Truda which, until some action was taken by Mlle Tourain, would give the girls the impression that the staff sanctioned it. She was alarmed. Maria-Teresa and Stephania had gone; she was alone now, with Ilse and Anna on her left, the German girls on her right, sitting between them like the referee at a wrestling match, she thought irritably. Everyone in the dining room was watching them now. Ilse and Anna were trying without much success to appear unconcerned, sitting with their eyes rigidly fixed on the table, but she saw that Ilse's lips were trembling again ... she was in no state to take teasing, that was the trouble. There was nothing which Truda could actually do, either in the dining room or the front hall, but Ilse was too close to hysteria to realize that.

The silence was becoming oppressive, making itself felt as something more than the mere absence of movement and conversation. Two of the maids poked their heads through the swinging doors at the other end of the room and then retreated into the kitchen again.

Mary bit her lip, mentally cursing her nerves and the state of her brain, both of which were apparently choosing this singularly inopportune moment to make thinking impossible. For lack of any better solution she decided to leave herself with Ilse and Anna, letting the school think what they liked of the staff's attitude toward the Truda-Ilse affair, when Theodora Cohen crossed the room, late for tea as usual, and sat down lazily with her back to the Germans.

She glanced over her shoulder at them, then said to Mary in her cool, drawling voice, 'Truda's still hungry. Do ring for more tea for her, Mlle Ellerton.'

The remark, spoken in Theodora's clear French, brought Truda to her feet saying roughly, 'You shut up!'

She got up very deliberately and, turning, faced the German girl. They were both unusually tall. 'Certainly,' she said good-humouredly. 'I know my place ... in a Nazi gutter isn't it, Truda?' She bowed with a slight smile and, turning, sat down once more with her back to the German girl fuming two feet behind her. She helped herself to some bread and butter and jam, apparently unconscious of the gaping school and the livid Truda, and remarked, 'There's going to be snow ... lots of snow. I suppose that'll mean bad skiing tomorrow ... bad for me, anyway. I'm trying to learn how to do a stem turn to the left. I can do it to the right, but for some reason not the other way. Funny, isn't it? I always thought open christies were supposed to be harder. C'est curieux, hein?'

'Très curieux,' agreed Miss Ellerton. 'If you'll come out tomorrow at four I'll give you some pointers. I'd like to do some longish trips at Gstaad. You'd better get into condition. Do you think you could do twelve miles a day?'

'It's a cinch,' said Miss Cohen, breaking unexpectedly into English.

Mary choked, then turned and said to Truda, 'Haven't you anything to do but stand there gaping?'

They left, followed after a short interval by Ilse and Anna. The remaining girls crowded out; Mary and Theodora, who was placidly consuming her bread and butter, were left alone with the two maids, clearing away the dishes across the room.

Mary stretched and said, 'Teddy, you're a brick. I couldn't think of anything to do but the reason for not doing it.' She looked across at Theodora and smiled. The Jewish girl from St. Louis, Missouri, grinned back, but said nothing. 'It's all impossible, and yet it's true. Another week like this and we'll have half a dozen girls all screaming for their mothers every time we say "boo" at them. Five years ago, for example, I suppose Truda and Ilse would have gone through the entire year without addressing more than half a dozen words to each other, but that would have been all. I can see that they're not naturally particularly congenial. Truda's an earnest, hardworking, humourless soul; Ilse's tired, worried out of her wits, over-sensitive and utterly lacking in self-confidence. Truda's all wound up in a retrogressive political movement. Ilse's ... just Ilse ...'

'Half Jewish,' said Theodora matter-of-factly.

'Yes. Well, anyhow, there in 1935 you have the basis for almost any sort of trouble. What's the matter with the world, Teddy?' she asked unhappily.

Theodora slid down in her chair, leaving her long, beautiful legs hanging over the arm and said peacefully, 'Don't upset yourself, darling. Everything works out for the good of those as loves God. We'll all murder each other in another ten days; somehow Vicky will be held responsible for it just on general principles, and that will be that.'

'Why?' demanded Mary.

She shrugged and sighed. 'Oh, Vick's just one of those people who are a sort of perpetual goat. They'd probably have burned her for witchcraft in the Middle Ages ... or ducked her a few times in the village pond in an effort to make her a little more comprehensible, anyway. She'll be kicked out of here sooner or later and then goodness knows where we'll go ...'

'Why "we"?'

'You don't think I'd let her walk out the front door alone, do you?' asked Theodora in genuine astonishment. And as Mary shook her head, she went on with apparent irrelevance, 'Do you know that game called "Cat's Cradle"?'

'Yes. Why?'

'This school makes me think of it.'

'Oh,' said Mary. And as Theodora continued to eat bread and butter without further explanation, she said, 'Come on, Teddy ... elaborate.'

'I was thinking that this school, from a psychological point of view, looks like the last grim stages of that game when your fingers are all tangled with crossed and re-crossed lines of string. The hands belong to our Amelia. Between her fingers is a piece of ... string ... connecting Ilse and Truda; another, in a very different way, connecting Consuelo and Marian; another Vicky and the two Andersons; another between the Andersons and the Cummings-Gordons; another between Truda and me; still another between Truda and ... Anna ...' she said with a change of tone.

'That's what Vicky thinks,' said Mary, with a puzzled expression. 'What's back of Anna, Teddy?'

'Ask me another. It's just that I feel something. I don't know anything. And there's a line between practically everyone and our little Ida Samuels ... between her and me, anyway. May God have mercy upon her soul for the sake of her *dear* parents residing in the Bronx,' she interpolated maliciously.

Her habit of rattling along inconsequentially and then suddenly becoming perfectly serious at the end of a sentence which had begun facetiously was rather exhausting for anyone trying to rest in her presence, Mary thought. She herself was startling, a series of contrasts and apparent contradictions. Her hair was dark red with streaks of gold; half the school maintained that it was dyed, the other half equally stubbornly that it was not. Theodora herself, when approached, said that she preferred to keep an open mind on the subject. Her eyebrows were plucked down to almost nothing; she had a clear, rather dark skin which was always liberally made up in spite of everything which Mlle Tourain could say on the subject of cosmetics; brown eyes, a nose which was a little too broad for any pretence to beauty, and a well-shaped, surprisingly sweet mouth. Her clothes were all bought in Paris and were conspicuous, though in excellent taste. Vicky had once observed, disclaiming any originality for the remark, that Mary Ellerton's were sports clothes, and Theodora's clothes *pour le sport*, two vastly different things. Theodora's language was fearful, and her conduct very frequently regrettable. She was rather bad-mannered and excessively lazy; she smoked incessantly in her room and was quite indifferent as to whether or not she was caught.

At the same time she was an exceptionally strong character. She had the highest form of courage ... the kind which is required to retain both self-respect and self-control in spite of constant jibes at her racial inferiority. She remained proud of being Jewish in the face of everyone. She had a few loyalties which remained fixed and dominated her behaviour at all times; she would have been quite capable of hitting anyone who criticized

Vicky. Her sense of humour never deserted her for more than a few seconds, no matter how intensely she felt, and she had a tendency to give away everything she owned and then spend three months' allowance replenishing her wardrobe.

She had learned to think late, and had been trying to organize her beliefs and her values in a rather disorderly and panic-stricken way since her arrival at the school in the beginning of September. No one had ever directed her thinking, and she had no knowledge of what could be got out of life ... only what could be got out of money. She had been brought up in the wealthy Jewish section of St. Louis society, the daughter of a railway man who died when she was twelve, leaving his millions to herself and her brother, along with a membership of three country clubs, two houses of extravagant size and ugliness, and one of the best art collections in that part of the United States ... all on the somewhat eccentric condition that his twin son and daughter acquire a knowledge of five languages before their twenty-first birthday.

She had already spent four years in Europe during which she had learnt enough Spanish, Italian, French and German to enable her to speak them without a trace of an accent. The only languge in which she had a distinct accent was English; to the end of her life her own speech would have 'St. Louis' stamped all over it. Her brother had inherited his father's perversity and elected to learn Rumanian, Danish, Dutch and Hungarian, although he had abandoned the last after eight months in Budapest, asserting that no one but a drunken lorry-driver could get his tongue around Hungarian vowels, and demanding from his sister the loan of two hundred dollars in order to get to Biarritz.

She was an aristocrat. Her particular friends in the school were Mary Ellerton, Vicky, Consuelo Deane from São Paolo, Brazil, and Anna von Landenburg; the others she ignored except when there was some occasion for generosity. She was observant, however oblivious she might appear, and her Cat's Cradle idea interested Mary.

She said again, 'But why Anna?' And a moment later, 'Where did you get that idea? Did Vicky say anything?'

'Vicky *never* says anything except things about art like, "It should be apprehended half by the mind, half by the emotions, and half ..." No that makes more than a sum total, doesn't it? Well, a third of each then ... no, I mean by all three together ... the third being the soul, whatever that is, Miss Ellerton. And on the basis of that she takes exception to the Beethoven Sixth because she says that you cannot apprehend a duck's quacking and a rooster's crowing by a third of your mind ... No, darn it, I mean a third mentally, a third emotionally, and a third spiritu ...'

'Shut up,' said Miss Ellerton rudely.

'I was only thinking that you might like to share some of the benefits of Vicky's wisdom,' she said, looking injured.

'That would be all right if you didn't misquote her so outrageously,' she said unkindly. 'I don't know what Vicky said about art, but I'll stake my soul on it's not being anything so involved as that.'

'Art is an involved subject, Miss Ellerton,' said Theodora loftily.

'I know it is. But you involve it still further, if you don't mind my saying so.'

'O.K. Anyway, she proceeded to develop a nice logical ... er ... logical ...'

'Are you stuck for once?' asked Mary solicitously.

'I was merely searching for the mot juste,' she said, in the tone of one who refuses to be disturbed by hecklers in the gallery. 'A nice ... logical ... refutation of abstractionism in painting, representationalism in music, and something or other in dancing ... anyway, she says that Mary Wigman and the like are too titanic; they make her feel that life is *most* terrific and filled mit stürm und drang ...'

'Whew!' whistled Mary admiringly. 'And?'

'She doesn't like that sort of dancing.'

'I rather gathered that. But Anna, Teddy?'

'I don't know, I told you. But ... there's something on her mind and what's given me the jitters is that it's something which shouldn't be known by anyone, particularly Truda ... and that Truda *does* know it ... or guesses it. Well, we'll soon know,' she added with a shrug. And a moment later, irrelevantly, 'She appears to like Jews ... Anna, I mean.' She contemplated the unusual spectacle of a Christian who really liked Jews, for a few minutes, and then laughed. A moment later, with a sudden change of expression, she said, 'How long is that bitch going to be allowed to pick on Vicky?'

'Vicky can take care of herself,' said Mary, but instantly looked rather concerned. 'What's she done now, Teddy?'

'She's taken away all her gramophone records. Vicky'd just got the *Royal Water Music* from London after waiting for it for three months, and a special recording of a Gregorian Mass which our little Dupraix dropped on the floor outside Vicky's room. I know, because I happened along and she told me to pick up the pieces. Vicky doesn't know that she broke it ... Dupraix isn't the type of person who'd ever own up to anyone about anything ... much less to Vicky. As for paying for it ... not a chance! But I'll get even with her,' she added, hugging one of her knees contentedly. 'I'll get even with her.'

'Come on, Teddy ... don't be so beastly smug about it. What are you going to do?'

'I went shopping with Fräulein Lange this morning. She was all excited about some book or other she wanted, and she let me go down Petit Chêne alone to that record shop. I ordered another

Gregorian Mass from Rome, and when it comes I'll take it to Dupraix, and say, "I knew you'd be worrying about this, Rose, ma petite vipère. La voici." Now isn't that neat?'

'Teddy!'

'Good heavens, you're not going to object, are you?'

'Certainly not.'

Theodora laughed, then said coldly, 'I can stand any amount of straightforward, honest-to-goodness rowing provided it's done in the heat of something or other, but when it comes to an unhealthy sort of obsession like this one of Dupraix's about Vicky, it gives me goose-flesh. It's got a sex basis, of course. That's what makes it so disagreeable.'

'You shouldn't say such things.'

'No? It's just my dirty American mind, Mary; think nothing of it. All the same, this can't go on much longer. Lately she's taken to trying to snag Vicky into talking about herself ... and you know what a mug's game *that* is. I've tried it myself ... I guess you have, too. Only once though, eh? It's the one thing which really bothers Vicky terribly, which is why I say that Dupraix will either have to let up or else ...'

'I think it'll be "or else," Teddy. Mlle Tourain's started to wake up to the fact that there's an awful lot going on in this school that she doesn't know anything about. It's begun to gall her a bit. Top that with the fact that there's someone who *does* know ... Vicky ... and my guess is that she'll be out before Easter, and there's nothing you or I can do about it. It's Mlle Tourain's own fault for being so astonishingly oblivious, and to make it worse she hasn't done enough headmistressing to get the knack of it ... she doesn't know how to deal with people. She's always putting her foot in it. If she did, she'd either pull herself into the position where she knows more than Vicky, or she'd avoid any conflict with her. But she won't. Sooner or later she'll get her on the mat about something publicly, Vicky will close up like a clam, and Mlle Tourain will come off worse ... probably make an ass of herself. Incidentally, this is not for public consumption ... though thank heaven I don't have to tell *you* that.'

'No, you don't,' said Theodora absently, looking straight ahead of her.

'As for Mlle Dupraix, she'll be out too, once Mlle Tourain really gets going. The only reason she's lasted this long is that she's part of the old régime ... incidentally, I wonder if Mlle d'Ormonde *will* ever come back? And what Mlle Tourain would do if she ... if she died? ... However, that's neither here nor there at the moment. I think Mlle d'Ormonde must have inherited Rose Dupraix from her aunt ... the one who gave her the ormolu clock, and the volumes on tropical fish.'

'Is that what they are?' She laughed, and shifted her position so that one leg was crossed over the other. 'I've been trying to find out for months, but Mlle Tourain seems a little sensitive about them. She always whisks you away before you have a good look. I thought maybe they were unabridged editions of Casanova, Cellini, Rabelais, and *Lady Chatterley's Lover*, and that Mlle Tourain read them in bed each night. Well, well, well, tropical fish, forsooth ... I suppose there's no chance of their being false covers?'

'No,' said Mary, looking amused.

'Anyway, I'm sorry Dupraix is so firmly anchored to the school. She's a great loss to the W.C.T.U., the Legion of Decency, and the Morality Squad.'

They got up and started toward the door, Theodora still munching a crust of bread and moving beside Mary with that loose, swinging walk which was so ungraceful and at the same time one of her chief charms. She managed to do everything wrong to such an extent that people watched her, fascinated ...

dominating most of the world about her by sheer individuality.

At the door Mary stopped, looking doubtfully across the dark hall at Mlle Tourain coming down the main staircase. 'Do try and keep some sort of order during that faculty meeting when no one's about to suppress Truda or Ida tonight, will you Teddy? It's not only for Ilse's sake, but also because if one row has a chance to get started, we'll have half a dozen to deal with within a week.'

Theodora looked down at her and shook her head. 'I'm a lousy person to pick,' she said. 'There are too many people here who have absorbed, maybe without knowing it, some of this anti-Jewish feeling that's drifting around the world now. I haven't much authority ... and I can't do anything with Truda. Of course if I just sat and let her call me names, that would undoubtedly help her to blow off some steam and keep her occupied for a while, but it won't do for the whole evening. Why don't you ask Vick? She can handle anyone.'

'I can't. Mlle Tourain has her back up about her. You'll just have to do your best, Teddy. I think she'd almost rather have a row than have to be grateful for Vicky preventing one. She won't give her authority a badge by letting her come down tonight.'

'Oh hell,' said Theodora. 'Us and the League of Nations ... you could see it, by the way, through a telescope ... if that point of land didn't get in the way.'

III

⁓

I

*A*nna von Landenburg sat at her desk, trying to compose a letter to her father. It was a difficult task and grew more difficult as time went on, for what was of vital importance to her was also of vital importance to the censors. For the past three months she had written an average of three letters a week without once saying anything which really mattered.

Her mind was too exhausted and her head too heavy with fever to concentrate. Between her eyes and the sheet of note-paper in front of her a series of strange pictures which had first come to her in her sleep and which had lately begun to remain with her all day, kept rising up and blinding her so that from time to time she raised her head to look at the icon hanging on the wall above her, trying to clear her thoughts. The crazy, horrible pictures continued to dance in front of her like an old-fashioned film: she saw her father being flogged through the streets; she saw the Cardinal standing before an altar praying, while a jeering mob at the back of the cathedral shouted insults and blasphemy.

Her brother Anton, at present interned in the labour camp 'Sulzbach,' near Nürnberg, had not written to her for several weeks, nor had he communicated with Graf von Landenburg in any way. She knew that her father was alarmed, for he had not made one single reference to Anton in his letters for the past two months. She had read and re-read every one, seeking some remark which might be an indirect method of letting her know that at least Anton was still alive. There was none.

The men interned at Sulzbach slept in wooden bunks covered with straw, a row down each wall. The floor was stone, and most of the windows had no glass ... only strips of canvas nailed across them. The stoves shed their heat in a restricted area; the rest of the room was cold and damp. The Arbeitsdienstler, 'labour service men,' as they were called there, got thirty-five pfennigs a day and two hot meals, or board, lodging and about six shillings a week in exchange for building bridges, trenches, fortifications and roads. Those six shillings were supposed to feed, clothe and lodge their families. Since the men were often politically undesirable ... or radically undesirable ... whether or not their families were fed, clothed or lodged adequately was of no great importance. If they refused to go to the camps ... and if they were permitted to refuse ... the unemployed got nothing, nor did their families. They worked in columns under armed overseers; they received no visitors, their mail was opened by the camp officials, and they could not leave. Each year seven thousand young Germans who could not help growing up and reaching the age of sixteen were drafted as labour service men, landhelpers, or emergency workers, marching about the German countryside working at anything which the government thought needed doing. If they refused to go when they were drafted, they were sent to a concentration camp to 'accustom themselves to discipline.' They were separated from their families and they could not marry.

Her brother had gone to Sulzbach more than a year ago, in December of 1933. Anton's lungs were none too strong; he should have returned to Basle where the air was good and where he was studying medicine, instead of going to Sulzbach.

Anna remembered the morning that he had received the order to report at Sulzbach; the four of them were sitting at breakfast in the dining room with the table drawn close to the fire, for it was already turning cold, and he had sat very still with the letter in his hand, while her father determined to use what little remained of his influence to get the order cancelled. Seemingly not even hearing what his father was saying, Anton had stated simply, 'I shall go.' An order to a member of the aristocracy was an unheard of thing, and Anton's imprisonment was a warning. He had refused to allow his father to draw attention to himself, and so he had gone, one bitter December day shortly before Christmas, and they had not seen him since. Her mother had had a weak heart which had not withstood her worry. One windy night early in March, she died, and then there were only her father and herself left in the house in Nürnberg. Now, there was no one. The house was shuttered up and deserted and the von Landenburgs who had lived there, who had been gay and sad, who had loved each other and had loved God a little more than most people, were gone.

If Anton had become so ill that he was unfit for any kind of work, what had they done with him? Anna knew that the Nazi point of view was based on the survival of the fittest; if you were weak you were better dead, for a high intelligence in a delicate body was only a nuisance. In fact a high intelligence was a nuisance anyhow. It was unlikely that they would bother much about a twenty-year-old boy whose father was concerning himself with matters which were not his business.

It was actually that they, her father and herself, were leaving Anton to die, as thousands of Catholics, Jews, Socialists and Communists were leaving their relatives to die, without protest. If they were members of the counter-revolutionary party; if they belonged to one of the Groups of Five in a factory, or ran crude printing machines wherever it was moderately safe to do so, or distributed those little pamphlets which were left on street corners, on vacant plots and out of the way places, by whom, one knew not ... in any case, they said nothing, for to remain inconspicuous was essential to their very existence.

A revolutionary movement in a thoroughly mechanized state like modern Germany was an entirely different matter from the Russian revolution, for example. The Ochrana could only get about on horseback for the most part, while the Gestapo of Fascist Germany had everything from radio-police to machine-guns. Its organization and technical efficiency forced the counter-revolutionaries to work alone, or almost alone, and it was not an infrequent thing for a man to learn that his brother also belonged to a Group of Five only when the police came to arrest him.

A few days before, her father had been forced to take refuge in a monastery outside Nördlingen, although his whole organization lay in and around Nürnburg, and the move alarmed her. He must be directing operations from there. It was the same monastery which had been raided by the police in the spring of 1934. The only incriminating evidence had been three printing-presses, which the brothers *might* have been using for religious purposes, but they were still under suspicion. One of them had been arrested and sent to a concentration camp, presumably to 'accustom himself to discipline,' on general principles, which had caused such a scandal that the others were left unmolested for the time being.

She had had a letter from her father that afternoon which had been carried over the border by a Dominican monk, on his way to see his invalid mother in Zürich. It was lying open on the desk before her, but she was sitting in the dark in order to rest her eyes while she tried to compose an answer.

She got up at last and dragged herself across the room to switch on the light, in order to read it again. There was still no news of Anton, although her father could have written in safety. No news was not good news, she thought with a wry smile ... it was bad. She found herself becoming dizzy; the flowered wall-paper was a sickly confusion of green, blue, and pink against a glaring white background. She resisted the temptation to open the window and try to clear her head, for the sudden draught would probably give her more cold and more fever, and returned to her chair by the desk.

The icon above her on the wall had belonged to her Russian mother, and a small lamp, suspended beneath it on a slender chain which ran from corner to corner of the frame, lit the Madonna day and night. Anna's prayer-book and crucifix lay on the enamel-topped table by her bed; beyond that the room was devoid of personality, with only the regulation basins in the alcove, as well as two beds ... although Anna occupied it alone ... over one of which was thrown a dark cover, for she used it as a couch. It was a large corner room with a full-length glass door leading to her balcony on the south side, and a casement window looking down toward Montreux and the valley of the Rhône to the east.

She sat at her desk reading her father's letter and shivering, in spite of the woollen dressing gown which she had wrapped around her on coming up from tea. Her head was heavy with steady pain, and her eyes so dried and blurred by fever that she blinked continuously in an effort to read more easily. Her father had written two days before from the monastery at Nördlingen:

It is a relief to be in such a quiet atmosphere, and the brothers help me with my work which has been piling up at an oppressive rate because the Gestapo kept me on the move so much. Last week it had got to a point where I was changing my office two and three times a day and getting nothing done. At last I was forced to leave Nürnberg altogether and take refuge here, for the police have got into such a state of nerves that you cannot look a Nazi in the eye without being accused of having an expression contrary to the spirit of the Fascist corporate state. Our work is going forward well ... of course that's the reason for the increasing number of Secret Police. I suppose after a while, everyone who isn't a counter-revolutionary will be a policeman ... and they will persecute and arrest and execute harder and faster than ever in order to take the mind of the public off the food shortage and the housing problem. The *Rote Fahn* reached four thousand copies its last issue. It's impossible to tell how many of us there are now, but we are certainly getting on.

I do not want to worry you with what I am going to say now, for I am merely taking the course I should take if I were a doctor or a lawyer or a businessman. If anything happens to me you will have a small income ... enough to get along on. I want you to go either to Königsberg to stay with your aunt, or back to the sisters, who could certainly do with your help, for they are working themselves to death collecting food and clothing. They need you, and love you, as you know.

Anna, my darling, I miss you very much. I don't know when I shall see you again. If things have not settled down by Easter you had better go to Königsberg for the holidays. I cannot have you anywhere near me for the present. In the meantime I want you to be as happy as possible, and keep well. Take care of yourself and try not to worry. God bless you.

She had heard of torturing and violence. The summer before, she and her aunt had been walking in the town; her aunt had suddenly caught her arm and pulled her into an alley, in time to prevent her from seeing some Communists being driven through the streets of Königsberg to a concentration camp ... but not in time to prevent her from hearing the whistling of whips in the air, the screams and wails of women.

Someone had told her ... was it Ida? ... of a small village where one of the men had flown a red flag. The Nazi Storm Troopers came in and beat up the men in full sight of their wives, mothers, sisters and children, then loaded them into lorries and took them away. When the Troopers returned the next day another red flag was flying, but when they sent a small boy up to get it, they found it was only a towel, soaked in the blood of the previous day.

That scene she could not forget; the village street lined with anguished women and children cut straight across her mind, forming a background against which there was the image of her father, beaten through the streets like the Communists in East Prussia, and the Cardinal saying mass, while the crowd behind him defiled and profaned the church. She knew that she was drawing too close to the slender border line between sanity and madness; she knew that no human being could stand continual contemplation of intense suffering, and she prayed to the Madonna above her:

'Heilige Maria, stop me thinking of these things. Give me strength and guidance, for I am so afraid ...'

2

'But I don't see,' said Elsa Michielsen of Copenhagen, 'why your politics are a concern of mine. Government in general is, I should think, a method of organizing a country so that its citizens are able to live peacefully, progressively, and prosperously together. You're as bellicose as you can be, you German Fascists; you're anything but prosperous, and as for progression ... if you'll excuse my saying so, you seem to be travelling backwards at an incredible rate. First you take all freedom away from your women, then you harass the Church, and *then*, if you please, you decide that Christianity is no good and start a movement for the worship of Wotan and Thor. Really, Truda. If you want to be a Fascist, go ahead and be one, but let the rest of us drift along our incompetent, racially impure way.'

'I'm not trying to make you be anything,' said Truda obstinately. 'I'm only trying to explain.'

'You're trying to excuse, my dear, which is a different thing.' She was sitting cross-legged on Truda's bed, sketching Truda on the chair in front of the dressing table and little Gretel and Lotta behind her on the floor with their backs to the radiator. They were known respectively as 'Little Klaus' and 'Big Klaus,' because they were inseparable, and because Gretel was so small that Lotta ... in reality of only medium height ... appeared huge beside her. Over on the other bed Christina Erichsen, the only Norwegian in the school, was curled up knitting a pale blue sweater.

'You don't know how awful everything was before Hitler was elected,' said Truda, in a more reasonable tone. She was able to discuss her opinions more or less rationally with Elsa and Christina because of their racial neutrality. At the same time, although they were two years older than herself, she despised them slightly for having no particular political convictions. Her Fascism was a species of religious fanaticism; in consequence she had the traditional view of the reformer toward those who, for one reason or another, have not yet seen the light. Elsa and Christina rather liked her, since they were naturally more drawn to English and German people than to any others, but they found her incessant political talk tiresome. They considered anyone with a desire to reform the world a meddler, and since they were surrounded on all sides by adolescents with that particular tendency, they had few intimates in the school.

'I have read that book, *Little Man, What Now?*' said Christina, laying down her knitting for the moment and pushing a strand of fine blonde hair off her forehead. She was a quiet-mannered girl of twenty, who believed in compromise and hated arguments, yet she had her own opinions and upheld them, as unobtrusively as possible, when she considered it necessary for the sake of her conscience. She went on dispassionately, 'When a country is in such a hopeless state as that, perhaps anything definite is better.'

Little Klaus said violently, 'I wish people would leave us alone. Ever since the war we've been treated like naughty school-children. It began with the Americans coming over and deciding to cut off East Prussia from the rest of the country. How would they have felt if we had gone there and handed over Chicago to Canada?' She was not very sure where Chicago was, and looked nervously from Truda to Elsa and Christina to see if they were laughing at her, but they were not sure where Chicago was either, so her remark passed uncontested, much to her relief. Contradictions always made her blush and stammer; actually never, until she came to the school, had she felt capable of holding an opinion on any subject. She had four brothers, three older and one younger than herself, all of whom considered her, as a girl, mentally negligible. The entirely novel experience of being listened to when she talked had gone to her head a little, and she was now anxious to express opinions on every subject. 'We don't want to interfere with other people; all we want is justice ...'

Elsa took her up on it, sketching in Truda's legs. 'People would believe Hitler and his "leave us alone" complex a little more easily if awkward things like that Swedish Fascist business weren't always turning up to contradict him.'

'What was that?' asked Truda.

'Oh, I don't remember it very well, but there was a scandal in the Stockholm papers over it a while ago. Apparently Göring ... I think it was Göring ... went up to Sweden and made a deal with the leader of the Swedish party by which Hitler was to contribute campaign funds in exchange for an agreement to turn over the Northern Provinces when they got into power. Only someone in the party was rather shocked, and spilled the whole story, which sort of spoilt things for a while.'

'Why the Northern Provinces?' demanded Truda.

'I don't know. I think they have iron ... or coal. I never *can* remember which it is that Germany needs so badly to make her steel. That's the reason she wants the Saar, isn't it?'

'Oh,' said Truda shrugging, 'she'll get the Saar.'

'Don't you be too sure,' said Christina.

'I'll bet you anything you like on it,' said Truda. And a moment later, 'I don't believe that story of yours, Elsa.'

'I didn't expect you to,' said Elsa coolly. 'Hitler's like the Pope;

84

once he ceases to be infallible and beyond reproach, he fades away, like a puff of smoke.'

'What do you mean by that, exactly?'

'Nothing, mon amie.'

Truda looked at her uncertainly. She was never very sure of either the Danish girl who never stopped sketching, or the Norwegian girl who never stopped knitting, and wondered for the fortieth time why she liked them in spite of it. She said rather hesitatingly, anxious to find some justification for Elsa's story in case it happened to be true, 'A German Empire mightn't be such a bad thing ...'

'But I don't want to be German,' said Elsa plaintively. 'Do you, Chris?'

'Not much,' she admitted.

'Voila! You see, Truda, we just don't know what's good for us.' There was something wrong with Truda's foot, she thought, and began to hunt for her eraser.

'It's underneath you,' said Christina, glancing across at her from her place on the other bed. 'You're sitting on it.'

'Thanks, Chris,' she said. 'What on earth would I do without you?'

'I've often wondered. I expect you'd end up with nothing to wear that hadn't holes in it, no books, no pencils ... no nothing. What you need is a nurse.'

'Why? Are you going to hand in your resignation?' Elsa extracted the eraser from under her, rubbed energetically for a minute, then began to sketch in Truda's foot for the second time. She was a dark girl with a pale skin and blue eyes, nervous, vivid, and rather intellectual, in contrast to the placid and serene domestic Christina. She could not sit still; out of school she smoked incessantly; within the school she sketched, and sketched well. Her pencil and pen-and-ink drawings were a complete record of her life at Pensionnat Les Ormes, for she caught and set down the people about her in all sorts of moods and attitudes. It was as good training as she could hope for at the moment. She was intending to study anatomical drawing, specializing in brain surgery and spending most of her life in operating rooms. The following year she would go to Brussels; in the meantime she had been sent to Switzerland to relax. So far she had not relaxed at all, for she had matured early, and the boarding school routine made her both impatient and irritable.

Truda got up, went over to the basin in the alcove and gulped down a glass of water. She was feeling bad-tempered, and was anxious to work off her general dissatisfaction on someone, preferably Ilse or Anna, chafing under the sense of frustration which had irked her ever since the scene with Theodora in the dining room. She leaned back against the basin and said in her fluent but poorly pronounced French, 'We have different ideas of what's good for us, from the rest of the world ... but it's not their business. Anyone who's lived in Germany for long knows what things were like until 1933. Ever since the war we've been poor; the little money there was, was all in the hands of the Jews who made it out of selling our soldiers paper-soled shoes and rotten flour and rubbishy materials ... even so they weren't beaten, they starved along with the rest of the country under the blockade. Outside the country, we were dogs with our tails between our legs; inside, the Jews had a stranglehold on the little there was left. No one thought we were any good; we didn't even think so ourselves. We had no nationalism ... the war had burst the country wide open, leaving everyone wandering around in it like a crowd of bewildered children.'

Little Klaus and Big Klaus nodded solemnly from their place on the floor by the radiator, and succeeded only in annoying her. She frowned at them and went on, looking from Christina to the oblivious Elsa, 'Then Hitler came into power. A little work is better than no work at least, a little money earned honestly, better than unearned relief. The unemployed were becoming a dead weight, unfitted for anything ... don't forget we starved during the war, which didn't do us much good physically, to start with. Now, in the labour camps, the men work in exchange for a little money ... they'll get more when it can be given to them ... and the landowners are able to keep their fields tilled with the landhelpers, instead of letting them lie and rot. You don't realize it ... but it's exciting to live in Germany now ... before, there was nothing but waiting, waiting ... for nothing but more waiting.' She looked at Christina, who smiled and nodded in confirmation.

'If you've got millions of people with different ideas from yours who simply won't co-operate, you've got to do something. In a time when everything's so desperate, it's no good sitting about and arguing all day, and letting people interfere with what you know has got to be done. When there's a crisis, the country comes first, and I say let the Jews go on wailing till all's blue ... trust the Jews to make enough noise to be heard right around the world! ... and the Communists and Socialists and Catholics can either shut up or go to work, or go to concentration camps and learn what's good for them. Even if they don't think it's right, they've absolutely no business to split up the country and upset everyone by squeaking their own little miseries from the housetops.'

'If they squeaked them,' remarked Elsa, 'they wouldn't be effective enough to bother anyone. And what about the German women?' The foot was all right now but she wanted Truda back in the group again. She could not ask her to return to her former seat by the dressing table when she was in the middle of a speech to the opposition. Elsa looked down at her sketch; there were

Little Klaus and Big Klaus all complete, there was nothing to do
to them. Truda's outlines, however, were a little vague. She looked
once more at the German girl still leaning against the basin,
then laid down her sketch pad and resigned herself to delay.

'We've got to play our part, too.'

'Certainly,' said Elsa. 'I'm always willing to play my part ...
provided it's recognized that my part is anatomical drawing and
not breeding children, like guinea pigs.'

Christina looked a little worried. 'I wish you wouldn't be so
... so direct,' she said mildly.

'Scientific language,' said Elsa.

'Well, after all, we're the ones who have children ... I mean,
men don't ...'

'They help,' said Elsa.

'Elsa!' said Christina reproachfully.

'All right, lambie.'

'And no woman wants to be married to a man who keeps
house while she goes out to work,' said Truda, continuing in
spite of them.

'I don't want to get married, though,' said Elsa. 'I don't mean
that I've any objection to marriage ... I dare say it's all right,
but I'm certainly not going to give up the work I've wanted to
do all my life for the sake of it, any more than I'd expect my
husband, if he were a doctor or a lawyer, for example, to give
up practising medicine or law in order to marry me.'

'Well, it's not up to you to get in the way, either,' said Truda.
Elsa raised her eyebrows but said nothing. 'And since it's a
choice between you getting a job and some man, who is either
supporting a family now or will in the future, getting it, then
you should stay home.'

'Why can't both Elsa and the man work?' asked Christina
unexpectedly.

'I told you,' she said impatiently. 'There's not enough to go round.'

'Why isn't there?'

'Well, because there isn't, that's all.'

'Too many people?' asked Elsa. 'In proportion to the number of jobs?'

'Yes,' Truda said unwillingly, because she realized that once more Elsa, with her infernal logic, was about to corner her.

'Then why this population of eighty-five million by 1960 or whenever it is?'

'Why are you always trying to trip me up?' she burst out, with a hasty glance at Little Klaus and Big Klaus. 'Do you think I know the answer to everything?'

'No,' said Elsa, looking rather mischievous. '*I* don't. And anyhow, my dear Truda, so far as this making a place for the men with ... or without ... families is concerned, I have twice as good a brain as the average man ... why on earth shouldn't I be allowed to use it?'

'Have you? It's nice of you to let us know about your wonderful brain, anyway,' said Truda rudely.

Elsa sighed, looked angry for a moment, then said calmly, 'You know perfectly well what I mean. The average mental age of the masses is about fourteen.' She yawned suddenly and unexpectedly; she was becoming rather bored, and took herself to task for it. After all, she was a woman and she ought to have Views, but she hadn't any. Provided she was permitted to do her own job, the rest of the world could get along as best it might. In Belgium and in her own Denmark, her life would be untroubled by all this dissension, and as a consequence she was incapable of taking much interest in it. That was deplorably egocentric, she thought, drawing blocks and triangles on the pad in front of her. All the same, politics tended to be rather childish, for only children believed that because one thing was true, the contrary must be false. It suddenly occurred to her that there was no reason why Christianity should be right and Taoism wrong ... why couldn't they both be right? She sat up, looking intently into space, quite engrossed with this new idea, and determined to start a discussion on it with Consuelo and Vicky and Theodora at the first opportunity. Thank heaven, she thought fervently, there are at least three girls in this school with some brains, and some interest in things other than politics or clothes and personalities.

'... so why does everyone pick on Germany?' the persistent Truda was asking the room in general.

'We don't,' said Christina, and scrambling down from the high bed she went over to the dressing table. She smoothed out the front section of the sweater and held it against herself, looking in the glass.

'It's awfully pretty, Chris,' said Elsa, anxious to change the subject. 'I wish I could wear that shade of blue ... it makes *me* look like a vegetable marrow.'

'Don't be silly,' said Christina, turning round to scrutinize her. 'You ought to have more self-confidence. You don't know how attractive you are.'

'I certainly don't,' Elsa said, looking amused. 'I'd agree with you instantly if you were to suggest that I was a genius ...'

'Remind me to suggest it some time, then,' said Truda. 'We've never agreed on anything yet.'

Elsa looked at her rather affectionately. 'You'd be awfully nice,' she said with a sigh, 'if only you'd stop crusading.' Then, for fear her remark would be seized upon as an opening for further Fascist propaganda, she went on hurriedly, 'I remember when I was little my mother used to say wistfully, "You know, Elsa, I cannot understand *why* it is that no matter what colour

you wear, your face looks dirty." My face usually *was* dirty, perhaps that accounted for it. My mother never knew it though.
We had a nurse ... a heavenly fat woman who was fearfully lazy
... who came from Germany, by the way, Truda ... and who told
us all those fantastic legends of the Harz mountains, while she
should have been washing us. We had a sort of standing agreement ... my brothers and I ... that no one should ever tell on her.
My mother's a sort of vague woman, anyhow ... that is when it
comes to domestic matters. She's a writer, you know ...'

'They should know,' said Christina. 'After all, Elsa Michielsen
is fairly ...'

'Her books are banned in Germany,' said Truda.

'I know,' said Elsa junior. 'When her publisher told her that,
she said, "Now I *know* I'm worth reading. At last I've had some
real encouragement," and retired into her study to begin another
trilogy.'

'I shouldn't like to have a mother who spent all her time in a
study writing books,' observed Big Klaus. 'She wouldn't be like
a mother at all ... she'd be like a ... like a father.'

'You don't know my mother,' said Elsa reasonably. She chuckled a moment later, and went on, 'She's sublime. She's an idiot.
I *think* she's also a genius, and she's madly funny. She's the most
entertaining human being I've ever known ... with,' she added
thoughtfully, 'the possible exception of my father.'

'How does *he* like it?' demanded Big Klaus.

'He doesn't seem to mind,' said Elsa, still looking amused.
'I think he *quite* likes it. At any rate, he quite likes her, so that
takes care of that.' She realized that her background was as
alien to the three German girls as the background of the two
Babaians, Natalia and Aimée, and decided once more to change
the subject. That's the trouble in a place like this, she thought ...
our home lives are all wildly dissimilar, and there's no basis, no

common ground most of the time, to make our lives at school of any particular value. Or isn't there? What about Theodora and Vicky and Consuelo? She shrugged; really her thoughts were becoming remarkably disjointed and incoherent ... in the middle of a political discussion she suddenly wondered why Taoism and Christianity were necessarily alternatives, and now, talking about her mother, she began to wonder how much good it actually did any of them to come to Switzerland to school ... It only seemed to serve as a reinforcement of their natural prejudices. Anyhow Elsa, she said firmly to herself, get your mind on something and keep it there for a change.

'Do you think Vicky's pretty?' Truda was asking the room.

'Heavens, yes,' said Elsa, who had not the remotest idea how the subject had come up, but was grateful because it did not contain the seeds of contention. 'She has one of the most beautiful faces I've ever seen. I've tried to sketch her time and again, and the only way I can get even the faintest resemblance is by just suggesting her features.'

Big Klaus joined Christina by the mirror and stared at herself intently for a moment. Her hair was light brown and stringy, and no matter how much strength of mind she exercised, she still ate too much chocolate. Her mother did not approve of pampering the young and giving them ideas, nor was she, in truth, very careful in the choice of her own clothes. Big Klaus was doomed to mediocrity at sixteen, or so she gloomily reflected as she looked at herself in the mirror. 'I think I should like to look like Miss Ellerton,' she said rather wistfully. 'It's too bad we can't choose what we look like, when we've only got one life, and always have to wear the same face. Miss Ellerton's so ... so glowing ... as though she had a lamp lit inside her.'

Little Klaus said slowly, 'I think I'd like to be Vicky,' and scarcely knew why she said it, for certainly Miss Ellerton was prettier with her red-gold hair and small features.

'I don't think Vicky's very attractive,' said Truda. 'Those high cheekbones and her dark hair and her eyes ... they're such a light grey that they're almost like water ...' And a moment later, 'She's so odd she makes me feel queer, as though she weren't quite human.'

'Whom would you look like if you could choose, Truda?' asked Christina, turning on the dressing table to smile at the German girl still lounging against the basin.

'I don't know. Personally I don't think looks matter very much, and I certainly don't admire anyone here enough to want to look like her. I think I'd rather look like myself, although I suppose you think that's very funny. You probably can't imagine anyone wanting to look like me!' The passion with which she spoke and the fact that she was obviously hurt in some obscure way caused Christina to deny her statement with unusual feeling, and Elsa to look at her with scientific interest. What was her background, that Truda should emerge from it so very unsure of herself?

'How much longer is Ilse going to be allowed the run of our purses?' Truda burst out in the embarrassed silence following her unexpected display of emotion. Christina had abandoned the chair in front of the dressing table for her old place on the bed, and was busy casting on stitches for the back of her sweater. Truda returned to her former position, and went on, her face working, 'I've lost twenty francs, and I needed them for a new pair of skates. Now I've got to go without any, for my father won't send me any more money till Easter. I suppose Ilse's such a pet of Mlle Devaux's that she'll *never* be blamed for it ... beastly little Jew!'

'Ilse's not Jewish,' objected Christina. Elsa was sketching Truda's face and could not afford the time to make an answer to her outrageous accusations. If Truda was going to get worked up all over again, she thought, she would soon find a sitting position intolerable and would either pace the floor or go back to the basin again.

'Her mother is, and if you're half-Jewish, you're Jewish. Ilse is *so* sweet and *so* gentle, she makes me sick. She hasn't any guts; she creeps in and out of class with her "Oui, Mlle Devaux. Non, Mlle Devaux," until I could scream.' She flushed, and spoke with an angry intensity which robbed her usually musical voice of all its charm. 'She's got on my nerves so that I'd give just about anything not to have to look at her for at least a week!'

'Everyone gets on your nerves who doesn't agree with you,' observed Christina quietly. 'If I were you I'd take on someone who can give you a good fight ... Ted Cohen, for example. There's someone who's really worthy of you, Trudy!'

'I hate her,' said Truda, ignoring Elsa's faintly mocking eyes, 'but I'll say this for her, she doesn't hide behind anyone's skirts. She at least doesn't sneak ...'

'That's what I always say,' said Big Klaus. 'At least you know where you are with her, which is more than you do with lots of others ... the Babaians, for example ... you never know what *they're* thinking. Anyhow, we just don't mix, most of the people here, and I don't see the point in coming. Supposing we did like everyone here, we'd only have to stop when we got home, because nobody there would agree with us.'

'I'm not so sure of that,' said Elsa, still sketching Truda who was sitting rigidly in her chair by the dressing table, her face stormy. 'Vicky likes everyone. She gets along marvellously with everyone, so I suppose it can be done, if you only start out at least moderately free of prejudices.'

'Vicky doesn't like me,' said Truda.

Elsa looked at her sharply, and said, 'Yes, she does, Truda.'

'How do *you* know?' she asked ungraciously.

'She told me yesterday ... or the day before, I've forgotten. As a matter of fact,' she went on deliberately, 'we weren't talking about you altogether ... mostly about Anna von Landenburg.'

'Anna! What's she got to do with me? If Vicky thinks I'd have anything to do with that ... that ...' She hesitated, for once in her life afraid to say what she meant. Christina dropped her knitting and stared at her, while the two on the floor by the radiator shifted a little and looked very interested, as people do when they are about to hear something malicious or unkind. Truda, however, still hesitated. She said at last, 'Well, I'm not sure *what* she is, but I've got a pretty good idea, and I mean to make certain. Then something will happen, you can be sure of that. I've got ways ... I can write to my father in Essen, and things'll be not too easy for Graf von Landenburg!'

'You mind your own business,' said Christina, so angrily that the three German girls, who had imagined that she was as gentle as she looked, were astonished. Elsa, who knew her very well, did not even bother to stop sketching. 'If you're so anxious to concern yourself with other people, see if you can cheer up Marian Comstock ... or try your influence on Cay Shaunessy. She needs a little. I'm afraid she'll be expelled, the way she's going on. Mlle Dupraix caught her smoking again last night, and this morning she went down to that chocolate shop without permission.'

'I'm not interested in Cay Shaunessy, thank you,' said Truda.

'I know you're not. The only people you're interested in are the ones you can persecute. It's time someone gave you a piece of her mind, and if you want to know what I think, it's about time you stopped and had a good look at yourself too. We've been sitting here with you for more than an hour, and in all that time you haven't made one single kind remark about anyone.

It's nothing but "what's wrong with other people" day and night. As for Anna, she's as sick as a dog, and if you so much as whisper a sentence to her, you'll deal with me, and you'll deal with Elsa, and Theodora, and Consuelo ... and, my dear Truda, you'll deal with Vicky. You wouldn't like that, would you?'

'I'm not afraid of Vicky,' she said.

'No?' said Elsa. 'Well, I don't mind admitting that I'd rather have a row with just about anyone than Vicky.'

'Yes,' said Truda slowly, 'maybe you're right.' The others were startled at the sudden change in the tone of her voice. For some unaccountable reason, even the mention of Vicky's name was enough to remind her of her grandmother, and she sat beside the dressing table in silence, unaware of the effect she created, looking rather childish in spite of her long legs and well-developed body. Her mind was suddenly filled with the image of old Mrs. Meyer who had lived with her son and his family for fourteen years ... or rather above them on the third floor, refusing to come down and share his home until the day she died. Like Vicky, she feared no one; she used to stand in the centre of the drawing room leaning a little sideways on her stick with her black moiré skirts falling to the tops of her black leather boots, looking up at her son, quite unawed, no matter what he said. He might be telling her that from now on she must stop her visits to the factory-workers' families, and stop meddling in other people's business, because from these trips she always returned depressed and troubled, would mount the stairs rather faster than usual, lie down on the couch of her sitting-room on the third floor and send for her son. He could never face her like that, apparently, but the following day when they were all in the drawing room after dinner and Herr Meyer was reinforced by the presence of his wife and child, he would issue his regular ultimatum. No more visits to the workmen, no

more meddling in other people's business. She would get up from
her high-backed chair by the fire ... she always said she could
think better on her feet ... listen to all he had to say, and when
he had entirely finished she would remark drily, 'Josef, my son,
your tie is crooked,' and once more retire to her own quarters
on the third floor.

She was the only one who ever contradicted him when he
talked about keeping the lower orders in their places, and women
in their homes, although she usually contented herself with quite
obviously paying no attention to him. Meyer was rather afraid
of her, and for a few months after her death he was melancholy
and more gentle with Truda and her mother than was his wont.
Then, gradually, he had become more stern and more dominating than ever.

Truda missed her grandmother. Her mother was essentially
the sort of woman in whom such characteristics as courage,
mental flexibility and intellect have to be taken for granted, but
Meyer was not the man to foster and cherish such qualities in
any human being with whom his relationship was at all intimate,
much less his wife. He was a stupid man, and Truda considered
her mother negligible, as a result of her father's attitude toward
his wife.

Old Mrs. Meyer had strongly protested against Truda's being
sent away to boarding school when she was ten. The day she
was to leave, her grandmother had come down from her rooms
to pace the floor of the library with short, quick steps, stopping
every now and then to utter some particularly damning criticism
of her son who stood silently with his hands clasped behind him
in front of the coal grate. Truda herself was sitting in the corner
by the door, her presence forgotten by both of them.

She remembered her grandmother standing by the desk at
the far end of the room by the windows, and turning to say, 'The

child is appallingly sensitive. I tell you, Josef, I know what I am saying. In the impersonal atmosphere of this ... this school you are sending her to, the love and understanding which are essential to the development of such a temperament as hers will be absent. If you persist in sending her away she will either go to pieces, or she will grow inwards. Truda demands love such as you, Josef, have made no effort to give her.'

She came back to the centre of the room and, gripping her stick, spoke with an intensity and depth of passion which partially revealed to the child in the corner all the bitterness of disappointment which she had felt for many years. 'You will answer for your stupidity toward your wife and your child. You are my son, but I do not excuse you. If I get to Heaven before you, I shall see that you answer for it ... that is a terrible thing for me to say, and yet I mean it. I am telling you that if you send that child away now, you will be making an error which may take years to rectify, which may never be rectified at all, for she may become a human being like yourself.'

He had said angrily, 'That is the worst thing that could happen to her, I suppose ... to grow up to resemble her father.'

She had stood her ground, but her face was colourless and her skin stretched like parchment on a drum as she answered, 'Yes, Josef. You bring no happiness to other people; if you died there would be no less goodness in the world. You would be no real loss to anyone.' And a moment later, 'You are not evil, Josef ... you are *null und nichtig*. You exist, and He does not see you, for you are a person of no importance.' She was breathing so heavily that Truda, hearing her irregular gasps for breath, on the other side of the room, was afraid that she would faint, but she turned and marched straight to the door, across the hall and up the stairs more quickly than ever.

Truda found herself thinking as she sat by the dressing table that this confused and unhappy state in which she lived would not have been possible if only she had seen more of her grandmother after she went away to school. During the holidays she had avoided her, and seldom climbed the three flights of stairs to her room, for when she got there all her grandmother seemed to do was to lie on her couch and stare at her ... since they no longer had anything to talk about. In the summer of 1933 she had died of angina.

In some strange way Vicky was like her, and yet not like her. They had the same way of dealing with people, the same quiet certainty, but Vicky made no use of her influence, and had, into the bargain, seemed to be avoiding the conflicts of others as much as she could ... she had not been there at tea that afternoon, for example, and Truda had a shrewd suspicion that when the scene between herself and Theodora was recounted to her, she would heave a sigh of relief because, for once, she had not been drawn in. That was not in the least like her grandmother.

The first bell rang for dinner. Little Klaus and Big Klaus leaped to their feet and ran out, followed by Christina at a more dignified pace. Truda stopped Elsa at the door, taking the sketch pad from her hand, without waiting for the Danish girl's permission. 'Let's see it, Elsa,' she said, and looked at it with an expressionless face. 'I do look charming, don't I?' she remarked and, returning the pad, went over to the window to close her shutters. Elsa had an idea that she was crying, but after glancing at her, decided to leave her alone, and went out.

3

Ilse Brüning, sitting in her room with a copy of *Le Cid* open before her on the desk, heard the first bell ring for dinner and stiffened with nervousness. She had been dreading and yet waiting anxiously for the sound ever since coming up from tea two and a half hours before, and had accomplished nothing during the interval. She was frightened; she had been frightened for weeks. The approaching Sunday constituted an abyss, a break in the continuity of time which seemed to widen as it came nearer and nearer. For some it would be a day of triumph, for others a day to be remembered as long as they lived, fraught with tragedy. Its political implications were of no importance to Ilse. Whether the Saar went to Germany, to France, or remained with the League of Nations was to her a vitally personal issue. Her father was too ill to leave Saarbrücken before spring; in the meantime their livelihood and the whole of Ilse's little world revolved around and depended upon a young Jew named Paul Mendelssohn. If, as Anna had said, Germany got the Saar on Sunday, then it would be brought to the attention of the authorities that Paul was active in the pro-League faction, and what then?

Ida had told her about a German Jew who was a relative of her family in New York, a gentle old man who had never harmed anyone, but he had been stripped of everything he owned. On the last night before his family left to take refuge in France, the police entered the house and dragged him from the table where he was sitting at dinner into the billiard room, where they spread-eagled him on the table ...

Du lieber Gott! If they did that to a defenceless old Jew who had never in his life dealt evil to a human soul, what horrible thing would Paul have to suffer, when he was even at this moment, in all likelihood, speaking against Hitler and his National Socialism? She was going to marry Paul in the summer; they had loved each other ever since she was fourteen and he twenty-one. He used to joke about it to her father, 'Don't forget, Herr Brüning, Ilse belongs to me.' Then he had come to live with them, and said it again one day when they were at lunch. Suddenly, as soon as the words were out of his mouth, he had looked at her across the table, and remained sitting motionless, still staring at her as though he had never seen her before, while she felt her cheeks growing hotter and hotter and no one seemed to be able to think of anything to say until her father cleared his throat and asked, 'Shall I tell Hans to prune the apple trees now, Paul, or is it too early in the season?'

After that he had been very polite and did not tease her any more. Then one day in the spring of the year before, when she had been picking lilacs, he had said, 'We shall be married next summer on your eighteenth birthday, Ilse?'

She had said, 'Yes, Paul,' as though she had known it all the time. It was growing dusk. Her memories of that early evening eight months before were a confusion of sights, sounds and feelings. She remembered that a cart had been going by on the other side of the high garden wall, that the moon was just rising over the apple trees and that the lilacs had suddenly seemed to send out more perfume than ever before as Paul took her in his arms.

She tried to remember the garden more clearly as she sat at her desk, having an idea that if only she could make herself believe that she was there once more ... would she ever be there again? ... in all that beauty and peace, then she would not be afraid of Truda, the very sight of Truda; then she would not go about the school scanning every face which was turned away from her, wondering if that girl too thought she was a thief.

How could anyone imagine that she would steal? Why should they think that she even wanted money? She wanted nothing in all the world but to marry Paul and see her mother and father settled in a little house with a garden close by. It was true that they were not rich, but at the moment she had lots of money ... she had more money than she knew what to do with ... she had a hundred francs. Paul had sent it to her two days before, instructing her to be careful with it and not spend it on something she needed. He had said in his letter, 'All your life it's been a question of "Do you really need it?" Now please go and buy yourself a pair of earrings, or two orchids, or a stuffed dog. If you *need* anything, let me know. Your father worries a lot about money but really we are doing very well considering everything, and you must be sure to tell me if there's anything you want. After all, we're practically married.'

Such a silly letter for a man of twenty-five to write! But she was glad he had written it, for he had said to her once, 'I can tell you anything I like. It's one of ten thousand reasons why I love you so much. If I were to say things like that to anyone else, he'd look at me with that ... oh, you know the look ... Young man, you'll soon get over this nonsense. That's what *that* look says. Isn't it terrible the number of things we're supposed to "get over," liebchen?' With everyone else he was so dignified; when all the family had come from Paris last summer to see them ... heavens, how many parcels they had! ... they had sat in the living room each night after dinner watching Paul, listening to him talk about the political situation, nodding to each other and smiling. 'Paul is a fine boy, he will go far.'

What would he say if he knew they suspected her of stealing? He would be very angry and would probably come at once and take her away, which would never do, for though she might be a coward ... and only she knew how frightened of everything in life Ilse Brüning was! ... still, she would stay at least until they found out who was doing it. She would not tell Paul anyhow; he had enough to worry him already.

Why did he love her when she was not pretty and not at all clever? Perhaps, one day, he might realize how plain and stupid she really was. She had said that to him once, and he had been quite annoyed. He had said, 'When you're with me, you're very pretty. If you're not pretty when you're with other people, it doesn't matter, because soon you'll be with me all the time ... and even if you weren't, what difference does it make? I think you always see what you want to see in the face of someone you love. Even if something awful happened to your face, and no one else was even able to recognize you, I would still see *my* Ilse.'

She had been thinking of Paul and the garden that day when Truda thought she was copying. When you were thinking hard about something, you simply did not see what was in front of you. She had said that to Miss Williams, who had understood, but Truda was not the sort of person who was ever absent-minded and she had not understood. Truda said that anyone who would copy, would steal. Ilse supposed that was true, but she was guilty of neither crime, whatever Truda thought, although now, when she came into a room, she was aware of looks, of silences and whispering, which were only natural perhaps, but she was so conscious of them and so afraid that the others agreed with Truda, that she'd have given anything to be able to lock herself in her room and stay there.

The second bell for dinner rang. Now she must go and sit at Miss William's table with Truda directly opposite her, and she felt sick. She always felt sick when she was very frightened. Suppose she *were* sick in the dining room in front of everyone?

Ilse got up and went out. At the door she stopped and suddenly darted away down the hall to the left, past the main staircase, for she had seen Truda's feet and ankles coming down the stairs from the floor above. She wanted Vicky; she thought that if only Vicky would sit beside her at dinner, she would be all right and she would not be sick. At the back stairs she paused, looking upwards. Vicky's room was on the top floor, and the sound of footsteps in the hall below was growing fainter ... they must all be in the dining room now. She could not be late, and be scolded by Mlle Tourain before the whole school. She fled back along the hall and down the main staircase, which only the staff were permitted to use, arriving at the door of the dining room just as Marthe, Mlle Tourain's personal maid who waited on the head table, was about to close it. Ilse Brüning of Saarbrücken thought of Paul Mendelssohn as she crossed the room to Miss Williams's table in the centre of the south wall by the French windows, overlooking the Lake of Geneva; if she could think of Paul sufficiently hard, she would not think of Truda or the stealing, or the elections on Sunday, and she would not be sick. That, at the moment, was more important than anything else.

IV

～

*M*lle Tourain was saying grace. Her mind was not on God, however; she was watching a stout middle-aged woman in dusty brown making her way slowly down a lane to a little house whose windows overlooked the gradual slope to Ouchy. On either side of the lane was a wooden fence, blackened with age and rotted by the incessant snows of winter, with lilacs hanging heavily over the top. The fence was broken here and there by little gates which led to other people's houses. The end gate on the right was her own; the stout woman turned there, glanced for a last time at the lilacs, then walked up the flagged path to the house, pausing now and then to lean over a little breathlessly and examine the hyacinths which grew in joyous disorder everywhere.

There was no one to look at the stout woman but Amélie Tourain, and she scarcely recognized her. Apparently she lived in that house and only went out through the gate once a day to take a walk at sundown. The remainder of her life was spent in the small tidy study on the ground floor, poring over books on Swiss Independence. There was something faintly ridiculous about her, thought the acting headmistress of Pensionnat Les Ormes rather uncomfortably, for she was utterly unaware of the passage of time, and indifferent to the facts contained in the newspaper which she read at breakfast each morning rather absent-mindedly. She seemed to live with her back deliberately turned to the rest of the world, to life itself.

The stout middle-aged woman in dusty brown had disappeared into her house. A few minutes later a light glowed in the windows to the left of the front door, and a shadow passed back and forth across the curtains. Then the shutters were closed, and catching a brief glimpse of the woman's face as she glanced up at the night sky, Mlle Tourain wondered again at her remote tranquillity.

The two people merged into one for a moment, then from the vision two separate entities appeared, the one demanding insistently what was to be done with the other. Either the head-mistress of Pensionnat Les Ormes, now engaged in saying grace, must cease to exist and Jeanne be informed that a substitute must immediately be found, or the lilacs hanging over the stout woman's particular section of fence be allowed to grow wild, and dust to gather on her books.

There was the sound of fifty chairs being drawn back and then pulled into place. Amélie Tourain discovered with relief that she had said grace and was now sitting at the head of her table with the west windows behind her. Turning her head to the left, she looked through the pantry door and observing that the soup was not yet in evidence, allowed her eyes to wander about the room. They eventually reached the face of Rose Dupraix directly opposite her at the foot of her table, were caught, and held. The Beaux Arts teacher was staring at her fixedly, as though trying to communicate some idea.

It was a determined stare. From the compressed lips and the general look of her, Amélie Tourain gathered that she was being reminded of some unpleasant duty. But what? What on earth did the woman mean by looking at her like that? It was excessively irritating.

Mlle Tourain suddenly recollected the girl whom Mlle Lemaitre was always pleased to refer to as 'the unfortunate Vicky,' and her cigarettes. Of course, that was what Rose Dupraix's eyes were referring to. The headmistress let out a barely audible sigh, and picking up her fork, rapped on the table. There was immediate silence which continued unbroken for some time after the headmistress's peremptory 'Victoria! Stand up!' It was not the headmistress's habit to so much as glance in her victim's direction until she had heard a chair pulled back and a, usually apprehensive, 'Oui, Mlle Tourain?' When she had waited, this time rather longer than ever before, she raised her eyes at last and saw the empty chair at Fräulein Lange's table which seemed suddenly, as everyone else turned to look at it, to be endowed with life, to have taken on a personality of its own.

Fräulein Lange stammered, 'She's not here, Mlle Tourain,' and then suffered a spasm of increased nervousness for having spoken when she had not been spoken to, and into the bargain having offered a piece of information which was perfectly obvious.

The headmistress let her off easily, however, with 'Even I can see that, Fräulein.'

Theodora darted a swift look at Fräulein Lange's embarrassed face and stood up.

'Well, Theodora, supposing you enlighten us. Where is Vicky?'

'She's with Rosalie,' answered Theodora briefly. She never wasted words in a matter of this sort, knowing that with every extra one added, Mlle Tourain's sarcasm increased. It was not that she was afraid of sarcasm, for, as she had once remarked coolly to Mary Ellerton, 'I was very good at it myself when I was Mlle Tourain's age,' but that she disliked public debate.

'I beg your pardon, Theodora?'

'I said, she's with Rosalie.'

'Oh. Am I to assume that you have already made arrangements for her dinner, or have you left that to me?' Such a remark, spoken in such a tone, was guaranteed to reduce any ordinary European girl either to tears or at least to miserable incoherence.

Theodora continued to stand motionless with one hand on the back of her chair, the other hanging loosely by her side, looking across at the headmistress with a face which was quite unmoved. The sarcasm she regarded as superfluous and indicative of either weakness or bad breeding; one was not even sarcastic to servants, and she would have considered herself a fool to be shaken by it from her habitually reserved and deferential manner. At the same time, she had seen a good many girls break down under it, and the sight rankled. She said, looking innocent, 'Why no, Mlle Tourain. Vicky assumed that she would not get any dinner, since we all know that we are only allowed to carry trays if our roommates are ill, and it's very good of you to let me do it ...'

'I am *not* letting you do it. Before you sit down, you might be so good as to tell me *why* Vicky is visiting Rosalie at this particular time, when less privileged individuals are ...' she stopped, horrified to discover that she was on the point of saying '... are forced to drink Mlle Dupraix's onion soup.' It was that silly woman's fault that she had got herself into this ridiculous position and apparently she wanted, senselessly and childishly, to be rude to her. She hastily sipped some water to cover her confusion and then added lamely 'eating their dinner.' The three words hung suspended in absurdity for a moment while the appreciative school waited in silence.

Theodora glanced in a leisurely way around the room, then said at last, 'I was with Rosalie, and just as the bell went she asked for Vicky so ... so urgently that I couldn't object or refuse to get her. Vicky was already on her way down to dinner when I caught up with her. She asked me to explain to you afterward, for she hadn't time to get your permission before you came into the dining room.'

The headmistress was not looking at her, she was watching one of the maids carrying a soup tureen across the room to Miss Williams's table. Theodora forced herself to go on, anxious to put Vicky in a reasonable light, 'Rosalie's been very homesick all day. You know Vicky's the only other Canadian here ...' Mlle Tourain's obliviousness made her thoroughly self-conscious, so much so that her voice seemed to belong to someone else. I really seem to be the only person who's listening to Theodora Cohen, she thought with her usual humour. The headmistress continued to ignore her; she was ladling out the soup for her own table now and had evidently decided to employ her customary method of closing a conversation which was proving either awkward or boring, by suddenly ceasing to pay any attention. That left the other person more or less stranded, until he or she made a bad exit.

With a shrug for Amélie Tourain's manners, Theodora sat down. Fräulein Lange, ladling out the soup which, after some nine hundred dinners at Pensionnat Les Ormes she was still afraid of spilling, said without thinking, 'Vicky shouldn't go without her dinner, it's bad for her,' and then cast a quick, embarrassed glance around her table, because it was not seemly for a teacher to express opinions contrary to authority, particularly before the girls.

Theodora slid down a little in her chair and said, 'Don't worry, Fräulein, Vicky won't go without her dinner.'

Yasha, usually so careful not to involve herself in anything, said surprisingly, 'If you're going to get a tray from one of the maids, I'll help you.'

Natalia's quick sidelong glance showed that she too was startled, but she said nothing. Theodora smiled. 'That's awfully good of you, Yasha, but I think I'll just tip one of the maids to do it ... it's simpler. I've been caught carrying trays to Vicky before this, too many times.'

There was a short silence as they began their soup. Then Stephania remarked as her eyes fell on Mlle Lemaitre's thin, feverish bird-like face in the opposite corner, 'You know, she looks worse ... she looks *much* worse ...'

The German mistress said, 'Mlle Lemaitre?'

'Yes,' said Stephania.

'I really think she ought to be in a warm climate, but when I said something to her about the south of France the other day, she wouldn't listen. She comes from Clermont, you know. She says, however, that they only discovered how bad the air of the Midi was for people with bronchial trouble when several thousand people who'd gone there to be cured, all died.'

'Maupassant had a short story on that,' observed Theodora, then corrected herself. 'No, it's in *Sur l'eau*, isn't it?' she asked Natalia, who nodded. 'You remember, it begins, "Des princes, des princes, partout des princes! Ceux qui aiment les princes sont heureux ..." Which always reminds me, for no reason at all, of that uncle of Bertie's who rushed down to breakfast one morning, lifted the covers off the dishes, peered into them, said, "Eggs, eggs, damn all eggs!" and retired to the south of France never to return to the bosom of his family.'

'As you say, there doesn't seem to be any reason why princes, princes, princes everywhere should remind you of eggs, eggs, damn all eggs,' remarked Yasha.

'I have that kind of mind,' she said loftily. 'It's subtle, that's all. I see relationships and connections which people of far coarser intellect miss entirely.' She turned to Natalia again. 'You remember that paragraph in *Sur l'eau* which begins "Heureux ceux qui ne connaissent pas l'écoeurment abominable des mêmes actions toujours répétées; heureux ceux qui ... qui ..." What is it?'

'"... ont la force de recommencer chaque jour les mêmes besognes avec les mêmes gestes ..." C'est nous, Teddy, hein?'

'"Heureux ceux qui ne s'aperçoivent pas avec un immense dégout que rien ne change, que rien ne passe et que tout se lasse,"' finished Theodora, her head nodding in agreement. 'It's certainly us, all right.'

'Disillusioned schoolgirl,' said Yasha sadly, 'admiring Maupassant and his impassioned cynicisms ...'

'Very good,' said Theodora. 'I take back my remark about your coarse and unsubtle intellect.'

'Oh, was that intended for me?'

'Mais, naturellement,' said Theodora.

Fräulein Lange was looking at them in dismay, wrenched from her troubled thoughts by what she regarded as still another incomprehensible exhibition of precocity. She shook her head helplessly, and said, looking from one to the other, 'I should think you were twenty-five, to hear you talk. How old are you, Theodora? And you, Yasha? And you, Natalia?'

'Practically twenty-one,' said Theodora. 'Too old for this intellectual vacuum.'

'Nineteen,' said Yasha.

'Twenty,' said Natalia, smiling at the German mistress.

'I don't know what's the matter with you,' said Fräulein Lange unhappily. 'None of you are in the least like ordinary young girls, except Maria-Teresa.'

'Well, I should hope so,' said Theodora. 'After all, she's only fifteen, and almost feeble-minded into the bargain.'

'Zitto!' said Maria-Teresa. 'Basta di te ...'

'Maria-Teresa,' said Fräulein Lange rebukingly. 'You're supposed to be learning French here.'

'Shut up then, you idiot,' said Maria-Teresa in French.

'Can't you be polite in *any* language?' asked Fräulein Lange despairingly.

'She's awfully ladylike in Mandarin,' said Theodora, and added a moment later, 'I see the Cummings-Gordons have at last found their own level. They're with Mlle Tourain,' she added, gesturing in explanation toward the head table across the room.

'Now, Theodora,' said Fräulein Lange reprovingly, 'they're good students ...'

'... and?'

'They're never disobedient. You would do well to follow their example ...'

Maria-Teresa said imploringly, 'No! Two of them are quite enough. Besides that, if you suggest anything to Teddy she takes you up on it. She's bad enough as she is. If she becomes virtuous as well, she'll be unbearable ... insupportable!'

'What do you think they'll talk about at Mlle Tourain's table?' asked Stephania.

Yasha yawned, looked at the remainder of her soup with an unfriendly expression and said, 'First of all, skiing at Gstaad. Then Swiss respectability ...' The word was out before she could stop herself and she looked apologetically at Fräulein Lange to see if she had taken the remark amiss, but the German teacher's mind was only half following the conversation; in the background was her intention of asking Mlle Tourain after the faculty meeting if she might go home that weekend. That had been Vicky's idea. At the end of her tale of worry and alarm, she had said, 'Why don't you go to Zürich Saturday morning, take your sister to a doctor yourself and set your mind at rest?'

It had not occurred to her that she could do that. 'We're only allowed one weekend a month,' she had objected, 'and I took that two weeks ago.'

'Supposing you did? Are you ten years old, Fräulein?'

'No,' she said. 'I am not, as you very well know.'

Vicky laughed. 'You can explain it all to Mlle Tourain. I'm sure she'll understand if you tell her your sister is ill and you feel it necessary to see her. You wouldn't be missing any classes.'

Of course, if you looked at it in that light, there was no reason why she shouldn't go. So now, sitting at dinner, she was steeling herself to remain behind after the faculty meeting and ask permission to take an extra weekend. In all her three years at the school she had never dreamed of asking a favour, and she was astonished at her own courage. Nevertheless, she would ask for it, and she would go. Only one more day and she would see Maria. Sylvia Lange, what on earth are you coming to?

Mary Ellerton, hearing snatches of conversation from Yasha, Natalia and Theodora at the next table, sighed rather wistfully as she served her six girls with dried beef and watery vegetables. None of them, taken separately, was very interesting, but combined they managed to produce quite disproportionate dullness. If brilliant conversationalists converse more brilliantly when stimulated by each other's minds, she thought, trying to divide the remaining carrots into three equal servings, the opposite is true of mediocrities. General interest here stopped at clothes and personalities.

There was, at the other end, one Henriette Martin from

Mulhouse, a strange girl with a sallow complexion and a puffy nose. She had an atrocious accent, her French never having recovered form the German occupation of Alsace-Lorraine. She said 'piang' for 'bien,' and 'maissong' for 'maison;' her f's were all v's, and her v's all f's. She hissed her s's and was liable to spatter you if you came too close. She never took baths. It was easy to find out whether a girl did or did not, because on Thursdays and Mondays if one wished a bath one called 'Bain,' instead of skiing, skating, walking, hockey, or 'en ville,' which denoted shopping, when the roll was taken for the afternoon recreation. Why, Mary asked herself heatedly, should baths be an alternative to skiing, skating, walking, hockey or shopping?

Next to Henriette was Rose Budet. Mary had nothing against her specifically, except a remark she had made on Mary's first day at the school. Hearing that the girl came from Brussels, Mary had said, 'Oh, then perhaps you know Natalia's family?' Whereupon the Budet ... her name lent itself to alteration with unfortunate ease ... stated with finality that she was not in the habit of associating with Armenians.

Opposite Rose were Cissie and Ruth Anderson from Manchester. They, and the two Cummings-Gordon girls from Philadelphia, were the chief exponents in the school of refinement and gentility. The four got along rather badly together, though, for whereas the two from Manchester believed that respectability and decency were confined to England, the two from Philadelphia considered that the only really enlightened country in the world was the United States. Cissie and Ruth were small and rather thin with heavy dark brown hair which was waved each week by the school hairdresser. Their eyebrows were plucked to a thin, unbecoming line and always looked a little raw. They put on their make-up badly and were over-conscious of the male sex. Cissie Anderson was the oldest girl in the school and consequently considered that she was out of her element. Mary would have sympathized with her a little more if she had not been twenty-two, and old enough, one would have thought, to be treated as an adult by her parents. Her sister Ruth was a year younger; her nose and chin were pointed and her features in every way less attractive than Cissie's, but she possessed more vivacity and more colour to make up for it. Mary had spent a month watching their crooked fingers as they delicately lifted their food to their mouths, and often wondered whether they would have been so unladylike as to chew at all, if they could have managed to swallow their food without doing it. As it was, they chewed with their front teeth as much as possible; that made the whole business of mastication less gross, apparently.

Of the two others present, Ida Samuels was a Jewish girl from New York ... 'or the Bronx,' said Theodora, 'which, my dear Mary, is an entirely different thing' ... with a general air of over-sexed vulgarity. Her one asset was her legs. The possession of even remarkably beautiful legs might not have greatly altered the course of anyone's life, but Ida did wonders with them. She had once bored Mary almost to tears with a story about a country-club dance in Westchester when she had spotted an attractive boy on the other side of the room whom no one knew but whom every girl there was dying to meet. She, Ida Samuels, had simply lifted her skirts a few inches and he had come right over. There had been a lot more of it, along the same lines, but Mary had managed not to listen. Ida had been tried out by all the other cliques in the school but none of them had been able to stand her and she had been forced to fall back on Henriette and Rose who considered her marvellously sophisticated, and also to a certain extent on the Andersons who were not very popular.

She would have been harmless enough, Mary knew, if her mind had not been of an extremely sensational turn; unlike Theodora she was very conscious of being Jewish and would have denied it if it had been possible. To excuse it, and endow both Jewry and therefore indirectly herself with importance, she read avidly everything the newspapers contained about Jewish persecution and ill-treatment, choosing Ilse and Anna as an audience to be preferred to any other, because it was on them that her words had their greatest effect. She and Theodora hated one another. On the famous occasion when Theodora had hit her across the face for describing the anecdote of the bloody flag to Anna von Landenburg, she had not hesitated to go straight to Mlle Tourain with the story. That stalwart soul told Ida that she had got no more than she deserved, then called in Theodora ... after Ida had returned, raging, to her room ... and informed *her* that she had behaved like a Billingsgate fishwife, which Theodora very well knew. Ten days later a cable arrived informing Mlle Tourain that Mr. and Mrs. Samuels were leaving for Europe in order to remove their Ida from the school, as soon as Mr. Samuels could leave his leather business, and that they would take the matter up with the American consul if Theodora were not immediately expelled. The headmistress meditated on the cable for a while, then dropped it in her waste-basket and did nothing. The Samuels did not arrive.

The only girl at her table whom Mary really liked was a red-haired child from Seattle named Cay Shaunessy. Hers was, thought Mary, the most extreme case of parental indifference she had ever come across. Her mother had deposited her at Pensionnat Les Ormes the preceding September, informing Mlle Tourain that she would return for her three years hence, and then immediately sailed on a freight boat bound for California, leaving her daughter to endure the worst case of homesickness which even Mlle Dupraix with her twenty years as housekeeper and eight years as Beaux Arts mistress had ever seen. It had taken the combined efforts of the whole staff to persuade Cay to stop crying and get up from her bed at the end of the first three weeks in the school. From then on, Mary had gathered from their reports, she had followed the pattern set down by thousands of homesick school-children of previous generations. She had recovered from her wild and hysterical unhappiness to drift into complete apathy, from there first to tentative and carefully concealed misconduct, and then to open and incessant disobedience. Mary knew from her own experience at boarding school, having seen other girls of Cay's temperament, that she would continue in this last stage until she was expelled, unless someone could influence her. So far no one, not even herself, had been able to get beyond that stony, aggressive exterior. Mary caught her smoking and said nothing about it to the headmistress; she tried to forestall her numerous ... and often successful ... attempts to break bounds; she tried to reason with her, but Cay was too appalled by the prospect of fifty-four endless months to be endured before she got out of Pensionnat Les Ormes forever, to care what was said or done to her.

Mary worried about her more than Cay ever realized, knowing that she could not keep her out of the limelight much longer, for she had other things to do besides watch that girl from eight in the morning to ten at night. She came to the conclusion that Mrs. Shaunessy and her husband had been supremely unwise in ever permitting such an issue to arise, for the school was bad for Cay, and expulsion would be equally bad for her by giving her her own way through anarchic means.

Mary was interested in the whole question of Catherine Shaunessy from a philosophic as well as a personal point of view, since the problem presented by Vicky's unusual temperament had first made her realize how grave an error is often committed by authority in allowing a difference to become an issue, in erecting an obstacle between itself and another person so that one or the other has to climb over it. For Cay either to gain or lose her point would be equally bad for her. Mary had seen similar situations between Vicky and Mlle Tourain. The headmistress would question her publicly about something which concerned someone else, Vicky would shut up like an oyster, and the headmistress would be justly angry because her authority had been outraged by a small, slender girl who merely refused to talk.

From Vicky, Mary's mind wandered to her husband ... or rather her ex-husband ... they being the two people in the world whom she most loved. She often found herself holding imaginary discussions with him when she was puzzled, for she knew his mind so well that in that way she could get an outside opinion. She never made the mistake of thinking of him as an extension of herself. Or did she? This new person which she had become and whom he did not know was at the same time born of him in some obscure way, for she had admired that part of him which was not concerned in their personal relationship. His clarity and profundity of mind, his passion for people, had all had their effect on her, she knew, for the Mary Ellerton she had been before marriage was a nice, but at the same time rather oblivious and limited outdoor girl. She supposed that it was she, and not the present Mary Ellerton, who found the Andersons and their crooked fingers so extraordinarily irritating. All the same, she thought, spearing the last piece of beef, there seemed to be no real and valid reason for the existence of such people as the Andersons, except in so far as they served as a reminder of virtues now ... fortunately ... almost extinct. Like the Albert Memorial, she added mentally, and then noticed that

Cay had scarcely touched her dinner.

'Eat some of that, Cay,' she said. 'You can't live on air, you know, even in Switzerland.'

The little redhead with her fine nose and thin mouth which would, Mary believed, have a twist of humour in it later on, did not even look up. She said in a rather muffled voice, 'This isn't beef ... it's horse. "Beef" is just a polite word for it.'

'Well,' said Mary, smiling at her, 'Beef or horse, you'd better eat it. You're quite thin enough already.'

'You know,' said Cay suddenly in English, 'if there were more people like you around here, I shouldn't mind it so much.'

At Mlle Devaux's table Consuelo Deane from São Paolo, Brazil, was thinking about her brother Juan. She visualized his dark face ... in such contrast to her own fairness ... his six-feet-three inches of ugliness, which for some reason seemed to reduce the average woman to gibbering idiocy, and hoped that Theodora was not going to disgrace herself by falling in love with him. She had seemed to be contemplating it when Juan departed for Paris the previous week; Consuelo knew them both too well, and she could not imagine which of them would emerge from the affair most shattered ... it would probably be Theodora, she thought. Still, there was no way of telling. After trying to envisage the outcome of such an unfortunate union ... well, perhaps the word 'union' was hardly apt under the circumstances, although you never could tell ... while she ploughed through her meat and vegetables for the sake of the necessary nourishment, she shrugged, summing up the affair in advance with, 'Of course, they'll both go nuts.'

A moment later she realized that Mlle Devaux had twice asked her a question. She looked across the table at the nervous grammar teacher, and attempted to bring back the remark from her unconscious mind, if that were the place where it had taken refuge, into her memory. She had heard it all right, but it had instantly been relegated to the background in order to make room for Juan and Theodora. She struggled for a moment, then recollected. 'Marian's not well, Mademoiselle,' she said.

'I know that,' said Mlle Devaux impatiently. 'Everyone knows that. But what's the matter with her?'

Consuelo looked down at her plate, straightened her knife and fork, then answered deliberately, 'She is indisposed.' The word referred to a specific condition; Consuelo knew very well what a deliberate matter it was, and knew also that the Swiss woman would not have the courage to pursue the topic any further. Some of the others at her table were not so inhibited; from their amused glances Consuelo gathered that they did not believe her.

She was quite indifferent to everyone in the vicinity, and devoted to her roommate. With one eyebrow cocked she looked blandly round the table, then dropped her eyes to her plate once more. What she saw there was not particularly pleasing ... a piece of rubber-like carrot, and a bit of fat. Consuelo did not like fat. She wrinkled her beautiful nose at it, folded her long white hands on the edge of the table, and transferred her gaze to the lithograph on the wall behind Christina's head opposite her. The lithograph was a peculiarly revolting picture of a distressed stag struggling down some perpendicular rocks, but during the past two years Consuelo had become accustomed to it. The preceding September she had been delegated by Mlle Tourain to act as escort to Vicky on her first day at the school; having completed a tour of inspection which lasted half an hour, during which neither the Canadian nor the South American said very much, for they were both rather silent by nature, Consuelo led her into the dining room, across to the far corner, and sat down in a chair looking at the lithograph quite intently, with a melancholy expression, while Vicky stood beside her, rather at a loss.

'You see that?' said Consuelo.

'Yes,' said Vicky.

'It's most interesting ... most interesting.'

'Really,' said Vicky.

'Yes. But you don't know why?'

'No,' admitted Vicky. 'I mean I've seen better things in butcher shops, haven't you?'

'That's not the point.'

'No?'

'No. It's the philosophy of the thing.'

'I see. I suppose it takes time to grasp it, or else I'm fearfully dense.'

'I've been looking at it for two years,' said Consuelo. 'It has now come to mean a great deal to me ... as an illustration of the principle that you can get used to anything. After a great deal of thought, I have come to the conclusion that I can now state with absolute honesty that I *am* used to it.'

'Really,' said Vicky again. 'Then it's certainly worthwhile to stay here two years.' But, with a further glance at the lithograph, 'I'm not sure that it wouldn't take me longer, though.'

Consuelo, remembering that conversation of the previous September, chuckled to herself, then once more her mind reverted to her roommate, Marian Comstock. She was not indisposed; Mlle Devaux knew it, and Consuelo knew that she knew it. She had taken to her bed ten days before, the afternoon following the receipt of a letter from her mother in South Africa, in which she had written that her trip to Europe from Port Elizabeth had had to be postponed until the summer of 1936, and that her daughter was to remain in the school for a further eighteen months. Marian had then behaved in a way which

Consuelo considered very alarming, for besides going to bed and refusing to get up, she was also refusing to eat. She was by nature a very gentle, unobtrusive girl, who had never been known to break a rule.

There was no point in telling Mlle Tourain about her, thought Consuelo, for all the headmistress would do would be to look up some book or other, find a passage headed 'Passive Resistance,' or 'Food-Strike,' or some such no doubt interesting but hypothetical case, and apply the treatment prescribed, to Marian. Or she would employ her usual exuberant manner and say, 'Now then, Marian, get up, there's a good girl. If you don't, you won't be able to go to Gstaad next week, you know ... and think how much you enjoyed it last year and the year before ... this is your third year, isn't it? I thought so.' As if that would do any good, thought Consuelo irritably.

What Marian needed was to get out for the weekend, see a few attractive men, do a little dancing, and have it proved to her that she was still alive, in the face of all the evidence supplied by Pensionnat Les Ormes to the contrary, she added mentally. Only, if she were to go out Saturday with Juan and herself, she would have to be induced to get up tomorrow ... Friday ... for Mlle Tourain would never permit Marian to go straight from a supposed sickbed to the Palace Hotel.

At Mlle Lemaitre's table in the corner they were discussing the coming performances of *Le Malade Imaginaire*, *Le Médecin Malgré lui*, and *L'Étourdi*, which a touring company from the Comédie Française was playing in Lausanne the following week. Mlle Lemaitre deplored the choice of that particular week for the removal of the entire school to Gstaad, and was trying to make up for it a little, by giving to her table as full an account of each play as possible.

She was excited; her habitually jerky and vivacious manner was, today, especially obvious, for she was feeling ill. Her cheeks were flushed, the rest of her face so white and dry and the ending of colour along her nose and chin so abrupt that she looked like an amiable vulture.

Little Klaus and Big Klaus sitting on either side of her were paying almost no attention to her long quotations from *L'Étourdi*; Elsa and Ina Barron, a small, plain English girl from Southampton, were attempting to eat and look at her at the same time, for neither of them wished her to think that she was not listening ... they *were* listening, but they had to give visible proof of their undivided attention, for Mlle Lemaitre was firmly convinced that modern girls had no manners; she was very exigeante and expected them to keep their eyes riveted to her face when she was talking, and if their glance wandered away for so much as a moment, she would suddenly stop and swoop down on her victim and accuse her of impoliteness. Anna von Landenburg, at the foot of her table, was quite obviously wrapped up in her own thoughts, but Mlle Lemaitre, for reasons best known to herself, ignored it. As a matter of fact, although none of her girls knew it, she was paying no attention to herself, having long ago reached that ideal point of concentration for a teacher, when one is able to talk on one subject and allow one's mind to revolve around quite another at the same time.

She was wondering whether mere existence for five or six years in Switzerland would be preferable to a year or so of life in Paris ... That was the most she could hope for in such a climate, and if she lived carefully, her savings would last her two years. She had no relatives; in Clermont, where she had lived and taught in her father's school until she was thirty, and had managed to scrape together enough money to put herself through the Sorbonne, there was no one who even remembered her very well. She had not been back since before the war, when she had spent two weeks there after getting her degree, in the belief that the climate of Clermont could work miracles with her health which had been badly undermined by three years of working for eighteen hours a day, with insufficient food. Her activities since that time she had once described to Vicky as, 'Ten years in a Lycée, one year in hospital as a result of it; eleven years in a private school at Passy, and three years at Pensionnat Les Ormes as a result of *that*.'

She was neither tolerant nor warm-hearted, but she was extremely fond of Vicky, although she would probably have overworked her as she had overworked herself, if Mlle Tourain had permitted it. She had singled out Vicky for special attention four months before, kept her in her room for many hours a week, giving her an extraordinary amount of miscellaneous information, as though she were racing against time. They had spent the last week of the Christmas holidays together, following Vicky's return from Stephania Carré's home in Milan, a week during which Mlle Lemaitre sat in her rocking chair and talked of Voltaire and Rousseau from nine in the morning to seven at night, sketching in the background formed by eighteenth century Europe with such vividness and clarity that as long as she lived, Vicky knew, she would remember those two men as that exhausted, vital Frenchwoman made her see them.

She had been told by her doctor in Paris that if she had devoted a twentieth of the time she had laboured with her mind to caring for her body, this would never have happened. 'This' referred to four attacks of pleurisy which had left her bronchial tubes in a state which, she had quoted once to Vicky with a humorous light in her black eyes, 'positively defy my powers of description, Mlle Lemaitre,' according to the doctor. But she did not regret it. 'What is the body? It is at best an inefficient and unpleasant mechanism, something which we use for a while and discard like an old coat. But the mind ... Ah, the mind, that goes on. It is immortal. The mind of Christ, of Bach, of Leonardo ... that is what matters. The rest ... pouf! It is nothing, Veecky.'

Miss Williams was trying without much success to interpose her personality between Ilse on her right, and Truda on her left. She had introduced various topics of conversation but neither of them listened ... Ilse *appeared* to be listening, but Truda would not even make that much effort. The little Saarlander sat with downcast eyes; every now and then she raised them to glance fleetingly and unseeingly at the English teacher's face for the sake of good manners, but Truda merely sat and ate with evident enjoyment, ignoring Miss Williams altogether, and appearing to be staring at Ilse across the table even when she was obviously not staring at her. Miss Williams became more and more flustered. Her face was rather more red than too many English winters had already tinged it; she upset her glass of water and kept clearing her throat from time to time as though she hoped in that way to clear the atmosphere.

She began to talk about spring in England. It seemed a safe topic but after a while she became so engrossed in it that she forgot all about Ilse and Truda, and scattered her remarks in a disjointed manner, pausing now and then to look at Aimée, the only girl at her table who seemed to be paying attention. Aimée, however, always appeared to be paying attention. In spite of Natalia's statements, Miss Williams suspected that the younger of the two Armenian cousins knew no English at all. There was no way of finding out. She wrote very proper and prim little essays for Miss Williams, but it was more than possible that

Natalia did them for her. She sat, at the opposite end of the table, her long black eyes fastened on the Englishwoman's face, expressionless, enigmatic, disconcerting.

Miss Williams ceased to be conscious of the eyes after a while, for she was in her father's rectory in Kent. It was tea time, and the dining room was rather dark, a long 'tunnel of green gloom' for the lilac bushes grew against the windows. The fireplace was brick, with some brass bowls of violets on the mantelpiece, the polished table was covered with blue china, and there were ferns hanging by the windows.

She was suddenly despairing of a life which so senselessly forced her away from the only place in which she was ever at home and at ease, that drove her out into a world which, however she might try to adapt herself, remained alien and unnatural to her. She thought that if she could only go back to her father's house on the Medway, if she could only stay there, forever watching the turning of the world through its four seasons, from the rectory garden, life for her would possess meaning, continuity and purpose.

She found herself silent again, and hastily asked the table in general if they had ever been in England. The table in general, consisting as it did of one German, one Saarlander, an Armenian, a Hungarian, and a small dark vain creature from Buenos Aires, had not. This Miss Williams very well knew, and in the mildly surprised silence which followed, she began to wonder if she had taken leave of her senses, and if her incoherent, unhappy thoughts were as audible to the others as they seemed to herself.

Broken sentences, pronouns, nouns, verbs, adjectives, clauses torn from their context rose from the six tables into the air, and then lapsed back into the medley of sound; dishes clattering, voices whispering, laughing, talking; forty-five girls fidgeting ... fifty-two human beings eating their dinner in the dining room of a Swiss school overlooking Lausanne and the Lake of Geneva.

'It's pure satire,' said Mlle Lemaitre, back on the subject of Molière.

'... six black Shetland ponies ...'

'... and my dear, they made us *walk* to Chillon! It must be at *least* twenty kilometres ...'

'I've never yet found a Swiss, man or woman, who knew the name of the president of Switzerland ...' from Theodora.

Then Mlle Tourain's voice, bored, pitched low, with an occasional lift which said that she was dutifully injecting a little interest into her remarks, 'They met in a wood, each man bringing six others with him, making twenty-one altogether, and that was the beginning of Swiss Independence.'

'... like Théophile Gautier's cats, only his taste ran to white mice. He had hundreds, all over the house.'

'Have you ever seen a flautist who wasn't bald? My brother took up the flute three years ago, and he's already getting thin on top. After all, if you persist in such an unnatural passion as blowing sideways for heaven only knows how many hours a day, you've got to expect something to happen ...' This was from Elsa, manfully making an effort to amuse Anna von Landenburg, who was sitting motionless at the foot of Mlle Lemaitre's table on Little Klaus's right, drawing innumerable lines on the table-cloth with a spoon.

'*Mlle de Maupin* is not suitable for young girls,' said Mlle Devaux severely to the imperturbable Consuelo.

'... so, of course with all *that* money, there's no chance of his going to a quiet little place like Gstaad this year ...'

'She was the sort of woman who keeps dead flowers around the place so that when her young men come by to call and remark on the depressing effect created by two dozen brown roses, she can sigh wistfully and remark, "Yes, but you know, even dead flowers are better than none at all," and they're morally obliged to step in at a florist's on their way home and do something about it.'

'... and *just* what every woman has always wanted ... a combination radio-vacuum cleaner.'

'Ilse,' said Miss Williams, 'you've eaten nothing. You will be ill.'

Ilse shook her head quickly and glanced up imploringly at the little Swiss maid who was clearing their table, and who evidently understood for she removed her plate without waiting for her to finish, and started across the room with it. She only got as far as the head table, for Mlle Tourain, seeing the untouched meat and vegetables, said sharply, 'Whose plate is that, Belle?'

She stopped and blushed. 'It's Mlle Ilse's,' she said.

'Ilse!' said Amélie Tourain, raising her voice. She began to say something, then thought better of it, and her voice trailed away into silence. Shaking her head slightly with a vague, wandering look about the room, she began to serve the sweet, which was some kind of thin cream flavoured with strawberry jelly.

She had a feeling of being smothered, mentally and physically, by the Cummings-Gordon on either side of her. Elizabeth was to her right, Helen on her left. They were both fat, although Helen was the fatter of the two. It is possible to be good in such a way that one's goodness, tempered by humour and understanding, shines as a positive and unvarying light over one's own life and the lives of those with whom one comes into contact; the Cummings-Gordon girls were good, but their goodness was not of that order. It was almost wholly negative; one could have described them by what they would never dream of doing, what they strongly disapproved of others doing, rather than what they actually did. When they returned to their home in Philadelphia, Mlle Tourain knew, their relatives and friends would say with satisfaction, 'They haven't changed a bit.' Anxious parents had often said to the headmistress, 'I do hope I won't find her changed when I come back ...' The headmistress snorted. Changed indeed! Of course not. Nothing ever changed these young women from England and America. Provincial they were, and provincial they remained, while their friends and relatives gave thanks for their safe return from that immoral, retrogressive, unenlightened and dangerous place, Europe.

Mrs. Shaunessy, mother of poor, homesick little Cay, had remarked of the Cummings-Gordons, 'such wholesome girls ... I'm so glad you have that type in the school.' The word 'wholesome' implies a richness and validity which the two sisters from Philadelphia did not possess, but Mrs. Shaunessy was too shaken by her encounter with Natalia ... who had come to Cay's room to find out if Cay's mother would like tea, or if there was anything else she could do for her ... to make nice distinctions. Natalia had, of course, been followed by the silent and equally Oriental Aimée, Aimée by Maria-Teresa Tucci, and Maria-Teresa by Yasha, and Yasha by Theodora. The four of them were like nothing Mrs. Shaunessy had ever encountered in Seattle, and Theodora was merely another vulgar Jewess, which alone explained her relief on sighting the Cummings-Gordon girls.

Their bedroom was garnished with silk pillows ... they were relentlessly feminine ... a Harvard pennant, and two French dolls which they thought daring. They were inoffensive, obedient, and from an academic point of view, fairly intelligent. Therefore, thought the headmistress irritably, she ought to like them. They were obviously ideal pupils for a tired headmistress. Pensionnat Les Ormes, inhabited entirely by Cummings-Gordons, would have run itself. She could have rested, assured that there would be no emotional outbursts, no stealing, no problems, no hope on the other hand of getting anywhere so far as the international aspect of the school was concerned, and could have returned to her analysis of democracy in Italy, France, Germany and Switzerland.

It was really bad enough having Mlle Dupraix at the other end of the table where she could not avoid looking at her and hearing her incessantly intelligent and improving conversation ... which was always devoted to cultural subjects. The head-mistress suspected that Mlle Dupraix did it deliberately, remembering her unkind question, 'Tell me, what is Beaux Arts? Or should I say what *are* Beaux Arts?' She was evidently determined to spend the balance of her life proving to the head-mistress that even if *she* were uncultivated, Rose Dupraix was not. At this moment, the Beaux Arts mistress was involved in a description of Mont St. Michel. Despite her florid adjectives, the great architectural marvel rising from its salt marshes appeared like the waiting-room of a small Swiss railway station. The woman seemed to possess the peculiar ability to make every subject stuffy. What a terrible misfortune, thought Amélie Tourain. If our bodies have an individual odour which enables dogs to distinguish between human beings, our minds also pos-sess an individual quality which flavours every subject we touch upon. Some people are boring because they are bored. Others may be equally egotistical, but there is sufficient vitality and life in their self-engrossment to offset it. Probably it depended on the size of the ego. Mlle Dupraix's ego was not on a large enough scale, apparently, and besides that ... remembering the analogous physical odour ... the personality of her mind was so obtrusive and penetrating that it affected every subject *she* touched upon for the worse.

She was too tired to think very coherently, she found. Back came her mind to the Cummings-Gordons ... really, it *was* bad enough having Mlle Dupraix as a permanent fixture at the foot of her table, without adding them as well. She would not have minded them so much if they had not been so well brought-up that they felt it their duty to make polite conversation. Parents, thought Amélie Tourain grimly, should take stock of their children's minds before they teach them that silence at meals is not golden, but inconsiderate and bad-mannered. The Cummings-Gordons had probably been informed from their earliest infancy that one goes through certain meaningless actions and makes interminable meaningless conversation that the wheels of society may turn more smoothly. Such people should have more respect for the human mind and less for convention, she thought, almost slamming her water down on the table. Here were these girls destined to go through life disturbing the few intelligent people they met ... disturbing their efforts to think, rather ... by talking about coming-out parties, wedding presents and showers, and in another few years, by talking about babies, golf clubs and dinner parties. Eventually, when they grew old, they would indulge in a great deal of malicious gossip and encourage all that was reactionary and narrow in their community, because, the dinner parties, babies and golf clubs now being ruled out by age, they would have nothing better to do.

Her excessive irritability startled even herself. She kept glancing impatiently about the room, watching for that blessed moment when the last spoon would be laid down, and she would be able to escape to her study. This behaviour was unlike her. Until now she had always been able to retain a certain amount of detachment. At the moment, in spite of herself, everything got on her nerves; instead of seeing individual problems in their relation to the whole, each person, her foibles and her eccentricities, was becoming her personal concern and she was ceasing to view anything in its proper perspective. That was because, with the loss of her detachment, she had the distorted view of one who looks from too near at hand. Sometime this afternoon her mind had emerged from its comfortable cocoon into a confused, noisy and silly microcosm which had no connection with anything but itself. She had almost, during the staff meeting a few hours before, brought herself to a point where she could visualize Amélie Tourain, head of Pensionnat Les Ormes, as a person who was indirectly, and to a small, though very real extent, influencing the world. She had since lost that vision completely, and was asking herself all over again what possible reason she had for being where she was, except her loyalty to an idealistic woman who lay ill with cancer across the lake at Evian.

She looked about the room again. There's Lotta ... she's always the last, and she's finished now, so I can go ... No, there's Truda, choosing this moment to ask for a second helping.

'Don't wait so long next time, Truda,' she said.

'No, Mademoiselle,' said Truda dutifully, from Miss Williams's table.

She resigned herself to further delay. It seemed literally an hour since she herself had finished; what was going to happen to her if she continued in this way? I suppose no one can help making other people the victims of one's moods occasionally, she thought, but I have no right to be here at all if I cannot rely on my judgment ... the judgement of my brain balanced by my emotions, not unbalanced by them.

'Are you looking forward to going to Gstaad, Helen?' she asked the Cummings-Gordon on her left, as though in penance for her neglect of the past few minutes, and then did not listen to the reply. If only Jeanne comes back in the spring, if only I *knew* that Jeanne would be back then, I could really take hold of myself and make a good job of this.

Truda was through at last.

Amélie Tourain stood up and sailed out of the room, her brown hair streaked with grey piled high on the top of her head, that curious walk, which was a relic of the nineteenth century and the tradition that ladies do not swing their arms, carrying her into her study where, a few moments later, she was joined by her staff.

2

The girls' living room, where everyone but the bedridden Rosalie, and Vicky Morrison, gathered after dinner, was a large room with windows on two sides, the north and east. The west wall was broken by the door which led to the hall, and the south by double doors which folded back and led into the main classroom. These were now pulled shut with a couch in front of them, on which Ilse and Anna were sitting in obvious isolation from the other Germans, six or seven of whom were gathered around Truda, farther down the wall on their left. The room contained a few glassed-in bookcases, with bits of statuary placed at intervals along the top of them, several large urns filled with artificial flowers, and far too many tables and chairs which, however, could not be eliminated, as the room had to seat fifty people each evening. The confusion was heightened by dull, flowered wallpaper and heavy dark-red velvet curtains at each of the long windows, as well as by an odd assortment of mauve antimacassars on the red and brown velvet-upholstered chairs. 'All it needs,' Theodora had remarked on first seeing the room, 'is a few lithographs of defunct Tourains and Dupraix, and two or three stuffed birds under glass.'

She was now sitting with Consuelo, Elsa and Christina, in her usual position, with her long legs over the arm of the chair, picking distastefully at the antimacassar by her left shoulder. 'I gave Belle two francs for taking the tray to Vick,' she remarked.

Elsa said, without looking up from her sketching, 'That was rather a lot.' She was sitting in a low chair trying to sketch the group in the opposite corner composed of the Cummings-Gordons, their English counterparts, the Anderson sisters from Manchester, Ida Samuels, Henriette Martin, and Rose Budet. She was doing badly, because her view was obscured by half a dozen intervening heads and shoulders, as well as by tables and chairs. She kept leaning far out to the right, then far out to the left, trying to see them better.

'What *are* you doing, Elsa?' asked Consuelo. 'Trying to do reducing exercises in a sitting position?'

'I'm trying to see them properly,' she said. In defiance of Mlle Tourain's expressed wish that the girls change for dinner, she was wearing a dark-blue tweed skirt and yellow sweater which had become separated as a result of her contortions.

'Do yourself up, woman,' said Theodora. 'Or pull yourself together, rather. You're coming apart.'

'Sorry,' she said hastily, and jerked down her sweater. The other three were wearing silk dresses, Consuelo in blue which matched her eyes and set off her fair hair and pale skin to such advantage that Theodora glanced at her admiringly from time to time; Christina in green, intent as usual upon her knitting, and Theodora in brown silk crêpe which was extremely simple but for a large tie of gilt rope round her neck, which made her hair appear a more improbable shade of red than ever.

'Look at the Manchester-Philadelphia sister-acts,' said Theodora, yawning. 'Isn't it wonderful how we women can sink our differences as soon as we start talking about clothes?'

'How do you know that's what they're talking about?' asked Consuelo.

'Have you ever known them to talk about anything else?'

'Yes. Men, actors and actresses, the social life of their respective cities, and who's-the-best-looking-girl-in-the-school?'

'Maybe I'm wrong then.'

'Do you like women, Ted?' asked Elsa.

'Not much,' she said frankly.

'Why not?'

'They're raised for men and marriage, so they're not interested in anything else much. If they are, they're conscious of it. I mean the woman who's genuinely intellectual, having been brought up, maybe just unconsciously but still brought up, to regard marriage as the ultimate goal, is usually rather defiant about it.'

'Defiant?' repeated Elsa.

'Yes. I mean she makes a parade of her difference ... runs around in collars and ties ... mentally speaking, if not actually ... and makes a song and dance about being different. When the average woman says something intelligent, she always gives me the feeling that she read it somewhere the night before. I don't think we're naturally less intelligent than men, but everything the average woman says and does outside the home or not connected with domestic things in any way, is bound to be second-rate because that's not her main preoccupation.'

'Yet you haven't anything you want to do, particularly,' said Elsa.

'What do you mean?'

'You've got to include yourself in the "average woman" group then.'

'But I don't want to marry either,' said Theodora. 'That lets me out of both classes.'

'Don't you like men?'

'No. Men,' said Theodora, 'are idiots.'

'How do you know?' asked Consuelo.

'Excepting your brother Juan,' she added hastily.

Consuelo looked at her, and said firmly, 'Now see here, Teddy ... I've got enough to do looking after Marian and trying to get her out of bed once and for all, without worrying about you and Juan ...'

'You don't have to worry about me and Juan.'

'I know I don't have to. It's purely voluntary. I like you both, and I'd hate to see either of you ...'

'Taisez-vous,' said Theodora. 'There are a couple of sweet young Scandinavians present. Less of your nasty South American realism.' She was keeping an eye on Truda, as she had promised Mary Ellerton, and so far, during the half-hour which had elapsed since dinner, her behaviour had been exemplary. Truda was sitting on a small table by the door, six or eight feet from Ilse and Anna on the couch, talking to her group of sycophants. At that moment, as Theodora glanced across the room at her once more, she saw Truda dart a quick look down the wall at Ilse and Anna, then she said something in German which Theodora could not catch. It was evidently something disagreeable, for she noticed that Ilse stiffened. She remarked vaguely to Consuelo, 'I suppose he'll be back from Paris tomorr ...' and stopped, pulling her body forward and upward by one hand on Consuelo's chair. She had heard Truda say, 'Ilse will be made into a good German when we get the Saar ... even if she doesn't think so. Lots of other Jews don't think so either ... but they learn,' and had seen Anna look up angrily.

Then again, Truda's deliberate voice saying, 'Why, didn't you know she's engaged? That's why she's been collecting ... er ... her dowry from us ...'

Theodora got to her feet with surprising speed. The others dropped their knitting and sketching; the group on the floor behind them, Natalia, Aimée, Stephania, Maria-Teresa and

Yasha, fell into silence, then the girls in the other corner. The knowledge that something was in the air, that something exciting was going to happen travelled from group to group and from person to person until the whole room was still, everyone watching the girls by the door.

Truda slid down from her table as Anna got up from the couch saying furiously, 'You shut up, Truda. You've done enough damage. You're disgracing every German girl in the school.'

Little Klaus across the room startled everyone by saying quite clearly, 'Yes, that is true. People will think German girls are not kind ...' then stopped, looking embarrassed and a little frightened.

The two by the couch standing facing each other did not hear the gentle little voice. Truda said, her voice hard and vindictive, 'If you want to talk about Germans and being German ... what kind of citizen do you consider yourself? Do you think you and your precious father make good Germans?'

Anna went white. She tried to speak, tried to control the trembling of her body, and struggled to control her voice. At last she asked, against her will, 'What do you mean by that?' wishing that some vestige of her former strength would return to her so that she could deal with Truda unemotionally, and with the dignity which was so necessary to her. Was it the fever which made her so weak, and made her feel so sick?

'I'm talking about your father,' said Truda. 'I'd like to know what he does for the government, and so would everyone else. He seems to be rather mysterious. Last week my *Zeitung* reported that the police wanted to get some information from him, but he'd disappeared. Where is he, exactly ... and *what* is he?'

'You ... you ...' Anna put her hand up to her face, too shaken with fear to be able to think, to be able to think even of a lie.

'Leave ... him ... out of this ...' Her voice had broken in the middle, which increased her terror, for she was as much unnerved by her own loss of self-control as she was by Truda's determination to trap her.

They had dropped into German, which few of the girls understood, but the room was still silent. They might not know what was being said, but the sight of Anna, usually so quiet and contained, utterly upset and almost in tears, held their attention.

Theodora, who included German among her many languages, walked over to the couch and got between them. Truda was still looking stonily at Anna, who began to sob. Theodora said coldly, 'Stop this, Truda. You're making a fool of yourself ...'

Truda said nothing, put out one hand and with a single vicious thrust sent Theodora reeling back until she fell against the nearest table. Caught in a sudden panic, the Jewish girl from St. Louis turned and yelled in Consuelo's direction, 'Con, for God's sake get Vicky!'

Consuelo, she discovered a moment later, had already gone. Theodora, hearing her footsteps racing up the wooden stairs by the door, two steps at a time, looked wildly round the room at the gaping school and asked herself, 'Why in hell do forty people have to stand in the background like a bunch of cows, even if they don't understand German? Can't they see Anna's going to scream in a minute? If I could get some co-operation I could stop this ...'

Truda was saying, 'I don't see why I should leave you out of this ... or your father either. Unless you want to talk about Ilse?'

'No ... no, you know perfectly well I don't.'

'You brought it up by saying something about being German.' Her face was disfigured by an emotion which was compounded of anger, shame, a determination to see Anna get what she deserved, and righteous indignation. She thought of the letter she would write her father, giving the information about Graf von Landenburg which was so badly wanted, and went on relentlessly, 'I shouldn't think your father would call himself a German ... he's more of an ... Internationalist, isn't he?'

Anna was too terrified to take any possible alley leading in another direction, obsessed by the one desire to shield her father. She repeated in her broken voice, 'Leave him out of this!'

'Why?'

'Because it's none of your business!'

'Isn't it?'

'No, and I'm not going to stand here letting you make your horrible insinuations just because you're never really happy unless you're making someone else miserable ...' Her voice gave way again. She put out one hand unseeingly toward the couch, trying to get hold of some solid object to lend her support, but the couch was too far away and her hand closed helplessly on air. It had the effect of further unnerving her, like a tired swimmer who feels for bottom while he is still beyond his depth, and increased her feeling of isolation. She thought that the whole expectant school behind her was waiting and hoping to see her go under.

'What does he do? And where *is* he, if I may ask?'

'He's ... he's ...'

'Where is he?'

'I don't know!'

'You got a letter from him yesterday, postmarked Zürich. He could hardly be in Switzerland, could he? Not if the whole country's looking for him. They'd know if he got over the border ...'

'They ... might not ...'

'Oh, yes they would.'

Anna shook her head again, unable to take her eyes from Truda's. They were green, compelling her to look into their depths. 'He's ... in Zürich. Yes ... yes, that's where he is ...'

'Oh, no he isn't,' she said derisively. 'They'd know if he were. Well, come on, Anna ... if he's not doing something he shouldn't be doing, what are you hesitating for?'

'I'm not hesitating ...' she said, her body and face convulsed by sobs.

'Where is he then? And what's he doing?'

She swallowed in a last desperate effort, then her self-control gave way, after the weeks and months of strain and worry. 'All right,' she said, 'I'll tell you ... I don't care if the whole world knows it! What chance have we got anyway? Everyone's against us ... I'll tell you, I'll tell you ... he's in ... he's in ...'

'Königsberg,' said Vicky from the doorway. 'And he keeps chickens.' Her voice was pitched low as usual, yet the absurd words carried to the far corners of the room. She seemed as she crossed the room, small and slender as she was, to dwarf both Truda and Anna, to relegate them once more to their own places in a group of forty-five. 'Really, Truda. What you need more than anything else is a rattle and a good spanking. Leave poor Anna alone, for heaven's sake ... she's got enough to worry about with a brother who's not strong and a father who's more interested in the welfare of the German Jews than your Adolf likes. But you can't have him arrested for that, can you? Or for keeping chickens.' She looked rather curiously at Truda and Anna, then at the gaping school which had begun to relax once more and was staring at her with some amusement. Her eyes fell on Theodora who had collapsed into a chair and was fanning herself with relief, and a smile flickered across her face.

She pushed Anna gently so that she sat down on the couch, then turned to Truda and went on quietly, 'She could have told you that weeks ago, but you've all scared her so with your tales of firing squads and concentration camps that she began to believe her father's Jewish charities were really a criminal offence ... besides, she's ill,' she added, still looking intently at the discomfited German girl, her disturbing grey eyes searching Truda's face for the reason behind all this. It was by character and the nature of her personality that Vicky dominated those about her, rather than through any desire of her own. She thought, really, I have the most unfortunate talent for transferring attention to myself, then remembered Consuelo's breathless remark as they rushed upstairs, 'She's been simply beastly to Ilse too ... accusing her of stealing money for her dowry.'

'You'd better apologize to both Ilse and Anna,' said Vicky. 'And leave them alone after this. If you *must* scrap with someone, scrap with Consuelo, or Elsa, or me. We don't mind it at all.'

Her intent, unemotional look had its effect. Truda bit her lip for a moment, then gave in. 'All right,' she said loudly. 'I'm sorry,' then turned, ran across the room and out the door.

Vicky said, 'Anna, brace up. You too, Ilse,' for the little Saarlander had forgotten all about Paul and the garden now, and was crying with her head buried in the sofa cushions. A moment later Vicky heard a door open and said dismally in English, 'Oh, lord, now I'm for it. Here comes the Light Brigade,' and sank down wearily in the centre of the sofa with Anna on her right and Ilse on her left.

'Sit down, everyone!' snapped Theodora as the footsteps approached the living room door. When Mlle Tourain entered at the head of her staff they were all in their accustomed places, except Vicky, who should have been upstairs playing her piano, and who, as Theodora remarked disgustedly to herself, 'stuck out like a sore thumb,' with a tear-stained girl on either side of her.

The headmistress caught sight of Vicky when she was half-way across the room, and stopped. 'What are *you* doing here?' she demanded.

Vicky stood up. 'I came down to try and get Anna to go to bed, Mlle Tourain.'

'Why?'

'She's not very well ... she's been feeling ill for the past week ...'

'Is that true, Anna?' asked the headmistress, turning to look at the Bavarian girl, who also stood up.

'Yes, Mlle Tourain.'

'Why didn't you report to Mlle Dupraix?'

'I ... I ... didn't want to be sent to bed ...' She had not yet recovered her self-possession, and was twisting a handkerchief through her fingers and biting her lip to steady it.

'Why not?'

'Because I ...' She stopped, looking helplessly at the head-mistress, who went over to her own table and sat down, while the rest of the staff scattered to their chairs in various parts of the room.

In the brief silence came Theodora's voice saying brightly in French, 'And when she told me that, I said "Josephine! How can you be so unmannerly and so ungracious? Give him your canary if he wants it ..."'

'Theodora!'

'Pardon, Mademoiselle.'

'Well, Anna?'

Vicky glanced at the Bavarian girl beside her, and said quickly, 'Mlle Tourain, this is entirely my fault. I got rather bored upstairs alone, and Anna provided a good excuse for ... coming down, and ...'

'That's enough, Vicky. Go to bed, Anna, and I'll send Dr. Laurent in to have a look at you tomorrow morning. You, Ilse, go upstairs and wash your face. You'd better go to bed after that, too.' She saw Vicky's worried eyes follow them to the door; apparently that girl's genius for self-obliteration was once more manifesting itself. She was constantly placing herself in a position where one could not avoid feeling that one was battling windmills. Her mind remained concentrated on other people even when she herself was bearing the brunt of an attack. 'We come to you, Vicky. But first of all, where is Truda?'

'She had a headache, Mademoiselle.'

'My entire school seems to be suffering from one ailment or another. Doesn't it?'

'Yes, Mlle Tourain.'

'You'd better return to your piano. At least you're not in mischief then.' And as Vicky reached the door, 'Your lies are not at all convincing. You must try to do better next time.' Then, as the door closed quietly behind her, Mlle Tourain said abruptly, addressing the whole room, 'If we have another incident of this sort, I'll expel every girl connected with it,' and getting up, went out the door and down the hall to her study, where she sat still until long after midnight, angry with herself and still more angry with Vicky, who had of course been responsible for her undignified position.

In the living room, Mary Ellerton joined Theodora and Consuelo on the couch. Theodora was saying furiously, 'It takes brains to make so many mistakes! Unless she's feeble-minded. Why in hell didn't she let Vick alone? She must have known she wouldn't get anywhere. But she never learns, our little Amelia, she never learns.'

Mary leaned back and closed her eyes wearily. 'Why does it have to be Vicky all the time? She certainly can't last much longer at this rate.'

Later Theodora and Consuelo went to her room, but she was

not there. She was not with Anna either, she had just left. They finally found her in the art room on the third floor, surrounded by the pale busts of Roman emperors, and long drawing-tables, playing Chopin on the school's one grand piano. She glanced up and smiled at them as they came in, but still looked rather absent-minded.

Theodora hauled herself up on the piano and sat swinging her legs in silence for a few moments. Then at last she burst out, 'Do you know how mad Mlle Tourain is at you now?'

'I can guess.'

'She's liable to think up a good reason for kicking you out, if you're not careful.'

She stopped playing and looked up. 'Yes ... I suppose she might. I do make an idiot of myself, don't I?'

'I shouldn't have fetched you,' said Consuelo from the window. 'Then you wouldn't have been dragged into it.'

'No,' said Vicky. 'But Anna was cracking by the time I got there.'

'What *is* her father? And where is he?' demanded Theodora.

'Et tu, Brute?'

'Just vulgar curiosity,' said Theodora lightly.

'Oh ... he's in a dangerous business, that's all.' She began to play "Au Clair de la Lune" with one finger. 'Poor Anna. Poor Truda ... poor Ilse, for that matter.'

'Poor you,' said Theodora.

'I'm all right.'

'Yeah, so it would seem.'

Vicky looked up at her anxious face, and said affectionately, 'You're very nice to worry about me, Teddy.' She smiled, then got up and joined Consuelo by the window, looking over a white and silent world toward Italy. Her eyes still seemed to be searching for something, as she said, 'Funny ... I'm the one person here who really likes it, and who really wants to stay ...'

Theodora had crossed the room and was standing beside her. The three of them looked out in silence. She said at last, 'It's not your fault, anyway.'

'Oh, yes it is. I haven't been victimized by anyone, and I'm not abused. Well, come along you two. We're supposed to be getting ready for bed.' They started toward the door, arm-in-arm, Vicky remarking with a return to her habitual, half-ironical humour, 'Just think, all over Lausanne, in fifty international schools, boys and girls are now preparing for bed. Now isn't that an inspiring thought?'

'No,' said Theodora.

PART TWO

Friday

V

~

The snow for which everyone at Pensionnat Les Ormes had been waiting, began to fall shortly before dawn. The whole external world was obscured by a dense white curtain so that the school was like a ship at sea, a seemingly frail human structure lonely and isolated from the invisible world beyond its windows. Vicky, pausing as she dressed, to look out, thought she discerned the outlines of the neighbouring insane asylum, and stayed to watch until an unmistakable section of white roof bordered with red tiles and eavestroughs appeared momentarily, then was lost once more behind the impenetrable white curtain.

She was a little late for breakfast. Fräulein Lange glanced at her with the required disapproval and murmured almost inaudibly, 'You're not very punctual, Vicky.'

She nodded, and sighed an apology. 'Yes,' she said, sitting down, 'I'm sorry. I'm always a little late for everything. I don't know why it is, and it's discouraging. I get up early ... I rush ... and then I'm late.' She scanned Fräulein Lange's face anxiously, wondering whether Mlle Tourain had given her permission to go home that weekend or not. Fräulein Lange had said that she was going to stay behind after the staff meeting and arrange it. From her long, thin profile Vicky could gather nothing, however, except that the German mistress was making an effort to appear more cheerful than she felt, this morning. Vicky picked up the jug of café au lait and filled her cup absently, her eyes still wandering in Fräulein Lange's direction.

'Jam?' suggested Theodora beside her.

'Thanks,' she said, looking into the china pot. 'Is it apricot?'

'Isn't it always apricot?'

'No,' said Vicky. 'On All Saints' Day we had strawberry.'

'Unfortunately, it doesn't seem to have established any precedent,' said Theodora. 'But for that one moment of weakness, Dupraix remains obstinately determined to feed us apricot and nothing but apricot.'

'Do you want some bread?' asked Yasha from across the table. Without waiting for an answer she stretched forward and deposited two slices on Vicky's plate, remarking in reply to Fräulein Lange's rebuke, 'Vicky doesn't eat unless you make her,' in the semi-indifferent tone which characterized most of her utterances.

'Butter?' said Maria-Therese who was occupying the foot of the table. 'Please allow me.' She got up, snatched the plate of butter from under Natalia's nose, rushed round the table with it and was back in her place again before Fräulein Lange could voice any objection. 'It's so nice not having to start the day with Mlle Tourain in the room,' she observed. 'I think she's quite right to take breakfast in bed ... or wherever she does take it.'

Theodora said with annoyance, 'I thought we had crescent rolls on Fridays ... in fact I *know* we do. Now, we start getting bread. What's this school coming to? On Wednesday we had custard instead of our usual ice-cream, and last night we had strawberry cream instead of custard. This uncertainty is bad for our nerves, and besides that, up till now I've always been able to tell what day of the week it was by the menu. I resent these ... these innovations.'

Natalia said, looking amused, 'The irregularity doesn't stop with custard, ice-cream and crescent rolls. There's a notice on the board saying that we're to have our woollen-drawers inspection this morning after assembly, instead of tomorrow morning.'

'Oh, Lord!' said Theodora in disgust. 'That puts the pants on it,' she added in English, and having delivered herself of an appropriate pun she looked quite good-humoured again.

Fräulein Lange frowned for a moment, then got it. She gave one of her rare laughs, and then helped herself to some bread which, she told herself a moment later, she could not possibly swallow without choking on it.

Yasha said, 'I don't see why Mlle Tourain won't believe we're wearing our woollen drawers without making us march by her and lift our skirts to prove it. We're not six years old.'

Mary Ellerton at the next table leaned over and touched Natalia's arm. 'Tell Vicky I want to speak to her a minute,' she said.

'Vicky,' said Natalia, 'Miss Ellerton wants you.'

Vicky got up, squeezed herself past Theodora and Stephania and said cheerfully, 'Hello, how are you this morning, Miss Ellerton?'

'I'm very well, thanks. How are you?'

'As usual. Each day I give thanks for my continuing good health, and I cannot but think that my constant appreci ...'

'Do be quiet, Vicky,' she said. 'Look here, I want to see you sometime today ... before lunch, if possible.'

'All right,' she said, nodding. 'I'm free from eleven on. I'm supposed to be practising in the art room, so let's meet there. What's the matter, Mary? Anything wrong?'

'No ... nothing special, except that Mlle Tourain is going to take your head off, if she can think of a good reason. I've just seen her. She looks as though she's been up all night.' She hesitated a moment, then went on casually, 'I'd go and see her, if I were you.'

'What for?'

'To explain about last night.'

'Explain what?'

'The ... the whole thing.'

'My dear Mary, she knew perfectly well Truda had been bothering Ilse and Anna. What good would it do for me to go and say that, if I felt like going and saying that, which I don't?'

'I didn't mean Truda and Ilse ... I meant ... Anna.'

'Anna?'

'Yes. Don't be so obtuse, Vicky. You know perfectly well what I'm talking about.'

'If she wants information about Anna, she can go to her for it. Then she won't be in the dark any longer.'

'It isn't that. She doesn't mind Anna knowing things she's not willing to talk about ... it's that she can't stand *your* knowing them.' Mary glanced up at the pale shadowed face above her, then down at her plate. Vicky's tone was impatient, but the expression in her grey eyes was impersonal as usual and therefore, thought Mary, who knew Vicky very well, she would accomplish nothing by further argument. In spite of that knowledge, however, she said matter-of-factly, 'I really advise you to try and straighten it out.'

Vicky shook her head again, tracing the long crease in the tablecloth with her eyes. She said nothing for a moment, then, 'She made a fool of herself last night,' with more annoyance than Mary had ever heard in her voice before. 'She should either have ignored everything, or have taken it for granted that *we* knew she knew, and therefore there was no need for her to establish her authority by having it out with me. She must have realized that I wasn't going to tell tales, and she shouldn't have needed the satisfaction of a public discussion in order to keep her dignity. She'd have kept *more* dignity if she'd paid no attention.' She frowned doubtfully, then her eyes came back to Mary's upturned, anxious face and remained there. 'It isn't only that, of course,' she said shrewdly. 'She's using me as a focusing point for her various uncertainties ... she thinks, if only I could get rid of that girl, then I'd know where I was. Everyone does that ... I mean they concentrate on one obstacle, and use it as an excuse.' She stopped and laughed. 'I sound as though I'm suffering from delusions of importance or something ...'

Mary let out a long breath, and taking a piece of bread, began to butter it absently. 'No,' she said in a tone of discouragement. 'You're right, that's the trouble. All the same, I do think it's time you opened up about a lot of things. You can't expect ...'

'I expect nothing,' she said quickly, withdrawing into herself again. 'It's my own fault.' She was aware of Cay and the others at Mary's table studiously not listening, and a smile flickered across her face.

'It's not your fault!' said Mary impatiently. She glanced at her mediocrities, then dropped her voice until it was scarcely more than a whisper, saying with quiet intensity, 'Vicky, you're going to be asked to leave if this goes on. One simply can't have a pupil who knows twice as much as the staff!'

'All I did was to arrive at the right moment. Anyone else

could have done it ... except Ted, poor lamb, who was the only one who was really trying, and of course being Jewish, Truda wouldn't pay any attention to her. Consuelo or Elsa or Christina might have stopped it, but none of them speak German, so they hadn't the faintest idea what Truda was saying. And she ... Truda, I mean ... was too worked up to let anyone stop her just on the general principle that rows aren't very pleasant. Well, supposing I do go and tell Mlle Tourain all that ... there's nothing to be gained by it. She doesn't want me in there elaborating my own ideas, keeping back what she no doubt regards as the essential piece of information ... what Anna's father actually does, and where he is ... and I'm certainly not going to tell her that! What's she trying to do? Turn me into a stool pigeon?'

'Yes,' said Mary. 'I'm not so sure that she isn't right ... at any rate so far as Rosalie is concerned,' she added deliberately.

'Rosalie!'

'Yes. She said yesterday to me, after the staff meeting, that she was afraid to leave her alone up there much longer. She knows Rosalie's suffering some kind of mental agony but she doesn't know what it is. She thinks you do.'

'Oh. I see. As a matter of fact I thought I'd try and see Dr. Laurent this morning. There's some talk of moving her to the Catholic hospital.'

'Is she worse?'

'Yes ... I think so. Last night during dinner and afterwards I was in there for an hour or so. She ... she frightens me a little now. I don't think she should be moved into a Catholic environment if it can possibly be helped.'

'But she *is* Catholic!'

'I know. That's the reason.'

'Are you mad, Vicky?' asked Mary helplessly.

She shook her head, smiling, then said, 'You're probably right;

I *shall* be kicked out. If I am, someone has to be left behind who really knows Rosalie ... I think perhaps ... I'd better ... open up, as you say. Not to Mlle Tourain, though. To you. Leave Anna's affairs alone for a while. I'm afraid it won't be necessary to keep quiet about Graf von Landenburg for very long. 'She spoke unevenly, trying to summon enough courage to face facts, for she did not want to leave, and she had an ordinary human tendency not to recognize a possibility by providing for it. 'I'll tell you something about Rosalie when we meet in the art room at eleven. In the meantime, I'd better get back to my breakfast.'

Under cover of Natalia's and Yasha's discussion of Villon's poetry which they were reading together, Vicky asked Fräulein Lange a few minutes later, 'Are you going to Zürich tomorrow to see your sister?'

She shook her head. Her face was hidden behind the cup which she held in her right hand; her left was clenched in her lap. She saw Vicky's angry look and smiling faintly, put her cup down. Her face was drawn and pale, even her thick brown hair seemed untidy and dull. She was usually a neat woman, given to small lace collars and cuffs which were always immaculate, Vicky had noticed, and she was troubled to observe that this morning they were rather soiled. Fräulein Lange said slowly, 'Mlle Tourain thought that this was the wrong time to ask for special favours.'

'Favours,' repeated Vicky irritably. 'What sort of a favour is that?' she demanded, then checked herself. It was certainly not going to do Fräulein Lange any good to hear her give vent to her opinions. 'It doesn't seem to me to be so much to ask,' she remarked less emotionally.

'Mlle Tourain said ... that with the stealing ... and everyone so on edge ... that I should have to wait until my regular time, and that if the atmosphere of the school hadn't improved by then, I'd be lucky if I got away in six weeks. By six weeks Maria will be ...'

'The baby will be just about born by then,' said Vicky matter-of-factly, in order to help her out.

'Yes.'

'How about phoning?'

'It would just upset her, Vicky. Besides that, Adolf would resent my interfering. He'd have resented my going there tomorrow, but if I'd been able to, I should have accomplished something, so it wouldn't matter.'

'Well ...' Vicky shook her head helplessly. 'I'm sorry I've run out of suggestions, Fräulein. I wish I could think of something ... I tell you what you might do. You might describe your sister's symptoms to Dr. Laurent when he comes this morning to see Anna, and find out if he thinks there's anything wrong. It probably wouldn't be much help, but if there *isn't* anything wrong with her he'd set your mind at rest ... a little, anyhow.'

Fräulein Lange nodded, but her face had not brightened very much. She was still trying not to cry, and was coming so close to it in spite of her struggle that she was almost grimacing. She went on unsteadily. 'What I mind is that after ... all these years ... I should be treated like a child trying to get out of its lessons.' That was the wrong thing to say; once you put a thing into words it became twice as true and had twice as much power to hurt. She raised her cup again with one red, shaking hand and held it in front of her face.

Vicky, realizing that the one thing she did not want was for anyone to notice or remark on her lack of composure, turned her head away quickly, and said to Theodora on her right, 'Talk, Teddy. It doesn't matter what you say, but talk.'

Theodora swallowed her bread and butter and said instantly, 'Of course I, for one, wouldn't be found dead by the roadside, in a pair of woollen drawers. I mean, is this the twentieth century or isn't it? That's what I always say. So I keep my beastly bloomers in the sound-chamber of my portable gramophone, and they're just as good at deadening sound as they are in keeping out the cold ... better, in fact. Personally, I've never felt the need of extra warmth in those regions. It's always the tip of my Grecian nose that freezes.'

'Your nose isn't Grecian,' said Maria-Teresa.

'There are a lot of noses in modern Athens that are much funnier,' she said. 'I was not referring to the classical Greek, but the contemporary Greek nose.'

'Well, go on about your drawers,' said Yasha, yawning. 'It's much too fascinating a subject to be dropped in the middle like that.'

'I'm not wearing any now, if that's what you mean, as Mlle Tourain very well knows. And how am I going to get into the damn things when they're at present buried in the depths of my gramophone, and we're expected to go straight from assembly to line up for the inspection?'

Fräulein Lange had recovered her poise. She felt that she ought to return favours, and after searching about in her mind for a moment she said, rather more airily than was natural to her, 'If you found that you had forgotten your handkerchief, I might excuse you now in order to get it.'

'Thank you, Fräulein.' She bowed, and got up. Halfway across the room she stopped, turned and came back again. 'As a token of my appreciation of your help in this crisis,' she said formally to the German mistress, 'you may have what is left of my apricot jam,' and wound her lazy way to the door again.

In the hall she was held up by Belle, one of the little Swiss maids, who was holding a telegram between the first and second fingers of her left hand. She had only that month come down from the mountains, and her experience of telegrams was confined to two visits to the cinema when the heroine in each case had been informed by wire of the death of her lover. Belle's expression was a mixture of anxiety and concern for Mlle Théodore, and an intense desire to get this thing out of her hands, as she said unhappily, 'It's for you, Mademoiselle. I hope he is not ill or ... or ... Collect,' she added uncertainly, not being any too sure what the words meant. Mlle Théodore seemed to know, however, for she fished down into her stocking for the chamois bag which contained the funds with which she met her running expenses, and paid the boy at the door, leaving Belle to flee into the kitchen and spend the next fifteen minutes in melodramatic speculations with the cook.

Theodora's room was on the second floor, facing the lake. She ran up the flight of stairs by the girls' living room two steps at a time, and rushed into her room, banging the door behind her as usual. Then she sat down on the radiator and eyed the telegram with disfavour. It must be from her brother Lewis because he was the only human being in the world with the nerve to send her telegrams collect. He was supposed to be at Juan-les-Pins, but was undoubtedly somewhere else, without funds with which to get back to where he was supposed to be. That much was certain, she thought with some pride, for he had never in his life remained where he ought to be for longer than a few weeks, and he was always short of money.

With the telegram still unopened, she got up and rescued her drawers from the interior of her gramophone which sat casually on one end of her overloaded dressing table, then started the record. It was a very old and worn record, but the entire suffering school was aware that Theodora's affection for it was undimmed by either time or constant repetition.

St. Louis woman, with her diamond rings,
Drags that man around, by her a-pron stri-ings.
Now if it wasn't for that woman
And her store-bought hair
The one I love ...
Wouldn't be gone ... so ... far ... from ... here ...

She put on her drawers and then ripped open the telegram, and above the voice from the gramophone on her dressing table could be heard her pained, 'Oh, my gosh!' as she looked up in order to glare at a photograph of her brother which, along with some aerial views of New York and St. Louis, two night-club programmes and pictures of six masculine movie stars, was decorating the opposite wall.

I've got the St. Louis blues
Just as blue as a gal can be,
Now that man's got a heart
Like a rock cast down in-to the sea
Or else he wouldn't have gone so far from me ...

She had been wrong about his whereabouts. He *was* in Juan-les-Pins, 'with bells on, too,' she groaned. The telegram read:

THEODORA COHEN

PENSIONNAT LES ORMES

LAUSANNE SUISSE

TED CAN YOU POSSIBLY LEND ME FIVE HUNDRED FRANCS
SWISS NOT FRENCH STOP AM BROKE BUT IN LOVE AT LAST
SO IT DOESNT MATTER FOR THE TIME BEING STOP BREAK
THE NEWS TO MOTHER IS SHE STILL MOPING OVER THAT
GIGOLO AT THE MONTMARTRE QUESTION MARK HER NAME

IS ANGELA SHES AN ACTRESS MAYBE YOUD BETTER NOT
MENTION HER TO MOTHER ON SECOND THOUGHTS AND
EXPECT THE FIVE HUNDRED IMMEDIATELY YOURS WITH
THE JITTERS LEWIS

'Oh, my *gosh!*' she said again, this time with even greater
emphasis and distress. She glanced at her wristwatch, observed
that the time was five minutes to nine, and hastily scribbled an
answer on the pad of telegram forms which she had thoughtfully removed from the Palace Hotel three months before, for
just such emergencies. She could get one of the school staff to
send it from the office in Place St. François during the morning.

LEWIS COHEN
HOTEL BEAU SITE
JUAN LES PINS FRANCE
THEY ARE ALWAYS CALLED ANGELA HAS SHE A STARVING
MOTHER AND TEN LITTLE SISTERS ANYWHERE I BET SHE
HAS YOU POOR SAP STOP AM SENDING TWO HUNDRED AND
FIFTY FRANCES AND NOT ANOTHER SOU UNLESS YOU COME
UP HERE AND COLLECT IT YOURSELF AND DONT BRING
YOUR ANGELA WITH YOU EITHER BECAUSE WE WOULDNT
GET ALONG WELL TOGETHER STOP WHY WERE YOU EVER
BORN ANYWAY YOU JIBBERING IDIOT YOUR LOVING SISTER
THEODORA

Feeling tomorrow ... li-ike Ah feel today
Ah'll pack my trunk, an' make mah get-a-way
Feeling tomorrow ... li-ike Ah feel today.

She dashed out the door and down the stairs with the voice
from the gramophone following her and fell into her chair beside

Vicky at Fräulein Lange's table as the clock on the wall struck nine. They were in the corner between the French windows which faced the lake and the glass doors leading out into the loggia on the east side of the building. Directly above them on the wall was a large map of North America which had been made in Germany and which fascinated Vicky because, as she said, it made the United States look like a suburb of Canada. At that moment, Mlle Tourain and Mlle Dupraix being engaged in an argument on the other side of the room, Vicky was once more on the subject of the map.

She was sitting half sideways in her chair looking up at it and addressing herself vaguely to Theodora beside her. 'I suppose it was made during the war,' she remarked. 'Germany had some idea of acquiring Canada then, didn't it? So they made maps like this. I mean their soldiers must have heard about the wealth and general desirability of the United States, but not so much about Canada, so if they made Canada five times the size of the U.S. then everyone would be encouraged to fight for it. There are only ... let me see ...' She took a long breath and pulled out an extraordinary assemblage of papers, pencils, rulers, odds and ends from the drawer in front of her, eyeing its extreme untidiness with an expression which combined annoyance with a certain fatalistic acceptance of life's unnecessary complications. 'There are only about eleven million inefficient Scots and French in Canada, who presumably wouldn't object so much to being annexed as a hundred and twenty million Americans.' She glanced at some papers and went on, 'One is either born with the faculty for neatness and order, or one isn't. I wasn't.'

'Do you imagine for one single minute that I'm listening to you?' demanded Theodora. 'Because I'm not.'

'What good can it possibly do us to know what the inhabitants of Bordeaux are called?' Consuelo across the table was asking

Yasha on her left with mild irritation. They were in the top class and since Mlle Devaux's grammar curriculum was designed to cover two years, and these girls had most inconveniently returned for a third, she was at her wits' end to know what to do with them until she had hit on a plan by which they memorized, among other things, long lists which began 'Nice — Niçois,' 'Lyon — Lyonnais,' 'Auvergne — Auvergnat,' 'Provence — Provençal.'

'It might be useful some time,' said Fräulein Lange.

'Why?' demanded Consuelo.

'What's the word for a person who lives in Manchester, Fräulein?' asked Yasha.

'Manchester?' she repeated, looking perplexed. 'I don't think I've ever heard of it.'

'Neither have I,' said Vicky. 'What is it?'

'Mancunian,' said Yasha.

'Mancunian?' said Fräulein Lange. 'What a peculiar word.'

'Did you ever need it during your three years in England, Fräulein?' asked Consuelo.

'No,' she admitted.

Consuelo yawned, and said, 'Then it ought to be possible for us to get through life fairly easily without being able to identify the people of Carcassonne.'

'Moi, j'ai vu Carcassonne,' remarked Yasha for no particular reason. 'Fréquemment,' she added rather absently.

'How nice,' said Consuelo. 'I hope you enjoyed yourself.'

'Oh, yes, it was delightful.'

'Elsa,' said Theodora, 'is thinking of becoming a Taoist.'

'Why?' asked Fräulein Lange in alarm.

'She intends to combine it with Christianity to see if it can be done, and anyhow she says that she doubts even Lausanne boasts a Taoist temple, and therefore if, when Mlle Tourain wishes to dispatch her to a church of her own denomination, she states loftily that she is a Taoist, that will dispose of the question of how she is to spend her Sunday mornings, and she can stay home and paint.'

On the other side of the room Mlle Tourain broke off in the middle of what appeared to be an interminable discussion with Mlle Dupraix, and stated with finality, 'Fräulein Lange's class will meet in the art room from ten to eleven.' Then raising her voice she said, looking from one table to the next so that her glance included everyone in the room, 'There will be no classes tomorrow morning. Unless the girl who has been stealing comes to me before noon today, I shall call in a city detective to question you all individually at ten o'clock tomorrow.'

Vicky started at the word 'detective,' and felt a wave of apprehension pass over her. She had an instant picture of a Swiss policeman grilling some of the younger girls ... Ilse, Little Klaus, Cay Shaunessy, for example ... and wondered impatiently what had got into the headmistress to give her such an idea. She looked idly about the room in the silence following Mlle Tourain's remark until her eyes fell on Ina Barron, her English roommate, sitting at Mlle Devaux's table in the opposite corner. Ina's normally rather vacant face was drawn tight with terror, and Vicky stiffened so suddenly that the papers fell off her lap on to the floor.

When she and Theodora had gathered them up she looked about the room again and became aware that half the girls were staring at Ilse Brüning, sitting at Mlle Tourain's long table with her back to the folding doors on the other side of which Truda and Anna had quarrelled the night before. She had gone white, and was moistening her lips with her tongue in a manner which was too plainly nervous to escape attention. An increasing number of girls began to look at her, one by one, becoming conscious of other glances in her direction, while Mlle Tourain and the Beaux Arts mistress farther up the table by the door, continued to disagree with one another, unaware of the growing tension.

Vicky watched Ilse, trying with one part of her mind to transmit some of her own strength and self-control to the girl, while the rest of her thoughts were in confusion. She blamed herself because she had not made a greater effort to help Ilse, because she had not made a point of being with her in view of the whole school and thereby backing her up ... Vicky knew her own influence ... and because, finally, she told herself angrily, she had gone her own remote, self-centred way, when a little extra consideration on her part would have made all the difference to someone else. Who *had* been looking after Ilse? Consuelo was fully occupied with Marian Comstock, trying to persuade her to get up and behave more rationally; Elsa never did anything but sketch, Mary Ellerton was busy with her games, and with Cay Shaunessy, not to mention a few others, while Theodora spent all her spare time trying to learn 'open christies,' or 'stem turns,' or whatever it was. Anna was too worried herself to be able to do much for Ilse. The little Saarlander had evidently been living all alone in an atmosphere of gossip and suspicion from which she, Vicky, had deliberately withdrawn herself.

Ilse was sitting motionless now with her back to the folding doors; Vicky had the impression, watching her, that she was almost on the point of making some sudden, hysterical sound in order to break the silence which had fallen on the whole room except for that little area by the door where the headmistress and Mlle Dupraix were still arguing. She seemed to grow more tense and more rigid with every second that passed; her hands were fastened to her Bible on the table in front of her and her whole body was straining forward as her terrified brown eyes darted from one face to the next. She was struggling to control herself, her mouth trembling as her eyes wavered back and forth, back and forth, searching the faces before her, some of which were accusing her, some pitying her, some curious, and some merely staring because she looked so strange.

The two voices by the door continued, low-pitched and persistent, completely external to the intense quiet over the rest of the room which seemed to the more sensitive ones to be rushing forward into some kind of wild outburst from Ilse, who did not look as though she could hold on for more than a few seconds longer. The teachers and the few girls with sufficient courage and ingenuity to take things into their own hands and divert some of the attention from Ilse to themselves, were powerless. So long as the headmistress was in the room they could not speak unless she spoke first to them.

There was the sound of a chair being shoved violently backward until it fell, shattering the silence, against the wooden doors, and Ilse was on her feet gasping, 'Stop it! Stop staring at me like that! I haven't done anything ... I haven't done anything!'

Vicky started up, only to be pulled roughly back into her chair by Theodora who hissed imperatively, 'Stay where you are, you sap!'

Mlle Tourain and Mary Ellerton arrived at Ilse's side at the same moment, the headmistress saying sharply, 'Ilse, control yourself! Control yourself, I say!' Grasping the girl's shoulders she shook her slightly, while Miss Ellerton stood helplessly beside them.

She seemed to have lost her breath entirely, until at last she gave a long, shivering sob. Her eyes seemed to be searching the headmistress's face for some sign of sympathy and understanding, but she could find none. The little Saarlander's face took on a look of hopelessness as she struggled to get her breath. It seemed to her that she was making a good deal of noise every time she sobbed, but she could not stop crying.

Mlle Tourain remembered the treatment for hysterics. It did not include gentleness, rather one was supposed to treat it by administering some kind of shock. She did not want to slap Ilse's face, so she continued to shake her, fighting down her impulse to take the poor child in her arms and let her cry to her heart's content. A moment later Ilse broke away from her and ran to the door where she stood for a minute trying to turn the stiff handle, and then disappeared.

The headmistress stared blankly at the door through which Ilse had gone, then went slowly back to her place at the head of the table. The staff and the girls had become accustomed to unconventional behaviour from her and thought that she was choosing this singularly inopportune moment to fall into one of her abstracted moods. Actually, she was asking herself with bitter self-reproach why it was that so many of her theories, put into practice, ended in failure and in the conviction that she would have done better to follow her instinct rather than something she had read. Amélie Tourain had been away from the world so long that she had forgotten how to deal with people, and she was afraid to rely on her emotions. She was very still at the head of her table looking down at the Bible before her, and indifferent as always to the fifty people who sat in silence, waiting for her to give some sort of signal.

Her voice came to them at last, speaking in a monotone, 'Notre père qui es aux cieux, que ton nom soit faite sanctifié, que ton regne vienne, que ta volonté soit faite sur la terre comme aux cieux' ... They joined in one by one ... 'Donne-nous aujourd'hui notre pain quotidien; pardonne-nous nos offenses comme aussi nous pardonnons à ceux qui nous ont offensés; ne nous induis pas en tentation mais délivre-nous du mal, car c'est à toi appartiennent le regne, la puissance et la gloire, Amen.'

A short silence, then she said, 'You will kindly collect your laundry at twelve o'clock instead of leaving it here until sometime during the afternoon. You may find the effect created by forty pairs of drawers very pleasing; I, however, do not. I therefore ask you to spare me the sight of your freshly laundered underwear, and request that you come down and get it before lunch.' Amélie Tourain was herself again.

Belle's rosy face suddenly appeared looking nervously round the door. 'Come in, come in,' said the headmistress impatiently. 'Don't stand at the door as though you thought I were going to eat you. What is it?'

Belle opened the door another six inches and said doubtfully, 'Dr. Laurent is here, Mademoiselle,' as though she were not quite sure whether or not her eyes had deceived her. She glanced quickly at the headmistress and then retreated. How in the name of the Blessed Saints, had even that old dragon Marthe managed to survive four years of Mlle Tourain?

The headmistress rose, saying to Mlle Dupraix, 'Please inspect the girls' clothing for me.' She turned and looked once more round the room. 'You,' she went on, addressing her pupils, 'will file by Mlle Dupraix one by one, then make your beds and go to your classes at nine-thirty as usual.' She swept out, and there was another noisy interlude while the girls collected their pens, pencils and notebooks to the accompaniment of a great many voices whispering, talking and laughing.

On hearing Dr. Laurent's name Vicky shook her head in answer to Mary's inquiring look from across the room, and said to Theodora, 'Darn it, why does he have to come so early? I thought I might be able to see him if he came sometime after eleven or during the afternoon, but I've got classes for the next two hours, so I can't. Why does he have to arrive at the crack of dawn, anyhow?'

'He probably owes his success to early rising,' said Theodora. She cast a despairing look around the table, then began wildly turning out the contents of her drawer in search of her French grammar. 'Who was it talked about the cursed something or other?'

'The cursed animosity of inanimate objects?' asked Vicky. 'Or inanimate things, I forget. Carlyle, perhaps. Then again, perhaps not.'

'Probably. I was never taught more than enough to prevent me from being illiterate. Anyway, I'll bet that lousy book is leering at me from under this pile of stuff. Well, it can go on leering. I'm not going to wait for it to come out any longer. I'll use yours.'

They started toward the door, Theodora still muttering imprecations against her grammar, Vicky's mind occupied with Rosalie. Even if she had been able to see Dr. Laurent, it was unlikely that he would be able to do anything for Rosalie, and when it came to what she would say if she did see him, Vicky realized that she would probably be quite unable to tell him anything he had not guessed already. She had no wish to appear a hysterical schoolgirl with a taste for melodrama, and no wish to appear an alarmist. Mlle Tourain had written Garcenot père to remove his daughter, and nothing further could be done in any case until the headmistress had heard from him, unless they seriously intended putting her in the Catholic hospital.

She had come to know Rosalie's background a few weeks before Christmas and the girl had seemed so much better after talking to someone, that for a while Vicky had ceased to worry so much about her. During the past week, however, she had had a mental relapse, and that unearthly quiet had settled down on her again and she seemed to Vicky to be trying to force herself by an extreme effort of will into another world. She was trying to die. There were hours each day when she lay in bed without moving, her eyes fixed on a reproduction of the head of Christ from *The Last Supper*, which Vicky had brought her from Milan.

Theodora was back on the subject of woollen drawers as they took their places at the end of the line which began at Mlle Dupraix by the study door and ended with Vicky and Theodora by the door of the classroom. 'It always seems to me there's something indecent about this performance. What do you think?' she asked. 'Of course there are no gentlemen present ... unless you count Bill Wallingford,' she added. 'I shall always have a soft spot in my heart for Bill Wallingford. I can never forget that it was she who brought us together. You remember our first meeting, Vick?'

Vicky glanced at Theodora, then away through the open door of the classroom to the windows facing the lake. 'I remember,' she said shortly, 'though I prefer to forget. You never did have any tact.'

'Sorry. It's a long time since I've been able to take things seriously enough.'

'Oh, don't worry. It *was* awful, though, wasn't it? I remember I was lying in bed reading by one candle when a movement of the light made me look up to see the door opening inch by inch. I nearly screamed, for some reason or other ... I'm not usually very nervous. Then Bill's face, distorted by the crazy light, appeared around the edge of the door. I couldn't imagine what on earth she was doing at that time of night. She hadn't the expression of one paying a social call, somehow or other. She just stared at me. I remembered the poor idiot had taken a fancy to me and had been sort of following me about ... walking when I walked, playing basketball when I played basketball, shopping when I shopped ...

but I didn't know anything about ... well, whatever you call that. She came and sat on the edge of my bed while I stared back, paralysed with fear.'

'And then I came along, forming a rescue squad of one.'

She laughed, remembering Theodora's casual, 'May I join you ladies?' and the next queer fifteen minutes during which the three of them had sat on the bed, Vicky almost weak with relief, Bill shaking as though she had been brought too roughly out of a trance, and only Theodora, calm and conversational as ever, her apparently unshakable self-possession still with her.

Immediately after Bill left, Theodora had said coolly, 'I don't like that woman's looks. I saw her pass my door and had a hunch she was up to no good ... I'm really unusually observant, Victoria ... do people call you Victoria, my poor child? They do? Well, sorry, I won't. Vicky, or Vick for short from now on. Anyway, she passed my door but I hadn't anything on at the time, so immediate pursuit was impossible. Sorry you got such a scare.'

She had gone to Mlle Tourain the next day and expressed herself somewhat too freely, so that the headmistress, incredulous and harassed, had heard her out and then told her to go away and rid herself of such ignoble and discreditable ideas.

Theodora had been devoted to Vicky ever since. She said thoughtfully as the line began to move forward toward the door of Mlle Tourain's study, 'I wonder why it is that women are not supposed to be capable of friendship and loyalty to such an extent as men? They're always pictured like Kipling's cat, walking alone, when it comes right down to it, and when they change their environment ... I mean after they get married, or fall in love with an unusual man or something, then their friendships alter.'

'Shakespeare knew better,' said Vicky.

'I know, but he lived four hundred years ago and since then people have forgotten. I guess it's because no one ever takes the trouble to find out about us. It's so much easier to talk about men as people, and women as women ... lumping us all together, and referring to the female sex as though it were an enigmatic and too, too baffling inanimate object. We're supposed to be all alike underneath ... men aren't, they're permitted individuality, when we're not. We differ in degree, but not in kind, apparently. I mean you're catty, but not so catty as Ida ...'

'Why am I catty?' Vicky wanted to know.

'Because you're not a man, darling,' she said patiently. 'Also, being a woman, you like gossip ...'

'I don't like gossip,' said Vicky.

'Stop interrupting me. Men don't gossip, they're always logical, and they never reason emotionally. Women do all of these things. "Oh, Mlle Tourain, in our hours of ease, uncertain, coy and hard to please ..." You see?'

'No,' said Vicky. 'I don't see.'

'"Truda is the lesser man and all her passions, matched with mine, are as moonlight unto sunlight and as water unto wine."'

'Oh, that's interesting.'

'Yes. Now, to misquote Beverley Nichols, "It is precisely because I adore and reverence Mlle Dupraix ..."'

'What's the rest of it?'

'It's because he adores and reverences women that he hates to see them at bargain counters, or wearing too much lipstick, or playing tennis in shorts ... one of those things, anyhow. "The worst thing you can possibly do to the Bonne Femme is to deprive her of a grievance."'

'What on earth are you talking about, Teddy?'

'I'm generalizing about women, only putting in the name of someone we know instead of the word "woman."'

'You're showing off,' she said severely. 'That's what you're doing. I had no idea until this minute that you were so cultured.'

'When a man wishes to praise something he says it's "completely masculine." That means it soars straight to the point, doesn't waver or jitter, is passionate but cool, logical, consistent, and devoid of frills. Wouldn't you like to be completely masculine, just naturally born with all these blessings?'

'No,' said Vicky.

'No?' she said, looking shocked. 'Oh, come now, Miss Morrison, you don't know what you're saying.'

'If I were a man I'd have to shave every morning and rush about pretending I knew things I didn't know ... like how to put a washer on a bathroom tap without flooding the house, and changing tyres, and the difference between the Conservatives and the Liberals ... or Republicans and Democrats. And ... good heavens! If I were a man I'd have to *be* a Conservative or a Liberal, a Republican or a Democrat ... I wouldn't be able just to vote for whoever was making the least ass of himself at the moment. Think how awful that would be.'

'Not compared to the unremedable ... unremedial ... Is either of those a word?' she asked. 'Anyhow, what I meant was ... what I ... what was I saying?' She looked distressed. 'That's the fourth time this morning I've forgotten what I was saying right in the middle of a sentence. Am I getting something? Amnesia?'

'You were holding forth on the advantages of complete masculinity,' said Vicky. Her eyes wandered from Theodora's face to the wall behind her, and up the wall until they came to rest on the portrait of a middle-aged man in side-whiskers. 'Oh, I say, Teddy! Look at that! Talk about complete masculinity ... did he ever suffer a moment of feminine indecision?'

'Never!' She too considered it, awe-struck. 'Why haven't we ever noticed it before? Here we had this inspirational work, this portrait of a man who could have shown us the way to better, finer things ...' She waved one hand in a vague gesture indicative of the impossibility of estimating the countless spiritual advantages to be derived from prolonged consideration of this work, and went on, 'Why do they stick him over an old oak cupboard filled with sweaters and worn-out ski socks?'

The subject of the portrait continued to glare down at them defiantly. 'Probably because of that expression of suspended animus,' said Vicky. 'No one would want him around for long ... I mean he has the sort of face one can't avoid looking at. Wait a minute! *I* know who that is ... it's Jeanne d'Ormonde's uncle.'

'How do you know?'

'Because only an unnatural and frustrated passion for gold-fish could produce that look of wistful bitterness.'

'You think so?'

'I'm convinced of it.'

'Well, perhaps you're right.'

'He probably assumed that glum appearance after his wife had refused to stop expressing herself by keeping a girls' finishing school. Incidentally, she must have been just as cuckoo as he was. Do you suppose they had any children?'

'But yes,' said Theodora.

'Who?'

'Mlle Dupraix.'

'Mlle Dupraix? Good heavens, how terrible for them. I expect she talked about basilicas and Corinthian arches even in her cradle.'

'Yes,' said Theodora sadly, leaning against the wall, 'she did. Having taken a good look at her and observed the unfortunate result of their union, they decided that it would be a better thing than they had ever done if they went their separate ways. So, in the middle of Place St. François where that public washroom now stands to mark and commemorate the spot, they parted forever, he carrying his five hundred books on goldfish under his arm, she with her ormolu clock, her six teaspoons, and her Pekinese dog in her hand. Life is sad, Victoria, life is sad ... Gosh, look where we are!' The line was halfway to the drawing room door now, and they rushed forward fifteen feet, closing the gap between themselves and the Andersons. 'Apropos of women,' said Theodora, settling herself against the wall again, 'supposing I were to fall in love with your husband ... no, supposing you were to fall in love with my husband, supposing again that I were to acquire one when drunk, or otherwise not in possession of my faculties ... what would happen?'

'I should go to Java and plant coffee, or write an autobiographical novel, or become a flagpole sitter.'

'Seriously?' She shrugged. 'Quite seriously, I should not fall in love with your husband.'

'Perhaps you couldn't help it.'

'My dear, I'm not the sort of person who "can't help" things, I'm afraid. Perhaps most people aren't, when it comes right down to it. The average person falls in love with the available ... and for people like us husbands are *not* available, so it would never occur to us to fall in love with them. For modern rugged individualists who don't give a hoot for anyone but themselves, and who believe that being in love excuses disloyalty, weakness and foul play ... well ... I can't say about them.'

'Have you ever been in love, Vicky?'

Vicky turned on her shoulder ... she was leaning against the wall two or three feet behind Theodora ... and looked at her in surprise. 'Yes,' she said simply.

'Much?'

'Yes.'

'That Englishman I introduced you to?'

'Right again.'

'What happened to him?'

'He went to Italy.'

'How thoughtless of him. Are you still ... keen on him?'

She was staring straight across the hall toward the front door. Without turning her head to look at Theodora she said, 'Yes, I think so,' quite matter-of-factly. 'At least, I'm not a ... a unit, as I was before. I don't quite belong to myself now ... but I don't know, though.' Her eyes came back to Theodora's face. 'Why did you ask that?'

'I ... was ... just wondering. You see, I've never been in love with anyone ...'

'I didn't think you were ever really out of it for long.'

She shook her head. 'I have some idea, somewhere in the back of my head ... I haven't the remotest idea where it came from ... anyway, some idea of what such things should be. So far, it's *just* an idea. I've too much sense to think that I've ever cared enough about anyone to ...' She stopped, looking rather bewildered. 'Oh, hell,' she said irritably. 'I don't know what I'm talking about.'

'Enough to what?'

'Enough not to be bored. God, how boring most men are, in their relation to women! You say, at a dance, "Let's go outside," because you're steaming with heat and want to cool off ... and they think you want to be kissed. The suspicion that they're not attractive to you never occurs to the little dears. You make some remark ... almost any remark ... and they immediately turn it round and aim it back at you. For example, you say "That *is* a beautiful girl over there," because you love beauty and see no reason why, merely because you're a woman, you have to make an exception to women. What you get back in reply is, "She's not as lovely as you," or something equally imbecile. You know you're not beautiful, you've got quite used to not being beautiful, and you don't *mind* not being beautiful. And telling you that you are is so obviously a lie that it embarrasses you, and humiliates you. It's nothing short of an insult to your intelligence ... only of course, being a woman and Sex being spelt with a capital S, you're not intelligent. You're just a woman, and all women just *love* being kissed and mauled by any man. Well, here's one who's been sent orchids when she was fifteen, who's acquired dozens of fraternity pins, who's never been a wallflower in her life, who's had no end of proposals, and yet who *still* says that ninety-nine men out of a hundred make her sick.'

'Gosh,' said Vicky. 'I just adore you when you start blazing, you blaze so beautifully.'

'Theodora Cohen on the male sex,' she said derisively. And a moment later, 'Of course it's our whole continent.'

'Explain, please.'

'I mean the way we're brought up. Isn't it?' And as Vicky shook her head uncomprehendingly, 'I mean this necking business. Here, in Europe, men don't seem to go in for it. Instead, they go in for things which my mother would say were much worse. But I'm not so sure. At least they call a spade a spade. In America we call it doing the done thing, or a parked car. Mix up an American girl and a European man and what have you?'

'A deadlock,' said Vicky.

'No, indeed. She lets him kiss her, and do everything else but, and then, because he has always thought, poor innocent, that the kissing and the everything else was only a prelude to the but ...'

'You're getting horribly involved,' said Vicky. 'You mean that she thinks he's a cad because, with his realistic mind, there seems little sense and little morality in going so far and then stopping. He doesn't grasp the American game of having your cake and eating it, or, alternatively, never getting past the prelude to the opera itself.'

'Sometimes they do,' said Theodora, 'without having intended to. Then it's a shotgun wedding, and neither the man nor the girl have any more idea at the end of their lives what it's all about than they had at the beginning.'

'How do you know?'

'Because,' she said deliberately, 'when I was sixteen, I sat in a parked car, and things went farther than *I'd* intended. You see, my mother taught me all the facts of life from a biological point of view. It was all very modern and exactly like a text-book. What she didn't bother to mention was the fact that men and women didn't always have babies in mind. In any case, because I was her daughter, any kind of desire was impossible so long as I wasn't married. I mean nice girls don't feel or do that sort of thing.'

'Were you a nice girl?'

'Certainly.'

'Poor Teddy! I'm beginning to understand you a little better.'

'So one day last July my mother woke up to the fact that I was no longer a sweet young thing. After running around in circles wondering how it had all happened, she dumped me here.'

'Because of that!' she said incredulously.

'Yes.'

'But what possible good can it do you to go to boarding school when you're almost twenty-one? How long have you been out of school?'

'Four and a half years.'

'Good lord,' said Vicky. 'Your mother must be ... well, a little cuckoo, if you'll excuse my saying so.'

'She is.'

'Where is she now?'

'Paris.'

'What does she do there?'

'I don't know. She's got a gigolo at the Montmartre to teach her French and the Argentine tango. She's a nice girl too, so of course her feeling for him is purely that of a mother. Honestly, Vick. She gives him things and calls him "poor boy," and tries to make him take cod liver oil.' And a moment later, 'We'll be going back to St. Louis in the autumn. In twenty years *I'll* be in Paris, complete with gigolo and maternal instinct.'

'Perhaps not.'

'There's no perhaps about it. If I had a little less money I'd go in for good works, and women's clubs. But I've got a lot of money, so I'll go in for Europe and gigolos.'

'You might, through a series of accidents, marry a man who *did* know what it was all about.'

'That's not very probable,' she said indifferently.

They were past the drawing room door now. The inspection was taking longer than usual that morning, as Mlle Dupraix was constantly interrupting herself to scold one of the girls for speaking too loudly, or speaking the wrong language; or being interrupted by a maid wanting directions from her in her capacity as housekeeper. The two girls continued to lounge against the wall.

On their way up the stairs a few minutes later, Theodora said suddenly as they reached the landing, 'If you get kicked out, I'm going with you.'

Vicky stopped and turned round. 'You couldn't do that, Teddy.'

'Oh, yes I could. When it comes to a fight, I can beat anyone hands down. That includes both Amelia and my mother. We've got enough money between us to live in a Paris garret till I come of age ... I mean for purposes of inheriting my father's wealth ... then we can do anything we like. We might go to Singapore.'

They moved over against the wall out of the way of the girls running up and down stairs. In the poor light from the stained glass window above their heads Vicky scrutinized Theodora's attractive face, and could think of nothing to say but 'Why Singapore?'

'I've always wanted to go there. Singapore, Rio de Janeiro, Madras, and Peking.'

'They're a long way from Paris,' said Vicky, looking up at the window.

'Never mind. There are almost no limits to what we can do on my sordid millions. I'll buy you clothes from Lelong and diamonds from Cartier.'

'I don't care so much about them, but I should like awfully to have champagne every morning for breakfast and all the Brandenburg Concertos.'

'They are practically yours,' said Theodora.

Little Klaus and Big Klaus passed them with Truda at their heels. She stopped as they caught sight of Vicky and said awkwardly, 'Could I see you sometime today?' ignoring Theodora who looked at her menacingly and remarked, 'I suppose you realize that after your maltreatment of last night, I am bruised beyond recognition.' She began to whistle 'Die Wacht am Rhein,' without waiting for a reply, and opened her notebook to stare intently and tactfully at a page on which was written in her large round hand:

me
te   le
se before la before lui before y before en
nous   les   leur
vous

Vicky nodded. 'Later ... this afternoon, if you like,' she said in the rather grave manner she habitually used with people whom she did not know very intimately. 'Are you going to walk or ski?'

Truda brushed a long string of black hair off her face and said, 'I'll walk, if that's what you're going to do.' Vicky nodded again, and she continued on her way downstairs.

Theodora stopped considering the position of pronoun objects, and raising her eyes to Vicky's, said hurriedly, 'Listen, Vicky, I'm perfectly serious about leaving. You know as well as I do that Amelia almost has apoplexy every time she looks at you. There must be something about your face that she doesn't like. Anyhow, there it is. So remember that if you go, I go with you.'

2

The snow began to fall less heavily as the morning wore on. By eleven o'clock when Vicky went to her room she could make out the faint outlines of the pine-covered point which jutted out into the Lake of Geneva a mile or so to the west of Lausanne. The sky showed brilliant splashes of blue here and there, although across the lake there were still some heavy clouds drifting closer in the still, cold air. The peaks on the opposite shore were out of sight. They said that you could tell when spring was on its way, even when there were still drifts of snow in the narrow streets of Lausanne, and in the corners of the cathedral, by the clouds which began to float beneath the peaks of the mountains above Evian, instead of hiding their faces as they did all the winter.

Her room was on the top floor which was, at this hour, almost deserted. She was grateful for the quiet all about her. She had only to shut her door and the school dropped away, almost, she thought, as though she were leaving it in an elevator rising from the roof. She was glad that Ina Barron, her roommate, was not there; she had just seen her in the lower hall with Rose Budet and Henriette. Vicky hoped that they would occupy Ina for the next ten minutes; she wanted, most decidedly, to be alone.

Somewhere beyond her conscious enjoyment of each leisurely winter day that passed, was a feeling of depression which was weighing down on her, though she could not account for it. She left the window with a sigh, and going over to the basin in the alcove, drank a glass of water. Between the alcove and the window was a blue-tiled dressing table; the wallpaper was the usual pink, blue and green on a white background. Vicky hated flowered wallpapers because she had been brought up in a house which had nothing else ... dull red and purple on brown trellis-work with a buff background ... but she found the school wallpaper gay and not in the least monotonous. She cast an appreciative glance at it, then wandered aimlessly across the room to sit on the edge of her bed.

Her eyes fell on a photograph of Ina's father, taken at Cambridge, which was standing on her roommate's side of the dressing table. Vicky liked his looks and wondered for the fiftieth time why he had never realized that his sister ... who had looked after Ina ever since the death of Mrs. Barron ... was anything but good to his daughter.

Mlle Tourain had asked in her hearty way where Vicky's parents were, and had received an answer so deliberately and obviously evasive when she pressed the point, that she had remained standing in the middle of Vicky's room for fully half a minute, at a loss what to say next. There was nothing in that room ... no photograph, no letters, no anything to connect Vicky with her home in Canada. It was unprecedented. The entire school wondered why; they speculated, they gossiped, and when they were there, their eyes searched the room for some tangible evidence that at one time at least, Vicky *had* had some kind of home, some background. They found none.

The only personal belongings, besides the toilet articles on the basin and dressing table, were her books. Between the head of her bed and the window along the west wall was a large bookcase containing over a hundred paper-backed French novels and plays, two calf-bound volumes of French poetry which she had given herself at Christmas, three dictionaries, fifty odd Tauchnitz editions, and several battered volumes of Greek poetry and drama, as well as an odd assortment of modern novels. There were also, on the windowsill, six bowls containing bulbs which she hoped would turn out to be hyacinths, for Rosalie, and a pile of music two feet high on the floor beneath them.

She sat on the side of the bed with her shoulders hunched a little, her hands lying loosely in her lap, looking across at the dressing table, absently following a crack in the blue tile from one square to the next. She was tired and her mind confused; she could see herself only too clearly, standing on the front steps of the school, wondering where she should go. She thought fleetingly of Theodora ... what would happen to her? And what kind of man had Cohen père been, not to foresee his wife's flight to Europe; not to realize that once there with her mother, Theodora at sixteen, seventeen, eighteen, nineteen and twenty would spend a good part of her life sitting in cafés and night-clubs watching her mother's shoulders moving in time to the music, realizing that her mother's eyes were searching, searching, for some cautious answer to her demand for diversion. It was all very well to be cosmopolitan, but why hadn't Mr. Cohen had the sense to see what would happen if a woman of Mrs. Cohen's temperament ... young, attractive, and bored as she was ... were turned loose on the Continent during all those years they must spend there if Theodora and Lewis were to learn their five languages?

She glanced at the clock on the dressing table; it was two minutes past eleven and Mary would be waiting for her in the art room. She did not yet know what she was going to say about Rosalie; she felt uneasy at saying anything, but at the same time she was afraid to take the sole responsibility for her any longer.

Vicky was on the point of getting up to join Mary, when the door burst open and Ina stood there crying, with a letter in her hand. She was a small, plain English girl whose mouth usually hung open a little, with straight fair hair, pale blue eyes and a neglected, unloved look.

She closed the door behind her and gasped in answer to Vicky's alarmed, 'Ina! What is it?' after a struggle to get her breath, 'My father's not coming this summer after all!' and rushing across the room, hurled herself at Vicky, winding her arms so tightly about her that she was unable to move for a moment.

She managed to loosen the arms a little and looking down at the fair head below her, said in a less sympathetic tone than was natural to her, 'I'm sorry, Ina. Is that letter from him?' She had been forced to adopt an impersonal manner in all her dealings with Ina, for the girl was almost hysterically devoted to her, jealous of Theodora and Consuelo, jealous of everyone Vicky knew, and even jealous of her piano.

She answered jerkily, with a quick nod of her head which was pressing against Vicky's shoulder, 'He says ... he ... can't afford to come ... and that I'm to stay here ... next summer ... and all next year!'

'That's better than going back to your aunt, Ina,' she said gently.

'I haven't seen him for five years.' The untidy blonde head on her shoulder was raised a little, and Ina stared at her. Then her face disappeared once more and she continued in her muffled voice, 'He promised I could go out, back to Ceylon with him, next year. Now he says I'm to stay here. I can't bear it, Vicky!' She began to sob convulsively again.

'Ina, try to control yourself a little, please.' She succeeded after considerable effort in loosening one of her arms so that she could put her hand under Ina's chin and force her to raise her head. 'You can't let yourself go like this; if you do, everything will seem ever so much worse.' She struggled free, and leaving Ina to sit on the edge of the bed, went over to the basin and got her a glass of water. 'Here, drink this,' she commanded.

Ina gulped it down, then raised her tear-stained face to Vicky, standing above her, 'Are you going to be ...' A sob caught her throat; she swallowed, and asked again, 'Are you going to be here next year?'

'Next year, Ina?'

'Yes. You won't, will you? I know you won't, it's no use your trying to put me off to make me feel better. All the girls are saying that Mlle Tourain's going to expel you ...'

'All the girls are saying that?' she repeated mechanically. 'How do they know?'

Ina was too wrapped up in her own bitter disappointment to notice that drop in Vicky's tone which, Theodora could have told her, meant that Vicky was hurt. She caught hold of her skirt, she began twisting it into a knot, staring up at her anxiously.

Vicky sighed, half-smiled down at her, recovered her skirt, then retreated to the dressing table and pulling herself up on it backwards, sat there swinging her legs and surveying the meagre little figure before her, wondering what she could do to make this fresh blow less hard for her. The child was highly-strung, and emotionally unbalanced; added to that was the fact that her mother had died eleven years before when she was only five, and her father had immediately returned to Ceylon, leaving Ina in the care of an aunt who apparently, from all Vicky could gather, hated her small niece. The aunt's letters to Ina were always full of small taunts and threats. The child's bogy was the reformatory; when she had first arrived at the school she had repeatedly wakened Vicky at night by calling out in her sleep, 'Don't send me away! Don't send me away!'

She suddenly slid down from the high bed and, running forward, caught Vicky's hand and held it against her cheek saying passionately, 'Vicky, don't go away and leave me! Don't go away! You remember, when Ted asked you to room with her, and I was so afraid you would, you said that someone had to keep an eye on me, and that you wouldn't go away then. I can't get along without you, I'll kill myself if Mlle Tourain makes you leave ...'

'Ina, if I leave, it won't be because I want to, you know that. Your going on this way makes everything much harder. If you're as fond of me as you say you are, why don't you try to depend on me a little less, to be less emotional? And there's something else that doesn't seem to have occurred to you ... your father's not exactly rich, is he?'

'No,' she said.

'Do you know how expensive this school is?'

'Expensive?'

'Yes, it is rather. He must have to work very hard to pay your bills here, and he wouldn't send you to a place like this unless he cared about you, and were counting on you. I'm not the only one, you know.'

Ina straightened up, brushed away her tears with the back of her hand, and said in a more reasonable voice, 'I haven't seen him for so long, Vicky, that's the trouble. But I'll try not to be such a nuisance, I promise.' She added, however, as Vicky went out the door a moment later, 'I simply can't help adoring you, though. No one could who knew you as well as I do.'

VI

❧

The art room was on the top floor, with windows facing Montreux and the valley of the Rhône to the east, and the mountains to the north. They were very large casement windows let into the roof at an angle, without curtains or any sort of shade. The room was very bright and almost shadowless all day long, with a strange and unearthly quality to the light which was first cast in by the snow and then thrown back by the smooth white plastered walls and ceiling.

There were three long drawing tables cluttered with paints, brushes, pencils, rulers and sketch pads; a grand piano in the south-east corner opposite the door, and busts of Julius Caesar, Augustus, Justinian, Hadrain, Beethoven, and Voltaire, each on individual columns placed along the four sides of the room at regular intervals. The glaring white walls were decorated here and there with etchings and photographs of the Forum, Carcassonne, Mont St. Michel and Chartres, as well as a few detailed enlargements of Notre-Dame.

Vicky was sitting on the long table by the east windows, while Mary, slightly to her left, was on the floor with her back against the wall, so that she had to turn her head to see her, and had straight in front of her an uninterrupted view of the orphanage roof ... or what could be seen of it now, for the clouds had already moved over from the opposite shore, and it had begun to snow heavily again ... the tops of the elm trees which grew close to the building and which had given the school its name, and the steep slope down to the lake where the Dents du Midi were visible only at intervals, in the distance.

They were talking about Rosalie, Vicky saying, 'I haven't yet got to a point where I can be sensible about her. In one peculiar way, she means more to me than anyone on earth ... it's that she seems to be inside me. I mean that I'm not objective about her, that's the trouble.' She rubbed her forehead in perplexity, then looking out the windows again, went on in a more matter-of-fact voice, 'It's very difficult for me to discuss her, not only because of my own feelings about her either. She's told me a great deal ... all there is to tell, I suppose ... but actually, if I say that she was born in Montreal on such and such a date, and her parents were this and that ... it doesn't help much. Yet the part which can't easily be put into words, and which could certainly not be added to Mlle Tourain's dossier, is the only part that really matters. It's something which must be felt, to be understood. It requires imagination, not reasoning. Perhaps some people would think it was all too intangible and too improbable to be real ... but it *is* real.'

Mary straightened up with a sigh, as Vicky fell into silence again, and said unhappily, 'I wish there was something in this idea that human beings can communicate a little of themselves to one another ...'

'There probably is something in it. At least I believe in it, I don't know to what extent.'

Mary looked at Vicky, who, after a quick glance at her, had turned her eyes to the windows again, and said meditatively, 'I wonder. Sometimes it seems to me as though it must be true.'

'What were you thinking about?'

'You.'

'Me?' Her grey eyes came back to Mary's face again. 'Why?'

'I was thinking that if only I could get something of you ... oh,' she added with a grimace, 'that sounds ridiculous. But I do wish that in some way or other you could transmit to me something of yourself ... I mean the part of you which is intuitive ... that amazing faculty you have for understanding other people. It isn't just sympathizing ... it's something far deeper. You really *understand* them, so that you know why they did such and such a thing, and what they will do in the future. There's a magic touch in dealing with people ... I suppose one is born with it, and that one can't possibly acquire it. You're a queer person, Vicky,' she said, looking up at her intently. 'You really *are* queer. I've never in my life met anyone in the least like you.'

Vicky detested the way her friends spoke of her and had an impulse to ask Mary to change the subject which she checked, aware that she usually had some purpose behind her remarks. She forced herself to say, 'Well, why am I queer?'

'I don't know. You've a streak of mysticism, haven't you?'

'Not that I know of.'

'It must be there, somewhere ... translated into something else, perhaps. You know, if you'd been born four hundred years ago, you'd have been very religious, possibly. You're the twentieth-century version of a mystic ... it's rather interesting. I mean you have all the requirements, even including some curious power over people ... but because you were born twenty-one years ago instead of a few centuries back, you do nothing with all your ...'

'Eccentricities,' suggested Vicky. 'Mary ...' She hesitated, then said as gently as she could, 'You know, we *were* talking about Rosalie, and it's rather important.'

'This is important too ... it's terribly important to me. Leave Rosalie for the moment ... I'll tell you why in a minute. I'm trying to get at something. Perhaps it's only the atmosphere of this school that's working on my nerves, giving me strange, distorted ideas that I wouldn't have if I were in a different environment ... but whether or not that's true, it's irrelevant. I have a feeling ... it's been growing on me for weeks now ... that *this* is the environment I'm going to fetch up in ... I don't know why, I can't explain. Anyhow, I do feel it, and I feel that if there were only a god of some sort to take pity on me, he'd make it possible for me to be a little like you.'

'Why?'

'Because you've a kind of wisdom that only comes with many years of suffering ... as though it had been distilled, and distilled within you. But because, more than that, you seem to be able to give things up, and not mind.'

'My dear ... I do mind,' she said quietly.

'But not madly, not with every atom of you so that you're ... so that you can't think of anything else. It's as though a bomb had burst inside you ... everything there is torn, ripped up with great jagged edges ...' She gave a long, shivering sigh and buried her head in her arms. She was crying. In a few moments she got hold of herself, lifted her head and said, 'Sorry, Vick. Do you know what I'm talking about?'

'Yes, I think I do. He'll be back, Mary. Try to believe that. It's just this place, as you say, that's been worrying you, turning you in on yourself.'

'Perhaps. But for some reason or other, I've been half out of my wits today.'

'I know.'

'*Do* you, Vicky?' she asked almost appealingly.

'Well ... I've guessed a lot. Are you waiting for him to come back?'

'Yes,' she said, looking straight in front of her. 'We made an agreement ... or rather I made it. We were to stay apart for a year, and if he still wanted me at the end of it ... and had wanted me enough during it, to ... play straight ... then we were going to remarry. You see, I *had* to do that, Vicky. Otherwise, it would simply have been so easy, so terribly easy ... too easy for him, to throw me over for another woman, then throw her over for me. I mean it was almost a case of Monday night with her and ... Tuesday ...' She stopped, and bit her lower lip. A moment later she looked up at Vicky, with a curious intensity in her glance.

'Don't stare at me like that, for heaven's sake,' said Vicky with a half-rueful expression. 'I don't know what I've ever done to deserve your making me feel as though I weren't quite human.'

She shook her head and attempted a smile. 'Right. But you know you do have a very unnerving effect on me sometimes, although I'm four years older and I've been around, as Ted would say.' Vicky did not answer. She was in one of her remote moods, Mary knew, when it was almost impossible to believe that she was only twenty-one, and to be regarded as a school-girl ... it was that, she thought, shifting her weight a little on the floor, which one couldn't help feeling ... that the girl was simply not like other people, for reasons which were either inherent in her, or the result of some strange background. 'Vicky, listen to me,' she said pleadingly.

Her eyes swung round to Mary's face and this time remained there. She was silent for what seemed to Mary a disconcertingly long time, and then said with visible effort, 'I wish you and other people wouldn't place so much responsibility on me. I don't know anything ... nothing about you or anyone else. You'd think I was a sort of oracle ... it's absurd. It's like going to a medical student who's just graduated, and demanding a brain operation.'

Mary got up, went over to the north windows and then sat down on the sill, with one hand on either side of her half supporting her weight. She heard Vicky say, 'You think it's a ... a "magic touch," you called it, didn't you? A magic touch given to a few specially gifted individuals at birth. Well, you may be right, but not about me. I haven't got it; people ... a few people ... merely think I have, and with me it's a curse, a silly delusion existing only in the minds of others, not in *my* mind. All the same, I'd do anything I could for you. You know that.'

Mary allowed her full weight to rest on the windowsill and began to twist a small signet ring on the little finger of her left hand. She looked down at it a moment, then back at Vicky, whose profile was turned toward her, and suddenly began to talk in a stream of words which startled even herself as she uttered them. She told Vicky, or rather that profile, about her childhood, her girlhood, her marriage, and her divorce from the beginning to the end.

Vicky said nothing. She did nothing, only turning her head now and again to glance at Mary, who at last got up, and coming over to her, began to pace up and down the floor between Vicky, still sitting on the drawing table, and the windows which faced Montreux and the valley of the Rhône.

'I'm all on edge,' said Mary, pausing to glance at the pale, immobile face beside her. 'It's curious ... I feel that now, everything in my life has driven toward this school ... as though it were a sort of funnel, and that only through it can I live, from now on. You know, I believe that people can, at least to some extent, visualize their future. I don't think that the totally unexpected very often happens, for the reason that the present and the future are far more often than not, an outgrowth of the past ... and that if one looks with sufficient detachment at things as they were, and at things as they are, one can at least guess at what will be. At any rate, I can see myself here ... next year, and the year after, and the year after that, while it becomes increasingly difficult for me to ... to identify myself with Barry. In some queer way, I seem to have gone past him now ... I can only look back on him; I can't look forward to him.'

Vicky said at last, 'You don't need to tell me that, Mary.' Her grey eyes went back to the window in front of her again; she was searching for the Dents du Midi but they were not there. The snow was falling so fast that she could not determine the descent of each individual flake at all; it seemed to hang like a sparkling veil between her eyes and the world beyond the windows, with only now and then a chimney, a long upward trail of thin smoke from the town, piercing it momentarily. Into and beyond the veil the whole visible world receded, leaving them isolated in this room with the photographs of the gargoyles of Notre-Dame, and the busts of dead emperors. The light, shadowless, unvarying and strained, made the whole scene fantastic.

'What an excellent place for hysterics,' remarked Vicky cheerfully. 'σκιᾶς ὄναρ ἄνθρῶπος ... you never studied Greek, did you? "Man is the shadow of a dream ..." That seems to me, at the moment, to be very apt. Our ambitions, our ideals, our suffering exist only in our minds, until we endow them with substance by translating them into words, or into actions. Yet what exists in the mind is, to me anyway, the only reality, the only certainty. God is within us all to a greater or lesser extent, according to

the magnitude of our conceptions. My views,' she added, looking amused, 'are excessively androcentric.'

Mary said nothing. Vicky looked at her rather anxiously, being
made aware of the silence which pervaded the room by the noise
of a door slamming somewhere below. The sound seemed to fall
away before it actually reached them, and her voice, when she
spoke again, was limited to the small living space by the east
windows where Mary was walking up and down, and she sitting on the edge of it, thought Vicky, conscious of the vacuum
behind her. 'Why do you stay here, Mary? It's so hard for
you. It's all right for me, and I love being here, simply because
everything which has to do with the material side of life is so
pleasantly inevitable. I mean, lunch is provided at twelve-fifteen,
and it would take an earthquake to make it twelve-twenty.
I'm left free to wander about and think in peace. I get a lot of
work done and I enjoy living with other people ... within certain
limits, of course,' she added, grimacing slightly. 'But all it's doing
to you is to make you lonely and introspective, and I don't think
it's good for you.'

Mary sat down on the sill facing Vicky and considered that
for a moment. 'It's odd, living in a girls' school, isn't it? We all
seem so detached from one another. Do women live within and
between their own personal mental horizons more than men?
I don't know. We're supposed to chatter incessantly about ourselves when we get together, we women. We're supposed to
gossip, and know everything about everyone else ... but here
we don't. We're all separated from one another. I've no point of
contact with anyone but you ... you have none even with me ...
with no one but ... Rosalie. Isn't that true?'

'Contact? What sort of contact?'

'I don't really know you, Vicky. I can tell what you're going
to do, but I can't tell why you do it. I never feel that you're quite

there, and you give me the impression that a great deal of what's gone to make you as you are is outside my experience ... perhaps even my understanding. Oh, I know we've wasted hours talking generalities ... like that afternoon you spent with me at the Centrale beer garden trying to convince me that the D Minor was César Franck's life ... incidentally, I still don't see that. Look at Tchaikovski ... he really had quite a decent time of it, all things considered, with that beneficent widow who gave him six hundred pounds a year or something like that, didn't she? No one could say that his life was in any way marked by misfortune, or unusual suffering, yet his music is tragic. On the other side of the medal is Mozart, whose life was a series of heartbreaks which seem to have found no outlet at all in his work. And Bach, the musician, was infinitely greater than Bach the man.'

'"Car de faire la poignée plus grande que le poing, la brassée plus grande que le bras, et d'éspèrer enjamber plus que l'estendue de nos jambes, cela est impossible et monstrueux; *ny que l'homme se monte au dessus de soy et de l'humanité ...*"'

'You're always quoting Montaigne at me.'

'He's a good antidote,' said Vicky.

'An antidote for what?'

She shrugged. 'Can you separate the mind into various compartments? Can you divide the body from the mind, the mind from the spirit? Can you subdivide all three into little sections labelled the religious sense, the moral sense, the aesthetic sense? I don't think so. I don't think you can split Bach into two, and call the two parts "the man" and "the musician." If you believe that it is only through truth, through beauty, and through goodness that man attains to the highest, then there has never been a great philosopher who did not seek beauty, nor a great artist who was not good.'

'You think Bach was good ... I mean in the absolute sense?'

'Is anyone ever good, "in the absolute sense"?' she countered.

'No, I suppose not. Leave Bach out of it then ... what about Michelangelo?'

'Do you believe in art for art's sake?'

'N — o,' said Mary doubtfully. 'But think of ... well, Gauguin, for example.'

'Think of Van Gogh, instead. He was the genius of the two. There's no such thing as a "mad" genius; it's rather the opposite. They are sane where we are insane. Van Gogh's sanity was the sanity of St. Francis of Assisi, Joan of Arc, Leonardo, Socrates. You were thinking of his "morals," ... using the word in its modern, limited sense of sexual morals ... which, if not exactly irrelevant, is rather begging the question.'

'You're being illogical,' said Mary.

'I usually am ... more so today, because I've got a headache. But why, particularly?'

'You can't say his conduct with women was irrelevant, and say at the same time that it's impossible to segregate the physical from the ... well, whatever it was you said.'

'You're using the word "morality" in the parochial sense of sexual morality; I wasn't. However, if you want to use it that way, it's still not easy to condemn him on those grounds. I don't know what your standards are, but I should think that one was immoral when, among other things, the physical elements were predominant ... and then I have a lot of old-fashioned notions about not hurting other people which might be described in a more dignified and learned way as the "relative importance" of the issues involved. But don't let's talk about sex ... it's only one aspect of life, after all. I'm afraid I find it rather dull, overemphasized alike by the puritanical and the exponents of free love. The one group endow it with too much negative importance, the other group with too much positive importance.'

'What do *you* believe, Vicky?' she asked suddenly.

'I believe in everyone minding his own business,' said Vicky.

'Apart from that ... and seriously?'

'I believe in God, and in miracles. I don't believe that the importance of the individual can possibly be underestimated ... in other words, I can't feel that my particular troubles are of any interest to Him, nor yours either.' She smiled suddenly, and continued, looking straight in front of her, 'I think He has "rather a take it or leave it" attitude toward us. Every little while a miracle happens, and a man of genius is born. Through him we are moved forward; through him we are given a glimpse of those three absolutes ... truth, and beauty, and goodness, and then left free to choose between them and the untrue, the ugly, and the bad. Genius can't be explained ... I believe that it's a miracle of God, and neither you nor anyone else can refute my statement ... because you can't explain it. I don't believe in ... well, Faure's theory of the man and the moment, because I'm more of a Platonist than anything else, and I'm therefore more inclined to think that the majority is always and invariably *wrong* ... I don't mean politically. You see, my training has been almost entirely classical. I'm not a romanticist. So far as my personal standards are concerned, I try, rather weakly, to be good. I love beauty, and I spend a lot of time reading aesthetics and metaphysics. I believe in the moral obligation contained in the words "I ought," ... and I don't believe that anything I've said for the past ten minutes is in the least original.'

'I never suspected you of being religious, somehow,' said Mary. 'I don't know why, exactly ... but I didn't. Perhaps because most of us aren't nowadays ... perhaps because we're accustomed to thinking of religion as belief in a personal God. Do you pray?'

'No, but I swear beautifully in several languages.'

Mary looked up at her quickly. That half-amused tone usually meant one thing and only one thing ... Vicky was heading her off. Evidently she considered that she had done enough talking about herself for one day. Mary said, anxious to catch her before she escaped once more, 'Be autobiographical for once, if you can ... will you, Vicky?'

'You mean explain my "mysterious past," my lack of photographs of mother and baby brother in 1921? All right. There's really no reason why I shouldn't. The reason why I haven't is, I think, fairly natural under the circumstances ... for one cannot dismiss a thing from mind, and babble about it to others at the same time.'

'No. Even my limited intelligence can grasp that.'

'However, if there's anything you want to know,' said Vicky, with an obvious effort to speak lightly, 'go ahead and ask questions. I can't just begin with "I was born on the 15th of August, 1913, of English and American parentage, in London, England ..."'

'What!'

'I observe that you expected something more bizarre,' she said, amused at Mary's astonished expression. 'What *did* you expect? An Indian squaw and the Siamese consul-general?'

'Where are your parents?' Mary asked, ignoring Vicky's last remark. 'Are they alive? And which was which?'

'What do you mean, which was which? You could tell my mother from my father ... Oh, I see what you mean. My mother was American, my father is English. That answers both questions.' An indescribable look flickered across her face as she mentioned Morrison, but it vanished before Mary looked up. Vicky was rather grimly determined to be impersonal.

'How and when did they go to Canada?'

'They came separately. My mother can't be said to have "come to Canada," at all. She only dropped in one night when she happened to be passing. I'll be as simple as possible. My father belongs to conventional, middle-class England. My mother belonged to conventional, lower middle-class America. They met in London. My father was at the time doing post-graduate work in archaeology at Cambridge. I ... occurred. Nine months later I was born, unfortunately. You needn't look like that, Mary ... it depends on how you view these things. If you believe in almost *any* morality, it's unfortunate, and that's all there is to it.'

'What happened?'

'My mother raised a considerable row, blackmailed my father's family, got some money from them, and then took me to the States. My father was then dispatched to Canada for the good of England ... what we call a "remittance man" ... No, darling, they were *not* married.' She was finding this even more difficult than she had expected, but her face was too disciplined to give her away. She was picking out fact from all the confusion of memory, trying to gain time in which to decide what to say and what not to say. 'He's in central Turkey now, on an American agricultural survey organized by Mustapha Kemal. I ran away when he'd been gone two weeks.'

'You ran away?' she repeated in astonishment.

'He left the first week in August, ten days before my twenty-first birthday. I inherited some money from my aunt ... about four hundred and fifty pounds a year. So I cleared out while the going was good.'

'Oh.' Mary waited for Vicky to go on, but she was silent again. It seemed to be becoming a sort of question and answer conversation, and she had no desire to appear curious. She scanned Vicky's face, and finding no irritation, no impatience, but merely that look of mental strain, went on hesitatingly, 'What was he like? ... your father, I mean. What sort of man is he?'

It was a long time before she answered. She was staring at the gargoyle on the wall to the right of the window, seeing beyond it, as the gargoyle faded, into a suddenly clarified past. One scene after another rose up before her eyes, but always fell away, giving place to the first again ... a long, tastelessly furnished room hung with dark-red curtains, and with a black marble fireplace in which some coal was burning, shedding an orange-bluish light on the furniture near by. There was a small, round brass table on six upright ebony legs inlaid with mother-of-pearl, in front of and slightly to one side of the fireplace. She was sitting on the floor behind a high-backed chair and leaned forward once or twice to run her fingers over the mother-of-pearl ... little diamonds and hearts of it set in the black wood ... somewhat fearfully, for her mother whom she could see round the left side of the chair, was drunk.

She was standing by a long table which was between the door and the fireplace, supporting her swaying body with one hand clinging to the edge, while the other held a glass of brandy. She was talking, crying, and swearing by turns, while, at the other end of the table, her father sat with his legs stretched out in front of him, staring into the fire.

She kept repeating, 'All right, I'm going, I'm going ... but that nuisance is not coming with me. Do you hear that? I'm god-damned if I'm going to lug her around any longer. I've had seven years of it, and I'm through. It's your turn now ... you keep her for seven years, then send me a wire when she's fourteen and maybe I'll come back for her.' She lost hold of the brandy glass and it fell to the floor, smashing into small pieces.

Vicky watched that small, eager child dressed in threadbare black velvet with a soiled lace collar, an incredibly thin child with long black hair and terrified grey eyes who was herself, and smiled a little. Here that child was now, swinging her legs as she sat on a drawing table in the art room of Pensionnat Les Ormes, Lausanne, Switzerland. Then her mind went back again: the man and woman quarrelled, her mother now moaning and whining, then shouting; her father sharp, bitter, hopeless. They both seemed immensely tall and out of focus, from her position behind the chair on the floor, and when her father stood up at last, his legs were cut in two by the round brass table, and she could hardly see his face, above the light cast by the fire, in semi-darkness. Her mother went away, having forgotten to say goodbye to her child, who, after a hasty glance at the door to be sure she was not coming back, continued to sit, silent and motionless, staring at the strange man's half-illuminated face. She had never seen her father before. She never saw her mother again.

She could remember nothing more with any distinctness, until her eleventh birthday. It was the same overcrowded room, with the same dull wallpaper of brown and red on a buff background. She had wanted to have a party, because she had been reading a book given her by her aunt in which the children had a party. She asked her father. He had said, 'You can't. No one would come even if I let you invite them. You're illegitimate. That means that people don't like you, they don't want to see you. That's the reason none of the children you know are allowed to play with you. Do you see?' She had nodded, then escaped upstairs, repeating the word 'illegitimate' over and over again to herself. She did not know what it meant, but it was evidently an important word.

Her mind returned to the present. She glanced at Mary, trying to remember her last question, then said, 'I can't describe him in one sentence. He was all mixed up ... he still is. There's nothing very simple and uncomplicated about him. You have to know a great deal about him, in order to understand even a little.'

'Your mother, then. What was she like?'

'Slovenly. Everything about her was slovenly ... her mind, her soul, also her clothes. I don't think she was really a bad lot in the beginning, but dragging a fatherless child about isn't very easy. She was rather incompetent, but I think she'd have held on to her jobs if I hadn't furnished such a good excuse for getting rid of her. I don't know why she didn't put me in a home ... I suppose she wanted to square herself as much as possible with her respectable ancestors and her respectable upbringing ... by doing *something* for me, at any rate. However, she just went from mediocre to bad, and from bad to worse. She eventually drank herself to death in Mobile, Alabama. There's something quite irrevocable about drinking yourself to death in Mobile, Alabama, isn't there?'

'I wish you wouldn't ... look like that.'

'My dear, you can hardly expect me to be sentimental about her. I never saw her after she dropped in on my father in Toronto one evening, and handed me over.'

'Were you fond of her?'

'She was all I had to be fond of. But now ... well, I suppose it was the best thing for me, and certainly he provided a better environment than she ever had, but *his* respectable upbringing never allowed him to forget the way in which he had degraded himself with my mother, and never allowed me to forget it either. I was not allowed to lose sight of the fact that I had been born in what must have been a singularly pointless and futile sin, nor to lose sight of the fact that I'm illegitimate.'

'Vicky!' she said in horror.

'I told you that,' she said.

'I thought you meant that they weren't married until ... well, until you were on the way.'

'No. They never married, and I'm still illegitimate. Does that shock you? I suppose it does,' she said meditatively, looking down at the floor. Then her eyes returned to Mary's face. 'I heard enough from my father of what Toronto thought about us ... people like us. But it's a provincial place and could hardly be called progressive so far as moral charity is concerned, so I thought ... Oh,' she added, half-smiling again, 'I don't really know what I thought. But what *do* you feel?'

'I ... can't quite describe it. But it makes you seem ...'

'Seem what?' she asked, looking at the gargoyle again. 'Different from the ordinary run ... an equivalent to a changeling, for example? A cuckoo in the nest ... a leprechaun ... a faun.' And as Mary said nothing she turned her head to look at her again and went on as quietly as before, 'At any rate, it puts me outside the ordinary society of ordinary people like *that* ...' she dropped her hand on the table, 'Doesn't it, Mary?'

'No, Vicky! No, it doesn't!' said Mary passionately. 'Why should it? It doesn't mean that *you're* not the same as the rest of us ...'

'Oh, but I'm not, Mary,' she said, shaking her head and looking at her with a faint smile.

'But why? Why *shouldn't* you be?'

'Why? What's "why" got to do with it? Do you expect, like Mlle Tourain, to find a reason behind every fact, before you'll recognize the existence of the fact itself? I'm not respectable ... I'm different ... I'm inconvenient, I'm awkward to have about. Reason hasn't anything to do with it.'

'It has usually,' she said almost unwillingly. 'Really, that's true, Vicky. Conventions are like ... like traffic lights, directing and simplifying the movement of society from generation to generation. Even things that are awfully unfair ... You said yourself, a moment ago, that you didn't agree with the modern tendency toward extreme individualism. You must have meant by that ... or whatever it was you said ... that it is the majority and not the minority ...' She stopped. Those grey eyes were looking at her again, Vicky's damnable ability to see through a remark into its implications and in spite of their possible reference to herself, to accept them without emotion and without prejudice, was once more in evidence.

She said quietly, 'And I still mean it. Because I happen to be in the unfortunate minority doesn't blind me to the fact that illegitimacy can hardly be accepted as the ... done thing.'

'What was your mother like?' Mary asked, anxious to get off the subject as quickly as possible. She bitterly regretted her defence of convention as soon as it was out. Perhaps Vicky thought that she was in agreement with ... the people of Toronto. 'I mean what else?'

'She was very genteel,' said Vicky tentatively.

'Genteel!'

'Yes. She used to drink sloe gin from the bathroom glass with her little finger delicately curved.'

'Like those dreadful Anderson girls!' said Mary, shuddering.

'Then she'd wipe her mouth in the grand manner with a dirty towel, when there was only me to see her ... and I was always as far away from her as the other side of the bed would allow me to go.' Her hands dropped down to her sides, and she sat relaxed, her face still expressionless except for the tense muscles around her mouth. For the first time, she was realizing that no matter how she struggled to attain a sense of proportion and to dismiss from mind all the evil days through which she had come to the present; no matter how she fought to prevent herself from harbouring any but the few good memories she had ... no matter what she did, her birth would loom large in the minds of others, ugly and unforgettable. She could blame her own sane and truth-loving mind, her unwillingness to rail against inevitabilities and against unalterable facts, for her present knowledge that though, if she were less self-controlled and more self-pitying, she might say entreatingly, 'Look at me as I am, not as you think I must be as a result of this,' it would do no real and lasting good, and might well endanger the integrity for which she had fought, and was still fighting.

She said, a moment later, 'I can't remember a time when I didn't feel sorry for my father. Even when I was very young, I sensed his great unhappiness. He had started life for a second time after he came to Toronto ... pulled himself together, got a job in the university, and was even engaged to a nice girl, when my mother deposited me on the doorstep. After that, perhaps partially because he expected the worst, the worst happened. He lost his job, lost his fiancée who had been brought up to believe that ... such conduct as his, nine months before my birth, was a fundamental and ineradicable blot on the character of man or woman. If a man would do that, he'd do anything ... commit murder, or become a drunkard ... anything in fact. People seem to forget, sometimes, that physical passion is not, like thieving or cruelty, or murder, an out-and-out moral issue. It's not simple, a straight question of right or wrong. It's more than that. I see nothing evil in what he did, but only in the punishment ... as self-inflicted and inflicted by others. I think he was an utter fool; I think he was a fool because in that moment he chose something shoddy, something cheap, something easy. All the same, his punishment was out of all proportion to his crime ... if I ever have children, I shall tell them that. I shall tell them that people are still of such a nature as to hang you for tripping and falling in the mud.'

'Do you believe that?'

'Yes,' she said slowly. 'I'm not thinking of the individual alone, in this instance any more than in any other, but of the fact that intolerance hurts the victims of it less than it does those who are guilty of it. To sin against others is worse than to sin against yourself ... though perhaps you can't ever do one without doing the other.' She paused, then went on reflectively, 'It seems odd to me even now, that my father, instead of reacting against the condemnation of society, came to see himself as others saw him. I can still hear him saying each morning, "we have left undone those things we ought to have done, we have done those things we ought not to have done, and there is no health in us." He was a puritan; he tried his best to impress upon me the doctrine of original sin. I remember saying to him once that if marriage was only a means of avoiding burning, if the highest ideal was life-long chastity, then it seemed to me that if we Christians were to live up to our beliefs, it would be race suicide. He said that since the evil of the world far outweighed the good, that was the logical conclusion. He remarked a few minutes later that my own existence was an indisputable proof of God's opinion on the subject.'

'What did he mean by that?' asked Mary, looking puzzled.

'That He deliberately contrived to make the punishment of adultery more severe than any other, by visiting the sins of the father upon the child.'

Mary said slowly, 'I've always admired you, but now I think you're simply unbelievable. How on earth have you managed to emerge from all that, not only sane, but saner than any of us?'

'With any kind of logical mind at all, it would have been pretty difficult for me to escape the realization that virtue and convention ... goodness, if you like ... have at least an immeasurably negative value. Just wait until you're stripped of both!'

'Did he blame you, or only himself?' Mary asked, turning to glance out of the window at the falling snow.

'I think it would have taken a heroic character not to blame me. After all, he'd have stayed in the university and married the girl he loved, if I hadn't upset the apple cart by turning up after seven years, during which he had tried very hard to straighten out his life. It mightn't have taken him so long if he hadn't had a puritan upbringing. But he had, so it *did* take those seven years, during which my mother and I wandered around the North American continent, for him to forget the mud in which he had wallowed ... for him to clean himself up a little. Then we walked in the door, and I think that same evening he allowed himself to slip back over all the ground he'd gained since he last saw us. At any rate, the door that closed behind my mother when she went out was never really opened again. For thirteen years we remained behind it, watching ordinary people go by in the street. Yet, perhaps through loneliness, and perhaps partly because he was resolved to do what he could for me, he kept me with him fairly constantly, and did his best for me, according to his lights. I remember one time he read me a description of the things they did to illegitimate children during the Inquisition. It was supposed to be an extract from Merekowski's *Leonardo*, and it wasn't until a long time afterwards when I could bring myself to read the book, that I found there was nothing about illegitimate children in it. You can see for yourself something in his character by that; you can imagine the state he was in by then ... the state that a man with a good mind such as his would *have* to be in before he could sit in a chair and read ... or rather fabricate ... such horrible things for the spiritual benefit of his small daughter.'

She seemed to Mary to be preoccupied, as though each thing she said, even as she said it, brought up a train of ideas to be followed and sorted out in her mind. Mary was anxious to make up for her lapse into obvious horror, for her silly remarks about conventions and traffic signals ... and she continued to prompt her. 'What happened after your mother left you there?'

She was looking through the window into the outer world again, as she said, shifting her position on the drawing table, 'He did nothing for ten years but study. He tutored me himself. I was harshly disciplined, mentally and physically. I was ready for university at fifteen, but he wouldn't let me go.' She ran one hand over her dark hair, and tried once more to smooth out the tense muscles in her forehead; her head was aching badly now. 'I never went to school. He taught me mathematics, a certain amount of science ... I think he was disappointed that my brain was not very scientific; geology was about the only subject in that group I ever did very well ... he taught me Latin and Greek and German, a good deal of history, a certain amount of archaeology, and a considerable amount of Mlle Dupraix's "Beaux Arts."' She paused a moment, then said with sudden enthusiasm, 'Here's something that might interest you. It isn't fair to him to give a one-sided picture of him, and I sometimes think that I wouldn't exchange that training ... that mental development ... even for a more balanced psychological environment. We really had a lot of fun. For example ... we did Plato, Socrates, Leibnitz, Nietzsche, and Kant, beginning when I was about fourteen ... coming to them through a good many others, of course. Anyhow, when I was about nineteen we started in on the English Empiricists, and then we really began to have a thoroughly good time together. My father is, as you can see for yourself, an utter empiricist. His judgement of everything is based on the proof of experience. Mine isn't. Anyhow, we started off with John Locke, and from then on had some of the best arguments I ever expect to have with anyone.'

'I suppose,' said Mary, 'that you read Plato in Greek at fourteen.'

'Yes. That's not so extraordinary when you consider that I had no playmates, so there was never anything else to do but work. Besides that, it was not such an uncommon thing up to the sixteenth or seventeenth century. I grant you that my upbringing is fairly weird for the twentieth century, but there'd have been nothing extraordinary about it in A.D. 1100.'

'But this,' said Mary, 'is not A.D. 1100, so you must forgive me if it seems a little odd, to say the least of it. What was your aunt like ... the one who left you enough to escape on?'

'She was a great deal older than my father ... my grandfather married twice, once at twenty-two and a second time at sixty-one, so you can see there was quite a gap between the two families! She was one of those women who should marry and have children, but men being the idiots they are, and because she didn't do embroidery or have a pretty face, but, on the other hand was wise, tolerant and scholarly, no one wanted her ... or rather, no one whom she respected very much wanted her. She tried very hard to adopt me, but my father, for reasons best known to himself, wouldn't give me up, so she came to Toronto and contented herself with doing what she could. My father hated his whole family for obvious reasons, but he allowed me to go to her house for tea once or twice a month. She was able to counterbalance a certain amount of what was really bad in my upbringing.'

'Was it she who taught you music?'

'No. My father. He loves music. He used to take me to concerts; we'd sit in the back row of the top gallery, getting there late and leaving early. Music acted on him the way drink does on some people ... a brief period of tremendous stimulation, and then black depression. He'd never let me go to bed when we got home, he always wanted to talk. We'd arrive at the house, go into the living room, he'd poke up the fire and I would sit, waiting for him to say something, rocking with fatigue. At last he'd begin to talk ... about the structure of St. Sophia or the Blue Mosque; whether or not the Basque people were of Celtic origin; whether or not their language *did* belong to the Ural-Altaic group ... everything, anything, on and on. Sometimes I wouldn't get to bed until three or four in the morning, but I had to be up at seven anyhow. My father never slept more than four or five hours a night; he said most people wasted far too much time sleeping, and that was all anyone needed.'

'Vicky ...' said Mary after another brief silence.

'Yes?'

'Don't you ever feel sorry for yourself ... don't you ever think that it's all ... well, rather unjust, to say the least of it?'

'No,' she said, looking surprised. 'Why should I? One doesn't expect justice from life ... it's the function of human beings to put it there, and I don't feel that my particular initial disadvantage has anything to do with God. If I did, then I should certainly be most unhappy ... but I don't. You see, I *am* very religious.'

Mary said doubtfully, 'I don't understand you. If you really were very religious, you'd believe that, even if it were not His responsibility, at least it was to Him that you should appeal for help.'

'For help? But it hasn't anything to do with Him! It's *my* problem ... the problem of society, if you like, but not His. What has He got to do with ugliness and evil? Nothing. I don't blame this on anyone; if I did I should be compromising in everything I believe. My whole scheme of things would have to be torn down and erected again on a basis which would certainly be rather egocentric, if nothing else. You see, I really believe in those three absolutes, those attributes of God, if you like. Their importance seems to be borne out by the evidence of past civilizations ... those that were purely material, those which were ugly, and those in which evil predominated, have all gone and left almost nothing behind them. Other aspects of life, except in so far as they contribute something to those three, are transient, negative if you like.'

And a moment later, as Mary said nothing, but continued to look uncomprehending, 'I know I don't explain this very well, because naturally it's not very clear to me. It's only something that I feel. I'm a very ordinary human being, with no exceptional talents.'

'Hasn't anything ever turned you upside down? Confused you, shaken you, almost destroyed your peace of mind?'

'Yes,' she said quietly. 'And again something quite ordinary ... a man,' she added. In answer to Mary's inquiring look she flushed slightly and went on, seeing that she expected something further, 'I was in love with him. He got fed up with me and went in search of a warmer climate.' She paused, then remarked in a carefully controlled voice, 'I suppose it threw me off centre rather more than it would have if I'd been used to ... being actively happy. I wasn't used to that ... my life has been ... I don't know how to describe it ... you might say "passively happy" which is different. I don't suppose you can quite imagine how entirely free of the ... little things which are so nice ... how free of them my life has been. I mean my ... my aunt ... was always ... glad that I was alive ... but apart from her, I was alone. I mean "alone" in the sense that I lived quite literally by myself. After she died, I might just as well have been on a desert island, so far as loving other people and being loved in return were concerned.'

Mary said, her voice trembling, 'Then everything which the normal person distributes among a dozen or more relatives, friends, and small love affairs, must have gone into that one person. How terrible, Vicky.'

'Well, it was the only time in my life that I felt like saying to God, "Really, this is a bit excessive. Aren't You going to let me have anything?" But I got over that, after a little while. One shouldn't try to make up for a lifetime in a short period. I expect,' she added lightly, 'that the super-saturation rather got on his nerves. I don't blame him. It must have been rather like the Sorcerer's Apprentice returning home with the river instead of just a bucket full of water. I think he was essentially the sort of man who preferred love in small doses ... not much at a time, but frequently, with changes to make it more interesting. I am not that sort of woman. I don't mean that I wept all over him or anything, but all my life I've loved beauty ... the truth and the goodness come to me through it, I'm afraid ... and my morality is based on that. When it was all finished, I realized that, like my father, I had not chosen the beautiful, and because I'd tried for so long, so very hard, to do just that ... it was pretty awful. Then, because I loved him, my life was full to overflowing, as it had never been before, and for the first time in my life I agreed with Spinoza,' she added, half smiling. 'I perceived that I was a bit young to exist entirely upon the fruits of philosophy.'

Mary was not deceived by the bantering manner. She continued to sit motionless on the windowsill, watching Vicky's face. Once more it was impossible to tell what she was feeling. There was no suggestion of emotion in her face, only that lovely quality of stillness, of passion and spirituality, which was unforgettable. Mary said at last, 'Then you've gone through what I've been through ... only you've come out on top. I haven't. You make me feel rather small ... because that brief interlude must have meant more to you, and taken more away from you when it ended, than most people would realize.'

Vicky said quickly, 'I suppose my intellect has the ascendance and the greater power over me. Except for a while after the man I loved left me, it has always been able to maintain a balance. I can remember so many times when I was utterly sick at heart during my childhood ... up to the time I left, in fact ... when the sterile unhappiness which pervaded every corner of that house would eat into my soul. Even at the worst of times, though, something could always pull me out of it ... Bach, Shakespeare, Montaigne. That sounds hopelessly academic, doesn't it? But it's not, it's the opposite. Through their minds we come closer to reality and to God, sometimes.'

She looked at Mary again, wondering how she could live without alternatives, without anything which had its origin in her mind, was revitalized by contact with other minds, and could sustain her through emotional havoc. If all you were, all your hope and your faith was poured into something as risky as a human being, and that human being let you down, what did you have left? Nothing, apparently.

Mary said hopelessly, 'This beastly winter looks as though it would last forever,' then went on with sudden intensity, 'Vicky, I'm so afraid. Everything I think about Barry now has a ... a dying fall. If I could only make myself believe that some day he'd be back ...' She got up from the windowsill and began to walk about the room again. Her voice came from behind Vicky a moment later, saying, 'If I could only see myself anywhere but here, in the future,' almost as though she were talking to herself.

Vicky slid round so that she was facing Mary, and said, 'What makes you think there's been another woman since the last time you saw him?'

'I don't know. But if I see him again, I'll know the very first minute ... and if he has done it again, I won't be able to bear it. You see, I did manage the first time, because going on alone, not as his wife but as the person who had been created by that marriage, who was alone for the first time, was ... not exactly interesting ... but ... Oh, I don't know how to put it. Then, slowly, I went back to identifying myself with him. You don't know how much I do that ...' She stopped, looked at Vicky, and saw that she did know. 'You must think I'm a fool, Vick. But you see, I was married very young. My father was in the Air Force, mad about flying and really not much interested in anything else. So far as I was concerned, he never came down to earth at all! Stephen, my brother ... there were just the two of us ... was ten years older than I. He inherited all my father's passion for speed and mobility. He eventually got himself killed in a smash at Brooklands,' she added quite matter-of-factly.

Vicky said, looking beyond her at a photograph of Mont St. Michel, 'You must have grown up almost as much alone as I.'

'No, because I was at boarding school most of the time. In the summers I used to go to Dieppe with a family of cousins, so I had plenty of companionship. But it wasn't, any of it, the sort of companionship which provides any intellectual stimulus. That's what I'm trying to get at. I was just a very ordinary middle-class English girl, healthy, bouncing, and fond of games, until I met my husband. My mental development, if any,' she interjected wryly, 'all took place after my marriage, so that there was no important aspect of my life which he hadn't touched upon ... more than that, really. No important aspect which he hadn't ... planted, tended, and helped along. When he left, he took almost everything there was of me with him. Husbands and wives should have their separate interests, if only to provide for such emergencies!'

'As a form of insurance,' said Vicky, almost inaudibly.

'Yes. Well, I had just managed to pull myself together and ... integrate the old Mary, the person who was largely my husband, and the new who was a combination of both, when he telephoned me, and against my will, at the very sound of his voice, I was pitched back to where I had been when he left me. I began to include him again. I found myself now mentally referring to him for an opinion, thinking about him consciously or unconsciously all the time. The idea of him is always there, in the back of my mind. I catch myself at odd moments ... halfway downstairs, opening a door, watching a hockey match, waiting for change in a shop ... and realize that my mind's only half on what I'm doing ... the other half seems to be saying his name, trying to visualize him, and ... more than either of those two things ... constantly imagining the happiness of being with him again. Daydreaming, if you like. *That's* what makes me different from other women here. They think, poor things, that it's because I have an independent income ...'

'Because ever since they can remember, and as far as they can see into the future, everything they do and everything they want to do but can't, comes down to money.'

'Yes ... but we need men just as much as we need money.'

'Possibly,' said Vicky, still looking critically at Mont St. Michel. 'Sex and money are rather alike, though. Both of them have terrific negative importance.'

'If you're going to generalize again,' said Mary warningly, 'I shan't listen.'

'I'm not,' she said hastily. And looking at Mary again, 'You wouldn't ever resemble Fräulein Lange, and Mlle Devaux et al, though, Mary.'

Mary was back at the north windows again, looking down into the snow-filled courtyard. 'Yes, I would!' she answered passionately. 'There's something sterile and static about a school, something that creeps into you and changes you without your knowing it. Eventually the place comes to stand between you and the uncomfortable business of living and adapting yourself to others. In a school, you don't have to adapt yourself, because it's so easy to make others adapt themselves to you.'

She relaxed and sank down on the windowsill again, while Vicky continued to look at her anxiously. 'And of course I'll stay, if my daydreams come to nothing. Not for any of those reasons ... they'll come later! ... but because here is something tangible, something difficult to do, something to set my teeth in, something to hold on to, to steady myself. Then after a while I'll grow older and begin to shirk in little things, and forget all about the silly, idealistic person I am now. Why that girl in 1934 and 1935 actually worried about Cay Shaunessy and Truda Meyer ... how absurd and childish of her! Stamp out their oddities, make them conform, make them uniform so that they cease to possess this awkward individuality, so that they're all alike on the surface at least ... as similar as loaves of bread. Supposing they're different underneath, supposing each one has her tragedies, her troubles, her own problems ... provided they don't bother *me*, what difference does it make? *That* will be my idea in ten years, and when I look back on myself, as I am now, I'll ... oh, it will be a case of

> *Gently she tombs the poor dim last time*
> *Strews pinkish dust above*
> *And sighs, 'The dear dead girlish pastime!*
> *But this ... ah, God! ... is ...'*

a really sensible point of view!'

Vicky threw back her head and laughed, then she said

meditatively, 'You and Mlle Tourain have exactly contrary points of view. I wonder which of you is right? Both, I suppose, according to your desires and ideals. You think this place is static and sterile, a half-world filled with shadowy people ... a wayside station, withdrawn from the world and from reality. She thinks it's a noisy, clattering, confusing microcosm, a kind of local Times Square and Piccadilly Circus. Unfortunately, she doesn't want life, though, she wants a little vacuum all her own in which to think and ponder on the lessons of history.'

'She's approaching sixty,' Mary pointed out.

Vicky shrugged. 'That hasn't much to do with it. Put her beside most of the twenty-year-olds here ... the Andersons, the Cummings-Gordons, Rose, Henriette, almost anyone, in fact ... and they pale into nothing beside her immense vitality, her strength, and her enthusiasm. As for Isabelle Lemaitre ... she has lived avidly, passionately, generously ... at fifty-odd she's dying, but she's had more fun out of sheer living than most other people, men and women who are husbands, wives, parents, and who in general fulfil their existences more completely ... in the conventional sense ... than she. It is an impertinence for the world to assume so smugly that unmarried women are to be pitied, as though the mere state of matrimony conferred blessings otherwise not to be experienced by spinsters. I think probably those who have not known love ... in its highest and richest form, the form in which it is pervaded by all the wisdom and experience which the two people have ... garnered ... during their lives, the form in which it is a blend and a harmony of passion and spirituality ... have missed *that* chance at greatness. But do the average husband and wife ever know intense happiness? Look at their faces as you see them at the movies, in tubes, in railway trains, in shops, and waiting for buses. Then look at Isabelle Lemaitre. All you learn from the two is that an outpouring of the spirit, an escape from the close confines of one's individuality is essential to a full life. Most people know that instinctively, and because love for another human being is the easiest and most obvious answer, they marry. Or they fall in love. Or both.'

'That's a rather peculiar way of looking at it,' said Mary. 'You think Mlle Lemaitre and the average wife are doing the same thing; in different ways each one is seeking an outlet.'

'There's no comparison between her and the average woman. Look at her face! Oh, I don't mean her poor nose, her chin, or her complexion ... but what there is in that face that charms you, and moves you, and gives you brief glimpses of what life may mean to you, if you're lucky. So might Héloïse have looked at fifty-four ... Incidentally, I wonder what she did look like? Abélard, I think, was rather like Delius.'

'Would you mind very much,' said Mary rather wearily, 'staying on the point for a while?'

'I *am* on the point,' she said without annoyance. 'I know that for you, with all your idealism and your simplicity, you will only love one man, give yourself, everything that you are, have been, or ever will be, just that once. I suppose your husband will be in possession of you as long as he lives ... perhaps that's a kind of punishment God inflicts on those of us who are so stupid as not to value what we have. But what I'm trying to say is that there's no real reason for you to cease growing outward, as though love were the only outlet for your individuality. It's because we think of marriage and babies as a *sine qua non* of a full life, that so many of us ... like the women in this school, just give up when men pass them by. I grant you that it's the easiest, that it's the most obvious ... perhaps it is also the most perfect ... that's what *I* have to discover too ... but it's still not the only way. That's all,' she added with finality, thinking that Mary expected something more.

'It sounds very simple,' said Mary. 'It's what's called "sublimation," isn't it?'

Vicky wrinkled up her nose. 'Yes, but that word has a holier than thou connotation which annoys me. As though the two things were necessarily alternatives, and sublimation the better of the two. It's not. I think it's probably the less desirable.' She paused a moment, then said suddenly, 'What time is it?'

'A quarter to twelve.'

'Then that leaves me fifteen minutes for Rosalie. It should have been the other way round ... fifteen minutes for you and me, and three-quarters of an hour for Rosalie.'

'Why? Is she ... so much more important?' asked Mary, looking a little hurt.

'I think so.'

'Why?'

'Because where you and I are battling with difficulties, she is struggling with a tragedy not of her own making; while you and I are trying to decide what to do with our lives, she is dying.' Her voice had dropped very low again. She was looking fixedly at the falling snow as she went on, 'I think I'll rush over it. You'll have to try to understand; you'll have to use a lot of imagination ... but even if I said a great deal and talked for hours, you'd either grasp it emotionally and intuitively, almost immediately, or you never would, though I might write whole books about it for you.' She paused again, then asked unexpectedly, 'Do you know anything about Roman Catholic psychology?'

'A little,' she said, looking surprised.

'Anything of the patience, the quality of endurance, and the long, timeless upward view which is inbred in some Catholics?'

'Yes,' she said quietly. 'Something that I knew and understood better through knowing Rosalie ... because I sensed it; you can't help sensing it, really, unless you're very intellectual in your approach to things ... than if I'd read all the books you might write on the subject.'

Vicky glanced at her, nodded, then went on quickly and unemotionally as though that were sufficient assurance that Mary would understand, 'Rosalie's mother is a Catholic ... a French-Canadian, of course ... but without the strength and intellect required to live up to the best in her Church. Her father, curiously enough, is a Scotch Presbyterian ... *his* father having been French Huguenot, hence the name Garcenot, and his mother, Rosalie's paternal grandmother, a Mc-something or other from Edinburgh. There are, it seems to me, at least two totally different kinds of devout Catholic ... those who are purely emotional, so that certain aspects of their religion verge on superstition, and those, equally devout, who love the Church for its scholasticism, its intellectual supremacy, its profoundly human wisdom. Madame Garcenot, needless to state, is in the first category, only unfortunately, though she hasn't enough wit to get into the second, she has too much to stay firmly put in the first.'

'Is she at all like Rosalie?'

'Not in the least. Rosalie has spent all her life, until a year ago, in a convent. Consequently she has ... or had ... the perfect devotion and obedience to her religion which I suppose only comes through unquestioning faith, or from a faith which has questioned everything, and yet arrives back at the point it started from ... a faith based on supreme ignorance, or based on great knowledge ... however you want to put it. Well, anyhow, Madame Garcenot fell in love with a Parisian, head of the Montreal branch of a French fur company. She then attempted to adapt her religion to the life she led with her lover, and since her religion isn't awfully adaptable, she didn't succeed. Shortly after Rosalie's fifteenth birthday her mother's amant was recalled to Paris; Garcenot père left on a business trip to the west, and taking advantage of his absence, she eloped, taking her young daughter along too.'

'But why?' demanded Mary in astonishment.

'Because she's weak ... like a lot of other people, she had to have her cake and eat it. I think, in some obscure way, she hoped to prove to God that though she might be a bad wife, she was still a devoted mother. She couldn't have done it to Rosalie if she really *had* been a devoted mother, of course.'

'But that's absurd,' said Mary, sitting on the floor with her back to the wall on the left of Vicky's window, and looking up at her with a puzzled expression. 'I should think she'd have left Rosalie in her convent as salve for her conscience.'

'I don't think it's as simple as that.' She picked up a pencil from the clutter behind her on the table, and began to draw a series of parallel lines on the worn, dark wood. 'She's a very vain woman, and an egoist. I think most people who do unconventional things, unless they do them from some sincere and profound conviction, are vain or egotistical at bottom, in their evident belief that they are different from others. Not that that has much to do with Madame Garcenot ... her vanity showed itself in a different way. I've an idea that the real reason behind, was her inability to face the prospect of Rosalie's being told by others that her mother had fallen from grace, of Rosalie being instructed by the sisters to pray for her mother's soul, and informed that one day she must try to make Madame Garcenot return to the Church.'

'Did the three of them go to Paris?' asked Mary.

'Yes, and there, with quite remarkable dullness of perception, she tried to give Rosalie, fresh from a convent and not yet sixteen, bewildered and lonely as she was, a ... a point of view which would not force Rosalie to condemn her mother. I mean that what Madame Garcenot did was to try and modernize Rosalie almost overnight. She took her about to restaurants, shops and theatres, and generally introduced her to gaiety. It was a rotten form of self-justification.' She was again speaking in that detached and unemotional way which Mary found so unnerving.

'She's a stupid woman,' Vicky added coldly, a little later. 'When she went to Paris, Rosalie knew less than nothing about life. We don't either at that age, all these reports of sophistication and precocity to the contrary, but she ... when she was suddenly uprooted, taken away from her convent ...' Vicky paused, looking upward, her face drawn and strained. She sighed a moment later, and went on, 'I know that place; it's a very old building in Sherbrooke Street, which is a street of old, grey buildings. There's a stone wall around it, with lilacs and fruit trees showing over the top. Everything within those walls *is* religion ... I think it must sometimes seem to the girls and women there that the whole convent is rocked in a cradle by God, for the feeling of peace and serene faith is so pervasive ... pervasive,' she repeated, still drawing lines on the table. 'You could imagine St. Francis of Assisi walking in the garden there, and neither time nor distance can quite make an idea like that absurd.'

'Yes, I know,' said Mary. She was ill at ease again, for Vicky's mind was in many aspects quite alien to her own. 'What happened to Rosalie? Why is she here?'

'She followed her mother and the man about from theatre to theatre and restaurant to restaurant for more than six months. I don't know what she thought about, except that she longed for her convent in Montreal, for that life which made sense while this did not, and which drew steadily farther and farther away from her as time passed. Her religion was so enveloping that none of her mother's veiled hints, subtleties and almost open statements got through to her. So that what happened in the end was a shock which was really horrible ... a shock such as neither you nor I could ever have, because we're too much in this world, too conscious of everything that happens to us for something to hit us suddenly, without any warning at all. I mean that fortuitous, irrelevant or cataclysmic events don't occur ... or occur so rarely that it doesn't affect us. Because we're unobservant and keyed to our environments, we see signs of future trouble, here and there, in odd and apparently disconnected things so that when the disaster comes, we're at least subconsciously half-prepared for it. Things don't suddenly come at us like a bomb from nowhere, unless we're remarkably obtuse and insensitive. Anyone else would have sensed something, but Rosalie had been jerked from her convent and thrown among people who wore odd clothes, who ate queer food, who spoke her language with an unfamiliar accent, who drank strange things, and said even stranger things, who danced, and swore, and never mentioned God or Christ except in blasphemy. It was all so completely alien to her that she didn't take it in at all. If there had been any similarity between present and past experience, it would have acted as an entering wedge, but there was none. You see, until they went to Paris, she had hardly even known her mother.'

Mary saw at last the emotion which she had sought in Vicky's face as she talked about her own distorted background, which she had sought there when talking about herself and her husband, and failed to find. It was there now, a look of suffering in the tense muscles around her eyes and mouth as she talked about Rosalie, the one human being with whom, Mary thought, Vicky was really involved. 'Everyone in the school knows that there's something on Rosalie's mind, something beyond a bad heart, anaemia, and homesickness ... something fatal. I think she's beyond help now. She won't even talk to her confessor.'

'But why doesn't Garcenot take his daughter away? Has he lost all interest in her?'

'He's probably thinking it's about time she was put in a Protestant boarding school. The Scotch Presbyterian mind has absolutely no conception of Catholicism ... I don't suppose that Rosalie and her father are intelligible to one another for more than five minutes at a time. Besides that, Mr. Garcenot is in the somewhat dubious and shaky position of one who deliberately closes his mind to the truth and chooses false doctrine, so far as Rosalie is concerned. He must have known that that was what she thought, and it would rankle him, to say the least.'

'But if you think she's going to die, Vicky, something has *got* to be done ...' said Mary straining forward impatiently.

'Mlle Tourain has asked Garcenot to take her away. So far he hasn't answered her.'

'Where's her mother?'

'On a cruise in the Mediterranean. No one knows just where.'

'Was there one specific thing? You said something about a shock, a moment ago. What was it?'

Vicky answered slowly, removing every trace of emotion from her voice. 'Rosalie was wandering about their apartment in Paris one hot night last summer, and she saw something which whatever deity there is who cares for lonely, innocent young girls, should have prevented her from seeing.' She looked down at the pencil in her hand while Mary stared at her. 'Well,' said Vicky, looking out into the world beyond the window again, 'That's what Rosalie thinks about. She doesn't want to live. She wants to escape from her body which was created in sin; she wants to escape from life because all life is rooted in carnality, and she desires no more of it.'

'Why haven't you told Mlle Tourain that?'

'Because,' she said quietly, 'I think Rosalie should be allowed to die in peace.'

'You think Rosalie should be allowed to die in peace?' repeated Mary incredulously. 'How *can* you think that? Vicky, are you mad?' she asked in horror. 'You ... you think she's dying ... you know it, in fact, and you take the responsibility for it. How can you, Vicky? You're ... you're doing something wicked ... you're answering for the life of another human being ...'

Vicky's face was impassive as she said, 'Quite. You see I'm inclined to agree with the man who said that we overestimate the sanctity of human life. Merely living isn't enough. She is, now, so far off the truth that no one can bring her back, no one but God. If He does it, she'll live; if He doesn't, she'll die. Either way,' she added, maintaining her low, steady tone of voice with great difficulty, 'would be right. No other way. What could we do for her?'

'I don't know. What have you done?' Mary asked more calmly now.

'I've ... only ... loved her. That was all I could do. Lately she's learned how to slip from consciousness ... or from what we think is consciousness ... into another world. If you speak to her suddenly she starts, and a look of physical pain crosses her face, only fading away very slowly.' Vicky was struggling to prevent herself from crying now. She searched for her handkerchief with one hand and went on, her voice shaking, 'There are some words which Odile in *Climats* keeps repeating ... "fatalement condamnée" ... "fatalement condamnée" ... fatally condemned ... I feel that about her. I didn't mean ... a moment ago ... that I was not ... trying ... but, you see, it's beyond me, and I don't feel that I have ... any right. There's nothing I can do but love her, and it's ... not ... enough.'

VII

Vicky sat through the first half of lunch in a state of abstraction, replying rather absent-mindedly when anyone asked her a question. Her face still looked drawn; she had been even more upset than she had expected by that conversation with Mary. For the first time she had put into words something which she had felt, half believed and feared for the past few weeks ... that Rosalie would really die. Vicky was unable to visualize any future for her; all those incidents which she had described to Mary, everything in the girl's past, led nowhere but toward her final destruction.

She became aware of Natalia's full, throaty voice asking impatiently, 'Why did we all behave like that to poor Ilse this morning? All of us staring at her as though she were a criminal in the dock ... I have never been so ashamed of myself!'

'That sort of thing often happens,' said Yasha calmly. 'I mean, if you stop in the street and stare fixedly at something, you'll have a whole crowd collected round you staring fixedly too, in just a few moments. Besides that, Ilse was so obviously terrified that some of us at least looked at her out of sheer surprise.'

Vicky glanced across to the next table where Ilse was sitting listening to some remarks of Miss Williams, smiling and nodding politely at the Englishwoman, but plainly very nervous. Vicky frowned anxiously, wondering how she could manage to see Ilse some time during the afternoon. There was also Truda, and Anna who was being kept in bed much against her will by Mlle Dupraix, and dosed with the inevitable cups of camomile tea. And there was Rosalie, all alone upstairs but for the efficient, unimaginative practical nurse whom Mlle Tourain had engaged to look after her. Vicky sank once more into her abstracted mood and remained oblivious to what was going on about her until Mlle Tourain's voice, speaking her name harshly, caused her to start and stand up with a bewildered look across the room at the headmistress. What was this?

Mlle Tourain cleared her throat and rapped on her glass, an action which she instantly realized was unnecessary, for the room was already silent. She raised her eyes for a moment, looked at Vicky irritably, and said without preamble, 'It has come to my notice that you have been bringing cigarettes into the school. Is that true?'

'No, Mademoiselle,' she answered immediately.

There was an indescribable sound of disbelief from Mlle Dupraix who turned in her chair at the foot of the headmistress's table so that she could look at Vicky more easily, and said with elaborate politeness, 'You must excuse me for contradicting you, but I am under the impression that I saw an unopened package in your purse day before yesterday. Possibly I am mistaken, Vicky?'

Vicky said nothing for a moment. She had bought some for Cissie Anderson on Wednesday afternoon, a fact which had completely slipped her mind a moment before. She was aware of Cissie's studied indifference at the next table, and half-smiled to herself. Her glance moved to Mary's angry face, then made a swift tour round the room and returned to Mlle Dupraix. Her face and her voice were quiet; she made a little gesture of apology with one hand and said quickly to the headmistress ... she had no intention of allowing this to develop into an argument between herself and Mlle Dupraix ... 'I beg your pardon, Mlle Tourain. I did bring some in with me. I happened to have them since my last weekend.'

'That was three weeks ago was it not, Vicky?' the Beaux Arts mistress cut in. She looked triumphantly at Mlle Tourain, then turned to Vicky again. 'And it was an unopened package, I believe.'

What *was* all this? To bring cigarettes into the school was not an offence unless you smoked them there. They must be having her up on the off-chance of proving indirectly that she had smoked them though they had not caught her at it, by asking her to produce them. Which, she thought, would be somewhat awkward because she had given them to Cissie and she had not the slightest idea where, in the Andersons' room, they were to be found. If, indeed, there were any left.

She said, trying to control her sudden spasm of nervousness by telling herself that even though this was an additional count against her, they could not expel her for it, 'Mlle Tourain knows that I do not smoke ... in the school,' she added as an after-thought, remembering her statement that they had been left over from her weekend three weeks before. She glanced down with a faint smile at Theodora who was making almost audible noises of fury at this grilling of her Vicky.

'I'm afraid that's a little difficult to believe,' said Mlle Dupraix, glancing at the headmistress with a smile which showed a certain amount of satisfaction.

'I assure you, Mlle Dupraix ...' began Vicky unwillingly.

'My dear, you might assure me that water is wet, and ice cold to the touch, and I should not believe you ...'

Theodora's self-control gave way. She shoved her chair back and ignoring Vicky's look of alarm, burst out, 'No, of course you wouldn't. Liars never do believe other people. I wouldn't admit a thing like that if I were you!'

'Sit down, Theodora!' said Mlle Tourain through clenched teeth.

'I will not sit down!' she said furiously. 'Now I've started I might just as well be hung for a sheep as a lamb anyway, and it's time someone told you what that woman is doing to Vicky! She comes into her room without knocking at all hours of the day and night; she hammers and hammers at her, trying to trip her into saying something about her past life; she takes her records away from her, drops them on the floor and breaks them and then doesn't have the guts to tell her. You listen to me, Mlle Dupraix, if I catch you in Vicky's room again, you'd better send for the police because once I get started on you there won't be much ...'

'*Sit down*, Theodora!' thundered the headmistress, half-rising in her chair.

Vicky turned round. 'Yes, *please* Teddy. Don't you see you're making everything much worse?'

'All right,' she muttered, and subsided into her chair. The entire school was staring at her aghast. She jabbed a fork into her salad, still shaking with rage.

'You will leave this school as soon as your mother can come to get you; in the meantime you will remain within the grounds,' said Mlle Tourain coldly.

'A fine person I'd be if I just sat here for fear someone would jump on me, and let that woman get away with saying anything she wanted to my best friend,' said Theodora under her breath in English.

Mlle Tourain took a sip of water, struggling to regain her self-control, surprised to find that she was as angry with Mlle Dupraix as she was with Theodora. She glanced across the room at Vicky, who looked really upset for the first time since the headmistress had known her, and felt a totally inexplicable wave of affection for the young, dark-haired girl sweep over her. Of all the curious, unprecedented emotions she had experienced during the last twenty-four hours, this was the strangest and the most unhappy, for she knew that Vicky would have to go. She said quietly and very seriously, 'Then you admit having brought cigarettes into the school, after first denying it, but you do not admit having smoked them, is that it?'

'Oui, Mademoiselle.' She was completely unnerved by the whole scene, following as it did upon that conversation with Mary in the art room. Too much had happened, too much had altered or changed, during the past day. She knew, instinctively, that these chaotic events were bringing her time at the school to a close. She bit her lip, then said with more feeling than anyone in the room but Mary and Theodora had ever heard in her voice before, so that once more they all turned to stare, 'Mlle Tourain, I have never in my life lied in order to save myself from anything ...'

'I believe you, Vicky,' she said simply. 'Sit down and go on with your lunch.'

Mlle Dupraix looked at the headmistress, then at Vicky across the room, then back at the headmistress again, with astonishment, and contempt. 'One moment, Mlle Tourain. Since I began this discussion, I think it only fair that you should allow me to prove my case ...'

Mlle Tourain looked down the table at her and said in a very low voice so that only the half-dozen girls between them could hear, 'Mlle Dupraix, you have not yet been installed as head-mistress.'

'I thought you prided yourself on a sense of justice,' she said, her face flushing.

'I do. It frequently happens that in order to be just to one, you must be unjust to another, so in this case I am allowing Vicky the benefit of the doubt. Not only that, but I do not wish this scene prolonged ...'

'Tell her to get those cigarettes,' said Mlle Dupraix, leaning forward suddenly. 'Then everyone in this room will be as convinced as yourself. I am so certain she is making a fool of you again, as she has so often made a fool of you and the rest of us before, that I should be willing to leave this school tonight if I am mistaken.'

'Mlle Dupraix, I must ask you to let this subject drop until later!'

She shook her head, half-smiling. Her expression said plainly, 'No, you don't get out of it as easily as that.' She looked at the headmistress for a moment in silence, as though she were weighing the odds, then turned in her chair, and said, 'Go and get those cigarettes, Vicky. Get them now.'

Vicky stood up. She looked at the headmistress who returned her look for a moment, then dropped her eyes. Amélie Tourain could do nothing, and the Beaux Arts teacher knew it. At last she had the headmistress where she wanted her, knowing as she did that Mlle Tourain would not tolerate a public difference of opinion between two members of the staff. The morale of the school would be even more badly shaken if she and Mlle Dupraix were to argue with each other now. The Beaux Arts teacher was banking on that, as she banked on the headmistress's determination to put up with anything rather than risk upsetting Jeanne d'Ormonde lying very ill across the lake in Evian, by dismissing her. She was the sort of human being who goes through life profiting by the goodness of others, the headmistress thought wearily. Perhaps goodness was not the right word; it was rather that she took advantage of those who refused to take advantage for themselves. So she had Amélie Tourain in this deadlock, knowing that she would not risk a loss of prestige among those in authority, knowing that the headmistress would not protest beyond a certain point.

She raised her eyes to Vicky's face again, gave a barely perceptible little nod of acquiescence to the Beaux Arts teacher's order, then dropped her eyes to her plate once more. She heard the door close behind Vicky and waited anxiously for her return, glancing briefly at Mlle Dupraix from time to time.

A little later she looked toward the door; that girl was taking an uncommonly long time to find her cigarettes. Mlle Tourain's eyes wandered to Mlle Lemaitre, whose habitual feverish flush was intensified now by her impatience with the weak-willed headmistress; from Mlle Lemaitre to Miss Williams who looked very distressed, from Miss Williams to Mary Ellerton, almost beside herself with anger, from Miss Ellerton to Fräulein Lange, where they stopped. What *was* the matter with that woman? Was it still her sister? Why couldn't she realize that the welfare of forty-eight young human beings depended at least partly upon her self-control, her strength, and her self-assurance? If Fräulein Lange wished to become thoroughly useless, by fussing about her sister many miles away in Zürich, Fräulein Lange should resign. Besides that, what *was* there to fuss about, when you came right down to it? Heaven only knew how many women managed to survive this ordeal; heaven only knew how many millions of women there were in the world, with so little intelligence that they were willing to go on producing offspring with something like an ultimate intelligence of fourteen years or less, in order to populate a world where everyone was mad and few attained happiness.

Where was Vicky? Why didn't she come back with those cursed cigarettes?

The headmistress drew in her breath sharply, then let it escape in a long sigh. She was very tired; her back was aching badly, and every nerve, every muscle in her body seemed stretched beyond endurance. For the first time she wondered what it was like to be old; were the final years of life a long period of frustration during which one had to battle with ever-diminishing mental and physical powers? Soon she would have to summon sufficient strength to get up and walk from the room; in the meantime she sat rather limply, asking herself what could be keeping Vicky all this time if she had been telling the truth. She signalled to Marthe to remove the plates. The stewed fruit was served and eaten before the door opened, and Vicky was standing beside her.

Speaking in a voice pitched so low that Mlle Dupraix at the foot of the table could not catch what she was saying, 'I could not find them, Mlle Tourain, I don't know where I put them. I'm so sorry for all this.'

'You couldn't find them? But Vicky ... where are they, then? If you haven't ... smoked them ... they must be somewhere. You leave me no alternative but to ... not to ... believe you. Really, you can't lose a thing as easily as that ...'

Vicky said nothing, buttoning and unbuttoning her sleeve, completely shaken out of her former self-control. She could either let Mlle Tourain down, or let Cissie down. Of the two the headmistress was incomparably the stronger. Cissie must have been trembling with fear for the past half-hour, terrified that Vicky would give her away, drag her into the open, let everyone see her as she was, stare at her, point their fingers at her, speak of her derisively ... she, the oldest girl in the school ...

Mlle Tourain said suddenly, without warning, 'Whom are you doing this for, Vicky?'

'No one, Mademoiselle.'

'Are you sure?'

'Yes, Mlle Tourain,' she said, biting her lip again in an effort to steady it.

The headmistress looked down at her plate, 'You would be doing me a kindness if you could ...' She stopped, half-smiled, and went on, 'But I know you can't.' She looked up, and with her eyes on Mlle Dupraix who was staring at them, and straining forward in an unsuccessful attempt to hear what they said, she continued so quietly that her words were inaudible to everyone but Vicky, 'You see, I don't believe you. I can conceive of you doing almost anything, but not ... not hiding in a cupboard, or lying flat on the balcony floor, or wherever it is my girls do their nocturnal smoking. All the same, if you haven't got them ... so that the school will know ... you put me in a position which ...'

'I understand, Mlle Tourain,' she said quickly.

'You've done it before. I suppose, if you're given a chance, that you'll do it again. And I can't have it.' She did not look up to see how Vicky had taken that, but rapped on her glass and said in her normal voice with a return to her old rather harsh manner, 'You will not be allowed to go out on Saturday or Sunday for one month.'

Vicky returned to her table, and sat down ignoring the puzzled glances which came at her from all directions. She remarked after a brief silence, 'Teddy, I love you very much, but you're an ass.'

'I know it,' said Theodora penitently.

'Still, I suppose it's partly because you're an ass that I love you very much, so forget it.'

'That's the nearest you ever get to blaming anyone for anything, isn't it, Vicky?' remarked Natalia.

'Look carefully and you'll see the beginnings of a halo round my head,' said Vicky.

'You had no right, Theodora, to be so impertinent to Mlle Dupraix,' said Fräulein Lange, who was very troubled by the whole affair. 'You Americans have too little respect for authority. It's your individualism ... you think everyone's free and equal, and if Mlle Tourain or Mlle Dupraix can say something to you, you can say it to them. That is not true. Don't you realize what a muddle and confusion this school would be in if every girl talked to a member of the staff in the way you talked to Mlle Dupraix?'

'What state of muddle and confusion would this school be in if Mlle Dupraix talked to everyone the way she talks to Vicky?' demanded Theodora, but looked rather apologetic a moment later.

'For that matter, what state is it in now?' asked Yasha. 'Accusing Vicky of smoking! Everyone knows she doesn't smoke. Why didn't Mlle Tourain take her word for it ... why doesn't anyone of them ever take our word about anything?'

'It wasn't Mlle Tourain,' said Vicky. 'It was Mlle Dupraix. But let's drop the whole thing, shall we?'

'But as Yasha says, everyone knows you don't smoke!' said little Maria-Teresa Tucci from the foot of the table.

'Well, they're all just a little too clever,' she said irritably. 'I've been smoking for years, for all you may know. I don't see why it is that Mlle Tourain or Mlle Dupraix doesn't believe me when I say one thing, and you don't when I say another.' She looked round the table and went on with unusual emphasis, 'I deserved no less than I got, and you and the rest of the school ought to have the sense to see it. You'd think I was some kind of super-fatted angel the way you go on ... but I'm not. And I'm not such a good little darling that I have to be let off when it's perfectly obvious from the facts that I don't deserve to be let off. I was sent to get those cigarettes and I couldn't produce them. There-fore, I'd smoked them. Now, for goodness sake let's talk about something else.'

'Why did you deny having brought them in at the beginning?' Fräulein Lange asked curiously.

'I'd completely forgotten,' said Vicky. 'Really, I had.'

'You are funny in the head,' said Maria-Teresa. 'Pazza,' she added in explanation. 'I don't know why it is, but sometimes, some days, it's impossible for me to speak this abominable French language. Perhaps I am suffering from exhaustion of the nerves?' she asked brightly.

'It's unlikely,' said Yasha. 'No one suffers from exhaustion of the nerves unless they've nothing better to do than sit about thinking of themselves.'

'Why Yasha, where did you ever learn about such things?' asked Fräulein Lange, looking startled.

'She reads dime novels,' said Vicky, knowing that Yasha was thinking of her mother, who suffered from nervous disorders which only periodic sea-voyages and periodic lovers could cure.

'And I have to live with Natalia,' said Yasha. She pushed her plate away and went on, looking down at it, 'Natalia's now entering another week of furniture moving. It's enough to wear anyone out. I have to spend most of my time helping her drag the bureau across the room, or sitting on my bed watching her drag it by herself. She does it regularly, once every two months. She gets restless, decides she wants to be a doctor, plans innumerable letters to her father informing him of it, and moves the furniture around. The three things always go together.' She turned, smiled at the Armenian girl, and said, 'I've always had an idea that if you once wrote that letter and really posted it, our furniture would stay where it is for a while.'

'It's not as easy as that,' said Natalia rather unhappily. 'All Armenian girls get married ... they don't study law, or medicine, or have careers in general. You don't understand how difficult it is to break away from family and racial tradition. Besides, my father would have a fit. I don't know what he'd do. He'd probably marry me off right away, and trust the rest to ...'

'The nature of the beast,' said Theodora.

Across the room Mlle Tourain was preparing to leave. Her eyes travelled impatiently from table to table to see if everyone had finished, then fell on Belle, the little Swiss housemaid, timidly crossing the room with the second of those dreadful telegrams to arrive that day. She paused, caught Mlle Tourain's eye and said in her breathless little voice, 'It's for Fräulein Lange, Mademoiselle.'

'Well, give it to her then!' she said shortly, and stood up. The rest of the school drifted out in her wake, leaving Fräulein Lange with Theodora and Vicky in the far corner of the room.

The German teacher had not noticed Belle's entrance. After rising with the others, she had delayed in order to calm Theodora who, after volunteering the information that she was going to see Mlle Tourain about the Beaux Arts teacher's attitude toward Vicky, refused to listen to any objections. The German teacher finally lost her temper and told Theodora to mind her own business, while Vicky leaned wearily against the table. She was very tired, and said rather dully, 'Leave the whole thing alone, Teddy, please. I'll have to go soon anyhow. Mlle Tourain won't let me stay if this sort of thing happens again.'

'I might just as well get it all off my chest now,' said Theodora obstinately. 'She's going to expel me anyhow. What difference does it make?'

'I don't think she will expel you,' said Fräulein Lange. 'Not if you behave yourself from now on. She'll probably send for you this afternoon and give you a good talking to ... perhaps make you stay within bounds for two or three months, but that's all. It isn't as though you'd made that scene on your own account. Mlle Tourain will take that into consideration ... not that that excuses you in any way,' she added, as Belle came up with the telegram and handed it to the German teacher.

She ripped it open and read it. A moment later she said, her face rigid and stiff, 'I was right, Vicky. It's kidney trouble. They've taken her to the hospital. She's ... she's ... dangerously ill, Adolf says.' Reaching up to her forehead, she shoved back a strand of brown hair in a childish, rather pathetic gesture. 'Mlle Tourain will have to let me go now, won't she? She can't ask me to stay here when my sister is ... perhaps ... dying ...'

They went out. Vicky and Theodora waited for her in the hall while she saw the headmistress. She stood in front of the desk, twisting the belt of her jersey with both hands as she talked. When she came to the end of her tale she said unemotionally, 'If my sister dies, I shall not come back. I suppose you can get another German teacher even at this time of year, there are so many of us.'

Amélie Tourain was to remember that remark as long as she lived. Sitting at her desk now, tapping the end of her pencil against the brass inkpot as she had done yesterday and the day before, as she would do tomorrow and the day after, she thought

SWISS SONATA

that half the heartsick world, buffeted and driven through life as they were, must at some time say with tragic simplicity, 'There are so many of us,' in many different circumstances, with many different meanings.

Fräulein Lange left in a taxi half an hour later. The two girls had packed her bag for her, as she seemed unable to make decisions or perform specific actions. She sat in a straight-backed wooden chair with a faded chintz-covered cushion on its seat, and looked blankly at a photograph of the Lion of Lucerne on the opposite wall, leaving Theodora and Vicky to choose what she should take, what she should leave behind.

In the clear, cold air of the courtyard she seemed to recover a little. They put her into a taxi, at a loss for anything to say, and closed the door, Theodora saying to the driver, 'She's going to Zürich on the 2:30. You'd better see she gets safely on the train,' and fished down into her stocking which apparently held an inexhaustible store of money.

The taxi went off down the drive with Fräulein Lange, who did not even glance up at the towering, snow-laden elms on either side, nor glance back at Pensionnat Les Ormes where for four years she had lived, and which she was never to see again.

The two girls ran back into the house shivering, and stopped undecidedly in the hall. 'Do you suppose it was all right for me to tell him to see that she got on the train? She wouldn't mind, would she?' asked Theodora, leaning with one elbow on the post at the foot of the stairs.

'She doesn't even know you did it,' answered Vicky. She glanced up the stairs, then said, 'It's quite early still. Let's go and get some dates from the Bonne Femme. What with one thing and another, I didn't manage to get much lunch.'

They made their way across the empty classroom, across the stone floor of the loggia, and down the short flight of snow-covered steps which led to the Bonne Femme's cellar shop.

The old woman greeted them enthusiastically, hoisting herself to her feet from her place on a barrel. 'Lovely weather, Mesdemoiselles,' she said, including the whole long lake beyond the roofs of Lausanne in one joyful sweep of her arm. 'So clear it is now. This morning I said to Georges, mon fils, that it will stop ... this heavy snow ... exactly on the stroke of one. He knows that at home they say, "You do not need an instrument to tell you the weather; merely consult Henriette Moussole," but he says to me, "Ça, c'est bien ma mère; doubtless you knew the weather in our little village, but the weather in a different canton altogether ... c'est autre chose. Vois-tu, we are no longer in the mountains, and these things require to be judged otherwise ..."'

'Some dates, please,' said Theodora, interrupting her, and apparently oblivious to the old woman's look of fleeting annoyance. Vicky sat down on the recently vacated barrel shivering a little, and looked about her. It was a small, damp, earthen room with an improvised counter made of two boards placed side by side supported on each end by a barrel, and loaded with huge golden oranges, bananas, dates in yellow and red packages decorated with camels and palm trees; figs, olives, apples which were polished till you could see your face in them, and small squat jars containing oysters, lobster, foie gras and marzipan.

The Bonne Femme, her face creased once more in a smile since she had recovered from her gloomy forebodings of the night before, swept a strand of white hair back under her lace cap and continued imperturbably, 'He thinks, because I am a woman, I am also an idiot. Such is the way of men, is it not?' She paused for confirmation, looking from Theodora, who was picking up apple after apple and examining it suspiciously, to Vicky, sitting on her barrel and watching her friend with amusement, and wondering how long it would be before the Bonne Femme realized that Theodora was insulting her produce.

'It is,' said Vicky, with only a rudimentary idea of what the ancient Swiss woman was talking about.

'Young as you are, I can see that you have a knowledge of men. So I said to George, mon fils, "That is all very well, and doubtless you are at liberty to belittle the intelligence of your poor old mother who has not long to live in any case ..." Mlle Théodore! There is nothing whatever wrong with those apples!' She reached forward and rapped Theodora's knuckles with her stick. 'There! That will teach you.'

Vicky leaned back against the dirty cement wall and laughed; Theodora retired to another barrel with an aggrieved expression, sighed gustily at intervals while the Bonne Femme continued her interminable, rambling tale. They would get nothing until Madame finished in her own good time; that they knew from experience.

'... and I said to him that he would see whether I was right or not about the weather, for it would stop snowing as the bell tolled the hour of one from the Cathedral in Place St. François, en ville.' The last two words indicated that the conversation had taken place somewhere in Ouchy, for although it is impossible to tell where Lausanne ends and Ouchy begins, the people who live down by the Lake of Geneva still think of the two as separate towns. 'And I was right. At one precisely, it stopped snowing. My son is quite toqué lately; he thinks of marrying one of these Vaudoises, when I tell him that he should take a girl from the mountains who knows a little something besides lipstick, the fashion in clothes, and the cinéma ... Une de ces sacrées Vaudoises!' she repeated derisively, and spat on the hard earth floor.

They accomplished their buying at last and fled up the stone steps into the house, Vicky remarking vaguely as they climbed the stairs to Consuelo's room on the second floor, 'Isn't it funny how people *will* subdivide themselves, no matter how little space they have? In my country we're all split up into provinces so that politically it's impossible to get united action ... I mean that the Federal government decides to put through some piece of progressive legislation and immediately the people of Alberta, or Nova Scotia, or whatever it is, get up and object. The result is that the welfare of the people depends on a lot of little, short views, instead of one long one. The little short views are never alike either, so that advancement is very difficult. I suppose Switzerland would fit nicely into one corner of Ontario, yet they divide themselves up into Cantons, in order to indulge in what would be provincialisms in Canada ...'

Consuelo opened the door in answer to their knock. They crossed the room to the bed where Marian was lying between the window and the balcony door. Theodora dropped down beside her and said with concern, 'How are you feeling today, Mouse? Any better?'

She shook her head. 'Not much.'

'Aren't you going to get up so that you can go out with Con and Juan tomorrow?' she asked, as though she were coaxing a small child.

'I don't feel like going out, Teddy,' she said in her low-pitched, rather flat voice. She looked transparent in the brilliant after-noon sunlight; she was ordinarily without natural colour but surrounded by all that brightness of sun and snow, white wood-work and flowered wallpaper, her face appeared thinner, paler and more lifeless than ever. Her cheekbones were high, her eyes pale blue and her hair soft, fine and dun-coloured, held in place now by a white silk ribbon across her head. She was lying on her back with three pillows under her head and shoulders, a pale blue shawl hiding her nightdress.

Theodora went off on an elaborate, inaccurate but very amusing account of Vicky's and her own misdemeanours at lunch. Vicky sighed, looked affectionately at Theodora and said, 'Don't believe a word of it, Mouse,' then retreated to the other side of the room where Consuelo was sitting on the bed shelling peanuts, with a waste basket held between her knees. Vicky took a handful and fell to helping her.

Under cover of Theodora's pleasant St. Louis drawl and the crackling of peanut shells, Consuelo asked anxiously, 'What am I going to do with her, Vick? I told Miss Williams about her today, and she said that if Marian would even get up tomorrow morning, she thought Mlle Tourain would let her go out with us though she wouldn't ordinarily allow anyone to go straight from bed to town, because she wants us all to have a change of scene. She's sending all the girls who haven't anyone to go out with to the movies. But Marian *won't* get up!'

Vicky glanced at the Brazilian girl's beautiful, slender face with its frame of lovely fair hair, then across at Marian, spiritless and silent against her pillows, and was touched again by Consuelo's loyalty to her roommate. 'I suppose if she stays there much longer she won't be able to get up. She'll be *really* ill after another fortnight of no exercise, no food, no sleep. She was anaemic to start with, wasn't she? She's always looked it, anyhow.'

'Yes,' Consuelo said hopelessly for one of her even and well-balanced temperament. "I'll have to try and explain it to Mlle Tourain if she goes on like this much longer. She won't talk to me ... I mean Marian won't. She won't tell me why she's doing it ... although of course I know why. Still, she doesn't confide in me now the way she used to. She just went to bed the day she got that letter from her mother, without saying anything except that she didn't feel well. Two years more ... it seems such a long time to us, when we're so young, and there's no *reason* for it! I mean, if they sent her to a university, it would be a different thing, but here ... well, it seems almost as though it were a convenient and simple way of getting rid of some of us. I know Mr. and Mrs. Comstock *can't* get away for two years, but Marian should be sent somewhere that's ... not just a matter of marking time, that's all. I mean it seems so stupid and so unkind. She just can't face it. I have an idea that she thinks it's a sort of bad dream, and that so long as she stays in bed she can keep it away from her ... prevent it from becoming real. As soon as she starts off on the school routine again, it will be there, two whole years of it, stretching as far as she can see.'

'Why don't you put the whole thing up to Mlle Tourain?' asked Vicky.

'Mlle Tourain!' said Consuelo scornfully. 'All she'd do would be to come and sit on the edge of Marian's bed and tell her how much she'll enjoy being at Gstaad skiing and skating just like any other healthy, bouncing young ten-year-old. And a lot of good that would do her!' She shelled a few more peanuts, glanced over at Marian again, and went on, 'She's tired out. They dose her with cod liver oil, but it doesn't do her any good. If you could have seen her when she came two years ago, Vicky! I wish you could have seen her ...' She raised her eyes momentarily, smiling at that image of Marian as she had been, then tossed a peanut into the bowl at her feet and picking up another one, cracked it between her long, slender fingers, a discouraged look on her usually composed face. 'Really, boarding schools are about the most irrational and illogical places yet devised by man. When there is such an interdependence between men and women, why in the name of common sense are we segregated from one another in this way? Take me, for example. My men friends are as essential to me as my women friends. No one would expect me to develop properly in some remote colony surrounded entirely by men, so why am I expected to flourish in an atmosphere which is entirely feminine? The theory seems to be that I am living a life natural to those not yet of a marriageable age ... I'm only twenty, so it doesn't matter ... which is the greatest rot, because it's putting a heavy, negative emphasis on sex. I need men because I'm alive, and because they are as much a part of my life as women. And *that's* what is wrong with Marian. We might just as well be realistic about it, as try to fool her and ourselves into believing that all she needs is a little skiing and skating, and some nice "wholesome" occupation to take her mind off herself. She's drying up here. Nossa Senhora, she hasn't been away from this half-world for two years!'

On the other side of the room Theodora was saying, 'She knew perfectly well Vicky doesn't tell lies, but she gets all her ideas about running a school from books. Vicky's just case 5f; sec. 240; vol. 19; ch. 62; page 7642, calling for the firm hand, the unemotional tone of voice, the quiet ultimatum, the ...'

'I wish you didn't have such a one-track mind,' said Vicky, sighing. 'You start on one idea and nothing on earth will get you off it. Why don't you turn it to some useful purpose?'

'I have just such a purpose in mind,' she said with dignity. 'Sooner or later I'll have worn you down to a point where you'll tell me who you got them for.' She was sitting with her hands clasped around her knees, immaculate and well-groomed as always in a brown woollen dress with a necklace of coarse, emerald-green glass. 'Sooner or later,' she repeated menacingly.

Vicky laughed. 'But it wouldn't do you any good if you did know, Teddy.'

'Yes, it would. I should intervene.'

'How would you intervene?'

'I should reason with the girl. I should put my hand on her shoulder and say gently, "Wouldn't it have been a finer and better thing if you had owned up?" and if that didn't have any effect, I should continue, still without raising my voice and still speaking gently, "Well, whether or not you think it would be a finer better thing, you'll go and tell Mlle Tourain it was you and not Vicky, or I'll hamstring you, dear heart."'

'Oh,' said Vicky, unimpressed.

Consuelo said, as Theodora and Marian began to talk about Fräulein Lange, 'She just adores you, doesn't she, Vick?'

'She's a combination watch-dog, lady companion and keeper,' said Vicky. 'Way down at the bottom of Theodora's heart is a conviction that I'm one of the most injured, maligned and incompetent people who ever lived. She does me more good than anyone I've ever known, though. I think I'm just as fond of her as she is of me; I hope she knows that. You know,' she continued thoughtfully, leaning with one elbow on Consuelo's pillow, 'it annoys me sometimes to realize that so few people here really do justice to her. That sounds silly, and I suppose it's inevitable that she should be underestimated. Purely as a spectacle, she's fascinating, because she's afraid of nothing. I thought at lunch how impossible it would be to run this school ... any school ... to run society, any society ... if it were composed entirely of people like Ted. The world would be anarchic and chaotic if everyone, like Ted, feared nothing. If she had wanted to go on with her outburst at lunch, she'd have gone on with it, and nothing short of knocking her out or murdering her could have put a stop to it. How frightful life would be if we were all like that! In general she plays the game according to the rules because she sees that it's the only way in which so many people can manage to live comfortably without too much discord. But there comes a time ... I suppose it will happen again during her life ... when she decides that the rules are not the essential thing at the moment, so she throws them over and does what she likes. And the only way of controlling her is to prove to her that she's being unreasonable; no kind of threat has any effect at all. She's going to have an interesting life, Con, to say the least of it. I wouldn't be surprised at anything she did.'

'No,' said Consuelo, 'neither would I. But gosh, what a temper!' She whistled appreciatively, then said a moment later, 'You know, I never thought of that before ... I mean the sheer fright which underlies society.'

'What are you two talking about?' asked Theodora from the other side of the room.

'Your beastly disposition,' said Consuelo.

'Oh,' said Theodora. 'Damn my beastly disposition!' she added after a brief pause. 'Look at the mess it's got me into. Do you suppose Mlle Tourain will really throw me out?'

'No,' said Consuelo. 'I've seen her do that before. She'd never throw anyone out for sticking up for another person. If you'd done it on your own account, or if Mlle Dupraix had been a little less poisonous, no doubt she would have. But don't tell me you're afraid of being expelled!'

'Expelled!' she said contemptuously. 'What difference does that make to me? I did the only thing I could have done and still look at my angel face in the mirror without blushing. I don't care what other people think of me so long as I don't agree with them. No, being expelled doesn't matter ... it's Vick I'm thinking about.' She glanced over at Vicky on the bed, with a worried expression. 'Vick, left to her own devices, hasn't even enough sense to come in out of the rain.'

'You see?' murmured Vicky to Consuelo.

'Well,' said Theodora, shrugging, 'I guess I'll just have to hang around Lausanne until Vick is dispatched to join me.'

'What about your mother?' said Marian.

'My what? Oh, you mean Mrs. Cohen ... she doesn't really come into it.' She got up and went over to the window, looking impatient and unhappy. A moment later she turned and said, brightening a little, 'Let's go out and get some skiing ... come on, Vick. You too, Con.'

Consuelo hesitated, looking doubtfully at Marian, who raised her head a little and said, 'Go along, Con. It will do you good,' then relaxed against her pillows again.

Vicky shook her head. 'I can't,' she said. 'I'm on my way to Rosalie. By the way, how's Ilse?' she asked Consuelo, who was keeping an eye on the little Saarlander as well as her roommate.

'Fairly nervy,' she answered shortly, walking over to her cupboard. 'She could hardly be anything else. I'm glad they're going to get to the bottom of this nasty stealing tomorrow.'

'There ought to be some way of doing it besides calling in a city detective,' said Vicky, fluffing up the thick, light duvet on Consuelo's bed. 'I don't think it's a bit sensible. Some of the younger girls ... my roommate, for example ... are simply dreading it. It's too ... melodramatic ... too drastic.'

'My sweet innocent,' said Consuelo, lifting down her red ski-suit, 'the man won't third-degree us. I'll bet he'll be scared to death and crimson with embarrassment.'

'They don't know that, though,' said Vicky, one hand on the door. She glanced at the three of them, 'Well, au revoir, my children. Don't break your neck, Teddy. I may get down for a while after tea if you're still out then.'

She stopped at Anna von Landenburg's room on her way to see Rosalie, and knocked softly. The Bavarian girl opened the door and sank back against the frame, leaning against it with her hands behind her. 'Oh, hello, Vicky,' she said, smiling.

'You ought to be in bed, Anna.'

'I was but I ... I got too restless to stay there any longer. I'll go back after tea, if Mlle Dupraix doesn't come back in the meantime and start fussing, and peppering me with questions, and talking her head off again. How's Marian? I heard you talking in there as I went past on my way to Ilse's room.'

'She's looking pretty badly. Consuelo's terribly worried about her.' Vicky raised her eyes to Anna's face, then looked down at the floor again. She was standing with her back against the wall opposite Anna's door, so that her feet and legs blocked the narrow passage. Elsa and Christina passed on their way down to the rink. The hall was dark, with a splash of light where the sun came through Anna's open door.

'Won't you come in, Vicky?' she asked. 'I'd like a chance to talk to you if you are not too busy.'

'I can't,' she said quickly. 'I'm on my way to see Rosalie. Is there anything special?'

'No ...' she said hesitatingly. 'Just ... one thing. I ... I don't want to seem to be ... poking my nose into other people's affairs, but Mlle Dupraix has been in and out of my room all day ... you know, bringing me dozens of cups of camomile tea and hot water bottles and things, and she's never stopped talking. She seems all wound up about something, particularly since lunch.'

'There was a row in the dining room.'

'Yes, I know, Ilse told me. Anyhow, she came in about an hour ago and said, "Well, I suppose you don't know anything more about that girl than the rest of us." She was nervous; in fact just fuming about something ... I suppose it was the business at lunch; then she said, "We'll all know soon, at any rate." I asked her what she meant. She said that there was a Canadian teacher here once who came from Toronto ... she left about five or six years ago, I think. Anyhow, Mlle Dupraix has been keeping up some kind of correspondence with her since and apparently she's written ... at the beginning of December ...' Anna stopped.

'To see what she can find out about me,' said Vicky.

'Yes.' And a moment later, 'I don't know how anyone could be so unkind.'

She bit her lip and said, 'Oh, well, I suppose there'll be others ... often ... who'll do that.' She looked up at Anna again, and went on. 'Tell me something. Is there the slightest use in trying? You're beaten before you start, anyhow, there are so many odds against you. Funny, I thought I could stand just about anything ...' she went on, half-smiling, though her voice was shaking, 'but I don't believe I want to have Mlle Dupraix make a public exhibition of me. I've got to get out before that happens.' She began to cry in spite of herself. 'I suppose they're all right ... I never should have come. It's a bit late in the day to try to live ... like ... other girls.' She mopped at her eyes with the handkerchief Anna handed her in silence, then said, 'I can think of better places than hallways to enjoy a good cry over spilt milk.' A moment's pause, then, with sudden alarm, 'For goodness sake, Anna, don't let on to anyone about this, will you?'

'Why?' she asked, astonished at Vicky's abrupt change of tone.

'Because if Ted comes to hear of it ... Oh,' she said weakly, subsiding against the wall again, 'Words fail me.'

'You really are the most amazing person,' said Anna. 'If you weren't so ... easily hurt ... and if you didn't mind things so terribly, I could understand you ... but I don't. If you were a Catholic ...'

'Some day you might try and convert me.'

'No,' she said, her face serious. 'I wouldn't be so impertinent.'

Vicky straightened up. She shook her head slightly, as though she were trying to clear away her unhappy and confused thoughts. There was no use in worrying about herself now when she had so many other people on her mind. She said with quick concern, 'How are you, Anna?'

'I think I'm all right. I'm ... depressed. It's probably just fatigue, I don't know. I'm not thinking of those crazy things since last night ... those ... ugly scenes I told you about. The Cardinal, and that street in Königsberg ... they don't bother me now. I'm sick at heart, I don't know why.'

'You're worn out, Anna.'

'No, it's not that ... I'm not worn out. I'm really very strong ... I've never been ill. I feel that there's no hope ... I can't tell you when that feeling came over me. I woke up with it in the middle of the night. There doesn't seem to be any use in even praying for my father now ... although of course I have been, all day.' She rubbed her eyes in her tired, perplexed way. 'I know I'm never going to see him again,' she said with such quiet certainty that no contradiction was possible. 'What's the use in trying to do what he's doing? We'll not get anywhere. The whole world is mad, rolling backwards, and sometimes I think we're farther from God than we were two thousand years ago.' Her eyes were following a crack along the floor. She looked up at last. 'Even my Blessed Virgin seems to have deserted me,' and turned her head so that her fine, delicate features were outlined against the light. She stared at the icon, dull and faded in the sunlight. 'You see, she doesn't live. You wouldn't even know the lamp was lit.' Her eyes came back to Vicky's face, wavering uncertainly.

'She does live, Anna,' said Vicky simply, as though she were talking to a child, and brushing past her, she went over to the window and pulled the curtains nearer together. 'Now look,' she said. 'You see, she's begun to glow again to prove to you that she *is* alive, Anna ... she *is* alive.'

VIII

⁓

*R*osalie lay on her back with only one pillow under her head. Above her bed on the wall was a plain ebony cross; on the table beside her a small blue bowl which Vicky and Theodora kept filled with sweet peas. The room was on the west side of the house, warmly and gently illuminated now in the late afternoon sun. The air of stillness which always pervaded it was enhanced by the mellow light so that Vicky, sitting by the bed with her feet propped on the rung of her chair, found it more difficult than ever to realize that she was still in the school. The atmosphere which surrounded the little Canadienne worried the other girls; though they might rush through her door laughing and talking, their voices gradually subsided and they grew more and more ill at ease as the minutes passed. They came because they were kind-hearted, but were glad to escape again.

Even Anna's visits were short, for she found the mysticism which she sensed in Rosalie disturbing, and tinged with a spiritual passion which frightened her. Vicky's temperament, however, was such that she was able to sit motionless and silent, thinking her own thoughts, without becoming either restless or nervous.

Rosalie had said almost nothing since Vicky's arrival almost an hour before; she seemed to be trying to clarify some idea in her mind, her eyes wandering about the room. Vicky leaned back in her chair at last and smiled at her. 'Talk to me, Rosalie,' she said. 'Tell me how you are.'

'I'm well enough, thank you,' she answered, her glance flickering half-unseeing across Vicky's face. She turned her head so that she could look at Vicky more easily and said in her quiet, almost breathless voice, 'I go to the Catholic Hospital tomorrow, Vicky. Dr. Laurent decided this morning.' She stopped and waited, her eyes searching Vicky's face as though she were seeking assurance.

'Are you glad, my sweet?' she asked in the gentle, unobtrusive voice with which she always spoke to Rosalie.

'I don't know.' She turned her head away again and raised one thin hand to brush away her dark hair from her forehead. Her small face was white, her shadowed black eyes glowing unnaturally. 'It's my heart now. I heard them, outside the door ...'

'Heard whom, Rosalie?' Vicky asked with no change of tone.

'Mlle Tourain and the doctor. I was not supposed to hear, but you know ... that door ... it doesn't close unless you lift it up a little, and it slipped open while they were talking outside it ...'

'What did they say?'

'They said I might live a year, Vicky.' Her eyes came back to Vicky's face and remained there with that curious trust which she had in Vicky, and in no one else but the Mother Superior of her convent in Montreal.

'If you wanted to live, darling, I'm sure it would make a difference.' She spoke rather tentatively, without emphasis; she knew, intuitively, that she must not make the mistake of expressing an opinion about what Rosalie *ought* to do or think.

'I don't,' she said. 'Even a year is too long, though he ... Dr. Laurent ... evidently he thinks that that's unlikely.' Her mind was clearly not on what she was saying; she seemed to be only half-listening to her own voice. She was staring at the door on which was pinned a reproduction of the Christ from *The Last Supper* which Vicky had brought her from Milan. She had bitterly regretted the gift soon after Rosalie had asked her to have it pinned up where she could see it without having to turn her head. The face was faint with all its colours washed by time, disembodied, tragic and resigned. Vicky had found herself thinking a hundred times as she sat and watched Rosalie look at it in silence, that the picture had the same effect on her as the spinning silver ball which some hypnotists use to put their subjects into a trance. The girl would lie still and look at it unblinkingly until her eyes were glazed, and Vicky knew that if she spoke her name suddenly she would start and look ill, then wrench herself away from it with difficulty, as though dragging herself back from unconsciousness.

Vicky was afraid that Rosalie would escape her again, and that she would be forced to spend the remainder of this visit in a silence which, for the first time, she found very troubling. Her mind was in a turmoil which was unfamiliar to her; the news of that letter which Mlle Dupraix had written set a definite limit on her time at the school, and in a few weeks, or a few days, she would have to go. Where she would go, she did not know. Then there was also Anna, whose quiet desperation might so easily indicate a turn for the worse in her father's anxious life; Mary, Ilse, Ina, and Marian. Apart from the desolation of leaving the school she loved, the idea of deserting the few human beings to whom she was of some use was impossible to face. Rosalie might very well die on the day she left the school. Her life now hung on a single thread, her relationship to Vicky, who alone had the power to translate the things of this life into terms she could understand. Her sole connections with the world which surrounded her lay through the dark-haired girl sitting beside her so quietly now. She had only that one link; the rest lay too far behind her, on the other side of the immense gulf which those eight months in Paris had created.

'Vicky,' she said suddenly, forcing herself to talk again, 'Is there anything else I won't have ... there ... which I still have here, in this world? Most people do not want to die because of all the things which they must leave, but for me, what is there?'

Although she knew that anyone else would have answered, 'You cannot know because you haven't yet begun to live,' Vicky could not say it, lacking the conviction that it was true. She had, less than most people, the sense of time which makes it possible for them to count a full, rounded life in so many years, months, weeks and days. With a wisdom which was purely intuitive she knew that a life may be lived to its end in a day, or even an hour, though years may pass before the hour of actual death. Rosalie had known her years of peace, serenity and trust; her months of terror and bewilderment, only in the end to have the vital stem of her being choked off in one night. There was that break in the continuity of her mental and spiritual existence which no extension, no prolonging of physical experience could heal. Sitting in her small, straight-backed chair Vicky thought that if God kept a record of His children, He must have written 'Finish' under the name of Rosalie Garcenot on the twenty-eighth of August, nineteen hundred and thirty-five.

She said at last, 'Your religion teaches that one ought not to hope for death, Rosalie.'

'But I have no duty to anyone. No one wants me.' She turned her eyes away from Vicky's face again, and went on with an effort, 'Soeur Catherine used to say that I should one day grow up, and then it would be my duty to ... to ... help my mother in every way I could ... by example, rather than by precept.'

It was one of her convent phrases which never failed to disturb Vicky a little. The words called up images of cloisters, of high, sweet voices, of the nuns walking two by two ... strangely alien to their noisy, modern surroundings of city streets and city people ... of the vast and eternal Church.

Rosalie was too exhausted today, she knew that by the way she spoke; her sentences were slow, hesitating and difficult, as though she had been so far from the earth that she had lost touch with it, and had to feel her way even in ordinary speech. She went on a moment later, still with that troubled, restless look which Vicky had not seen in her before, 'Surely Soeur Catherine would not ask me to stay with my mother and ... with ... with them?'

'I don't think so,' she answered simply, moving her chair a little so that she could look out the window. 'It's so lovely out there, darling. Wouldn't you like to go with me somewhere this summer? Somewhere that's beautiful and quiet, so that you could get strong and well again.'

'I want to go back to the sisters,' she said, glancing at the window, then turning her face away from the light again. 'Do you know what I see now as I lie here, Vicky?'

'No, darling,' said Vicky.

She looked toward the picture on the door again and was silent for a moment. Then she said slowly, 'I see Soeur Catherine, walking up and down.' She looked at Vicky and continued more rapidly, 'The walls of the convent face each other on one side ... the side that looks toward Mount Royal. There's a sort of ... of ... square,' she added and with a visible effort to be more comprehensible went on, 'I mean that from the window of my room I could see the parapet along the opposite wall. There was a long narrow space there with a low, iron railing along the outer edge ... it made a sort of balcony. Soeur Catherine used to walk up and down there, looking out towards Sherbrooke Street. She used to walk very fast with her skirts swinging out behind her, then stop suddenly, gripping the railing with both hands for a minute, looking straight down four stories to the courtyard where the statue of the Virgin Mary is, then she would start to walk again. I saw her there often when I woke up at night.'

'What was she like ... Soeur Catherine?' asked Vicky.

'Like? She was ... she was a little frightening. I used to feel ... awkward, and silly when I looked at her, but I'd have done anything she wanted. Soeur Catherine was a saint, the girls said. She was not worldly. The other nuns envied her ... no, envy is not the word I want ... but they wished they were like her, for she had never been anything but a nun.' She looked upset and bit her lip as she stared at Vicky and through her to the nun walking along the parapet. 'I'm so sorry, I say everything wrong.'

'Do you mean that she had always lived in the convent, ever since childhood?'

'Yes,' she answered, with a long sigh of relief. She became more and more easily shaken as time went on; Vicky had seen how, from one week to the next, small perplexities took hold of her and worried her. 'Since she was four. So you see, she could know nothing of the outside world, and nothing of evil.'

'No,' said Vicky. 'What happened to her?' There was something else in this, she could see that as she watched Rosalie's face.

'She died,' said Rosalie dully. Her look of sudden animation, which had appeared as she described the sisters and the convent, was gone; she seemed spent and flattened back on her pillow.

'Was she ill?'

'No, she just died. That was all we were told. She was at vespers one evening, then we never saw her again. Next morning the Mother Superior said that she was dead.' Her breath began to come in gasps and she said with sudden urgency, 'I want to sit up. Please, Vicky, help me up ...'

Vicky got up and bending over her with one hand under each shoulder, said uncertainly, 'You're not supposed to sit up this week ...'

'Yes ... yes, I know, but I want to sit up ...' She spoke with such surprising force that Vicky raised her almost to a sitting position, putting under her head and shoulders the pillows from the other bed. Rosalie smiled faintly. 'I feel as though something's lying on me like a heavy weight when I'm flat on my back, sometimes. I remember once when I was about twelve, I became hysterical, I don't remember what it was about now. I lay on my bed and thrashed about and I was almost beside myself. Soeur Catherine came in and held me down with one hand on my chest ... it was the same feeling. I've had it from time to time ever since. Vicky, I'm so afraid sometimes ...' She reached out and took Vicky's hand, holding it in a painfully tight grasp, 'I don't know what it is I'm afraid of. I lie here, day after day, and I don't want to go on living because I'm so tired. But I know I'm not good and I'm going to die ... it's not that, though, for I do not fear death ... it's something else. Sometimes I feel as though I am very far from God ... I seem ... like a person in a dream ... looking for something they can't find, trying to touch something which always escapes before you can quite reach it.'

Vicky said nothing. She continued to sit and watch the sad, anxious little face on the pillow while Rosalie stared straight in front of her, holding her hand as though for safety. Vicky's other hand was gripping the side of her chair as she sought about in her mind for something ... just one small thing ... which she might recall to Rosalie in order to bridge that gap between her years of serenity, and her months of confusion. Vicky had very little knowledge of Rosalie's childhood; she knew that the Garcenot's house had stood halfway up the mountain, that from its windows you could see over the smoking city and beyond the St. Lawrence River for fifty miles south-west toward Lake Champlain, south to Vermont, and south-east toward Lake Memphramagog. The mountains across the river lay against the horizon, long, blue and mysterious in the distance. Nearer at hand was the St. Lawrence with its ships going westward into the heart of the continent, and eastward down to the sea, winding its way across the wide, flat valley, a white, curving expanse in winter and a band of bluish silver when the ice went out. But Rosalie had no associations with those physical surroundings which Vicky could recall to her memory, and the life she had led in her convent school existed only in her own mind, beyond Vicky's reach and separated now from Rosalie herself. She had said once, 'It's as though I were on a long pilgrimage, and had an immense chasm to cross which, when I had crossed it, was too wide for me to be able to look back and see the place I had come from, except very indistinctly, like a land in the mist.'

That land in the mist, her convent in Sherbrooke Street, where she had known God and the reality of Christ, was now gradually eluding her, destroying her composure and putting a terrible strain on her faith. These many months she had been living on the memory of a spiritual affirmation which was slowly ceasing to have any reality, as it faded farther and farther into the past. Because she was so young, and her heart still so childish, her concept of God could not be without a large element of time,

and place, and circumstance, and was dependent upon her recol-
lections of things now lost.

Vicky would remember her first sight of Rosalie as long as
she lived. The girl had been standing in the hall waiting to be
admitted to Mlle Tourain's study with that quiet, self-contained
patience in her attitude which distinguishes many convent-bred
girls. Coming down the back stairs Vicky had stopped; she
remembered leaning against the banister and watching her,
struck by the melancholy cast of the child's face and her quiet,
patient bearing.

During the day and the night before Christmas, Rosalie had
said a thousand Aves, oppressed by her sudden realization that
Vicky was as alone in the world as herself, and determined to
make some return for all that Vicky had done for her. She knew
that if she could say a full thousand, she would be granted anything she asked, and had intended to beg the Holy Virgin to
send her back to the convent in Sherbrooke Street. She had
barely completed the first dozen when the image of Vicky rose
up in her mind, and she cast aside the idea of requesting something for herself. She tried to think of the best thing to ask as
she intoned her last Ave ... *'Dominus tecum benedicta tu in
mulieribus et benedictus fructus ventris tui, Jesus ...'* What did
Vicky need most? What could little Rosalie Garcenot do for her
to show that she was grateful? *'Sancta Maria, ora pro nobis ...
nobis peccatoribus, nunc et in hora mortis nostrae ...'* In the end
she had asked the Holy Virgin to see that Vicky was happy ...
'You know, Holy Mother, she is already very good, so I don't
need to ask for that.'

Her mind was more occupied with Vicky than Vicky herself
ever realized; often during those hours of silent companionship
Rosalie was not thinking of herself at all. Sometimes she was
half-praying that the quiet girl sitting beside her would never be

hurt, sometimes her mind went back to her first sight of Vicky, watching her from the shadows of the back staircase, then coming forward with that curiously unobtrusive manner of hers and asking, 'Is there anything I can do for you?' She had known then that Vicky was her friend.

She turned her head suddenly and said, with her eyes appearing to look through Vicky into that future in which she saw Vicky alone, after her death, 'I can't tell you how much you've done for me.'

Vicky shook off her preoccupation with Rosalie's background ... she was still trying to visualize the interior of the convent, to lose herself in its atmosphere as she imagined it to be, with a lack of success which made her impatient ... and said, 'Don't think about that, darling.'

Rosalie smiled and said, looking at the ceiling, 'I was telling Teddy about that one day last week, and she taught me a little poem ... it's in English ... to say to you.' Her eyes came back to Vicky's face again. 'Would you like to hear it? My English isn't very good, but Teddy said that I'd got it quite well.'

'Yes, say it for me ...'

She looked up at the ceiling again, and repeated very slowly and carefully, like a little girl:

I'll keep a little tavern
  Below the grey-eyed crest
Wherein all high hill's people
  May sit them down and rest.

There shall be plates a-plenty
  And mugs to melt the chill
Of all the grey-eyed people
  Who happen up the hill.

There sound will sleep the traveller
  And dream his journey's end,
But I will rouse at midnight
  The falling fire to tend.

Aye, 'tis a curious fancy —
  But all the good I know
Was taught me out of two grey eyes
  A long time ago.

She did not know that Vicky was crying, and remarked with her pathetic simplicity, 'Of course, the last line isn't right because it's not "a long time ago," but now, and during the past three months.' There was a brief silence. She went on a moment later, 'I don't know what I'd ever have done without you, Vicky. I wish they wouldn't take me away from you, and send me to a strange place and strange people. I've never been in a hospital. What is it like? Will they come and ask me questions?'

'I don't think so, darling. The sisters there may be just like the sisters in your old convent.'

'But it's not the same. I don't know how to explain it, but hearing suddenly that I'm going to be moved, has brought me back ... I mean that I ... I seem to be living in the world again ... and that I've got to try and ...' She stopped, shaking her head hopelessly, at a loss to know how to make herself intelligible. She turned her head again and looked almost imploringly at Vicky, 'I'll have to talk to people, and tell them things ... won't I?'

'I don't think so, darling,' she said again.

'I wouldn't mind so much if you were going with me.' She thought, if only they'd let Vicky come so that I shouldn't be alone, for she *could* not talk any more. Her exhausted mind was unable to face the prospect of further explanations; she did not want people looking at her curiously, pityingly, trying to understand. During the past three months she had slowly succeeded in throwing off the limitations of the physical world which surrounded her; now, with the discovery that she was to be moved into an unfamiliar environment where she would once more be forced to adapt herself to strange people and strange things, God had taken away her mental refuge and left her alone in the world again. Something like panic took possession of her as she tried to make herself believe that He had not forgotten little Rosalie Garcenot.

Her grip on Vicky's hand slowly tightened as she began to pray in a final attempt to escape from herself, 'Hail, Mary, full of grace ...' What came after that? '*Ave Maria, gratia plena ... Ave Maria, gratia plena ...*' Her mind was blank. Even the Holy Virgin was far away, lost somewhere in the past. She repeated the four words again, her forehead damp with perspiration, 'Hail, Mary, full of grace ...'

It was at this moment that Mlle Dupraix knocked on the door. She entered, unnoticed by either of them; when she spoke Vicky started, and Rosalie bit her lip in a spasm of nervousness. She heard the Beaux Arts teacher say to Vicky, 'Mlle Tourain wants to see you in her study, immediately,' and saw Vicky getting up, freeing her hand from Rosalie's grasp.

She said, in a voice which seemed to Rosalie to be very faint, 'I'll be back in a minute, dear,' as the door closed behind them.

Rosalie continued to lie motionless for a while gripping the sheets with both hands. She was trying to remember her Ave still.

'Hail, Mary, full of grace ...' she said again, but the other words would not come. She could remember nothing, nor experience once again the relief and happiness of knowing that she was not alone. She looked about the empty room, as though seeking visible proof of God's presence, but there was nothing there. Beyond her frantic efforts to remember, her mind was filled with scenes from her childhood, and beyond those again was the figure of a nun walking along the parapet to the very edge where only a low iron railing separated her from the stone courtyard four stories below ...

She saw a tall thin man sitting in a chair reading a book, and two people, a woman and a child, standing in the doorway. The child's eyes were fixed on the man; she was trying to summon sufficient courage to ask him to come with them, but she turned away at last in answer to a slight pull from her mother, and went out of the door, leaving him there alone. From the city below as they walked down the drive came the sound of innumerable bells tolling Mass. It was Lent, and yet the man had eaten meat on both Wednesday and Friday.

There were apple trees blossoming in the convent garden; the Mother Superior had given her a small plot of ground by the stone wall where she was digging. She wanted to grow enough flowers to keep the altar beautiful all summer, and was busy planting seeds. There was a slight breeze, and the blossoms kept drifting down into her shallow furrows. She stopped digging at last and turned to look up into the heart of the tree from which they came, and remained lost in her dream until another bell rang.

Both those scenes faded at the sound of a bell. She remembered a hot living room in a Paris apartment, her mother in the man's arms, unmistakable, although the light given off by the city beneath them was dim, then the chimes of Notre-Dame tolling three o'clock, and that scene slowly left her mind.

The school bell outside the door of the girls' living room clanged loudly, and the black-haired girl standing beside her, looking at her with those queer, incurious grey eyes, said quietly, 'It's no use your waiting any longer for her. Come and have tea, there's fresh bread today ...'

Vicky's face vanished. She raised herself on her pillow still farther, trying to bring it back so that the figure of the nun would not grow larger and larger, but Vicky had gone. The nun moved back and forth, outlined against the illuminated night sky of the city, and other pictures of her appeared in the background. Soeur Catherine was standing beside her low bed; she seemed immensely tall with her thin, passionate face very far above little Rosalie Garcenot. She reached over and put one hand on the child's chest, holding her down as she said, 'It's wrong to give way like that! It's wrong! Control yourself, Rosalie, control yourself!' What had it all been about? She could not remember now.

'Soeur Catherine is a saint,' the girls said ...

The nun still walked back and forth, back and forth ... Hail, Mary, full of grace, *gratia plena, gratia plena* ... then before Rosalie's terrified eyes she stopped, holding the railing with both hands, looking downward. She stood there a very long time, then, so quickly that Rosalie could hardly see her, she put one foot over and was gone, her skirts flying out as she fell.

'Vicky!' she screamed. '*Vicky!*'

Rosalie threw back the covers and half fell to the floor where she lay for a moment trying to get her breath, then struggled up and over to the door. It wouldn't open ... please, Holy Mother, open this door ... yes, she remembered, that you had to lift it, for the lock was wrong. She made a tremendous effort, and wrenched it open. The hall reached out and away before her eyes; if she could get to the stairwell and call down, Vicky, who was in Mlle Tourain's study three floors below, would hear her.

'Vicky!' she called from the top of the stairs. 'Vicky, where are you? ... Oh, please come ...' She began to sob, and started down the stairs, but something caught her and she fell, straight down to the landing, and lay there.

PART THREE

Saturday

IX

❧

I

At ten the next morning the detective arrived. He was seen waddling up the long drive from the gates to the corner of the house by a dozen or more girls who were standing at their windows, aimlessly seeking something to occupy their minds. Rosalie had been taken to the hospital at four-thirty on Friday afternoon, and died a few hours later. The news of her death was whispered from girl to girl at breakfast; when Natalia told her, Vicky got up and left the dining room, while Mlle Dupraix and Mlle Devaux, on the point of protesting against such unconventional behaviour, checked themselves and remained silent as they caught a glimpse of her face. After that the girls finished their breakfast in complete silence, the first time that such a thing had ever occurred in the school. No one spoke, not even to whisper, as they rose and left the dining room to climb the stairs to their rooms half an hour later.

Mlle Tourain, crossing the hall from her study to the kitchens, stopped by the door of the dining room puzzled by the silence, opened it a little, then closed it again, saying nothing. She forgot her errand to the kitchens and returned to her study where she remained for more than an hour lost in thought, and making no effort to restore a more normal atmosphere. When the detective was shown in she was very distraite; it was three-quarters of an hour before she had answered all his questions and the bell rang to summon the girls to her study. She forgot the beginning of his sentences before he had reached the end; her 'Pardon, Monsieur?' interrupted him repeatedly, and several times he looked across at the middle-aged woman sitting behind her desk, puzzled by her behaviour. At last she noticed his expression and said quietly, 'You will excuse my being somewhat upset; one of my girls died in hospital here last night.' She paused a moment, looking upwards, then went on incomprehensibly, 'You must understand that I blame myself because I knew nothing about her. I hold myself responsible for her death through my ignorance.'

He coughed awkwardly and continued his questions, appalled by the silence all about him. No sound reached the study; the girls were all in their rooms, too bewildered and too sad for talking. The mail, arriving at ten o'clock, was distributed by Belle, tiptoeing from room to room; no one went near the front hall where it was usually sorted and left on the table for the girls themselves to collect.

2

Ilse sat at her desk once more, her feet twined around the legs of her chair as she read Paul's letter. He told her that her father's health had improved a little but that he had been ordered to the South of France. By the time she received the letter they would be on their way to Uncle Isaac Lehmann's little villa in St. Raphael. Uncle Isaac had arrived at Saarbrücken on Wednesday morning and had spent the whole day arguing with Herr Brüning about the house. If someone did not go and occupy it immediately it would fall to pieces; he, Isaac Lehmann, had no wish to go near the place again, for now that his wife, Sarah, was dead, the house held nothing but unhappiness for him.

So your father agreed. We are leaving on Saturday morning ... a few hours before you get this even. I should like to have stayed and seen the elections through, but the doctor is afraid that the strain of the next few days might undo all the good of the past year, and prove a serious setback for your father, so that's that. I expect you're terribly glad, liebchen. Uncle Isaac has it all settled that your mother and father should remain at St. Raphael forever; at any rate, I've offered this house for sale and I hope we shall be able to get rid of it.

Now for two bits of marvellous news. The first, I shall be seeing you in Lausanne on Thursday or Friday of next week, on my way back to Paris from St. Raphael. Won't it be heaven to be together again, darling? Your father says it's only two weeks since you were home for Christmas, but he's a silly ass and I told him so. It's months ... years ... in fact, centuries. And Ilse, they're going to let you leave Pensionnat Les Ormes and all its works, at Easter. I shall come for you and we'll go to Paris to buy your trousseau ... we'll stay with Uncle Isaac and Aunt Naomi for two weeks, then go to St. Raphael and be married, then to Italy for a month before we go back to Paris and my father's law business again.

She had begun to cry, pierced by this undreamed-of happiness, and had to blink several times in order to finish the letter. She had not told him how miserable she had been, but some of her anxiety and fear must have seeped through her actual words, for the last paragraph expressed his love and understanding in a way which made her think that he had guessed more than he said:

I have never a moment's doubt that we shall be happy together as long as we live. I think it's because I believe in you, and know just what it is that I must give you. You need to be believed in; lots of people do, men as well as women, and often they can do great things in the end, because of that conviction on the part of someone they love who loves them, that they can and will accomplish the impossible. Without that love they might equally well be nothing. I have the whole world when I have you; without you I should be unreal, and only half alive. Till next week, my darling Ilse, — Paul.

3

'Marian, listen to me ...' said Consuelo, sitting down beside her on the bed. 'I've had a letter from Juan. It was mailed from Paris on Thursday and says that he's leaving Friday night for Lausanne ... that's last night, so he must be here now. If you'll only get up right away ... this very minute ... we can go out for the weekend and not come back until Monday morning. We can dance, and drive, and play ping-pong, and enjoy ourselves.'

Marian said nothing, but she looked at her friend intently as though, for the first time, she were really taking her seriously, thought Consuelo. That was something. 'I've never in all our time together asked you to do anything for me, but I'm asking you now, because I think you're mad to go on this way. If you don't try to get back to normal, you'll ruin your health. In another month, you'll be really ill, and no good to anyone. This would be all very well if you were alone on a desert island but you're not; you're living in the world; you have duties and obligations to other people ... to your mother and father, to Mlle Tourain, to the other girls here ... and to me. You're lying down on the job. If you don't snap out of this, I ... well, I won't think much of you, that's all.'

She had never heard Consuelo say such a thing before, and looked rather hurt for a moment. Then she said with difficulty, 'I haven't thought of it from that point of view. What difference do I make, Con? What does it matter to anyone if I do this, or that, or the other thing? None that I can see. To you, perhaps ...'

'Yes,' she said. 'To me, as well as a good many other people. One would think you were living in a sort of vacuum, but you're not. You know, it really *is* true that you get out of things more or less what you put into them. So long as you spend your life thinking about Marian Comstock, your life won't be worth living. I grant you that it isn't now.'

'Don't talk to me like that,' she said, her mouth trembling.

'I *will* talk to you like that! Heaven knows, I'm no fool, I'm perfectly aware of what you're up against, but I refuse to sit and sympathize with you any longer. I'll *do* what I can ... I mean I wrote my Mother a couple of days ago and asked her if she'd invite you to come and spend the summer with us on Lake Como ... she's renting a villa near Bellagio, and lots of Juan's friends will be there, so it will be fun. Next year Juan and I are going to have an apartment in Paris with one of our aunts from London to chaperon us, and you might come along too. I wrote

Mother about that as well, and she'll see if she can arrange it with your parents.' She hesitated a moment, then went on, 'I didn't tell you that because I wanted to see you have the guts to get up and face things without putting a lot of jam on the bread to make it easier to swallow. And if I thought that you'd just prefer to lie here for the rest of your two years, moping, I'd move out tomorrow and room with Teddy. I haven't the right temperament to nurse a ... neurotic.'

They stared at each other in silence for a moment, Consuelo's face rigidly uncompromising, Marian half tearful, half angry. Her expression changed a moment later; before Consuelo's astonished eyes, she began to look amused. The amusement spread from her eyes to her mouth, until at last she threw back her head on the pillow and began to laugh. She laughed helplessly for a moment, then said, 'Excuse me, I think perhaps I'm adding hysteria to all my other ailments. But it struck me suddenly what an ass I am, and the contrast to what I've imagined I was all these weeks is so ... so ... overpowering, that I have to laugh or cry. I'd rather laugh. Well, get up, Miss Nightingale; I can't move while you're practically sitting on top of me.' And a moment later, rather thoughtfully, 'By the way, is there any chance of Peter Vinen being at the Palace this afternoon?'

'Perhaps,' said Consuelo.

'And I haven't got anything to wear!'

'You can wear my new blue dress,' said Consuelo unselfishly, and then sighed. 'Though someone told me I was simply devastating in it. Still, thy need is greater than mine. But I'm going to take you shopping next week. I'm fed up with being the mainstay of your existence, sartorially as well as emotionally.' But she smiled, and for the first time in many days her face had its old serene, untroubled look.

Marian said suddenly, 'Thanks, Con. Thanks ... for everything.'

'You're welcome, my dear ... as we say in São Paolo, Brazil.'

4

Catherine Shaunessy had a letter from her mother. She was lying down on her bed, with her chin on her hands, reading it for a second time when Mary came in the door and silently sat down beside her. She saw that Cay's face was streaked with tears but she said nothing for a while, not wishing to interrupt her. The little American rolled over on her back at last and sat up, with her feet straight out in front of her. 'Well,' she said, as unemotionally as she could, 'Mother says that if I don't stop kicking about this place, she won't write me at all. This is the first time she's written in six weeks, so I wouldn't be missing much.'

'Do you ... kick ... much?'

She shook her head and said, with that air of bravado and challenge which had become habitual with her, 'No. Why should I? This is my idea of a perfect way of putting in three years, without causing anyone any trouble. I may have remarked once or twice to her that it would be nice if I could look forward to seeing her and Dad in the summer, instead of two and a half years from now, but that's as far as I went.'

'Cay, perhaps if you did well here, they'd let you leave as soon as you were ready for college ...'

'Oh, yeah? I've been in boarding school ever since I was eight! Besides, I don't want to go to college if I have to board there. I'm sick of being cooped up! I wish to goodness my dear parents had known a little more about birth control ...'

'Cay!'

'Well, what do you think?' she demanded. 'Do you send your

kids to boarding school for nine months of the year and to camp for the other three if you want to have them around? No, you don't.' She was silent a moment, drawing her knees up and resting her chin on them. She was trying to make up her mind whether or not she should tell Miss Ellerton of her recent inspiration. At last she decided in the affirmative. 'Well, it doesn't matter. I've hit on a sure way of getting out of here, anyway.'

Mary got up and walked over to the window. Looking out over the lake toward the mountains of France she said casually, 'I've wondered how long it would be before that occurred to you.'

'Before what occurred to me?' she asked, eyeing Miss Ellerton narrowly. 'You don't know what I'm talking about, do you?'

'Yes, Cay, I do. But I'm afraid it wouldn't work.'

'Why wouldn't it?'

'No one would believe that you had sneaked in and out of the girls' rooms, ransacked their bureau drawers, turned out their pockets, sat silent and watched Ilse taking the brunt of it ... No, Cay, not you. I know you too well, and so do a great many others. You'd just be laughed at.' She saw Cay begin to cry again, but continued in the same casual tone, 'I wonder if you could be any good at sports, if you worked hard at them ... skiing and skating, for example. Basketball too.'

'Why?' she asked, looking up.

Mary sat down on the windowsill with a sigh, and said wearily, 'Heavens, what a week this has been!' And a moment later, 'I'm going to have to ask Mlle Tourain to let me have an assistant ... someone to coach the beginners.'

Cay suddenly sat up. She stared at Miss Ellerton. She took her handkerchief from her pocket and dried her eyes, started to say something, then checked herself. She waited, for what seemed to her at least an hour, but Miss Ellerton was apparently engrossed in counting the flowers on the strip of wallpaper above the door, and said nothing. At last Cay's self-control gave way. She burst out, 'Let me do it! Oh, *please* let me do it! I could. Really, I could ... I ... well, when I was in school in Portland I was the junior ... I got the cup for the greatest number of points among the younger girls. Honestly I did, Miss Ellerton!'

'I don't doubt it,' said Mary rather dryly, 'but I'd like to see you with my own eyes. Ever since I've been here the only thing you've done with any success is breaking bounds and smoking after lights out. It's the only thing you've really put your mind on.' Her eyes suddenly contracted: she thought with a sudden wry smile which had vanished before Cay noticed it: You see, Vicky, I may turn out to be some good at it after all, then brought her mind back to Cay, who had jumped down from the bed and was looking at her entreatingly, her short, red hair almost standing on end from its recent battle with her pillow.

'If I ...' she said, and swallowing, made a fresh start. 'If I don't break a single rule ... if I'm as good as gold for the next month, would you ...?

'I'll think it over. But you've got to promise to stop making such an ass of yourself.'

'I promise,' she said, blowing her nose energetically. She had now committed herself, and her feelings were somewhat mixed, as she thought of what she had let herself in for. Anyway, if she *had* succeeded in getting herself expelled, her parents would only have put her in another, stricter school, so this was certainly the best solution. On the whole, things looked a good deal brighter than they had an hour ago.

Mary paused with her hand on the doorknob. 'You don't know where Vicky is, do you? No one's seen her since she walked out ... since breakfast.'

'She may be in Ted's room,' Cay suggested.

5

Theodora was speechless with rage when Mary walked in. She waved the telegram which she had just received by way of explanation, unable to articulate. At last she said, collapsing into a chair, 'It's my brother.'

'Your brother?' repeated Mary. 'I didn't know you had a brother. I thought you just had a moth ...'

'I've got a brother all right! The long-legged, feeble-minded, son of a ...'

'Leave it to my imagination,' Mary said hastily.

'All right. Let's see what your imagination can produce in the way of ... of ...' She ran one hand through her hair and gestured hopelessly. 'Well, what do you think he's done? I give you ... I give you ... Oh, millions of guesses. You'll never hit on it.'

'Motor-accident?'

'No.'

'Assault and battery?'

'No.'

'Arson?'

'No ... No! You're way off the track,' said Theodora.

'Gambling?'

'No.'

'... er ...?'

'Certainly not,' said Theodora. 'Don't forget he's an American, and therefore a sentimentalist.'

'I give up.'

'He's married a girl named Angela.' She paused for breath, looked up at the ceiling for a moment, then said with a sweet smile, 'My brother is just twenty. Angela says she's twenty-two. My brother believes her. He sent me a photograph. I looked at it. She seems to me to be a ripe thirty-five, but perhaps she was tired when it was taken, so we'll give her the benefit of the doubt and say she's thirty-four. My brother comes in for half a million dollars in six months ... *Oh!!*' she said, gritting her teeth, and hurled her hair brush at the photograph of Lewis. The glass fell to the floor in pieces.

'Feel better?' asked Mary, then continued conversationally, 'I knew a man once who always threw gramophone records at the fireplace when he was annoyed. Then there was another ... a second cousin of my mother-in-law by marriage ... who always broke china.' She saw that Theodora was really unhappy and sought about in her mind for something to say, but failed to find anything. The girl looked rather bewildered, and was tying and untying a series of knots in one of her beautiful chiffon hand-kerchiefs. 'Never mind, Teddy,' she said at last. 'Perhaps ...'

'It's not my idea of a marriage,' she said in a low voice. 'You don't know Lewis. He's ... nice, for all he's so scatterbrained ... an idealist if there ever was one. He's always thought I was absurd to be so cynical; I'll bet that poor baby thinks little Angela's like Diane in *Seventh Heaven*. He's probably even now estab-lishing her in a Paris attic and looking for a job as a waiter or a ditch-digger.'

'What will your mother say?' asked Mary.

Theodora shrugged. 'She'll probably be furious, and then help-less, and then forget all about it.' Her hands dropped to her sides; she looked about the room aimlessly and remarked, 'It all makes me feel more like an orphan than ever. It's funny how many of us there are who really haven't anyone at all, isn't it? I mean we're alone, with no one to stand between us and our sense of ... the strangeness of living. Vick, Cay, Yasha, Stephania, Rosalie ... Rosalie,' she repeated unsteadily. 'She was ... a sadder ... spectacle than any of us.' She stopped, trying to blink away her tears, and stared out the window for a moment. 'None of us really tried to help her ... no one but Vick. Now I know I won't ever forgive myself for not having made more effort to ... to ... help. I suppose that's the way with everything as long as we live ... so many regrets, so many things left undone, so much falling down on the job. Sometimes I think I'm so inadequate, such a mess, and wonder if I'll ever be anything else.' Her tears got the better of her, and she buried her head in her arms. Mary watched her for a few seconds, then got up and went out, closing the door quietly behind her.

6

Anna von Landenburg was reading a special delivery letter from Nördlingen.

> My daughter, I can think of no way to make what I have to tell you less hard to bear. Your father was arrested this morning just before sunrise and taken to the prison in Munich. He is to go before the military tribunal on Monday. I think you had better come to Munich at once, for I know that you could not remain inactive in your school without news, and it takes too long this way. I do not wish to intrude upon you at this terrible time, but I am taking the liberty of asking Sister Constance to leave for Lausanne tomorrow morning on the early train so that she should arrive almost as soon as this letter. I hope to see you both on Sunday.
>
> Remember that you need never feel lonely and uncared for, since there are many of us here in the monastery and in your convent, who pray for your happiness and welfare and who love you as a daughter. Your father suggested to me that you might like to train as a nurse or a doctor; whatever you decide to do, let it be started as soon as

possible for your own sake, and also because I think it would make him happy to know that his work would be carried on, though in a different way of course. He said to me yesterday, before this blow fell, that he had only one stipulation to make ... you must not concern yourself with politics. Perhaps it is a weakness in him and in me, but neither of us could bear to see you endanger yourself in any way ...

She raised her eyes to the icon above her head, the remaining sentences lying unread before her on the desk. Now that the worst had happened she was calm; she neither wept nor gave any outward sign of her despair as she sat, looking up at her Virgin.

'Holy Mother,' she prayed, as the brothers at Nördlingen were praying, 'Intercede for my father ...' and a little later when she could no longer control her tears, 'Give me courage, Holy Mother, give me courage; I have so much to do.'

7

Natalia said, rather perplexed, 'Do you suppose the room would look better if we put the bureau over there?'

'I do not,' said Yasha, for once moved to protest. 'I've let you put the desk in the alcove where there isn't any light; I've let you put the dressing table so close to the door that you can hardly squeeze past it getting in and out, but I draw the line at putting the bureau where we can't open the windows. There are limits, Natalia, and this time you've overstepped them.' She was sitting on her bed cross-legged, eating an apple. 'I wish you would make up your mind on the subject of career *v.* marriage once and for all, and leave the furniture alone!'

'The furniture hasn't anything to do with it,' said Natalia.

'Of course it has. Why did you let yourself get involved in this engagement, anyhow?'

'It just ... well, it just happened,' she said, her heavy dark face very unhappy.

'Is he nice?'

'I expect he's all right,' she said indifferently.

'You expect he's all right!' she said incredulously. 'What a perfectly splendid reason for marrying a man. The poor soul,' she went on reflectively. 'I feel rather sorry for him. He'll probably never know from one day to the next whether the marital bed is in the greenhouse or the vestibule. How did it happen?'

'Our families just ... well, they arranged it.'

'Don't you Armenians ever realize that this is the twentieth century? I didn't think they did that sort of thing any more, except with royalty.'

'We still do it,' she said, sitting down on her bed which was at this moment occupying the centre of the room. 'You see, I'm almost twenty-one. As a matter of fact, that's rather late for an engagement.'

'When do they expect you to get married?'

'In the summer,' she said hopelessly.

Yasha sat up and stared. For once her face had lost its impassivity; her brown eyes were wide open as she said forcefully, 'Natalia, stop being such a jellyfish!'

'How can I? Everyone I know gets married ... One just *does*, that's all ...'

'And what happens? After six months your husband takes a mistress. You either take a lover, or you spend your time producing children. Marriage!' said Yasha contemptuously. 'Pouf!'

'Is that what happens?' she asked, her black eyes narrowing.

'If it's a mariage de convenance. What do you expect? Why should Akim be faithful to you? He probably says, "I expect she's all right," in exactly the same enthusiastic, lovesick way that you just said it.'

'Do you mean to tell me that I ... that I'm going to spend the rest of my life being ... well, being ... deceived?'

'Undoubtedly,' said Yasha.

'Then what's the point of it?' she asked.

'What, indeed,' replied Yasha, shrugging. 'That's what I've been trying to find out ever since I've known you.'

'But ... but ...' she stammered in complete bewilderment, 'I don't understand!'

'You don't have to. You just be a good girl and do what you're told, and then, forty or fifty years from now, a few helpless young women will have to do what *you* say. That's your reward.' And a moment later, in a tone of mild exasperation, 'What on earth did you expect?'

'I thought it would work out. I mean I thought being married changed everything ... that afterwards one grew to love the other and ...'

'Parbleu, but you're an ass! Something like the movies, hein? Moonlight, and roses, and romance, and the magic spell of marriage. My God,' said Yasha, with feeling. 'Look at him!' They both considered the photograph of Akim, very seriously. 'You expect *that* to turn into Valentino after a week of your society. Well, he won't. He'll still have that funny mole on the end of his nose, and that smug look. In fact he'll look even smugger by the end of ten years, having put it over on you in a way he'll think quite clever, telling you that he's going to such and such a place when he's really going to see his little cabbage, and then after a while not bothering to tell you anything.'

'Well, what would you do?' she asked.

'I'd write a polite letter home saying that you won't marry him, and that you want to go to a university. You do, don't you?'

'Yes,' she said with an intensity which would have astonished anyone but Yasha, who knew her very well. 'Oh, *yes*, I do!'

'Well, then I'd get Mlle Tourain to write to your family and point out to them that you've had excellent grades ever since you've been here, and that she thinks you should go. That would be a help. If you went to the Sorbonne, you could live with Aimée's family, couldn't you?'

'Yes, and they'd help too, if there was a quarrel ... and there would be one,' she added ruefully. 'Aimée's going next year,' she remarked a moment later. She continued to sit motionless for a minute, looking thoughtfully at the photograph of Akim, then she said decisively, 'I'll do it. I'll do it now!' She got up, went over to the desk, and seizing her pen began to write. The letter took her about twenty minutes, during which Yasha ate a second apple, watching her out of the corner of her eye. At last Natalia sat back, sighed, and picking up an envelope, put the letter in it and sealed it up.

'Have you got a stamp, Yasha?' she asked.

'In my writing-case.'

'Thanks. Well, that's that.'

'Give it to me,' said Yasha. 'I'm not going to take any chances. If you want to get this thing back, you'll have to murder me.' She stuffed the letter inside her blouse, then observed, with a return to her old, indifferent manner, 'I suppose there's no use asking you to move the furniture back where it was before?'

'All right,' said Natalia. Together they shoved the bed back to its former place along the wall, and the bureau into its original position between the door and the alcove, Natalia remarking vaguely, 'I've often wondered what you'd do when you got out of here.'

'I,' said Yasha shamelessly, 'am thinking of getting married.'

8

Ruth Anderson was sitting in front of the dressing table, in the room which she shared with her sister ... the room which Vicky had ransacked the day before in her unsuccessful search for the package of cigarettes ... plucking her eyebrows, with now and again a quick glance at Cissie's reflection in the mirror before her. Picking a fine hair from her tweezers, Ruth remarked rather impatiently, 'Mlle Dupraix must have a pretty good idea that there was something queer about that business yesterday. She came in here after lunch ... before I'd had a chance to straighten up the room. Vicky left it in an awful mess. I must say I don't see why she had to turn the bureau drawers upside down and ...'

'What did Mlle Dupraix say?' asked Cissie rather anxiously.

'Nothing. She just looked wise. It's a good thing for us it was her and not anyone else, or we might have got into trouble. But she loathes Vicky, so that I suppose ...'

'Yes,' said Cissie shortly. And a moment later, 'God, I hate this place!'

Ruth glanced swiftly at the reflection in the mirror, and sighing, set down her tweezers exactly parallel to the pink-backed brush, comb, mirror, nail file, nail scissors, buffer and shoehorn which were all arranged in a neat row at an angle of sixty-five degrees to the edge of the dressing table. She scanned her face in the mirror for a moment and said, 'I wish to goodness I could get a few facials ...' Her skin was pink, too pink, from the point of her chin to the arch of her tortured eyebrows which now looked more raw than ever from too-frequent plucking. She had been endowed with that cast of middle-class English face which never permits its owner to look like a member of the upper classes. She saw Cissie's almost perfect profile, softened by a certain innate sweetness, outlined against the brilliant outer world as she stood by the window, and fell to brushing her hair with renewed energy. Cissie might be better-looking, but she wasn't half so popular with men.

'Have I got time to give myself a manicure before that police examination?' asked Ruth, putting down her brush ... exactly parallel to the other toilet articles.

'I don't know. Do as you like,' Cissie answered indifferently.

Ruth settled herself on the bed with a towel, polish-remover, orange-stick, nail file and the rest of her expensive paraphernalia, and began to file her nails. She glanced once more at Cissie; really, thought Ruth, her sister was so silent and morose these days that she was almost unfit for human consumption, and for the past twenty-four hours she had only uttered a few, ill-humoured words when someone spoke to her. The remainder of the time she had said nothing, but had wandered restlessly about, paid no attention in class, and was so nervous and irritable that one didn't dare to ask what was bothering her.

The two sisters were inseparable, but it was an association which was the result of habit, and of the same interests in life ... or the same lack of them ... rather than of any deep-seated emotion. Cissie was engaged; it was immediately after their father's first meeting with her fiancé that Mr. Anderson had disinterred himself from his factory and ordered them abroad for another year. He had met his wife's objections by stating that he had not the time to argue about it; he was due in Munich for a business conference in forty-eight hours, and would leave the two girls at Pensionnat Les Ormes on the way. He did not even allow them any time to shop. They disliked their father. He, in his turn, disliked them. He asked little of anyone, even of his daughters, but sincerity, humour and generosity; qualities in which Ruth and Cissie were conspicuously lacking. He was not a domestic man; he had never in his life believed that he should love his daughters because he happened to be their father, and was totally lacking in conventional, paternal feeling.

'Well,' said Cissie suddenly, whirling about and facing her younger sister, 'Why don't you say something, for heaven's sake?'

Ruth's mouth dropped open in astonishment. She ceased filing her nails in order to stare at her sister. 'What's the matter with you?' she demanded.

'You know perfectly well what's the matter with me! It's Vicky ... and if she isn't on your mind, she ought to be.'

'Oh, rot. She brought them in.'

'Bringing them in isn't against the rules. She was gated for smoking them ... and it was you and I who smoked them, not Vicky.'

'Now see here, Cissie, it's not going to do any good to rake that up all over again!' Ruth said, becoming impatient. 'It's bad enough being here at all without having everyone treat us as though we were ... well, just children, like everyone else. I *won't* have the staff start looking down their noses at us, and the younger girls think we're the same age as them. I won't have it! You couldn't stand that either,' she added a little more calmly, and began to file her nails again.

Cissie looked at her almost contemptuously, then turned her back, her eyes once more fixed on the mountains across the lake. Something had happened to her during the past two hours ... perhaps it was Rosalie's death. No young person whom she knew had ever died before. It had not occurred to her that such a thing could happen. She thought, Rosalie has gone, and nothing will bring her back, nothing at all. I might travel everywhere, I might look in every corner of the world, and I should never find her.

She said suddenly, hesitatingly, as though she only half perceived the truth in her own words, 'How unimportant we are. How tired God must be of the silly, rattling noises we make ...'

The nail file fell to the floor with a soft click. Ruth said, her face aghast, 'Are you going mad?'

'No.'

'Well, you're talking sheer drivel, if you want my opinion.'

'I don't want your opinion. For the first time in my life I don't care about your opinion, or anyone else's either. And I'm going to try not to care, ever again.'

'Cissie! For heaven's sake pull yourself together!'

'That's what I'm doing. Hasn't it occurred to you that ... that ... Rosalie's dead ... and yet you and I ... are worrying about being found out ...' She suddenly started toward the door, paused, then resolutely went on, and opened it.

'Where do you think you're going?' asked Ruth.

'I'm going to find Vicky.'

'What are you going to say to her?'

'I'm going to say that I ... that I'm so ... so utterly futile ... that I've got to do something about it. I've suddenly realized that I'm going to live with myself for the rest of my life; I'm twenty-two, and if I don't try now, it may be too late. I've just got to straighten this out ... it isn't much, but it's a beginning.'

'Do you know what you sound like? The last chapter of a penny dreadful!'

'I don't care what I sound like!' she said impatiently, and then increased her sister's pained astonishment by smiling suddenly. 'I don't, Ruth,' she said almost joyfully. 'I *don't*! For the very first time in my life ... ever since I can remember, I've worried about what I looked like, and what I sounded like ... if I ever thought or felt anything really deeply, I didn't say anything about it because ... because of being laughed at, for fear of having people think I was different, or ridiculous, or some kind of ... of ... female poet ... but now I don't care, and it's nice. It's frightfully nice. Do you know something? I'm free ... I'm free of a whole lot of things ... I'm just beginning to know that not many things are really worth bothering about ... but that there are a few things that are worth ... a lot of bother ... Oh, *oceans* of bother!' she added, throwing out her hands in a wide gesture.

'So you start to reform yourself by getting us both into a mess ...' began Ruth, but her voice trailed away before she got really started. Cissie had gone.

9

Vicky was in Rosalie's room, huddled in a chair which she had drawn close to the window on coming up after breakfast, and where she had been sitting ever since, motionless, without tears. The room had been stripped of all Rosalie's belongings except the black cross which was still nailed to the wall above her bed; soon someone would come to take it down, someone would wonder what to do with it. Perhaps it would be sent back to Canada with the rest of Rosalie's things. In a little while another girl would move into this room, next term probably. After her would come still others, each a little different from the one who preceded her, and the one who followed her, each lending to the room a little of her own personality for a few fleeting months. Already the atmosphere which had disturbed so many girls was gone; there was now nothing left of Rosalie, who had suffered, and prayed, and repeated so carefully the day before, 'I'll keep a little tavern, below the high hill's crest,' nothing but Vicky, of whom she had become a part.

Vicky did not hear Cissie open the door and only looked up as she spoke her name. She wondered why the English girl's eyes filled with tears when she saw her face. I suppose I must look queer, she thought, and stood up. 'You wanted to see me?'

'Yes.' She came forward a little and stood by the other side of the window, so that there was a shaft of light between them. She had never seen such grief in another face, and had to bite her lip in an effort to steady it. She could not bear to look at those grey eyes, and said, 'You shouldn't be alone here like this ...' watching the smoke rising from a distant chimney. She did not know why she said it; Vicky was really almost a stranger to her. In all their four months together they had only spoken very casually to one another, a fact which Cissie now bitterly regretted.

'I'm all right,' said Vicky mechanically.

'Vicky, I ...'

'Yes?'

'I want to say something to you. It's about those cigarettes. I don't know now how I could ever have done such a thing ...'

Vicky raised one hand to her eyes, and stared at Cissie uncomprehendingly. It seemed impossible to drag her mind away from Rosalie; impossible to make herself think. She had heard the words spoken to her across the window, but she had to repeat them to herself before she grasped their meaning. She said at last, 'Don't think about it. It's over and done with,' wondering why Cissie had come to her about such a trivial and silly thing at a time like this.

Cissie said almost passionately, 'No, it's not over and done with! Don't you see? I've got to do something about this ...' She shook her head, then began to talk in a confused rush of words; she told Vicky why she had said nothing in the dining room, why, all her life, she had been afraid to say and do what she felt and what she knew she ought to do, in a series of words, phrases and sentences of which Vicky understood nothing.

She interrupted Cissie halfway through her recital with an apologetic, 'I'm so sorry, I can't ... make myself ... think properly. I don't understand you ...'

'But you must!' She knew now why it was that she must

make her peace with Vicky, and why it was that all her life she would bitterly regret not having known her better. 'How I could do such a thing to you,' she said, her voice shaken with sobs, 'and how any of us could fail to ... to ... realize what you are, I don't know. To think that I should drag you through such a miserable, petty business, and force you into a position where someone could ... humiliate you ... like that ...'

Vicky watched her unseeingly. Her mind was gradually clearing. She had no idea what Cissie was talking about, it sounded like nonsense, but she kept repeating to herself, 'It must matter very much to her or she wouldn't be doing it,' over and over again until at last she had brought herself into the present. Her voice, low and clear, suddenly reached the English girl's ears, 'It's all right, Cissie. I understood why you did it, so it wasn't important. Things like that only matter if you don't understand them. That applies to both of us, to you as well, so don't think about it any more.'

'What can I do now?'

'Do?' What did the girl mean? 'You can't do anything now, why should you? It's all finished and forgotten.'

'I'll go to Mlle Tourain,' she said.

'No, please don't do that.'

'But I can't go on letting everyone think that you ...' Cissie began.

Vicky had a mental picture of Cissie further troubling the headmistress who already had quite enough on her mind, and leaning back against the window-frame, every line of her body betraying her exhaustion, she tried to explain. 'Don't you see, you'll just cause more confusion, more worry. It really means so little to me ... don't you understand that?'

'Yes,' she said, staring at Vicky. 'Yes ... yes, I do.' She began to say something else, but checked herself as the school bell clanged three floors below. 'That's for the cross-examination,' she said. 'Are you coming, Vicky? Or would you rather I ... I asked Mlle Tourain to ... to let you ... skip it?'

'No, no. I'm ... I'm all right. I think I'll get a glass of water before I go down, though,' she said, as she walked toward the door. She had a feeling, as the door closed, that behind her, in that room, somewhere in the past, Rosalie's voice could still be heard saying, 'I wish they wouldn't take me away from you, and send me to a strange place, with strange people ...'

X

⚘

*V*icky stopped in her room to brush her hair slowly and care-fully, indifferent to the headmistress's specific order to line up outside the study door as soon as the bell rang. Her immediate surroundings had become hazy, and she was unable to infuse any sense of reality into her movements. She was standing by the dressing table, looking blankly at her reflection in the mirror and trying to remember why it was that the bell had rung, when her small roommate, Ina Barron, came slowly into the room and sat down on the edge of her bed. She had evidently run upstairs, for her breathing was loud and rasping; she was not crying, but she was obviously very frightened, for her mouth was work-ing and she was slowly tearing one of Vicky's handkerchiefs into small pieces.

'What's the matter, Ina?' she asked.

Ina moistened her lips and said, 'I ... I couldn't bear it, down there. I had to run away. You ... you tell Mlle Tourain. I just couldn't stand it ...'

'Stand what?'

'Waiting outside there with all the others for the ... the policeman to ...'

'Oh. Yes, I remember now. But it's no worse for you than anyone else ...' She stopped, her alarmed eyes searching the child's face. She seemed to be almost stunned with fear. Vicky remembered the nights in September and October when Ina had dreamed that she was being taken to a reformatory and wakened Vicky by her sobbing; she supposed that this was a return of that apprehension which had been instilled in the girl by her aunt, as a means of discipline, apparently. She said as reasonably as she could, 'Mlle Tourain got the man up here, hoping that the girl who actually did it would react exactly as you're reacting, but there's no need for *you* ...' She stopped again. 'Ina!'

The peremptory note in her voice forced Ina to meet her eyes. For a few seconds she held on, then flung her head down on the pillow and began to sob, while Vicky watched her in dismay. 'You did it,' she said. 'Why?'

Ina was crying uncontrollably now, her feet beating a tattoo on the mattress, and could not answer for a moment. Vicky waited, so appalled that she could think of nothing to say. She could not think, and yet she *must* straighten the thing out in her mind before she began to consider the consequences or tried to decide on a course of action. Ina's voice, muffled by the pillow, reached her at last, saying incoherently, 'It was for you ... a watch. I just *had* to give you something, but I never have any money. Ted gives you things ... and Consuelo, even Maria-Teresa, and I hadn't ... anything. You haven't got a watch and I've often heard you say that you need one. You're always being late for things.' She spoke so simply that there was no doubt she was telling the truth.

I might have guessed it anyhow, thought Vicky, reaching out with a vague gesture for something to lean against. She was almost too tired to stand. She half sat on the dressing table, too discouraged to think at all clearly, for a while, then she said dully, 'Where is the money?'

'In the pocket of my jersey.'

'All of it?'

'Yes.'

'How ... much, altogether?'

'About six hundred francs.'

Vicky went over to the cupboard, took the bundle of notes from the pocket, and threw it down on the dressing table. She said, looking out the window, dragging out the words in a voice so unlike her own that Ina raised her head to glance across at her in perplexity, 'I couldn't ... want ... that kind of ... present. You might have known that. How could you dream that I would ... like ... anything which had made other people unhappy? Have you such a low opinion of me that you think I would be pleased with a present which had ... hurt ... Ilse, and so many other people, so much? It wouldn't have been your gift anyhow. Don't you see that?'

'I didn't think of that. I didn't think of anything except that they've such a lot of money and I haven't any at all to buy you something with. I couldn't even buy you an apple, and I wanted you to know how much I ... care ... about you ...'

'You don't care about me, Ina.'

'I do!' she said passionately. She scrambled to a sitting position on the bed and went on, 'I'd do anything for you, anything in the world ...'

'You don't care as much for me as you do for yourself. Don't you see, this is all ... vanity ... You wanted me to be grateful to you ...' She shook her head, unable to maintain such a difficult attitude, and said, 'I wish I could make you see it as it is, and not as you want it to be. I'm no good at scolding; I don't want to abuse you or anything, but surely you can understand that, apart from taking what isn't yours, you've done something wrong ... something terribly wrong, in hurting, and worrying other people so much, and making them so unhappy ...' She paused, having suddenly lost the thread of her thought as it occurred to her that the end of this whole business was not here, but downstairs in Mlle Tourain's study. The headmistress would make a public example of Ina; possibly she would expel her. Her aunt would come to hear of it, and the few chances there were now that Ina would ever become a valuable human being ... Vicky shook her head hopelessly and began to walk up and down the room, twisting a handkerchief through her fingers and paying no attention to the small figure on the bed. She could think of no solution, and was on the point of saying so when the door opened and Theodora came in.

She sat down on Vicky's bed and said cheerfully, 'I just thought I'd come and remind you, darling, that the bell went fifteen minutes ago, in case you've forgotten.'

'Is Ilse all right?' asked Vicky, and before Theodora had had time to answer, she continued, with a long sigh, 'Oh, Teddy, Teddy, I'm so glad you're here!'

'So am I,' said Theodora, looking rather bewildered. 'But why, particularly?'

'Oh, just because,' she said, rather amused at her own outburst. 'Because you're so sunny, maybe. Because of your ridiculous red hair, and your gorgeous sanity, and ... oh, everything.'

'My hair isn't ridiculous,' she said, looking injured. 'Most people think I'm nuts, and no one has ever thought I had a sunny disposition. Love is certainly blind.' Her brown eyes contracted as she looked at Vicky, and she saw what the past few hours had done to her; like Cissie, she wanted to cry, but unlike Cissie, she was almost grimly determined not to. Instead she continued, 'Apropos of Ilse, it seems our Paul is even now galloping in her direction, so all is rosy. Mlle Tourain told her that she didn't have to descend for a scene with The Law, but she's so ecstatic now that the entire police force of Lausanne wouldn't bother her, so she came down. Love must be wonderful. I sometimes think ... but we'll go into that some other time. There are still about twenty girls to go, so don't hurry yourselves ... just come when it's convenient,' she added politely. Her eyes fell on the money, and she whistled. 'What's that?' she demanded.

'It's ...'

'Well, what is it?' She stared at Vicky, then turned to Ina and began, 'You tell me, then, because Vick ...' and cut herself short. She looked at Ina, first incredulous, then horrified. Her voice dropped, as it always did when she was angry. 'Oh. You don't need to tell me,' she said coldly. 'So it was you, all the time. I might have guessed it. No one else would be so wrapped up in themselves that they could stand seeing Ilse and everyone else so miserable ...'

'She did it for me,' said Vicky quietly.

'For you!'

'Yes. She ... she wanted to ... buy me something ...'

'How nice of her,' said Theodora. 'In fact, how clever of her to live with you all these months and imagine that that would please you. Oh, stop bellowing, Ina!' she said with sudden fury. 'Instead of enjoying a good cry you'd better think up some way of getting Vick out of this ...'

'Getting Vick out of this?' repeated Ina, trying to dry her eyes with the back of her hand. 'Why?'

'Why?' said Theodora. 'Don't you see why? You go and tell Mlle Tourain that you did it for Vick, and in the first place she'll never believe that Vicky didn't know about it all the time ... the way she knew about Ro ... about everyone, and in the second place it will all ... this whole damned mess ... will wind up at Vicky's feet as usual. Short of planting the money on her and having it fall out of her pocket at dinner, you couldn't have involved Vicky any more neatly in this if you'd tried!'

'There's no use in going on like that, Ted,' said Vicky. 'It's done, anyhow. What are we going to do? How can we ask Mlle Tourain to ... to ... deal with it herself, so that ... the aunt ... well, you know what I mean. I can't think of anything, I've run out of ideas.'

'Let her stew in her own juice,' said Theodora irritably. 'She can't be babied all her life. She can take what's coming to her ...'

'No, because if this is just settled in the ordinary, boarding school way, she'll learn nothing by it. She won't understand the ... the truth of what she's done, any more than she does now. Having everyone know she's a ... that she's ...'

'A thief,' said Theodora coolly.

'Yes. Well, having everyone know that ... will just emphasize the money aspect. *It's* not the important one. She's got to learn something besides the sanctity of property ... I mean the way she's hurt other people. That's *got* to be brought home to her some way.'

'God, don't you ever get tired of ... Oh, well, let it go. Personally, I don't give a damn what happens to her.'

'Teddy,' she said pleadingly, 'Forget that I'm involved in this for just one minute ... or even half a minute, will you *please*?'

'How can I forget it? The whole business will end up by doing only one thing ... convincing Amelia once and for all that no matter what happens, no matter how trivial or how serious it is, if she looks long enough and hard enough, she'll find you at the bottom of it. And I will not have you dragged through another grilling today. I simply won't have it! I don't give two hoots for Ina, so far as I'm concerned she can jump out the window now or go and drown herself, but the idea of you going down there and being hauled over the coals for this, after everything you've ... you've been through during the past three days ... *No*, and that's final.'

'Then what are we going to do about it?'

Theodora pondered for a moment. 'I'll say I did it,' she suggested brightly.

'Splendid. Then we can all gather round and have a good laugh.'

'What do you mean, a good laugh?'

'Don't be ridiculous, Teddy. Go and take a good look at yourself in the mirror. That's about the wettest idea I've heard from you so far, and most of your ideas are pretty wet, when it comes right down to it.'

'All right. You think of something. Personally, I still don't see what all the bother's about.'

Vicky glanced at Ina, still terrified, her eyes wavering back and forth as she stared uncomprehendingly at first one, and then the other. She said, 'Ina's just sixteen. She's got about sixty years of life ahead of her. At the moment, she doesn't know anything at all. If she's sent back to England in disgrace to that aunt of hers, she never *will* know anything. She's got to stay here, live this thing down, and be made to understand it a little.' She paused, then sighed, and went on with a half-smile, 'I suppose the best thing is for me to take her loot down to the study and tell the whole story. If Ina does it, she'll only get in wrong from the beginning. Besides, I know her, and her background, much better than she does herself ... I can explain it better. I know I've done enough butting in to last a lifetime, but I don't see any way of getting around it.'

'I think that's a rotten idea,' said Theodora.

'It seems to be about the best thing you or I can think up,' she said quietly.

'Why doesn't Ina *really* do something for you at last?' demanded Theodora, turning to look at the little girl on the bed, though she was still talking to Vicky. 'Why doesn't she go down there, tell Mlle Tourain she wanted a new pair of skis or something, and leave you out of it?'

Ina swallowed. She turned her head, and said with unusual decision, her eyes on Vicky's face, 'All right. I'll do it. I think Teddy's right.'

Vicky smiled at her. 'I won't let you do it, Ina.'

'Of course you'll let her do it,' said Theodora impatiently.

'No.' She shook her head. 'I won't, and that's final.'

'Vicky,' said Theodora, leaning forward and speaking with an odd catch in her voice, 'I know how much this place means to you. I know how much you want to be allowed to stay, and live like ordinary people. I know that ... that you haven't ... any place to go, and that the ... the few people there are in the world who ... who ... care about you, are all here ...'

'Stop it, Ted,' said Vicky.

'All right.' There was a brief silence, then Theodora said, 'Mlle Tourain won't pay the slightest attention to what you know about Ina, what you think about her and about this whole business, and what you think ought to be done. She'll just resent it. Don't you know that?'

'Yes,' said Vicky. Her face was more drawn than ever, but she went on, matter-of-factly, 'But under other circumstances, she'd listen. She'd listen to me if I weren't ... one of her pupils. And if I were to ... to give her a choice between Ina and me ... she'd take

Ina. Wouldn't she?' asked Vicky. And as Theodora said nothing, 'Wouldn't she, Teddy?'

'I think you're a sap,' said Theodora. And glancing down at her wristwatch, 'I'll stay here with Ina till eleven-thirty. That gives you half an hour, before I bring her down.' As Vicky went out the door a few moments later, Theodora began to cry, and remarked to Ina who was staring at her, never having seen Theodora in tears before, 'Well, do I look so funny? Maybe I do, but I've got something to cry about, even if you haven't ... Oh, Vicky,' she sobbed into Vicky's pillow, 'You ass! You bloody ass!'

2

Vicky saw the headmistress's startled, angry look as she laid the notes on the desk. She glanced at the fat, good-natured and harassed detective, at Ida, whose turn it was to be questioned, then back at Mlle Tourain. 'Might I ... speak to you ... alone? I've just ... found out ... who's been ... stealing. That's the money there.'

Amélie Tourain said brusquely, '*You* have just found out! Why didn't you do your investigating a little sooner?' and turning to the detective, 'You must excuse me, Monsieur. This girl is the worst problem I have to contend with. I'm sorry she's given you all this trouble for nothing. You may go, Ida.'

The detective nodded solemnly, picked up his notebook, and with a disapproving glance at the small dark-haired girl standing by the desk, followed Ida into the hall. The headmistress ordered the remaining girls back to their rooms and returned to her desk, her breathing audible in the silent study as she made a desperate effort to control her temper. 'Well? Perhaps you'll be good enough to enlighten me?'

She said, 'Please ... may I sit down ... I'm almost ... done up ...'

'No,' Amélie snapped, 'Stand up!'

Vicky said, drawing a long breath, 'It's my roommate, Ina Barron. I only found out a few minutes ago. She was evidently down here, with the rest of the girls in line, and got panic-stricken. She came up to our room ... and I found out then. I should certainly not have said ... not have ... kept it to myself with Ilse ... and Anna ... if I had ...'

'You don't need to bother with all that, Vicky,' she said, her lip curling. 'There have been too many other instances of your ... taking it upon yourself ... to keep back many things which I should have been told.'

'I'm sorry.'

'It's a little late to be sorry. Really, I've had about as much of you as I can stand. However, since it all seems to involve you more or less indirectly, I don't see that there's anything to be done about it at the moment. Why isn't Ina herself here? Is *she* hiding behind your skirts too?'

'No. I wanted to try and ... and explain it for her. I felt I ought to. She ... she did it for me. She wanted to buy me something ... a watch, as a matter of fact. She hasn't any money of her own. She's ... too fond of me ... much too fond of me. Her mother died when she was very young; her father lives in Ceylon. She's been brought up by an aunt who has been much too strict and unkind to her, and who doesn't seem to ... to love her at all. The result is that after years and years of frustrated affection, she has poured all her feelings on to me.' She stopped. Somehow she must try to be more coherent. A moment later she began again, speaking slowly and carefully, trying to make the head-mistress see Ina and her background as *she* saw it, so that she would understand.

The headmistress said nothing. She sat and watched Vicky for fifteen minutes, obsessed with the idea that she must get rid of this girl or she could do nothing. She could cope with everything and everyone else, but she could do nothing with Vicky. It was not a personal animosity; it was something far more subtle and more troubling. What made Vicky so strange, so utterly unlike everyone else? What *was* she?

Mlle Tourain swept aside the problem of Ina Barron, and continued to watch Vicky's face, puzzled and ill at ease. She interrupted Vicky a moment later to say almost roughly, 'Sit down, for heaven's sake,' becoming aware of the girl's unsteadiness. She seemed to be almost wavering on her feet. Vicky sank down into the nearest chair and continued to talk about Ina Barron in a tone so level, in a voice which was pitched so low that Amélie Tourain could hardly follow what she was saying. The headmistress was making almost no effort in any case, for her mind was concentrated upon the personality of the girl before her.

She was trying to sort out what little she actually knew about Vicky, from pure hearsay, and discovered with a slight shock that she *knew* absolutely nothing except that the girl came from Toronto, Canada, that her father was an archaeologist on an expedition in central Turkey, and that she paid her own bills. The headmistress tried to remember how it had happened that Vicky had not given more personal information when she arrived. Had she just appeared at the door? No, that was not it; she had telephoned first, and then come to see Mlle Tourain. It was the first day of school and the headmistress had been too busy to address more than a few conversational remarks to the girl, and then rush out to attend to a more recent arrival. She thought that Vicky had gone away and returned some time later with her bags; all she was actually sure of, all that she could recall from the hazy days of the previous September was that Vicky was there at meals and occasionally visible in the halls, quiet, unobtrusive and inconspicuous.

The headmistress shook her head in perplexity; none of this served as any sort of explanation for Vicky Morrison, and she was impossible to question. Amélie Tourain could conceive of no one with so little sensibility that he or she could ask, without blushing, 'What are you? What kind of life have you led?' No, no, she thought, jerking impatiently in her chair and staring at the wall behind Vicky's head, that could not be considered. She became aware of the girl's voice again, and once more tried to keep her mind on what she was saying.

Mlle Tourain had undoubtedly realized that Ina was une hysterique, and that she was a case for a psychologist. She was certain that Mlle Tourain knew that as well as she did, and the headmistress must excuse her impertinence in assuming that she did not know and attempting to give as full an explanation of Ina's background as was possible, for she, Vicky, had lived with Ina for four months and had come to understand her, for that reason, perhaps more completely than anyone else.

If Ina were expelled and sent back to England her aunt would never let her hear the end of it; she might very well be useless to herself and everyone else from then on. Her aunt was evidently a woman of little imagination; she would doubtless have been an excellent guardian for an insensitive girl, but she had already almost broken Ina, who was anything but insensitive, who was starved of affection and therefore emotionally unbalanced. She herself had had to make an almost continuous effort to hold off the girl by speaking to her less kindly than she felt, chiefly because Ina overflowed with the affection which under normal circumstances would have found an outlet in her family. She had attached herself to Vicky because she needed someone on whom she could lavish that affection. Ina's feeling for herself had now, however, gone beyond all reasonable bounds and seemed something like an emotional fixation. There appeared to be only one solution to the problem ... that she, Vicky, should go. If it were convenient for Mlle Tourain, she would pack her belongings and leave immediately after lunch.

Vicky stopped, and waited. She was giving the headmistress a way out. Amélie Tourain's eyes swung to her face, and for a moment they looked at each other, a stout middle-aged woman in dusty brown, a young, dark-haired girl in a black dress, who sat gripping each arm of her leather-covered chair, as she saw that beneath her deliberately impersonal look, the headmistress was relieved. And rather grateful, thought Vicky, with a brief, wry little smile.

The tension which had always existed between them snapped suddenly. Amélie Tourain said, 'So you know me as well as you know everyone else. I wondered if you did. How old are you, Vicky?'

'Twenty-one, Mlle Tourain.'

'Where did you learn so much?'

'I had a Classical training,' said Vicky, looking rather mischievous.

The headmistress laughed. 'So had I, but, in some respects at least, I haven't learned as much from books as you.' She was silent a moment, then said, looking across her desk at the girl who was sitting with her head against the back of the chair, 'You can say what you like now, Vicky. You know a great deal more about this than I do. What shall I do with Ina?'

'Have her with you as much as you can,' she said quickly. 'Perhaps there's some little job she could do in here three or four times a week ... both as a punishment, and also because it would

give you a chance to talk to her without seeming to ... to be paying too much attention to her. She needs an impersonal contact
with someone much older and much wiser than herself, and it
would be good for her to know that there was a job which
depended on her for being done. I think she should have as much
responsibility as she can take.' She glanced at the headmistress
and said apologetically, 'I ... naturally I'm no authority on ...'

'It's all right,' she interrupted. And a moment later, 'Tell me
something. I don't want to ... to trouble you, but if you could
explain something to me ... What *did* Rosalie think about, Vicky?'
remembering that a long time ago ... a very long time ago! ... she
had said to Mary Ellerton that she supposed she would, in the end,
have to ask Vicky for information about Rosalie.

Vicky fought down an impulse to avoid the question, as she
would have done before, realizing that now it would be a
kindness to the living to talk. She said slowly, 'You know that
Rosalie was very devout, and knew none but the religious life
until, a little more than a year ago, her mother eloped with a
French businessman in Montreal, and took Rosalie with her to
Paris. The three of them lived in an apartment there. Rosalie
had no idea of it all until one night, when she found out ... she
saw her mother in the man's arms. It was, of course, the most
horrible kind of shock. She came gradually to a point afterwards where she believed that all life was rooted in evil and
ugliness ... it was the scarlet touch, which was unendurable to
her. She did not want to live. I think perhaps it was as well she
died, for she had nothing to go on ... no sense of the beauty of
ordinary human things.' And a moment later, when she had
steadied her voice, 'Nothing in her past had led up to anything.
I mean, we gather impressions, experiences, a little wisdom and
a great deal of enjoyment, each day we live, from which our later
life is an outgrowth. Living should be a process of continual

enrichment, and there should be no break. Rosalie's sixteen years, however, were a series of distorted and violent impressions and experiences, so far as everything which did not have to do with the convent was concerned ... impressions and experiences which led to nothing of truth, and nothing of value. When she came here she had only her faith in God, and her soul certainly belonged more in heaven than it belonged on earth.' She dropped her eyes, so that the headmistress should not see the tears in them, and said, 'I'm trying ... to persuade ... myself.'

'Yes,' said Mlle Tourain, her face tense. 'I know that, Vicky. I need that ... persuasion ... even more than you.'

'I suppose we all do,' she said, smiling a little. She looked across the desk at the headmistress, sitting just behind the light which streamed through the French windows. The face she saw was strong; the whole figure of the woman much too uncompromising for this room with its trivial attempt at ornament, with its potpourri jars, its cactus plants, and its china shepherdesses. Only the big desk seemed to have any relation to her personality; the rest of the room appeared to be a casual and irrelevant background, as she might pause in the street with a cake-shop behind her. 'Are you going to stay, Mlle Tourain?' asked Vicky on an impulse.

'Stay?' she repeated in astonishment. She had not imagined that anyone knew of the conflict within her, never having realized that it was obvious to every sympathetic observer. 'I don't know,' she said, unwonted discouragement showing in her face.

'How is Mlle d'Ormonde?'

'She's had a relapse.'

'Oh, I'm sorry, Mademoiselle.'

'You were saying that one's future is the logical outgrowth of one's past, and you were right. It is. Usually, as you look back, you realize that there have been no wild inconsistencies; rather, everything has been interrelated and dependent upon everything else.' She glanced briefly at Vicky, then lowered her eyes to the brass inkpot, knowing that the girl had understood her. In the back of her mind was a fleeting amazement that after all this time, it had only taken a few minutes with Vicky to make it clear to her why it was that everyone talked to her without self-consciousness and without restraint. The headmistress half smiled to herself as she remembered that conversation with Mary after the emergency staff-meeting on Thursday afternoon ... only two days before. She had said irritably, 'The girl apparently concerns herself with everyone and everything.' Now, once more, she remembered a few words of Mary Ellerton's ... were they spoken in answer to that statement which the headmistress now realized was ridiculous? Ridiculous, she added to herself, because here *she* was, doing precisely what everyone else had done ... Anyhow, Mary ... Miss Ellerton ... had said 'She has the gift of self-dismissal,' which was, perhaps, as near as anyone would ever come to explaining Vicky.

She said suddenly, 'If, some time in the future, you should feel like coming back, Vicky ...' then stopped. The future! Where would she herself be, five years from now, ten years from now? Would she still be here, struggling to bring order into this little world which could not but reflect the chaos of the great world which surrounded it on all sides; battling with problems which had no solution, constantly striving for the impossible? These girls were returning to their homes and all their differing back-grounds, countries, ways of thought and ways of living; they would always return to them ... why should she concern herself with them? What was one or two years in a foreign country compared to seventy in one's own? Besides that, even supposing that she and Mary Ellerton revised the whole curriculum and created a fresh basis, these girls would still come on the *old* basis

... would still come to be 'finished,' whatever, Blessed Saints, that word might mean. Finished! One was never finished. Here she was, at fifty-eight, beginning the gigantic task of running a girls' school, though, until four years ago, her life had run towards an entirely different conclusion.

In the old days before 1930 the school had not existed for her, save on those days ... once or twice a month ... when Jeanne would come to tea in Amélie Tourain's little house down the lane from Avenue Ruchonnet, and would talk about one Nancy O'Brien who was constantly in mischief, or someone named Antoinette something-or-other who came from Nantes and who was incurably homesick ... what did it all matter, Amélie Tourain had asked herself in those days. It was all very far away; she had only been a few times to Pensionnat Les Ormes, and had disliked intensely the sudden outburst of noise when there was a clattering of feet on the stairs, or the bell ... that dreadful bell ... rang for classes. In recent years she had avoided going there at all, and had begged her cousin to come to her house down the lane when she wished to see her. The school had always faded from her mind as soon as the door closed behind Jeanne, and Amélie Tourain was once more at work in her study. Until her cousin's next visit, it remained vaguely in the back of her mind, a large stone and brick building halfway up the hill behind Lausanne which was filled with noisy, bewildering young girls who came and went each year and who were, most strangely, the entire and sole preoccupation of her cousin, Jeanne d'Ormonde.

There had come a day in the spring of 1930 when she was to call a taxi and ride up to the school in answer to a summons from Jeanne, but she had spent the morning digging in her garden and planting hyacinths along the flagged path; she wanted them to grow in the grass here and there, not to be arranged in straight stiff rows.

Her life, her quiet orderly life! What had become of it? Here there was no time for thought, no time for study and learning; here no time for peace, but merely a succession of days which she spent, constantly interrupted, in her hopeless, self-imposed task of emptying the ocean with a sieve. Someone else could do it as well; someone else could probably do it much better. Why had Jeanne stood in the hall with the nurse holding the door open, waiting for her to come, and said, 'Promise me that you'll stay until I come back, Amélie. If I should not come back at all, think of me; remember that I have been here for many years, because *I* thought it was a task worth doing. I should not rest if I ...' She had hurried out the door with the sentence uncompleted, leaving the stout figure standing silently in the hall behind her, saddled with fifty-odd girls who had come, Blessed, Blessed Saints, to be 'finished.'

Her mind returned to the girl sitting across the desk from her; she said unexpectedly, 'I think these past two days have been the strangest I've ever known, Vicky, and perhaps you are the strangest part of all.'

Vicky smiled. 'I'm sorry I've been such a nuisance. I was ... attempting the impossible. I know that now.' She turned her head and looked out the window, trying to force herself to realize that in one hour, two hours, she would be standing on the steps of the school with nowhere to go. What would she tell the taxi-driver? She was not mentally ready to leave yet; she dreaded the idea of being alone, and of saying goodbye to her only friends. Once away from the school, there would be nothing left of Rosalie but the memory. She had an impulse to say, 'I won't go! I won't go!' to refuse to take the responsibility for herself, to allow herself to break down, just once. No one had ever said to her, 'Vicky, are you happy?' or 'Vicky, can I help?' God, God, she said, her fists doubling up on the arms of her chair, am I ever to find a home on this earth? Am I going to be alone as long as I live? No answer came to her from the silent room, and a moment later she relaxed, her head falling against the back of the chair.

There was a knock on the door, and an appreciable length of time after Mlle Tourain's 'Come in!' it opened, and Anna stood there with the empty hall behind her. As though some invisible voice were prompting her, she walked the few steps to the desk and stopped, saying nothing.

The headmistress stood up hastily, without knowing why she did it. 'What is it, Anna?' she asked, her voice shaking with sudden fear.

In a voice which she had carefully emptied of all emotion during that moment when she had stood outside the door with her hand on the knob, she said, 'My father was arrested in Nördlingen on Thursday morning, just before sunrise. There is no question about the trial. He comes before the Military Tribunal on Monday; he will be ... executed ... on Tuesday morning. He was working for the overthrow of the Nazi government. I am leaving ... this afternoon ... with ... a sister ... from my convent in Munich.' She made no movement as though she wished to go, now that she had finished, but remained motionless like a blind person waiting for a guiding touch, her face turned towards the light coming from the windows.

The headmistress struggled to speak, gripping her desk with both hands. She managed to say at last, 'Anna, I can't think of ... anything ... that would be any ... help ... to you, except that ... if there's anything I can do for you now ... or at any time later on in your life ... I should be glad.' She could go no further, and turning abruptly, went over to the window. 'Vicky, go upstairs with Anna. I will be up in a moment,' she said unsteadily, searching in the pocket of her dress for her handkerchief. She heard them go out, and leaning against the glass, began to cry for the first time in many years.

She took hold of herself at last as one of the maids knocked on the door and entered with a telegram. The girl saw such a look on Mlle Tourain's face as she had never seen before, and waited in alarm, one hand half held out to give the headmistress support if she should need it, while she read the telegram. A moment later, with her face unchanged except for a sudden tightening of the muscles around her mouth, she muttered thanks to the girl for waiting, and putting the telegram down, went out, followed by the maid. It lay face up on the desk, its eight significant words scrawled across the sheet in the handwriting of the telegraph operator down on Place St. François: 'Mademoiselle d'Ormonde died at ten-thirty this morning.'

XI

❧

I

A little later Vicky left Anna, still controlled and speaking unemotionally to Mlle Tourain, and started on a search for Theodora and Mary Ellerton. She found Mary at last in her room, stretched out on her bed sound asleep, and went out, closing the door quietly, not wishing to disturb her. She decided to see each member of the staff ... leaving her favourite, Mlle Lemaitre, to the last ... and then do her brief packing. Mary would probably be awake by that time. But where was Theodora? No one seemed to know. She asked Mlle Devaux, Miss Williams, and Mlle Dupraix as she said good-bye to each in turn; none of them had seen her.

Still puzzled by Theodora's complete disappearance, she knocked on Mlle Lemaitre's door and entered the Frenchwoman's

room in answer to her sharp 'Entrez!' She was sitting in a
rocking chair, which she had procured form the attic some time
before, reading with her horn-rimmed glasses slipping as usual
down her nose. She was wearing a shabby, unbecoming black
dress and looked tired, her face drawn and pinched, for she
had been sleeping badly. Only her black eyes retained their
light and energy, the rest of her face and body was wasted and
colourless.

Vicky had spent a great many hours in Mlle Lemaitre's room
and took her accustomed place on the bed automatically; there
was nowhere else she could sit, for the room was very narrow.
The bed occupied almost the whole wall on the left of the door,
and a desk was placed at a slight angle to it across the corner
by the window. The remainder of the space was taken by a large
bureau, a cupboard door, and Mlle Lemaitre's rocking chair.
The size of the room seemed further diminished by the clutter
of paper-backed books and pamphlets which overflowed from
the bookcase under the window to the top of the desk, the
bureau, and even the floor. Vicky, looking about this room which
she would never see again, asked herself once more how many
rooms like this Mlle Lemaitre had lived in ... small, dusty, disorderly rooms, up under the eaves ... rooms in Clermont, where
she had been brought up and where she had taught in the local
school; rooms in the Quartier Latin, which she had occupied
during her years at the Sorbonne, in Passy, where again she had
taught school, in various parts of Italy during holidays, and
now, in Pensionnat Les Ormes.

'Your crocuses look as though they'll be out early this year,'
said Vicky, glancing at the row of little pots on the windowsill.

'Yes. The light is good. What are you here for, young lady?'

'I came to say good-bye. I ...'

'Good-bye!'

'Yes. I'm leaving this afternoon.'

'Oh.' That was all Mlle Lemaitre said for a moment, lowering her eyes to follow the barely distinguishable chain of roses in the threadworn strip of carpet which ran between the bed and the desk. A moment later, still looking at the floor, she observed matter-of-factly, 'Of course you've been impossible.'

'Yes,' said Vicky. 'I don't see how I could have done anything else, though. The trouble is that I ... I'm much too real, to other people. I exist much more clearly in their minds than I do in my own ... I mean that I don't *want* to ... to be a bother ...'

'You're too old, Vicky,' she interrupted, looking at her directly now. 'Sometimes I think you were born old. You're so much wiser than you should be at your age. I'm afraid you're going to have this sort of experience time and again. It isn't only your queer background, and the fact that your parents didn't trouble to legitimize you ... Yes, my dear, I guessed that months ago ... It's you. Thank God!'

'You've always overrated me, Mlle Lemaitre.'

'I could not overrate you,' she said simply. 'And I'm glad to have known you. It isn't often one meets people of whom one can say that ... I'm glad to have known you ...' she repeated, looking upwards. Then she went on, with her old acidity, 'I suppose you will spend the next fifty years frittering away your time, dabbling in this and that?'

'I hadn't intended to,' she said with amusement.

'See that you don't, then. It's very easy, though, and you'd better be careful. You think now, perhaps, why should I work and work? What do I gain in the end? But Vicky, you won't be such a fool, will you? You must submerge yourself in something else ... it is a necessity of the human spirit. Some women manage to submerge themselves in their husbands, but that must be rather difficult for a woman of any intelligence.'

Vicky was accustomed to that kind of dry cynicism from Isabelle Lemaitre, and merely smiled in answer. A moment later she said, 'I don't really know yet what I'll do.'

'Go to the Sorbonne.'

'I'm not sure that I want to.'

'Why not?'

'My mind is neither scholarly nor academic.'

She said shortly, 'It's possible that your mind might become one or the other with a little encouragement,' but she said it without conviction.

'I thought of the Paris Conservatoire,' said Vicky tentatively.

'Music! No, no. You're not good enough. You would only be a dilettante, one of those innumerable young girls no one had ever heard of, who manage one recital at great expense, and then starve to death. No, my dear. Save your piano for your spare time.'

Seeing the anxiety in those over-brilliant black eyes Vicky said, 'I haven't had time to make up my mind yet, Mlle Lemaitre. You know as well as I do that I have no special talents ...'

'You have a fine mind,' she said shortly. And with a curious unsteadiness in her voice, 'You have a very unusual talent for people, Vicky, which is perhaps more.' She sighed, then said, 'It's your decision in any case ... your life ... your life. I do not want to live it for you; I am glad that my own has few years to go. I would not be young now, in these days, even if I could.'

'Why, Mlle Lemaitre?'

She said slowly, 'I think that human beings have always known periods when life was terrifying, but I doubt if those periods were ever so frequent, or so long, as they are now. There is nothing in the world so dangerous, or so overwhelming as stupidity; perhaps there is no more of it now than there has been at any time, but I do not think the witless of past generations had so much power. The powers of darkness are the powers of misdirected knowledge ...' And a moment later, with a barely perceptible shrug, 'It has really been most illuminating, this experience of observing the world at close quarters ... see what a muddle we are all in, here, in this cross-section of life, and you begin to understand the world a little.'

She suddenly recalled Vicky's remark that she had not yet made up her mind what she was going to do. 'Where are you going from here?' she demanded abruptly.

'I don't know,' said Vicky.

'You don't know!' she repeated, aghast, and began to suggest pensions in Lausanne, Paris, the Italian Lakes, about which she knew nothing at first-hand but which she vaguely remembered having heard about from respectable-appearing fellow-travellers in the past. Then she was off on one of her frequent tirades against the disasters which befall unchaperoned young girls, but checked herself just as she got well under way, suddenly realizing that it was no use ... indeed it was cruel ... to worry the girl about situations which she could not help. Who was to chaperon the child?

Vicky shook her head. It had not occurred to her until now that she was rather young to be turned loose in the world. It had not occurred to anyone else either, even to Mlle Tourain. Mlle Lemaitre stated that since such was the case, she herself would illuminate the headmistress on the subject.

Vicky objected. 'If you do that she'll only keep me here and everything will be more awkward than ever. I've already gone past it ... don't you see that? I can't go back now. Besides that, does it make any difference whether I'm twenty-one, or twenty-one and a half, or twenty-two, when I leave?'

'Yes, because you would be a little older at least.'

'You can't set down an arbitrary age-limit like that, Mlle Lemaitre.'

'No, I suppose not,' she said. And after a brief pause, with renewed concern, 'I had not thought that it was possible for any-one to be so ... so alone ... so rootless.' She looked at Vicky for a moment in silence, then she rose to her feet and taking a small earthenware jug from the bureau, began to water her crocuses. She did not wish Vicky to see her so upset. Her affection for Vicky was inexplicable; it was not in the least maternal, thought Isabelle Lemaitre, for she had no desire to see that Vicky kept her feet dry and wore woollen underwear, and she told herself that she would go mad if she were forced to live with the girl. Yet her heart and her thoughts were more with Vicky than they had ever been with anyone else.

She put down the jug on the floor, then returned to her rocking chair. She sat motionless, looking critically at Vicky's face and apparently unaware of the embarrassment which she created in its owner by doing so. If anyone had said to her that Vicky was beautiful, she would have replied impatiently, 'Yes, yes, of course she is!' irritated by a statement of what she considered the obvious and the trivial, exactly as she would have been irritated if someone had remarked in her hearing that Voltaire was ugly. She dismissed the girl's beauty as irrelevant, which it was not, for it was the outward aspect of an inner harmony of character and spirit. Her features were good, but not remarkable. Her forehead, which no one but Isabelle Lemaitre had ever noticed, was her one native asset; it was moulded in a way which was more masculine than feminine, high and broad, with three horizontal lines already etched on it.

She said at last, 'I don't see any weakness in you, Vicky. I don't think I need to worry,' and made one of her indescribable French noises with which she invariably signified that she was finished and well satisfied with her present task. It was half 'huh,' and half 'hein,' and it belonged to herself; a thousand girls and half a hundred fellow-students at the Sorbonne had tried and failed to imitate it.

She got up and opened the door. She said, as Vicky went out, 'I shall see you in Paris next year, perhaps. You can always get my address from Monsieur Bernard ...'

'Then you ...'

'I also am leaving. It seems incredible to me that I should have hesitated this long. There is no comparison between Paris and Lausanne as cities to live in ... or die in,' she added, with another shrug. And seeing a flash of pity in Vicky's face, 'Ma chère, I do not mind dying. Death,' said Isabelle Lemaitre, 'will be interesting. Most interesting.'

2

Mary came into Vicky's room just as she was closing her trunk, having packed all the lunch hour. She said, 'Your records, Vicky; I just retrieved them from Mlle Dupraix,' and helped her to do them up one by one in newspaper ready for travel, remarking as the last record was sandwiched in among the books, 'I rather imagine that my first action as assistant head will be to give Mlle Dupraix the sack.'

'Assistant head?' repeated Vicky in astonishment.

'That's Mlle Tourain's latest idea. She just informed me of it a moment ago. Incidentally ...'

'Yes?'

'Jeanne d'Ormonde's dead.'

'Oh,' said Vicky, straightening up and staring at the wall. 'So what does Mlle Tourain do?'

'She sits behind her desk, watching a small house off Avenue Ruchonnet go up in smoke,' said Mary. And a moment later, 'How good is your Shakespeare?'

'Oh ... so-so,' said Vicky. 'Why?'

'I've been thinking of something all morning,' she said, and looking straight ahead of her, repeated softly:

You do look, my son, in a moved sort,
As if you were dismayed; be cheerful, sir.
Our revels now are ended; these our actors
As I foretold you, were all spirits, and
Are melted into air, into thin air;
And, like the baseless fabric of this vision,
The cloud-capped towers, the gorgeous palaces,
The solemn temples, the great globe itself,
Yes, all which it inherit, shall dissolve,
And, like this insubstantial pageant faded,
Leave not a rack behind. We are such stuff
As dreams are made on, and our little life
Is rounded with a sleep.

She sat down on the bed and said, giving up all effort to be cheerful, 'I'm going to go mad without you, Vicky.'

'No, darling,' said Vicky, locking her trunk. 'You've too much to do. Besides, we'll be seeing each other at Easter. I'll be ...' She laughed. 'Of course, I keep forgetting that. I'm darned if I know where I'll be!'

'But you can't just leave like this!'

'I'm going to prove it can be done by doing it.'

'Where are you going to spend the night?' she demanded.

'At the Palace, I suppose, with Juan and Consuelo ... I don't know. Hotels are beyond my means, generally speaking.'

'But, Vicky ...'

'Mary, please don't start feeling sorry for me or I'll burst into tears. I've cried so much during the past twenty-four hours that

I'm almost melting anyhow. That's the trouble with being a person who finds it rather difficult to cry properly, once you start you can't stop.'

There was a knock on the door and two cartage men appeared. She said, in answer to their question, 'Take it to the station. I'll call for it later.' She found some money in her purse, gave it to them, and watched them carry out her trunk in silence. Then she took down her coat, hat and purse and laid them on Ina's bed.

'My gloves,' she said, and began to search distractedly through bureau and cupboard drawers while Mary looked at her, weighed down by the knowledge that something of herself would go with Vicky. She sat with her elbows on her knees and her chin in her hands, her legs swinging from the high bed, and seemed absurdly young. Vicky, catching sight of her in brief glimpses as she turned from one drawer to the next, felt herself beginning to share Mary's terror of the school.

She found her gloves at last in the pocket of her coat, and sat down on Ina's bed. 'I don't know what to do,' she said. 'I ordered that taxi for two-thirty, it's twenty past now, and still no Teddy. Was she at lunch?'

'No,' said Mary. 'Everyone was too upset to notice.'

'Where *is* she then?' demanded Vicky. 'I've combed the whole school. She's simply disappeared. You don't suppose that she's decamped, do you?'

'No,' said Mary. 'I would put nothing past her *except* leaving without you. She'd never do that.' She sat up straight, as though she were trying to shake off her unhappiness, and said, 'Well, I *shall* see you at Easter, anyhow, with or without my husband. You should get along well together ... he's of a literary turn of mind too, and he paints quite well. That's his reason for going to Sicily, I suppose.'

'All the best men seem to end up there,' said Vicky. 'Or all the worst,' she added, smiling rather mirthlessly to herself.

Mary stared at her. 'Why did you say that?'

'I don't know why I said it,' she replied, looking a little startled.' I was referring to the man whom Theodora is pleased to describe as "That wet smack, your ex-boyfriend," not to your husband.'

'Do you think anyone is ever going to be able to polish up Teddy's English?' asked Mary, shuddering.

Vicky laughed. 'It seems unlikely. By the way, what's your husband's name?' she asked idly. 'Do you know that all the time I've known you, you've never mentioned him except as "my husband," or "Barry."'

'It's Gilchrist,' she answered.

'What!'

'Gilchrist,' she repeated.

'What's ... his ... first name?'

'Christopher. Barry's his second name ... I'm the only one who calls him that. I knew someone once named "Christopher," whom I simply hated ... you know, just one of those silly things. He didn't mind being renamed, fortunately.' She looked at Vicky, and said, 'What's the matter? Why do you ... what *is* it, Vicky?'

'Nothing,' she said, moistening her lip.

'You look so queer,' said Mary, in a voice which was almost frightened.

'Do I?'

'Yes ... I ... I ...' She shook her head. 'You didn't ... you didn't ... meet him, or anything, did you, Vicky? Before school opened ... before he went away?'

'No,' she said steadily. 'I didn't know him, Mary.'

'Are you sure? You didn't ... hear anything ... about him?'

'No! No!' she said passionately. 'How could I? There are so many people in Lausanne ...'

'Oh, I don't know ... it's pretty small. Sooner or later one seems to run into all the foreign colony at the Beau Rivage or the Palace, or hear them mentioned.'

'No ... I ... I didn't,' she said.

'Teddy ran into him once or twice, I think. She said something about it ages ago ... but I ...'

'Teddy knows everyone. She was here all summer with her mother.' She had to avert this thing in some way; she might have been arguing with God as she thought, You can't expect me to tell her the truth. Someone else will do it sooner or later ... someone else. He's no good, he'll never be any good ... there'll always be ... someone else. But how could she let Mary go on believing that in the spring ... in the spring, she repeated to herself in sudden horror, that was what he had said to *her*. Why was it that she had to answer so many fearful questions; what curse was this which linked her with other people, and loaded her with such responsibility? This frightful confusion ... this frightful confusion ... Her mind kept beating out the words over and over again, until she saw that Mary was staring at her, saw her start forward and cross the room, felt her gripping her arms and heard her say,

'Vicky, what are you trying not to tell me?'

She shook Mary off and went over to the window. She could feel Mary's eyes on her, but she did not know what to do or what to say. There was the alternative of saying nothing and allowing Mary to go on in her unjustified faith, or of destroying this friendship. With that knowledge between them ... that knowledge which would block both their minds ... Mary could never bear to see her again. Vicky noticed that one of her hyacinths was sprouting and wondered why such a thing should insert itself into her mind now. She had grown those hyacinths for Rosalie; now, Rosalie was dead. She would leave them behind for Mary; Mary loved hyacinths, though she might not want these ... she might not want these. He had said, 'In the spring,' never thinking that his wife might come to Lausanne, and turn his little, convenient life into a distorted, drawing room comedy.

She turned at last, her face white, and said, 'Yes, I knew him, Mary.'

Mary continued to stand motionless by Ina's bed, then after a while moved back until she was leaning against it, without taking her eyes from Vicky's face. She was seeing not her friend ... her greatest friend, one part of her mind realized, for she knew without really seeing Vicky's face how little she could endure this, how much agony of mind and heart those five words had cost her ... but two people in a canoe on the Thames. The man was saying to the girl that he loved her, resting his arms on the paddle which lay across the gunwales. Ridiculous to remember that now!

Her mind began to clear a moment later and she said oddly, 'You know, Vicky ... I think I'm going to get over this. Do you know why? It's because, though I was fool enough to forgive him for myself, I'll never forgive him ... for you.' The net had dropped down on her now, and she knew it. She said, 'Christopher Gilchrist is out, one wife. Mlle Tourain is in, one assistant. Which balances the score a little for them, though not for me, yet. I suppose, in a while ...' She stopped looking into the future in one of those rare moments of foresight. She would go back to London in the summer, perhaps at Christmas and Easter as well, but everywhere she went she would see the school, standing on its hillside, never again quite happy when she was there, never again quite happy when she was away from it. What strange mad compulsion was this which made her stay where she could be of some use? Was it another baseless fabric which she was weaving to replace the old?

She almost thought that she would ask Vicky, and then decided to leave it until she saw her at Easter. They went downstairs together, and Vicky said good-bye to the headmistress, although that had really been done earlier in the day. They reached the front door, opened it, and saw in the courtyard a taxi, a taxi-driver who was eyeing eleven pieces of expensive luggage in disgust, and Theodora Cohen.

'Teddy,' said Vicky in astonishment. 'Where on earth were you?'

'In the trunk-room. Packing,' she added vaguely.

'Packing?'

'Packing,' she repeated patiently. 'You know, putting things in trunks.'

'What for?' asked Mary.

She looked from one to the other with frank disapproval. 'You know, you two ask the silliest questions. Why does one pack? Because one goes from place to place and extra clothing is essential both en route and following arrival.'

'Yes, but Teddy,' said Vicky helplessly. 'You don't think you're coming with me, do you?'

'No,' said Theodora. 'I know it.'

'You can't, Ted,' said Mary, but she said it without any force, having already seen enough of this weird girl now standing before her dressed in what she had not been able to get into her eleven pieces of luggage ... a mink coat, a black velvet turban with a diamond clip, a green wool sweater combined somewhat unsuccessfully with a bright blue skirt, and high-heeled brocade evening sandals, with a single, white elbow-length glove clutched in her left hand ... to doubt if there was anything that Theodora could not do. 'What about Mlle Tourain?'

'I put it to her like this, "Mlle Tourain," I said, "can I go peace-
ably or must I employ force?" "Go," said Mlle Tourain to me,
"Go," she said, "And my blessings be upon you, dear child ..."'

'Bunk,' remarked Vicky. 'Tell us the truth.'

'That is substantially the truth. Are you admiring my costume?
Chic, isn't it? ... all the latest things from various parts of the
Galleries Lafayette.' She glanced up at Vicky, standing above
her on the steps and looking as though she might cry. She said
hurriedly to the taxi-driver, 'Well, my good man, you might just
as well deal with those bags now, because you'll have to sooner
or later in any case.'

'I have a feeling,' said Vicky, observing the taxi-driver's expression as he hurled one bag after another on top of his car, 'that
our progress through Europe is going to be marked by a series
of brawls.'

They got into the car a few minutes later, leaving Mary watching them from the doorway. Vicky saw Mlle Tourain come
hurriedly into the hall and put her arm around Mary, then the
car turned the corner of the house and started down the long
drive to the gates which led out into the world. She heard
Theodora say, 'I've always wondered what it would be like to
be a lady with no destination. Here, Vick, weep into my handkerchief, it's bigger.'

'Where to, Mademoiselle?' asked the driver.

'Singapore,' said Theodora.

12/22